AS OUR WORLD FALLS
A Post-Apocalyptic Survival Thriller

JACK HUNT

DIRECT RESPONSE PUBLISHING

Copyright (c) 2020 by Jack Hunt
Published by Direct Response Publishing

Copyright © 2020 by Jack Hunt

All rights reserved. Direct Response Publishing. No part of this book may be reproduced, scanned, or distributed in any printed or electronic form without permission. Please do not participate in or encourage piracy of copyrighted materials in violation of the author's rights. Purchase only authorized editions.

This Book is licensed for your personal enjoyment only. This Book may not be resold. If you would like to share this book with another person, please purchase an additional copy for each person you share it with. If you're reading this book and did not purchase it, or it was not purchased for your use only, then you should return to an online retailer and purchase your own copy. Thank you for respecting the author's work.

As Our World Falls: A Post-Apocalyptic Survival Thriller is a work of fiction. All names, characters, places and incidents either are the product of the author's imagination or used fictitiously. Any resemblance to actual persons, living or dead, events or locales is entirely coincidental.

ISBN: 9798636878285

Also By Jack Hunt

The Renegades
The Renegades 2: Aftermath
The Renegades 3: Fortress
The Renegades 4: Colony
The Renegades 5: United
Mavericks: Hunters Moon
Killing Time
State of Panic
State of Shock
State of Decay
Defiant
Phobia
Anxiety
Strain
Blackout
Darkest Hour
Final Impact
And Many More…

Dedication

For my family.

Prologue

Los Angeles, California

A week after collapse

Unlike most, he was born into violence.

Deep in the heart of the Rampart District, a notorious stretch of neighborhood bordered by the Santa Monica Freeway and the Harbor Freeway sat the Church of St. Peter's. Framed by black smoke, it stood out like a light in the darkness, a beacon of hope to the lost, the only holy place left in L.A. Inside, Leo Henriquez surveyed solemn faces as he handed out gray blankets and bottled water to a room full of survivors. Twenty-six, short in stature, he was as much an oddity as was the untouched church people claimed God had protected.

With the summer in full swing and more than the usual turnout, it was stifling hot inside. Warm bodies filled pews. Some slept on the ground, others crammed into corners, the rest leaned against walls and stood out on the church steps.

None complained.

Service to others gave him meaning, atonement for his sins. It felt good to help.

An elderly woman with blackened skin looked up. She paused for a moment to study his inked face before offering a strained smile and thanking him in Spanish. He'd seen that expression countless times, though more so over the past two years since his departure from Barrio 18, otherwise known as the 18th Street Gang. All of the ink revealed his past association to a life he'd rather forget. Although he'd endured multiple painful trips to remove the tattoos, they still were there, faint, but visible.

"God bless you," he said. Leo cupped her wrinkled hands in his and said a prayer before moving on to the next.

Since the attack on America, an event known widely as the U.S. bombings, Leo had been assisting a local pastor ministering to those in need — and how great the need was. Barring the clothes on their backs, the distinction between the homeless and the wealthy was almost invisible. The divide that had once been there had vanished in the grip of desperation — the bombings had seen to that, the attack had leveled the playing field, brought the haughty to their knees, and humbled the self-righteous.

So much of California had vanished in an instant.

Hundreds of miles of rich coastal property was drowned by the Pacific, the result of a monster tsunami that had rolled inland on the first day, wiping out everything in its path. Further inland, huge swaths of the city were now buried below rubble, and anything that had survived was now valuable real estate, fought over by rival gangs. The same gangs that had once plagued the county and had been kept at bay by LAPD now ruled.

Law and order was amiss.

Police a novel sight.

Martial law had been imposed within days but enforcing it was a challenge too great for the country. Rumor had that any and all surviving military personnel were assisting FEMA — protecting them more like it, as he still hadn't seen help arrive.

Survivors forced out of homes, either by a gun or by ruin had taken to sleeping in tents, cardboard boxes or anywhere they could find a bed for the night. Others fled the city only to return when they realized the surrounding country was just as bad.

In many ways, the entire City of Angels now resembled Skid Row — the once-famous community left to fend for itself — a poverty-stricken knot of young and old reliant on the kindness of strangers and meager handouts.

After the initial wave of destruction, churches were the

first to open their doors, and the last to turn people away.

"Leo," Pastor Robbie called to him from across the chapel. "Bring out another case of water." Leo raised a hand of acknowledgment and went out back to a locked storage room. Inside, only a few brown boxes of canned goods and several twenty-four packs of water remained. A far cry from months gone by. Before the collapse, the church had offered meals twice a week to the homeless. Most of the goods were donated by local stores that had items close to expiring. As he loaded a few cases onto the cart, the sound of a gunshot startled him. It came from the sanctuary. Locking the door behind him, he hurried down a narrow corridor and entered to find Robbie on his knees with his hands up and a familiar face holding a gun to his head.

"Ramiro?" Leo said.

Ramiro Lopez was bald but had so many tattoos on his head, it looked as if he had hair. That day he wore baggy cream-colored pants and a black baseball T-shirt with the number 18 on the front. His eyes were covered by shades.

"Shorty."

Shorty was the nickname Leo went by in the gang. Ramiro was known as Gator for his reputation of violence.

Hurrying over to Robbie, he put a hand between them.

"Please. This is a house of God."

Ramiro looked around with a grin. "Didn't you hear? God left the building a long time ago." The eight guys with him smirked. Despite the display of aggression, gangs had an unusual association with churches. In fact, it was one of the most predominant ways to leave a gang that was accepted. Fleeing only ended with being dragged back. That never ended well. He'd seen his fair share of runaways beaten or executed. With the 18th Street gang so widespread, attempts to run were not only hard but foolish.

After twelve years as a member, Leo had worked his way up through the ranks; first as a puntero, or lookout, then as a seller of drugs. After that he became a gatillero, a triggerman killing rival gang members, before finishing as the compa — which meant friend and boss — the one who oversaw and coordinated operations.

Narrowing his eyes at Ramiro, he asked, "Why are you here?"

His lip curled. "Can't I visit an old friend?"

"I'm no longer in the gang."

Ramiro removed the 9mm from Robbie and looked him up and down before swaggering in front of the room full of people, waving his piece in the air. "Calmado," his voice echoed. He drew out the last letter as if playing with it, or enjoying the power it had over Leo. He didn't need to explain, Leo understood. While many gangs released their members upon request, walking away from 18th Street wasn't so easy. However, they did offer something, a kind of negotiation to gain a status known as calmado. It meant a member could leave but couldn't walk away entirely. Simply put, he couldn't disavow the gang but he would no longer be required to participate in activities or hold on to the structure anymore. But, and there was always a but, just like an army reserve, if a gang found itself in a tight spot he could be called back.

Two years, he thought it was all behind him.

He truly thought he'd carved out a new life.

Some might have said that he should have fled the country while he could but that would have only given them a reason to kill him. Their reach was far and wide and there was always one looking to work his way up the ranks with a kill.

No, instead he figured he would live in plain sight, be right there on their doorstep in the hope that they would leave him be, see his work in the community and allow him peace.

However, not every gang member held the church in high regard. Ramiro was one who didn't.

"What could you possibly want from me now? There is nothing left outside."

"Oh but there is," Ramiro replied. "It is business as usual, my friend, and you have work to do."

He shook his head as he glanced at Pastor Robbie, now

fearing for his safety. "I'm already doing work. God's work."

Ramiro chuckled as he walked back over to Leo. "This God you speak of, where was he when the bombs hit? Hmm? Where was he when people lay crying out for mercy? And where was he" — in an instant he turned and fired a round into a middle-aged man's forehead, his body slumped, and his wife screamed — "right then?"

Leo's hands balled as he took a step forward. Ramiro never flinched. "Go on," he said, taunting him to follow through. Pastor Robbie appeared at Leo's side, placing a hand on his shoulder. He whispered a scripture into his ear.

Though the rage never left, his hands relaxed.

Ramiro grinned, continuing to prowl as he spoke. "Um, just as I thought. Life serving your God has weakened you, Shorty, but I will make you strong again. Come, Alvaro has a mission for you."

Missions could mean anything from stealing a car to killing a rival member, however, if called back, it was a given that he wouldn't participate in any violent acts, or kill anyone. Calmado prevented him from doing that. The missions would be simple like hiding weapons, passing on information, moving money around or serving as a messenger.

Still, resistant to returning, Leo dug his heels in. "What could he possibly want that he doesn't already have?" Like a flash, Ramiro came back at him, though now his smile was gone and he was all spit and fury. He pointed the 9mm at an angle toward his chest.

"You are testing my patience, homie."

"All I'm asking for is clarity."

"And you will get it but if you don't come now, perhaps I might be persuaded to kill a few more of these fine people, huh? Maybe that will give you clarity," he said. He turned and waved the gun around, causing women to cry and duck, and men to wrap their arms around their children. "See, homie, it's not God they fear, it's me."

He had no choice.

He looked at the woman who was still clutching her dead husband, then back at Pastor Robbie. "I'm sorry," he said, feeling the weight of guilt as if he had brought this upon them. Under the watchful eye of Ramiro's guys, Leo headed for the exit.

"Peace be with you," Ramiro said in jest to those left behind as he followed his men out.

Chapter 1

Denver, Colorado

The projectile from the drone exploded upon impact.

A burst of hot air full of glass, metal and stone blitzed the street, tearing through anything in its path. A swarm of black dots vanished overhead. Alex and the others took cover inside a café and watched as a group of survivors vanished below falling rubble. There was nothing they could have done to escape. The attack came out of nowhere.

It was just another notch in the belt of hell they'd been wearing since day zero.

"Sophie!" Alex yelled, holding his hand out as she ran toward him.

He wrapped an arm around her, and they looked out in horror, watching the new wave of terror. For almost eight hours they had been stuck in this hell, running like wild animals from drones in the sky.

Where they had come from was a mystery.

"How can this be? The power grid is down," Sophie said.

"Depends how they're powered," Alex said squinting into the afternoon sunshine.

Thomas stepped forward. "Yeah. Even though UAVs are often powered by batteries and only last around thirty minutes before they need recharging, the military has been known to use hydrogen fuel cells which can increase air time up to eight hours, and that's just those big ones." He pointed up. "You see those high-speed suckers," he said. "That's some high-level autonomous tech. It makes me wonder if our foreign friends don't have an inside man." He looked over at Ryan and raised an eyebrow.

"Do I look like I work for the government?" Ryan shot back.

"You did."

"Yeah, to get out of a box, not to put society in one."

Thomas snorted, turning his attention to the air. "Wouldn't be surprised if they're using state-of-the-art facial recognition."

Alex shook his head. "Hardly see the point unless they're after someone, which it doesn't look like as they're dropping payloads on everything that moves."

Cars exploded farther up the street. No one escaped.

"Aren't you glad we didn't drive through here?" Thomas said, a smile forming. He had a dark sense of humor, one that Alex still wasn't getting used to after he agreed to let him come with them.

Seven days on the road. If America hadn't been crippled by the bombings, it shouldn't have taken more than three driving straight through.

Although vehicles were working, the power and internet were down and with that came a host of trouble. State after state they had witnessed the aftermath of the coordinated attack unleashed by hackers and it wasn't pretty — buildings flattened, homes burnt to the ground, bodies littering the streets.

If the widespread destruction wasn't hard enough to deal with, the panic that followed was worse. Everyone dealt with it in their own way. Some locked themselves inside their homes, others jumped on the bandwagon and raided stores. The few honest ones paid in cash. It was like watching the Los Angeles riots. Monkey see monkey do. If one person got away with something another followed suit, and why not? There was no CCTV that would capture them breaking into a store, and law enforcement was running on skeleton crews and wasn't capable of handling the increase in crime. So was it any surprise when people took survival into their own hands and stepped over the line between right and wrong?

As for martial law? The very mention of it was met with laughter. The truth was the military and government had their hands full. Sure in the first few days they'd seen them at checkpoints, directing traffic, checking vehicles, and many roaming towns and cities, but that soon became less frequent.

Why?

Dangerous people. Defending the nation. Helping FEMA. Protecting the line of government. Pick one. For them it was dangerous. The first half of the journey from Elizabeth City to California to be reunited with their daughter had been one hell of a ride. They'd experienced first-hand the perils of a lawless country. Alex's body still sported the cuts and bruises suffered at the hands of Cowboy, a tobacco-spitting madman with a taste for punishment.

If it hadn't been for Ryan, he would have drowned.

Since then, the obstacles hadn't stopped. They'd encountered a number of issues that had slowed them down. Multiple vehicles gave up the ghost, others were stolen right out from underneath their noses, and a couple were destroyed when they were forced to use them as battering rams.

Food. Well, that was an interesting challenge. In the first few days he'd blown through what little cash he had. After that they'd taken to eating anything they could get their hands on — handouts, vending machines were pretty good, abandoned lunch room refrigerators at businesses had yielded a nice selection. With store shelves emptied, it was a case of thinking outside the box, and they'd had to do a lot of that over the past week.

Drinking water was easy enough, they resorted to freshwater springs, streams, and rivers, then boiling it. At night they tied a plastic poncho between trees to catch rainwater. It had worked and it might have been easier if they had stayed in one place but they had to keep moving.

Ten miles east of Denver, in the shadow of the Rocky Mountains, they'd blown a tire. To be honest, it came as no surprise.

Luck was running short.

Attempting to swap out the tire, he found the spare was missing. Of course a valuable lesson was to be learned — when stuck in a bind, always check the vehicle for a spare tire. The problem is, when you're trying to avoid getting shot, a spare tire is the last thing buzzing in your head.

Continuing the journey by foot they'd made it into the Mile High City, or what was left of it. Denver was a shell of its former self. Rubble dominated; fires released toxic black smoke that spread across the concrete graveyard making it hard to breathe.

Alex was embarrassed to say that buying survival equipment had never been at the forefront of his mind. Like many Americans, reliance on infrastructure, government and community was the norm for him. Now all those talks with Charlie about making his own bug-out bag came back to haunt him.

Arriving in the dead of night, they'd holed up inside the Denver Public Library, figuring they wouldn't encounter trouble there. They were right. Books were the last thing on survivors' minds and yet for them that short stay had been valuable.

They obtained several maps, a list of businesses in the city, and found a tiny café full of stock. He'd filled his bag with muffins even though they were as hard as concrete. That night, Alex browsed the survival section, taking two of the books with him and spending an hour or two brushing up on ways they could ride out this shitstorm.

That night he slept like a baby.

That morning he'd awoke to a band of sunshine streaming on his face through a large window. For a moment it even felt like the horror had ended.

Faulty thinking, that's what that was.

"The drones must be targeting the state capitals as we never saw any of these on our way through other cities," Sophie said.

"This whole event is one targeted attack," Ryan replied. "This is just the second wave."

"I get the distinct impression you still know more than you're telling," Sophie said. Alex had backed off giving Ryan a hard time since his rescue. There was little they could do now to change what had happened. How much of a role he played was pure speculation but there were only a few who had access to the capabilities that were used and he happened to be one of them.

Glass crunched beneath Ryan's feet as he walked

farther back in the café.

Alex leaned against the doorway looking out. Small pockets of fire burned all over the city and smoke blew over streets of rubble. "One thing for sure is that technology is way ahead of its time. I've never seen drones move that fast or cluster together like that."

"I have," Ryan said. "You'd be surprised at the tech the military is using today. Most of those unidentified flying objects that those UFO nuts have video of are ours. Just our government won't say a thing."

Ryan climbed over the counter and dug through a cupboard of coffee. He pulled out a package, tore the top open and brought it up to his nose to smell the aroma. Sophie was keen to know what else Ryan knew but she figured it would lead to an argument. Thomas joined in sifting through the store for anything they could use while Alex remained at the door keeping a watchful eye on the drones.

A plastic wrapper of a brownie crinkled in Ryan's hands. He opened the packaging and went to toss the whole thing into his mouth when Sophie took it out of his hand. "Remember, we're rationing."

"Oh come on, you had plenty to eat at the library, besides, there's a whole box down there."

"Where?" Thomas said, ducking down only to come up empty. Ryan chuckled. Thomas gave him a jab. "Asshole."

"Ryan."

He shot her an annoyed look. "Oh God, what?"

"Where?"

"Where what?"

"Did you see drones like that?"

"Where do you think? I had access to top-secret files in the Pentagon's system. I saw videos of high-tech equipment, planes, drones, stuff the public still hasn't seen. Now can you give me the brownie?"

She tossed it back but not before taking a bite and breaking another piece off.

"What else do you know?" she asked.

"I told you everything."

"Not everything. We nearly died out there."

Ryan lifted a hand. "How would telling you this beforehand made the outcome any different?" he asked. "I didn't know there were drones here."

"I don't like secrets. Okay?"

He threw his hands up and huffed as he continued to search. Sophie walked over to Alex and offered him a piece of brownie. He might have gobbled it up but he was still full from the stash they'd found in the library's cafe.

Sophie leaned against the doorway. "You think we should move out this evening?"

"Depends."

"On?"

"Those things could have FLIR."

"In English," she replied.

"Forward-looking infrared. It uses thermographic cameras that detect heat."

"Why didn't you just say that?"

He shook his head and looked out again. "They can't stay up there the whole time. At some point they have to come down to be recharged even if it is for hydrogen fuel cells. The question is where did they come from and where will they land?"

"The better question is who is controlling them?" she replied.

"Someone miles away!" Thomas said coming up behind them. He was holding several bottles of cold coffee. "Here, we might need to stay awake." Alex took one and looked at the front of it.

"Nice find."

"Thought so myself," he said before chugging back the contents of his bottle, then wiping his lips with the back of his sleeve.

"What do you mean miles away?" Sophie asked.

"Hackers. Do you think they were up in the air when they released that shit on us? They're controlling all of this remotely from some location."

"Offshore?" Sophie asked.

"Possibly. A lot of military drones are controlled from thousands of miles away at an airbase in Nevada. Those suckers up there are top-grade tech. We're not talking about some crappy drone that you buy from BestBuy. Nope."

"How do you know that?"

He laughed, then took another swig and looked over his shoulder at Ryan who was digging through some box. "Your boy back there isn't the only one with golden fingers. I've dabbled. I took over control of a few drones in my time. Should I tell her about Creech, Ryan?"

"Knock your socks off."

He laughed. "Creech Air Force Base in Nevada is where a lot of the drone pilots operate from — you know, the guys who take out insurgents 8,000 miles away in Afghanistan — the ones who drop Hellfire missiles from Predator and Reaper drones. Anyway, a couple of years back I figured it would be interesting to give them a little scare. Me and your boy hacked into their system and took over one of the drones and made it crash into the mountains. Rumor has it those pilots were canned."

"Idiots. They were just doing their job," Alex said.

"Oh and what a job that is. Killing people like they were stepping on ants. Come on, you don't honestly think that every single person they killed down there deserved it, do you? What about the kids and mothers who died in those blasts?"

"Casualties of war," Alex muttered.

Thomas chuckled. "Jeepers, who needs enemies when we have them in our own backyard?"

As he continued to rattle on about morals and ethics, something caught Alex's eye. A flash of light, too bright to be sunlight reflecting off steel. "Did you see that?" Sophie stepped forward as he pointed. "Out there." Another flash. "There. You spot that?"

"Yeah."

It continued to flicker, leading them to believe someone was tilting a mirror and signaling. Were they trying to get their attention? Alex turned and shouted to Ryan. "Hey, grab a piece of that cracked mirror and bring it over."

"I'm busy."

"Ryan!" Sophie bellowed with all the authority of a mother.

To that he responded, hopping over the counter and returning with a shard. "Not exactly a good time to be checking your hair."

Alex rolled his eyes as he took it and went to walk out. Sophie grasped his arm. "Hey, careful."

"Always."

He scanned the skies for drones before darting out to a vehicle and getting into a position where he could angle the mirror and use sunlight to signal back. The street had an eerie feel to it; smoke rising, bodies strewn across rubble and smoldering vehicles. Alex brought up the mirror, his heart pounding fast. The last attack by drones had been so sudden they hadn't heard them until they zipped overhead and unleashed hell. Squinting into the afternoon light he waited for a response. Nothing. Then it occurred again. This time, however, he heard movement but it wasn't coming from the direction of where the signal was, but from off to his right. A small figure, cloaked in a black hood, wearing a blue jean jacket and bright Converse, burst over a mountain of stone, jumping from one large slab of concrete to the next like playing hopscotch.

His eyes scanned the blue sky.

He could feel the pulse in his neck beating hard and hear the blood in his ears rushing at the sight of black dots in the distance. Anyone else might have thought it was a swarm of birds.

"Hey!" he yelled out. "Over here!"

The hooded figure turned toward him but continued on.

There was no way the stranger would make it, they were about to run into an open stretch of terrain where there was nothing except the metal bones of vehicles, and those drones had made easy work of those. Alex looked back at the others standing in the doorway. Sophie shook her head, indicating no as if knowing what he was contemplating.

A moment of hesitation then Alex burst out from

behind the car and darted through the maze of debris. His eyes bounced between the figure and the drones that were getting closer. He called out to the stranger but instead of slowing they picked up the pace. The stranger's small legs weren't a match for his. He slid over the front of a vehicle, launched himself off a slab of concrete and pounded the asphalt. He scooped the figure up even as they cried, then he darted into the nearest building. Adrenaline pumped through his body; he didn't even look at the stranger until he was sure the drones were gone.

"You shouldn't have done that," a young girl's voice said.

He turned to see her drop back her hood to reveal short pink hair, and piercing blue eyes almost reminiscent of an Arctic wolf.

"I just saved your life, kid."

"No, you've just killed me."

He frowned, puzzled, as she slumped on the ground, despondent.

Chapter 2

Mendocino County, California

Shotgun at the ready, Officer Garcia kicked the door wide.

Grandfather Theo's cabin was situated two hours north of Petaluma. Nestled among the majestic redwoods, close to Lake Ada Rose and ten minutes from the small town of Willits. It had been in Liam's family for as long as he could remember, a home away from home. His grandparents would often have him there over the summer break just to give him relief from his overbearing father.

Although Elisha had told Garcia they could make their own way, he insisted on giving them a ride. Since the run-in with Carlos, Garcia had kept a close eye on her, the way a father might watch out for his own.

The first sign of trouble was seeing the door ajar. As they rolled up in the police cruiser and parked, Liam had noticed it. Garcia told them to wait in the vehicle while he and Andre made sure it was safe. Andre went around the back while Garcia entered through the front door. Elisha peered out the windshield and waited with bated breath as Garcia disappeared inside. A few seconds later he emerged giving the thumbs-up.

Liam struggled to get out with his arm in a cast. Both of them had suffered broken arms but unlike hers, which occurred in the initial attacks, Liam's had come from a brutal display of violence. She still couldn't get the image out of her mind, his arm between those two chairs. She was now staring down five weeks of recovery, while for him it would be six.

"Bastards!" Liam said as he entered the cabin to find the place in complete disarray. A table had been overturned, a loft-style bed torn to shreds and the pantry had been emptied. Though Liam seemed more concerned with a storage room at the rear of the cabin. The door was open, and a broken lock on the floor. As he entered, he banged a fist against the wall. "They took everything."

"What was inside?"

"Survival gear. You name it, my grandfather had it. That's why I wanted to come here. If anyone was ready to ride this crap out, it was him."

"Was he a prepper?" Garcia asked.

"Some might have called him that but no, just an avid hunter and outdoorsman, you could say. Everything that was in that room he'd accumulated over twenty years. Backpacks, emergency gear, tools, food, water, cooking gear, shelter, security items, stuff for creating fires, medical, hygiene. You name it, he had it." Liam reeled off the items as if he was holding a list. "I used to come in here when I was a kid and rummage through it all. Craziest thing ever. Damn guy could have opened his own survival store. Most of it never got used but he always said it was better to have than not."

"Did he have any friends in the area?"

"Many and they would have known about this." He

shook his head as he sat down on a bench. The inside reminded Elisha of a sauna — pine paneling, a few small vents to let air in and out. "He wasn't exactly one for keeping things to himself. Probably that's why this happened." He groaned. "He was a good man. He would have given you the shirt off his own back." Liam sighed, running a hand around the back of his neck. "I'm just glad he passed away before this shitstorm."

Elisha stepped inside and placed a hand on his shoulder. "We'll figure something out."

"Like what? I was banking on this being here. There would have been enough freeze-dried food to last us for the next year."

"Where did he buy it all?"

"A store in town. Forest City Surplus. It was owned by a buddy of his, Harry Moore. He would take me in there and shoot the breeze with him. I knew his grandson."

"Well I imagine that place was one of the first to be wiped out," Andre said appearing behind them. Andre was a strange fella, a huge man but soft-spoken. He looked as if he'd just stepped out of a penitentiary. Similar in appearance to Garcia, his body was covered in ink.

"Doubt it," Liam said. "Harry is a force to be reckoned with. A few folks in Willits call him Dirty Harry — you know, after the Clint Eastwood movie." He chuckled. "Damn guy would put a hole in you with his .45 if you tried to walk out without paying."

"Well maybe we should head into town and find out if he's still selling," Garcia suggested.

Liam got up and shook his head and brushed by them. "Ah forget it. We might as well head back to Petaluma."

"There's nothing there worth staying for," Garcia said. "Trust me on that."

"Well at least there's more than here."

Elisha frowned. "But you said this area is good for wildlife, fishing and…"

"I said a lot of things, okay! I just thought…" he trailed off. "Ah, forget what I thought." He looked at his hands in frustration. Since losing his parents, he was finding it hard to cope. It was to be expected.

Elisha looked at Garcia. "What do you think?"

Garcia set his shotgun against the wall and with the help of Andre began cleaning up the place. They put the table up again, set the four chairs beneath it and found a black bag to start placing anything that was broken into. "I think you're better off here than in the city. I think we all would."

She frowned. "But…"

"Petaluma is no more," Garcia said setting the black bag down.

"But the emergency committee?"

"As of yesterday, it's no longer in operation. Carlos' crew saw to that and as for the police department, it's down to ten officers, the rest are either dead or missing." He took a seat at the table. "We have to start thinking of our own survival."

"Mayor Fischer?" Elisha asked.

"Some say he skipped town after my conversation with him, but knowing him, he could just be hiding like a rat."

Elisha walked over to the main door and looked outside. Birds chirped and she could hear crickets. If she hadn't experienced the collapse, she could have almost imagined that everything was well in the world.

"Is that why you brought us up here? You were planning on staying?"

Garcia smiled. "No, I meant what I said. I just wanted to make sure you were both safe but by the looks of this, not even here is safe." He paused. "Of course, Andre and I won't stay here, we'll probably pitch a tent down near the lake."

"Why? There is plenty of space." Elisha pointed to the rooms. The cabin was a good size with two bedrooms on the main floor and another in the loft area which was accessible by a ladder.

They looked over to Liam who was turning a silver ring on his finger and looking down. He lifted his eyes. "What? If you want to stay here, be my guest. I'm not."

"But we came all this way," Elisha protested.

"Yeah and what do we have to show for it?"

"I know you're disappointed but the alternative isn't exactly better."

Silence stretched between them.

"What if we can get more supplies?" Garcia said.

"Man, it doesn't matter. Besides, without sounding rude, I don't know you, you don't know me. I mean I appreciate all you did for us back in the city but…"

Garcia nodded. "No, I get it."

"Don't you have family or something?" Liam asked.

"Never married. No kids," he replied. "Figured we could stick together. Safer that way."

"He's right," Elisha said. "Whoever did this might come back."

Liam got up. "Let 'em, there's nothing left to take." He walked out and Elisha looked at Garcia. She raised a finger before stepping outside to speak with him. Liam kicked his feet into the dry earth. He walked over to a tire swing and looked through the trees toward the lake. Sunlight glistened on the surface. It was a beautiful area, quiet and teeming with wildlife. Liam leaned against the tree, cradling his cast.

"So, you used this when you were a kid?"

"Yep," he said, not expanding upon it.

Elisha gripped the weathered rope and tugged at it. It was strong, attached to a large oak tree. She took a deep breath. "I know you're disappointed and I can't imagine what it must have been like to bury your mother and father but Garcia is right. We need to start thinking about our survival now, and… well… we can't do that alone." She looked at him but he wasn't paying attention. He looked lost in thought. "Liam."

"What?" he said with a frustrated tone.

"If you don't stay here, where else would you go?"

"My parents' home."

"Really? After what happened there? C'mon, be serious."

"Look, you know what. Maybe I just don't want Garcia here. Have you thought about that?"

"Why? He got us out."

"He also put us in that situation. Think about it,

Elisha. If it wasn't for him arresting those gang members, we would still be back in Petaluma, my arm wouldn't be broken, and my parents wouldn't be dead."

She stared at him, slowly shaking her head. "All right. I get it. You're looking for someone to blame."

He lifted his eyes. "No, I'm stating facts," he shot back.

"He was doing his job, Liam. You think he wanted any of this to happen?"

"I don't care. It happened because of him."

"Bullshit! You want to blame, go ahead, blame him. You want to wallow, go ahead, wallow. But I'm not spending another minute listening to this. We are alive because of that man. He didn't need to come back for us but he did. He put his career, his very life on the line. Show some appreciation."

"I did." He chuckled. "You know what. Inviting you up here was a bad idea."

With that said he walked off heading down to the lake.

"Yeah, perhaps it was," she yelled back, unsure if he

heard. She gave the tire swing a push in frustration and walked back to the cabin. Garcia and Andre were cleaning up the place and chatting. One look at her face and Garcia knew it hadn't gone well.

"Guessing his answer was no?"

"Let's just leave. He wants to be alone."

Garcia smiled placing a hand on her shoulder. "What guys say and what they mean are often two different things. We'll give him some time to cool off. In the meantime, let's head into Willits and see what the situation is like. I'll run by the police department, and then maybe we can find the infamous Dirty Harry."

It was only as they were backing out did Liam return. Garcia yelled out to him that they were going into town but would return soon. He shrugged and disappeared into the cabin. "Sure has a chip on his shoulder," Andre said.

"Wouldn't you if you lost both parents in one day?" Garcia said.

Finding people like Garcia who were level-headed was rare, having them watch your back was even rarer.

They followed Lilac Drive out to Clover Road, a little north of the lake, and joined Birch Street which ran down into Sherwood and the town. They'd briefly passed through the town on the way up and by any measure it appeared to have fared well in comparison to Petaluma. Shutters were down on stores, a few buildings had been reduced to rubble but beyond that there was nothing to stop it from continuing to function, at least to some moderate level.

Willits was a fraction of the size of Petaluma with roughly five thousand residents. It stood out from the rest of the towns nearby with an arch over the main road. It had been donated from the city of Reno. The problem was, if you blinked passing through, you'd miss it. Besides a Safeway grocery store there really were no brand-name stores, most of the businesses along Main Street were locally owned, mom-and-pop stores. Strangely for a town of its size, the building used for the police department was large. Located just off Commercial Street, it crouched beside city hall and was only a few blocks away from

Children's Services and the famous Skunk Train. As they swerved in front of the department, they noticed how the glass at the front was shattered and the doors were no longer attached.

"Maybe you should show me how to fire one of those," she said as Garcia made sure he had a full magazine.

He glanced at her. "Later. For now stay here."

There was no hesitation. He got out and ran at a crouch toward the main doors with Andre, who was holding a shotgun low. Both went inside while she remained in the cruiser, the engine running. One minute turned into two, then four, then six and she began to think something had gone awry. Sitting in the back seat, Elisha nervously turned her head. Was someone watching her or was it her mind playing tricks?

Right then, a hand slapped the window and she flinched only to see Garcia. She brought the window down and he told her to turn off the engine and follow him inside.

"Where did you come from?"

He pointed to a side door.

"Anyone in there?"

"We found a couple of dead cops but that's it. Andre is seeing what he can salvage. I didn't want to leave you out here." He looked toward the street.

Inside, glass was everywhere. There was blood on the walls, floors and counters, where someone had been shot and stumbled through the department only to come to rest beyond the main help desk. Paperwork was scattered like confetti.

"Find anything?" Garcia asked.

Andre shook his head. "Whoever did this wiped it out."

While they continued searching, Elisha walked down a corridor and peered into different rooms. At the far end of the corridor was the office of the chief of police. The door was partially closed but there was blood on the handle. Using the tip of her boot she pushed it open only to find the chief slumped over the desk. A single bullet wound to his temple, his face resting in a pool of congealed blood. Elisha felt her gag reflex kick in and she braced herself against the door.

Garcia appeared behind her and she put a hand on her heart. "I wish you would stop creeping up on me."

"Figured you heard me."

He looked past her and shook his head. "Damn it. I knew him. Good man." He stepped inside and looked around the room. "What in God's name happened here?"

"Gangs?" she asked.

"No. There's no incentive."

Elisha backed up. "Perhaps we should just leave. See if we can't find that surplus store."

"Yeah." As they turned to head out, a chorus of gunfire erupted. Elisha went to go check on Andre but Garcia wrapped a hand over her mouth and pulled her back into the room.

Chapter 3

Denver

Star, as she liked to be called, was a spunky little kid with a hooped ring in the corner of her lower lip, and a nose stud to boot. She had all the swagger of a twenty-year-old but was only thirteen. It was disconcerting to say the least. After saving her life Alex had brought her back to the café and was trying to get her to understand the danger but she acted like she was untouchable. "You're wrong. I wouldn't have died. Now I need to go or they'll kill me."

"Kill?"

"Not literally." She rolled her eyes.

"Who then… your parents?" Alex asked. "Is that who was signaling to you?"

"No, that was Meadow."

"Do any of you go by regular names?"

Star scowled.

Sophie could tell they weren't getting anywhere so she tried to work her magic. "Sweetheart. Where are your parents?"

"In a graveyard."

Awkwardness followed.

"Oh." Sophie shared a glance with Alex. "I'm sorry."

"I'm not." She bounced off the stool and tried to bolt for the door but Alex grabbed her arm. "Hey, man, get off me. I need to go."

"Just let her go," Ryan said.

Alex ignored him. "Where do you live?"

"Outside of the city."

"Where?"

"On a ranch."

"Do you want to be more specific?"

She pointed randomly. "You know the town of Golden?"

"No."

Star snorted. "It's west of here about 35 minutes by Jeep."

"Jeep?" Thomas perked up. "You got a ride, kid?"

Star acted like it was obvious. "Yeah."

"So this friend of yours. Meadow. She brought you into the city?"

"Not exactly."

Everything that was coming out of her mouth wasn't making sense.

Sophie bent at the waist and did her mothering act. "Hon, how did you get here?"

"Oh gee, Mom, I just told you. The Jeep."

The sarcasm was strong with this one.

"And Meadow, is that your sister?"

"No."

Alex shook his head, getting a little frustrated. "Thomas, keep an eye on her," Alex said as he motioned to Sophie to head to the main doors so they could talk. Thomas grinned as he walked over and stood in front of her, tapping a finger against his rifle to impose his authority.

Star folded her arms defiantly.

Once out of earshot, Alex shifted from one foot to the next. "So what do you want to do?"

"About?" Sophie asked.

"Well." He motioned toward the girl.

"Should have thought of that before you went and got her."

"What did you expect me to do? She's a kid."

"Yeah, and now we're responsible for her." She shook her head. "We didn't need this, Alex. We have enough to deal with."

"I figured of all people you would understand."

She set a hand against the wall. "No, I understand you were trying to help but now it's put us in an awkward position."

He bit down on his lower lip as he looked at Star.

"She mentioned a Jeep. Might be fate." A smile formed.

"Yeah, and this whole event might be fate. C'mon,

Alex." She leaned back against the wall and let out an exasperated sigh.

Alex got closer to her, his eyes narrowing. "You think I like this situation any more than you? We've been stuck here for far longer than we should. We should be in California by now but we're not. Why's that? Oh, that's right, Ryan wanted to make a pit stop by his so-called brother's house."

"You said you wouldn't bring that up again."

He exhaled hard. "I know. Look, I'm just frustrated, okay?" He looked back at Star. "The kid sounds as if she knows the area. Now we can use the maps and spend our time darting in and out of buildings, and maybe, just maybe, we'll get out in a couple of days if those drones don't kill us first but… perhaps with her Jeep we can get out of here faster."

"And perhaps she can get us killed."

He stared back in astonishment. "What's the problem?"

"My problem is exactly what you just said. We are a

week into this and still haven't reached our daughter. I don't want to get sidetracked. We did that once and look how that ended."

He chuckled, unable to hold in his amusement. "I'm pretty sure you were the one who agreed to stop in Asheville. It was also you who backed Ryan up."

She gave him this long look. "Are we back to that again?"

He groaned. "I don't want to fight. I just want to get out of here and if that kid has a faster way, then I'm all ears. So?"

Sophie pursed her lips and motioned for him to lead the way.

"Star," Alex said. "How long have you been in the city?"

"A day."

"How have you managed to avoid the drones?"

"The same way we've managed to avoid them since this started."

Thomas chimed in. "They've been here since the

beginning?"

"No. Two days after the event they showed up."

Alex brought up fingers to the bridge of his nose. "So you've been in the city how many times since this started?"

"Daily."

"Looking for provisions?"

Star smiled back but didn't say anything.

"Kid, can you stop being so cryptic and get to the part where you tell us how you've managed to elude those damn drones? Because from what I've seen, they kill everything in their path."

"They're not out at night," she replied.

"Well if that's the case, then why are you here in the day?" he shot back.

"I have my reasons."

"Oh great, another Ryan," Alex said looking over to him. Ryan wasn't paying attention. He was too busy ferreting through boxes.

Alex turned to Sophie. "So we wait until sundown."

He took his eyes off Star for but a moment when she bolted for the door. Not even Thomas could grab her in time. There was no hesitation, she burst out of the café, leaping over slabs of concrete and bouncing from one to the next with all the prowess of a panther. She hadn't been in the open for less than a minute when drones darkened the sky. Alex couldn't have made it back or even to a place of cover in time. All he could do was look on in horror as the young girl climbed, jumped and sprinted from one mound of debris to the next. He wanted to close his eyes to avoid seeing her disappear in an explosion but then something remarkable happened. The drones flew overhead and didn't engage.

They were dumbfounded.

Thomas' jaw dropped. "Well, I'll be damned. She was telling the truth."

"No. That's impossible," Sophie countered. "Those drones took out anyone that was moving or in sight."

"Obviously, she's an exception," Thomas said.

"The question is why?" Alex said.

Star stopped running and looked back at them, a smile danced as if it was all a big game. She shouted back, "If you want a ride out of the city, meet me tonight at the Denver Country Club at eight. If you're a minute late, we leave without you."

And just like that she turned and continued, darting around vehicles until she was out of sight. Alex contemplated following but the drones flew over again and he saw them strafe a building and unleash hell, sending large segments of glass and concrete to the ground.

What did she have that prevented her from getting hurt?

Why hadn't they engaged?

Not wasting any time he pulled out a map of the city and a list of businesses they'd gathered from the library. He cleared off the counter, sending paper cups and a metal rack to the ground. He scooped up a pen and smoothed out the map. "Okay, we are here. Quebec Street." He tapped the paper. "First Avenue is over here.

That area there is where the country club is," he said pointing to a large patch of greenery. "I estimate that it will take us around an hour to reach it on foot. If those drones are out tonight it could take far longer."

"She's playing with you," Ryan said, strolling in from the back with a half-finished cigarette in his mouth. He stubbed it out before Sophie could take it from him.

"And how would you know?" Thomas asked, folding his arms.

He lifted a hand. "Because she lied."

"Go on," Sophie said.

"She said the reason she was able to dodge those drones was because they visited the city at night and the drones are only here in the day. However, she didn't stick around until night before she left. Why? Because she knew those drones wouldn't touch her. The question you should be asking is, why not? My guess, she has something to do with it or she knows whoever is behind it." He took a seat on a stool and tore apart a packet of cookies. "Which leads me to believe whoever is controlling those eyes in the sky is at this ranch or closer."

"What if we could stop it?" Thomas said.

Sophie lifted a hand and pointed at him. "No. No. We are not getting involved. I am getting home to my daughter and that's all that matters to me," she said.

Thomas looked at Alex and he raised a hand. "Don't look at me. I'm with her."

"Ryan?"

"Do I look like I give a shit?"

"I would have thought you would."

"Oh right, because I started it… Is that what you're saying?"

"If the boot fits."

The two of them went at it again.

It was hard to ignore what they'd seen. How could a young kid escape under the nose of drones unless she knew something they didn't? Alex wondered what might come next if this was the second wave of attacks. Even if they could survive. Even if these attacks were focused on the capitals and they managed to get out. What then?

Days, weeks, even months from now society or what was left of it would need to pick up the pieces, reunite and rebuild what had been torn down. How could they do that if this kind of threat still existed? Then on the other hand, who were they to stop something of this magnitude? He looked at Ryan. Maybe fate had brought them together.

Still.

Who was this girl and how did she fit into the bigger picture?

* * *

For 18 seconds straight four gang members beat on the man before taking pocket knives and stabbing him until his intestines could be seen. After, Alvaro Fernandez gestured to his foot soldiers to drag the rival gang member outside and dump his body. Gang signs were thrown in the air and the rest continued drinking and partying as if nothing had happened.

Leo wanted to throw up as a flashback of his time in the gang came to him, and the day he asked permission to leave. Looking back now it all seemed so foolish but at the age of 12 he was naïve and lacking a father figure in his life. They offered him brotherhood, strict rules, protection and stability when he had none. With few options or prospects, and seeing so many of his friends get caught up in the drug scene, it just seemed like a no-brainer to get involved.

However, it didn't take him long to see through the smoke and mirrors.

Before looking at him, Alvaro raised his voice to the other sixty or more members that were jammed into a plush hotel lobby that once catered to the rich and famous. Now it was overrun with the worst of society like rats in a sewer. As a general might when rallying his troops, Alvaro paced before them raising two fingers. "There are only two roads for all of us in this life. Prison and death. At some point all of you will face these. But that's okay. That's what we signed up for. There is no escaping who we are. You've pledged your life to this gang, and we live or die by that pledge. No matter what happens, 18th Street is forever."

They roared and cheered.

At one time he would have been in awe, now he felt only shame, shame for his past.

Alvaro turned and his face changed to an expression of glee.

"Shorty. A long time, huh?" He looked him up and down and walked around Leo assessing him. "Been a lot of change around here. You kept your nose clean, I see, remained true to your word. Tell me, what was it like?"

"What?"

"Leaving the gang."

Leo shrugged.

"Must have been hard without an army behind you."

The few who were granted permission to leave usually suffered greatly and either died at the hands of another gang who had no idea they'd left, or they had problems finding employment as society blocked their path to a better life. "I survived."

"Survive. Yes you did, and that's why you're here. I

have a very special job for you."

Alvaro got close to him, his nose inches away from his face. Alvaro had dark hair, sunglasses and a mustache that made him look like Freddie Mercury. It didn't help that he was rarely seen out of a white muscle shirt. Age, however, was catching up with him. Leo eyed the silver flecks at his temple.

"Alvaro, with all due respect, surely there is someone else who can do it?"

"If there was, you and I wouldn't be talking now."

He cracked his neck in front of him by cocking it to the side before continuing to prowl his domain. "You will be heading north to provide support to La Primera."

"What?"

"I want you to go with twenty of our guys. You understand?"

He frowned. "I understand, but why? La Primera…"

"They are a leading source of narcotics in the northern district of California, allowing us to branch out. If they suffer, we suffer. Understand?"

"I understand but Ramiro surely…"

Before he could finish, Alvaro grabbed him by the throat and forced him back against a wall and squeezed hard. "Your days of giving orders, Leo, are gone. You relinquished the seat the day you walked out. Now I give the orders, you hear me?"

He gritted his teeth. This wasn't about need; it was a power move. Alvaro had at one time been below Leo, a triggerman like himself. Leo's rise to power had never sat well with him because he believed he should have been given the position. Now that he was at the helm he wanted Leo to know, he wanted him to feel what it was like to serve under someone else. Leo nodded. "I won't kill anyone."

He cocked his head. "You won't?"

"Calmado. There are rules that even you must follow."

Alvaro chuckled. "Those were the old rules. I make the rules now, homie. And as for Ramiro, he will go with you just to ensure that you do your job." He released his death grip around Leo's neck and backed up but not before slapping him on the side of the face. "It's good to see you again, Shorty. Remember, without loyalty the gang is nothing." He laughed as he walked over to Ramiro and muttered something to him. Ramiro grinned and looked at Leo before Alvaro returned.

He wanted to protest but he could see Alvaro was looking for a reason to show his dominance, and make Leo look less than a man in front of his men. Leo didn't care how he looked but knowing Alvaro, he wouldn't stop with him, he might punish the church and innocent people, and he couldn't have that.

"Oh by the way, Leo, I have something that belongs to you." He crossed the room and returned holding a 9mm. It was Leo's old piece. He recognized it instantly. Alvaro handed it to him with a smile on his face. He knew he was against killing. "Remember your first kill? Of course you do." Leo took it and looked at it. "Officer Felix Garcia. Find him. Then report back. I have more work for you to do."

Chapter 4

Willits, California

Two, maybe three. Garcia couldn't quite make out the conversation but he'd heard Andre's voice. He was alive. Possibly injured but alive. "Stay here," he said, quietly opening the door and shuffling out at a crouch. He looked back and saw Elisha close the door behind him. Cautiously he weaved his way around debris — reports, a tipped-over filing cabinet, even a snapshot of someone's family inside a cracked frame.

"I'm telling you the truth," Andre said loudly.

"You expect us to believe you waltzed in here to see what you could salvage?"

Garcia made his way up to a doorway and peered around. Two guys, ordinary looking, baseball caps, early twenties, one had shaggy blond hair coming out the back, the other was sporting one hell of a shiner.

He wanted to burst out, gun raised but needed to make sure they were the only ones. The two men continued to question Andre, apparently interested in where he was from, why he was in Willits and where he was staying.

Convinced they were alone, Garcia shuffled into the next room and made his way over to the counter. He'd use it for cover if they got trigger-happy and took a potshot. "Take a look, Travis. Our boy here has gang tats."

"Where's the rest of your crew?" Travis asked.

"I told you. It's just me."

"No, you boys don't travel alone. Where are they? Looting homes, businesses, raping someone?"

"I…"

"You better start telling the truth and…"

"Put your weapons down!" Garcia said rising from behind the counter, his shotgun leveled, his finger on the trigger. Both men looked his way, their eyes widened.

"He's not with the gangs."

The guy with shaggy hair set his rifle down immediately but the other, the one going by the name Travis, held on to his. "Can't do that."

"C'mon man, I don't want to shoot you," Garcia said.

"Yeah? What cop did you steal that uniform off?"

"Put the gun down!"

"If I do that, we're as good as dead just like these cops here. You did this, didn't you?"

"We're not even from the area. We're visiting. I'm an officer with Petaluma."

"Then you're a long way from home."

"Brought a friend here."

"Yeah? Who?"

Garcia was beginning to lose his patience. "Put the gun down."

"Sorry, compadre, but it looks like we are at a stalemate. By the time you squeeze that trigger, I will have squeezed mine and you'll have to pick up your pal's brains."

"Listen, I'm going to reach into my pocket and get you some ID. You cool with that?" Garcia asked.

"I'm cool with you putting that shotgun down."

Garcia chuckled. "Not happening."

"Oh I think it is," Travis said, a smile forming.

Just then, Garcia heard movement behind him. He turned his head ever so slightly to see a 9mm pointing at his cheek. A tall thin guy wearing a beanie grinned at him. He looked a little rough as if he hadn't slept in a week. "Lower the gun. Nice and easy."

As Garcia contemplated doing as instructed, the sound of someone racking a semi-auto was heard a short distance away. "You took the words right out of my mouth," Elisha said. A gun came into view from around the doorway, pointed at the same guy who had a 9mm to his head.

Beanie dude closed his eyes. "Shit!"

"Drop it," Elisha said with confidence and authority.

The clatter of the 9mm was met by further instructions from Garcia. "Unless you want your buddy to die, I recommend you put the rifle down."

Travis gritted his teeth, hesitated for a second and then lowered it.

As soon as he did, Andre swooped in and collected their weapons and then told them to get up against the wall so they could pat them down.

"You know this could have all been avoided had you listened," Garcia said.

"You won't make it out of town," Travis replied.

"Really? Why, are you head of some kind of posse? Huh?"

"Screw you, man."

Garcia chuckled.

"Are you going to kill us?" Shaggy asked.

"Oh I'm not planning on killing you boys," Garcia said after patting them down. "Take a seat on the ground with your hands locked behind your heads." Travis frowned, looking confused, as Andre kept his rifle trained on him.

"Here," Elisha said handing over the 9mm. "It wasn't

loaded."

Garcia chuckled and Travis turned to his pal. "You idiot!"

Beanie shrugged. "What? I didn't know."

Garcia went on to show them his ID. "Like I said, I'm not planning on killing you but I do have a few questions. What happened here?"

"You're asking us?" Travis glared at Andre.

"He was telling you the truth," Garcia said.

"Yeah, maybe he was, but I had good reason to not believe him. We've seen an influx of guys who look like you come through our town over the past week. How are we to know any different?"

"They did this?" Garcia asked.

"What do you think?" Travis replied. They were cocky but in years of working with different people, he'd gotten a feel for those who would slit your throat and those who only had courage when they were in a group.

Garcia's gaze washed over them. "So you guys are local?"

Travis laughed. "Of course. Next question."

"You think we can hurry this up? My knees are killing me," Shaggy said.

"Forest Surplus. You know it?" Elisha asked.

Shaggy looked at Travis and he shook his head. "Can't say I do."

Garcia caught the look on his pal's face. Dishonesty was an everyday part of his life. No one told the truth, at least very few did and cops were quite adept at seeing through the smoke and mirrors. "Interesting. How long have you lived here?"

Travis flashed a toothy grin. "Long enough."

"Huh. You see, we were told most folks knew who Dirty Harry was."

Travis' eyes fixed on him.

"Ah, there we go," Garcia replied. The lights were finally on.

"How do you know that name?"

Garcia shifted from one foot to the other, fine lines appearing on his forehead. "Everyone does, don't they?"

Travis looked at Shaggy. "There are only a few who call him that."

Garcia chuckled and eyed Elisha. "Maybe we should ask Liam."

That really got his attention. Travis lowered his hands. "Liam? Liam Carter?"

"Put your hands back where they were," Andre said.

Travis tossed him the bird but complied.

"You know him?" Elisha added.

Travis burst out laughing. "Do I know him?" He looked at Shaggy then back at her. "Of course I do, he's an old friend of mine." His face brightened up and he went to get up and Andre shoved the barrel at him.

"Whoa. Whoa! You want to call your dog off?" Travis backed up with his hands raised.

"Andre. It's okay, man," Garcia said. Andre took a few steps back as a precautionary measure but kept the rifle on them as Travis rose to his feet. "You might want to fill us in before my friend here changes his mind."

"Okay. Look, me and Liam go way back. He used to

spend his summers here. His grandfather Theo owned a cabin about ten minutes from here by the lake. That good enough for you?"

"Who broke into his place?" Elisha asked.

Travis glanced at her. "What?"

"The cabin was ransacked. Tables flipped over, ripped bedding, even the flooring had been pulled up in some areas. They took all the supplies."

"Listen, I don't know anything about that but I can tell you where the supplies are. They're with Harry, my grandfather. That's how I know him. Theo used to bring Liam into the store when he came into town. I used to help my grandfather and we hit it off. Though I haven't seen Liam in a long time."

Garcia frowned and Travis filled in the blanks.

"No one stole his stuff if that's what you're thinking. Before Theo passed away he put every single item into storage at my grandfather's. Said he could resell, or give it away to someone who could use it. He was worried about someone breaking in. I guess that answers your question about the ransacking."

Garcia nodded. "Possibly. Your grandfather still alive?"

"That guy will live to a hundred. He's as strong as an ox, isn't that right, Tate?" He said turning to the shaggy one. "Oh by the way, that's Tate, and slim boy there is Joe." They both gave a nod but still looked a little apprehensive because Andre hadn't taken the rifle off them.

"Andre," Garcia said motioning for him to lower the weapon.

"Yeah, well how about you take us to see Harry? We need supplies."

Travis's gaze bounced between them. "Well hold on a second, where's Liam?"

"At the cabin," Elisha replied.

"You'll need to get him. You could say my grandfather is a little skittish right now with all that's happened. His store has already had people try to get inside."

"How did that work out?" Andre asked.

Travis laughed. "Come and see for yourself. But first,

get Liam."

"I guess we're all going for a ride then," Garcia said, prompting them to exit.

* * *

Liam couldn't believe it was all gone. While the others were in town he dug through a shed out back to see if the old generator was in there. Nope. That was gone. He kicked an empty paint can across the yard just as he heard the sound of gravel crunching beneath tires. He brought a hand up to his eyes to block the glare of the afternoon sunshine. A truck rolled in behind the cruiser but he couldn't see who was driving.

"Liam!" Elisha called out his name.

"Around back," he bellowed as he made his way up to the cabin.

"Brought an old friend of yours."

"What?"

Travis strolled around the corner, a smirk on his face. "Liam."

He stopped walking and squinted. "Travis? Holy shit,"

he said jogging over. They gave each other a manly pat on the back as they hugged it out before parting. "What? When? Where?" he said trying to find the words as he looked over at Garcia.

"We had a bit of a run-in," Travis said thumbing over his shoulder.

"Not hurt, I hope?"

"No, we're good."

"We're?"

"Tate and Joe are in the truck."

"What?" He hurried over to see them. They hopped out and greeted one another. It had been years since he'd seen them. "Man, you guys are a sight for sore eyes. What's it been? Three years?"

"Something like that," Tate replied.

Liam's smile faded. "I'd invite you in for a drink or something but I'm afraid we've been ransacked."

"Actually…" Travis began to speak.

"His grandfather took it," Garcia said.

Liam shot back. "Why would he take it?"

"Theo told him to hold on to it."

Liam offered a confused expression. "He gave it back?"

"Liam, you haven't been back here in years. I don't even remember seeing you at your grandfather's funeral."

"I was overseas."

"Well, a lot has changed. Theo gave strict instructions for Harry to take it. He didn't want to have your mother deciding on where it went, I guess."

"Oh. Right." He nodded. "Well."

Travis placed a hand on his arm. "Look man, don't worry. I'm sure Harry will give you a few things."

"A few?"

"It was years ago, Liam. Most of what he had was sold or given away."

"You're joking, right?"

Travis shrugged. "Look, I don't know what to say."

"How about you tell me who broke in?"

"How would I know that?"

"Not much happens in this town without Harry knowing."

"That was before this event. There have been break-ins all over the town. Harry hasn't left that store in over a week. He's holed up there. Sleeps, eats, shits, you get the picture. And as for break-ins. Your grandfather wasn't the only one. Harry had to shoot two guys who tried to use a tire iron to tear off a lock from the shutters. And that's not the worst." He looked over to Garcia.

"I'll fill him in," Garcia said.

"Look, how about you all come back with us. Have a meal. We can catch up. You can tell me what you've been up to." He gripped Liam by the arms. "Man, it's good to see you again."

"You too, brother."

Travis got back in the truck and Elisha sidled up to Liam and they looked at them as the truck roared to life. "So… changed your mind on staying now?"

He smirked. "We'll see."

* * *

It didn't take long to reach Forest City Surplus. The one-story brick building had steel shutters covering the windows. It stood out like a sore thumb painted in emergency red with white lettering across the top. An American flag gently flapped in the breeze. It was attached to a pole on the left side of the building. An A-frame chalkboard outside had the words: CLOSED FOR BUSINESS. Multiple signs had been erected around the property with a warning that if anyone came within ten feet they would be shot. The two bodies not far from the main doors were proof of that. With survival gear in high demand and the uncertainty of sustainability hanging in the balance, everyone wanted a slice of the pie. Harry had been smart enough when he built the place to install large concrete barriers directly in front of the windows and doors so that any attempt to drive a vehicle through the front would fail.

"This grandfather of yours. How old is he?" Elisha asked.

Travis smiled. "Seventy going on eighty-four, he likes to say."

"And he shot these guys?"

"Hell yeah. Guy was in the military before he got into this business," Travis said as he guided them around the back to a steel door, then banged several times.

"Didn't give you a key?"

"How stupid would that be if I got caught?"

Garcia nodded. "Good point, and yet he gave you a special knock?"

They waited for Harry to appear at the door but he didn't. Instead, he emerged on top of the slanted roof, rifle aimed at them. "Who the fuck are they?" the old man said, with a cigar stuck in the corner of his mouth. *Eighty-four?* He didn't look a day over sixty. His hair was as white as snow and he was wearing an American flag bandanna. Reminded Garcia of some '80s action hero.

Travis took a few steps back and gazed up. "Grandfather, you remember Liam Carter."

"Who? Speak up?"

"Liam. Theo's grandson."

The man squinted through his round glasses. "Tube Steak?"

"Tube Steak?" Elisha asked, an eyebrow rising.

Liam closed his eyes and went red in the cheeks. He cleared his throat. "It's a long story. Toilet humor. Hey there," Liam replied to Harry.

"What are you doing back here?"

"You know… just taking in the sights."

Harry burst out laughing and took out his cigar. "Well, did you see those two guys? Cause that's exactly what they said until I put a hole in their heads."

Liam swallowed hard.

"Grandfather, just open up."

"And who are the other two pinheads?"

"A cop and …" He turned toward Andre who was scowling at him. "Another cop. I think," Travis said in an unsure tone as he shrugged.

Harry grumbled. "Cops? We still have some of those left?" No one answered. "They gonna be a problem, Travis?"

"No. Just open up."

"All right, all right. But if any of you try to take

anything, I'm warning you. I'll shoot you and throw you to the buzzards to chew on." He cracked up laughing and disappeared out of view. Two, maybe three minutes later came the sound of multiple locks being undone, then the door groaned open.

"Come on in, just... well... don't touch. Anything," Travis said. "With the amount of LSD he consumed in the seventies, he's been known to have flashbacks and—"

Harry cut him off. "I might be losing my sight, boy, but I can still hear you."

Travis laughed, patting him on the shoulder as he brushed past.

Chapter 5

Denver

The threat was real, the challenge great.

How did anyone traverse a city as huge as Denver when every time they stepped out they risked being annihilated? Alex gazed at the swarm that blackened the sky as drones scoured the streets for fresh targets. How many were there? Too many to count. Certainly enough that dozens could vanish, recharge, reload and take flight again without them noticing. Had they targeted the other capitals across the USA? And more importantly, who was in control?

Thomas and Ryan threw out ideas about certain hackers but at this point none of it was of any use to them. All they had to go on were the words of a stranger, a thirteen-year-old girl who appeared to defy logic. It wasn't just that the drones hadn't attacked her, she believed that she wouldn't be touched and that struck them as odd.

Multiple attempts to gain ground in the city had been met with force. Thomas had come dangerously close to death on their last run.

He was starting to think that perhaps they might have to rely on a child to escape this madness.

Alex looked at his watch.

He glanced over his shoulder, shaking his head. Hours had passed and they hadn't made it far. The café was still in sight. July meant the sun wouldn't set until roughly thirty minutes after eight. That was too late. Star would be gone by then. Not that they'd planned on heading to the country club. "I think Thomas is right. We might have to go with Star."

"No. We don't have time for that," Sophie said.

"Look at how far we've gotten over the past few hours. It's time to face the facts, we are not getting out of this city anytime soon unless we meet up with her. Now I have no idea how she is managing to elude these drones or if she'll even be at the location but that's a risk I'm willing to take if it means getting out." She stared at him as he continued. "Even Ryan is considering it."

She looked at Ryan who was talking with Thomas and then nodded in agreement. Alex pulled out the map and pushed it against a crumbling wall. He ran his hand over it to smooth out the creases. "We are here. She is here. That's a lot closer than us trying to get here." He pointed to the far side of the city. "Without a vehicle we are screwed, and even if we found one, you saw what those drones did to those last two vehicles. We don't stand a chance."

"No. There has to be another way," she said. "Let's wait until the sun goes down. You heard what she said. The drones aren't meant to be out at night."

"And what if they are? Hmm? What if we wait until then only to discover they are out and we've missed the opportunity to get out with Star? Look, as much as I don't want to get distracted, common sense tells me this girl knows something we don't, and if she thinks she can drive a Jeep out of here without getting blown to pieces then I want to be inside it. We can always get out and continue as soon as we are out of the capital but right now we have limited options."

Thomas and Ryan were eavesdropping.

"Finally, now you listen to me," Thomas said, looking at a red 4 x 4 truck that had only minutes earlier been filled with a family trying to flee. The truck was on its side. None had survived. Black smoke billowed above it as orange flames consumed the interior. After discussing a plan, Alex used the map and compass to pinpoint their location and which way they could go and certain stores they might be able to take cover in. It wasn't like they could time it. There were moments they were moving down the street and not one drone was in sight, but then they'd round a corner only to find a dozen tearing up the sky.

Alex shrugged his bag over his shoulder and adjusted it to make sure it didn't slip, wrapped the strap of his rifle around him and prepared to run the gauntlet.

"You ready?" he asked as they prepared to sprint.

Each of them nodded, looking like runners at a starting line.

It might have been easier had the streets been clear but with so much of the sidewalk and road covered in rubble, it felt like they were navigating an obstacle course. His thighs burned as he sprinted down the street, slaloming around obstacles, climbing over concrete, and launching himself off the top of crushed vehicles. They made it to East First Avenue, a stretch of road that ran adjacent to a once thriving neighborhood.

"Alex!" Sophie yelled as she took a tumble. He returned and scooped her up but didn't check to see if she was okay. There was no time for that. Limping, she groaned as they soldiered on though now even slower than before. The familiar and frightening hum of drones caught his attention. Alex scanned the sky. Where were they? Ryan and Thomas were at least twenty yards ahead. He bellowed for them to take cover but they didn't hear him because his cry was instantly muffled by an explosion as the army of drones came into view, racing toward them. He saw the two of them veer right onto Newport Street, they did the same but one street over.

Alex had no choice but to take cover inside a home. The door was closed. There was no time to make it to the next so they began banging on the door. From beyond they heard a female. "Go away."

"Let us in, please."

The woman refused, fearing for her life.

The only cover they had was a small overhang.

"Over here!" a voice cried from across the street.

An old-timer had opened his window and beckoned them across.

As they went to step out, the old man shouted for them to stop, his hand outstretched, his eyes widening. Seconds later two drones came into view, hovering above the street, rotating as if scanning or searching for them. Neither of them moved a muscle as the drones got lower.

The door behind them cracked open and the owner

waved them in. They backed up but not before Alex waved a thank you to her neighbor.

The woman was young, early twenties, short, dark hair and almond eyes. She was juggling a baby in one arm while two little boys no older than five hid behind her legs.

"Thank you," Sophie said, smiling to put the woman at ease. She was frightened and turned to look out the peephole again.

"How many are out there?"

"The drones?" Alex asked.

She nodded.

"Hard to tell. A lot." Alex looked around, and saw a photo on the wall of the woman with her kids and a guy. "That your partner?"

"Was," she said. She brushed by without explaining, she didn't need to. How many had lost their lives?

"We won't stay long," Sophie said limping into the living room. "I just need a moment to check my ankle." The woman set her baby into a portable crib and gave her boys some toys to play with before turning and looking at Sophie, who peeled down her sock to reveal an angry, swollen ankle.

"I'll get you something for that," the woman said, looking back at her kids then at Alex as if he might be a threat, especially since he was carrying a rifle. She stepped out of the room but returned only moments later with an instant ice pack. Sophie removed her boot and sock and thanked her as she wrapped it around her ankle and the woman tucked a few pillows beneath it.

"The name's Sophie."

"Crystal," the woman replied with a smile.

Her boys tossed a few plastic toys across the room and she apologized.

Alex smiled. "No need. Been a long time since ours were that age."

"You have kids?" she asked.

"Two," Sophie said.

"One," Alex said at the same time.

The difference created confusion. She bounced a finger

between them. "Together or…"

"Long story but…" Sophie said. "We have a daughter in California."

"And a son who's no longer with us," Alex said.

"I'm sorry. It seems we've all lost someone."

Alex looked at Sophie and neither of them chose to explain that Michael had died a long time ago. "My husband went out a few days ago to see if he could find supplies. He never returned." She looked at her children and Alex could see the pain in her eyes. "I couldn't go because of my kids." She sighed. "I'm sorry I don't have much to give you."

"You haven't been out in a week?"

She shook her head no.

"What have you been eating? Drinking?" Sophie asked looking at the kids.

"I'm breastfeeding my young one. Thankfully I had a lot of canned food in storage before this all happened. Though we were getting low when my husband went out." Tears welled in her eyes.

"And you?" Alex asked.

"I haven't eaten much."

Sophie looked at Alex and he recognized that look.

"Do you know your neighbors?" he asked.

"Not really. Everyone pretty much keeps to themselves."

Alex nodded. "Every man for himself." He thought back to Tarboro and the community helping one another. That's the way it should have been but that place was minuscule compared to Denver. "What about the guy across the street?"

"Don't know him."

"He seemed eager to help us."

She shrugged.

Alex shrugged off his bag and unzipped it. He took out what food he'd obtained from the library. It wasn't much, mostly muffins, chips, cookies, a few packets of peanuts and some coffee, but he figured she was in greater need. "Here, take this."

"No. I couldn't."

"It's fine," Sophie said. "You helped us. Let us help you."

They could see she wanted to take it but was hesitant. "Careful though, you might break a tooth on the outer part of that muffin," Alex said. "But once you get beyond that it's pretty good."

She chuckled and thanked them.

Right then, there was a knock at the door and Alex went to see. Through the peephole the large face of the old man across the road came into view. "It's your neighbor. You want me to open?" Alex asked. Crystal gave a nod so Alex opened the door.

"Oh, hi, I wanted to check in. Saw you made it. Figured you might know what's happening out there." He poked his head in but didn't cross over until Crystal invited him in.

He was a tall fella, early seventies, full head of gray hair but physically strong. "The name's Daniel." He shook his hand and walked into the living room and saw the kids. "Looks like you have a lot of mouths to feed. How you coping? My wife has been urging me to come over but with those drones out there I didn't want to take the risk. Then I saw you guys and… well… what's it like out there?" he asked.

"Hell, pure hell," Alex replied.

Daniel pursed his lips and nodded. "Where you heading?"

Alex glanced at Sophie and Daniel caught it. "Ah, it's fine, you don't need to tell me. I know people are a little skittish right now of each other. Um, I have something for you," he said motioning to Crystal. He went back to the main door and opened it. As he did that, Alex unslung his rifle just in case. Daniel returned with two plastic carrier bags. "Gina, my wife that is, told me to bring these over. We have enough but figured you could use some more." He set them down and Crystal looked inside. She withdrew cans of soup and looked up at him, her eyes welling. "Oh, and there is something in there for the kiddies. We're just across the road if you need anything else," he said turning to leave.

"Thank you. Really."

Alex felt like a fly on the wall witnessing human kindness at its best.

"Nice to meet you all. I should get back." Crystal got up and thanked him again.

As soon as he was gone, Sophie smiled at her. "Seems you do have an angel watching over you."

"Seems so. Here, you can take back what you gave. He's given us—"

"No, keep it," Alex said.

"Are you sure?"

"Positive. I was only telling Sophie this morning that we shouldn't have pigged out so much." He smiled. "You keep it, honey." Sophie looked at him, knowing that he wasn't telling the truth. Her lip curled ever so slightly. He turned his attention to her. "How's your leg? We should get moving."

Sophie stood up. "Still sore but better than it was."

Crystal hugged them before they parted ways. As soon as they were outside they stared toward the street, preparing to break into a jog. "Pigged out?" she said.

He smiled but didn't look at her. "What? That muffin filled me up."

She chuckled. He took her hand and they double-timed it down the block, his heart pounding in his chest just waiting for the first sight of a drone. Strangely they never reappeared. Although they were both concerned for Ryan and Thomas, they'd made it clear that if they got separated just to continue, keep going until they reached the country club.

The streets were empty. No one except them was crazy enough to play roulette with their lives. As they jogged together, Sophie turned to him. "Doesn't it seem odd to you?"

"What?"

"Star was able to run and walk beneath those drones without being targeted and presumably she can do the same in a vehicle, so why make us come to her? Why not tell us to stay put and bring the vehicle to us?"

He nudged her and pointed up ahead. "I don't know.

Maybe you can ask her. There she is!" It was the first sign of hope they'd had since arriving in Denver. Seeing Thomas and Ryan waiting for them brought a smile to Sophie, the thought of Crystal and Daniel brought a smile to his. Amid the pain, death and suffering there was still good, still people looking out for each other. Perhaps that was Star's intention, nothing more than someone looking to pay back kindness.

They would soon find out how wrong they were.

Chapter 6

California

It was baptism by fire.

Leo watched as Ramiro extracted the knife from the councilman's throat after seeking the whereabouts of Officer Felix Garcia. On the ride up to Petaluma, he'd learned a lot from Ramiro. A loyal foot soldier for Alvaro, he was careful not to speak out of line, perhaps fearful that one of the twenty that came with them might misinterpret his words and use them against him later. And, well they would if given the chance as there was no honor among thieves. Years in the gangs had taught Leo that many would take advantage of another if it meant rising through the ranks.

It was strange to be among them, running with the wolves. It should have felt normal and yet it was far from it.

Much had changed in two years away from gang life.

Rumor had that Chepe, the previous leader of 18th Street, had been taken out by a rival gang member in a drive-by shooting. While another gang had claimed they were responsible, those in the know said that Alvaro was behind it. It made sense; he would have been the first to benefit. The only thing standing between him and running the ship was a man twenty years his senior. Those at the top rarely stepped aside unless they were shot or jailed and even then he'd known some to run a crew from the inside.

Chepe had been a close friend of Leo's, someone who may not have been a good person but he understood fairness, and the true meaning of calmado, unlike Alvaro. Since taking the helm, Alvaro had discarded the old ways, the traditions passed from one member to another, and instead enforced his own rules, rules that changed on a whim depending on how he felt. Like a president choosing to go to war because they rolled out of bed on the wrong side, Alvaro was impulsive, bad news, bad for the gang, and bad for him. His rise to power couldn't have come at a worse time.

Moving on to the next council member after killing the first, he continued his line of questioning. "Where is he?"

The woman babbled, spilling words as fast as she could. "He lives at the end of Hidden Valley Drive, a few minutes from here," she said as Ramiro wiped blood from the blade on the woman's shirt.

"Now we're getting somewhere."

He chose not to kill her. Why? To be perceived as unpredictable.

As they exited the room in City Hall, they left behind a trail of blood — one dead security guard and one council member. The two remaining council members have given the name of the mayor and told them he hadn't been seen in over a week.

"Ramiro," Leo said pulling him aside, another attempt at persuading him to see the lunacy of this. "Why does this guy matter? We are facing unprecedented times. The country is in ruin. Surely even you can see there is no purpose to this mission."

"Are you seriously asking me that? If we let some homie shoot up our crew, what happens next, huh?"

He turned to walk away, ignoring him.

"I knew your brother Rudy," Leo said. Ramiro stopped and looked back at him. "He wouldn't have wanted this for you. Did you know he was close to leaving 18th Street before he was shot?"

"Bullshit."

"You think I would lie?"

Ramiro narrowed his eyes and slowly made his way back but not before telling the others to wait outside. As soon as the door closed he got up in Leo's face, stabbing a finger against his chest. "I won't have you undermine me in front of my men."

"Is that what I'm doing?"

"You know what you're doing," he said, narrowing his gaze.

"Your brother wanted out. I'm telling you the truth. There are rumors that it was Alvaro who put the hit on him."

Rage welled in his face, the vein in his neck pulsed hard as he brought up the knife to Leo. "I'm warning you."

"Alvaro doesn't need to know. We can say we found this Garcia guy and killed him. He won't know any different."

He snarled. "I will know."

"Does it mean that much to you?" Leo turned his back knowing Ramiro could stab him but he had to believe his reputation, even though it was marred, had earned him some level of respect. "Rudy and I used to run the streets together. We worked our way up through the ranks. We have blood on our hands to show for it but he wanted out because of you. Did you know that?"

"I'm warning you, Leo."

"Kill me then. I'm sure Alvaro would be pleased." He glanced back at him with a smile, not wanting him to see fear.

Ramiro turned the knife in the air pointing at him. "I could kill you right now. Alvaro wouldn't know the truth."

"Then how's what I'm suggesting any different?" Leo walked over to a window, feeling as though he finally had him, caught in his own words. He knew it was true, that's why he was still listening. Before leaving L.A., Alvaro had ordered at least two of his guys to watch over Leo to ensure that he didn't try to run. As if he would do that? Although Leo hated calmado, it had given him the ability to walk away from the gangs without being murdered. He could have run but he didn't. To disrespect that rule would have been to disrespect 18th Street, Chepe and all that it stood for. "Who is this Garcia to you?" Leo asked.

"An enemy."

"No, he's just another face, homie, nothing more than blood on your hands."

"It won't be my hands but yours."

Leo glanced at the dead councilman. "Rudy never

wanted this life for you. He wanted something better."

Ramiro laughed. "What, like the church? Huh? Is that better? Praying to a God that doesn't intervene?"

"Maybe he's intervening now."

His features screwed up as he closed the distance between them, tapping the knife against his head. "I know what you're trying to do, Leo. Trying to get in my head. But I won't let you. You hear me?"

"Look at the way Alvaro treats me, someone who at one time was Chepe's right-hand man. Do you think he will treat you any different, homie?"

He knew why Ramiro was following Alvaro's orders. It had little to do with loyalty and everything to do with power. Ramiro was like most foot soldiers, they craved the prestige that came with rising through the ranks, having others at their beck and call. No one wanted to be a lookout, a seller or even a triggerman, they wanted to be top dog and call the shots. That required praising the one on the throne until they could figure out a way to take it from them. "I'm telling you the truth. Rudy didn't want this for you."

He sneered. "You lie."

"Do I? Ramiro, you desire the very thing I had. Ask yourself. If it was so great, why would I walk away from it all?" With that said Leo let his words linger as he walked out of the room.

* * *

He was getting the hell out of town while he was still alive. When word reached Ken Fischer of gangs fighting in the streets, drive-by shootings and eventually the downfall of the Petaluma Police Department, he took that as a red flag to get out of Dodge. Sure, there were still cops out there doing their job, holding on to some slim hope that life would be the same, but not him. Oh, he was smarter than that. He wasn't sticking around to watch the curtain close. No, get out now and don't look back.

He'd told his wife, Colleen, to pack while he collected some valuables from the storage locker, mostly silver and gold that he'd kept outside of the home in a safe. Right now cash still had some value but eventually it would only be good for wiping your ass. Still, he wasn't taking any chances. He glanced over his shoulder, nervous every time he heard a gunshot. Had anyone seen him enter the self-storage facility? Colleen told him he was crazy to keep valuables outside the house but she soon changed her tune when they had a break-in a year ago while on vacation. They'd taken the TV, computers, and torn the place apart. No one would think to break into a self-storage facility as most of the crap people stored in there was furniture.

Nope. Not him. He'd installed a high-tech safe, and jammed it with gold, silver, a few thousand dollars and his wife's most expensive jewelry. Even as he tucked it all into a duffel bag and zipped it up, he couldn't help but toot his own horn in his mind. How many others would have been this smart?

He thought about the rest of the council members — idiots. All that talk about community spirit. What a crock of bullshit. It was every man for himself. Sure, at first he put on a big show and pretended to care for the people of Petaluma but once that twit Garcia waltzed into the room, spouting off about the gangs, he knew their days were numbered. In many ways he had him to thank for the heads-up. Had he not said anything, there was a good chance he could still be there, sitting around that table, listening to the boring crap coming out of Agatha's mouth. *We need to assist emergency management. We need to discuss ways to help the elderly. We need to...* Blah, blah, blah. Who cares? Not I, he thought as he slung the heavy duffel bag over his shoulder, and went to his truck and loaded it in the passenger side. He returned to the locker and collected several boxes of canned food he'd taken from the food drive the police had run a month ago. It was meant to go to the food bank in the community and it did, barring six boxes which he'd taken. What? He was the community. Didn't he deserve to have a little slice off the top? After all the shit he had to put up with, especially Officer Garcia. Who in their right mind hires an ex-gang member? He'd fought to get him fired a few months back but the chief refused to listen.

He adds value.

It offers diversity.

Oh he was so sick and tired of hearing that putrid bull crap.

It only existed to appease the masses, to keep the social justice warriors at bay. He shook his head as he loaded another box into his top-of-the-line 4 x 4 Titan truck, a beauty that the city had paid for with their hard-earned money. He'd embezzled almost a million from the city over the past three years. No one had noticed because he'd opened a secret bank account and named it the Sewer Capital Development Account and made it look like it belonged to the city. With him as the only signatory, he'd created an elaborate way of having money deposited into one account, then creating false invoices, and writing checks that were payable to the treasurer which of course was him, and the money ended up inside his new account. It was beautiful to see it growing like wildfire right under their noses.

He'd even given some spiel at the council meeting about not having a large enough budget to pay for this or that, after that meeting, the money train kept rolling.

Now of course, for a brief while he thought someone would catch on but they didn't. They were too busy listening to Agatha's crap or buying into all the social diversity nonsense to be worried about what the left hand was giving to the right. Two more years and he would have had quite the nest egg.

He chuckled at the thought as he brought another case of food to his truck. The only downside was he hadn't managed to retrieve the money. Right now it was sitting in his account, nothing but digits on a computer. No ATMs were working so he couldn't get it out but he figured, give it six months, maybe a year at the most of hiding in his cabin and the government would get the power grid back up. As soon as they did he would sweep in and empty that account, then it was bye-bye Petaluma and hello Margaritaville.

He brought the shutter down on the eight by ten

storage locker feeling proud of his ability to stay ahead of the curve. Seventy-two hours from now he would be sitting in a recliner, inside his cozy cabin north of Santa Rosa, drinking a brew and thinking about all these idiots running around the city trying to survive.

All those banners — Support Your Community.

Ah, fuck the community.

It didn't take long to return to his two-story home on Hidden Valley Drive. His house was one of only a few in the cul-de-sac. The truck bounced up into the driveway and rumbled as the engine idled. He jabbed the horn twice to let Colleen know that he was home and to get her ass in gear. With music playing lightly through the speakers, his fingers drummed against the steering wheel as he whistled and thought of ways he would kill time at the cabin. Fishing, and maybe he could do a little work on the 1933 Ford Roadster he'd bought two years ago. It was meant to be a side project, a reason to get out of doing work around the cabin. Ken lifted his eyes at the house. Where was that woman?

The horn blared as he placed his hand against it, this time holding it there for longer. "Come on!" If he had to go in, there would be trouble.

Another two minutes passed.

He huffed as he leaned out the window and yelled. "Colleen. C'mon, honey. We need to get going."

There was no response. She was probably doing her hair, or deciding which outfit to take. She was lucky there were any outfits. One street over had been hit so bad that many of the homes were nothing more than rubble. He honked the horn again before lighting a cigarette. He blew smoke out the corner of his mouth and narrowed his gaze. He glanced down the street.

Were they on to him?

No. No one knew he was leaving town. He'd made damn sure of that. He didn't want to answer questions. *Oh, why are you leaving? Who will make decisions? Shouldn't you stay until the ship goes down?*

No. No, and no!

He cursed under his breath as he got out and trudged

up the driveway and opened the front door. "Colleen, come on. I said we were leaving by five. You know I don't like to wait."

He turned into the living room and the cigarette fell from his lips.

Chapter 7

Forest City Surplus was a survivalist's wet dream.

Floor to ceiling shelves, clothing racks throughout, all of it stocked with essential camping gear, backpacks, tents, survival supplies, Airsoft rifles, electronics and military surplus, most of it modern, a few items dating back to the '50s. Elisha passed by a glass counter and gazed inside at countless gleaming knives of different sizes. Her eyes drifted to the wall behind which had a rack of swords and crossbows. "Sweet mother of Abraham. How on earth have you managed to keep this place under wraps?"

Harry snorted as he went behind the counter and took a seat on a stool. "Look, but don't touch. Not unless you've got the green and right now every item you see is worth three times the number you see on that red ticket."

"Grandfather," Travis scolded, walking close to Elisha and placing a hand on her shoulder. "If you see anything you want just let me know. I'm sure we can make it happen."

Harry leaned forward, removing the thick four-inch cigar from his lips. "Boy, are you hard of hearing?"

"No, but your memory isn't doing too well. I've worked up quite the tab in this place."

"Worked? When?"

Travis leaned against the counter, tapping it with his finger. "For the umpteenth time. I have been working for you for over three years. Some of which I might add I haven't been paid for. Remember those summer months?" He paused expecting Harry to reply but he didn't. "Of course not, ugh! Once this world goes back to the way it was, I'm getting you checked for Alzheimer's."

"Hey!" Harry pointed his finger at him and Travis grinned. He turned to Garcia who'd picked up an emergency hand-crank radio which also operated using solar power which charged batteries. "So what department are you from?" Harry asked.

"Petaluma." Garcia turned over the unit.

"Shouldn't you be there — you know, protecting?"

"Maybe."

"Sounds like you've lost faith."

"Not sure I had it to begin with," he said, setting the radio down then turning to him. "We got hit hard by the bombs, and then La Primera became a thorn in our side. Killed a lot of good people."

"But you managed to survive. Convenient."

Garcia's brow wrinkled. "What's that supposed to mean?"

"Look in the mirror."

"Grandfather," Travis barked. Harry scowled and got off his stool and walked away as Travis continued. "You'll have to forgive him. My grandmother was murdered in the first week. Some asshole carjacked her. They shot her and left her for dead. Someone saw it and said the one responsible looked—"

"Like me?" Garcia interjected.

Travis nodded. "They managed to get her to the hospital but she only lasted a day. Understandably he was torn up about it and that's when he shut the store down. He hasn't been himself since. Myself, Tate and Joe here were out there looking for the one responsible. The witness said he had a tattoo with the number fourteen."

"Like this?" Garcia asked. He rolled up his sleeve and showed him the rest of a partially hidden XIV. Travis squinted and got closer before nodding. Garcia exchanged a glance with Andre and they immediately knew he was referring to a Norteño gang member. They were the only ones who had that tattoo. Fourteen represented the fourteenth letter of the alphabet which was N. It was their way of paying homage to Nuestra Familia. His thoughts returned to Marco, and Santa Rosa. For the most part gang members from there didn't make their way north unless they were conducting business, collecting guns or drugs, and none of that was happening right now. Stepping out of gang territory could mean death if they weren't careful. "This witness. Did they only see one of them?"

"No, there were at least four," Travis replied.

"That's who we think are responsible for the raid on the police department," Tate said, removing his baseball cap and running his hand through his shaggy blond hair. "When we saw you guys, well…"

Garcia nodded. It made sense.

Just when they thought it would be safe to head out of Petaluma, they walk into this. He knew heading back to Santa Rosa and asking Marco would be of no benefit, especially after the warning. "You still think they're here?" Garcia asked.

Both of the guys shrugged. "Possibly. Graffiti has shown up."

Were they responsible for the break-in at Theo's? If they were, the question was why? An hour and a half north of Santa Rosa was a long way to travel unless they had a reason.

Garcia continued to browse, sifting through camo jackets.

After everything he'd gone through in Petaluma, the thought of facing more trouble didn't appeal to him, especially if it meant going up against an old friend of his. There would be no coming back from something like that. Although he'd turned his back on the gang, he couldn't help but still feel a close association with them. Norteños were his roots, his tradition. In many ways they'd made him who he was today.

"So?" Travis asked.

"What?" Garcia replied, lifting up a camo jacket and seeing if it fit him.

"You have any answers?"

"Yeah. Stay inside like your grandfather. It's safer."

Travis made his way around the silver racks of hanging clothes. "That's it?"

"Three of you weren't able to deal with us, trust me, the Norteños don't play around or tell you to lay your weapons down. You go down first, your weapon follows after." He set the jacket down.

"So you know who they are?"

"Of course I do, we just dealt with them," he replied hoping that he would drop the subject. Of course, he wouldn't. Travis followed in his shadow.

"That tattoo. How can you be a cop and one of them?"

"That was my past, this is my present."

Garcia reached for a large machete on the wall.

"Okay, so you had some inroad with this gang?"

"Had is the word. Not anymore."

"But…"

"Drop it, Travis. Okay?" Garcia said, turning around and speaking loud enough that he got the attention of Elisha and Liam who were browsing items across the store. "I'm telling you, these kinds of people don't play games."

Harry returned to see what all the commotion was about. "Yeah, well neither do we." Travis turned and jerked his head toward Tate and Joe. "Let's go."

"Travis. Don't start a war you can't finish."

"I never started it but you can be damn sure if they are still here, I will finish it." He shot Liam a look as if expecting him to follow but Liam remained.

Chapter 8

The Denver Country Club was an exclusive private establishment at the southern boundary of a wealthy subdivision. Catering to the who's who through amenities such as golf, racquet sports, swimming, and fitness, it had something for everyone. The oldest country club west of the Mississippi now looked a shell of its former self with one half of the two-story structure in ruins. Dark smoke rose above, some drifting their way bringing a pungent smell of toxicity. Alex turned his head toward the building as they jogged up the driveway. Was that a plane? The closer they got, the clearer it became. It looked like a jet wing and engine, charred and sticking out of concrete as if a military plane had crashed and split through the facility like a hot knife through butter. Had the military attempted to fight back? Was this the first sign of force? Beyond that was a golfer's paradise with 18 holes spread out over a rich green landscape. It almost looked out of place amid the rubble, and disaster that had befallen the city.

A bright red Jeep Rubicon idled out front with Star sitting on the hardtop, legs crossed with a lollipop in her mouth. She leaned back taking in the rays of sunshine. She had this grin as if she knew something they didn't. Another female, fifteen, maybe sixteen, sat on the passenger side. She had long dark hair with a strand of green through it, and piercing dark eyes. Thomas and Ryan were in the back, beckoning them on.

"Better speed up," Star bellowed, drumming her fingers on the roof and gazing up at the sky as a fleet of drones zipped their way. Alex turned back; panic caught in his chest. It felt like he was in a nightmare where his legs wouldn't move fast enough.

Reaching the Jeep, they dived into the back, breathing heavily, expecting a barrage of gunfire or a missile to end their misery but instead the drones flew over and Star let out a hoot as she hopped off the roof and slid behind the wheel. "Strap in, it's gonna be a bumpy ride. Meadow, you want to do the honors?"

"It would be my pleasure."

She cast a glance over her shoulder and Alex got a better look at her. She had smoky brown and green makeup, and one eyebrow pierced. She was also still sporting a pair of braces which she flashed as she smiled.

Meadow took a black package from the center console and unzipped it to reveal a selection of CDs. "Nope, nope, nope, nope, ah!" Thumbing through them, she pulled out one and winked at Star and stuck it in the CD player. Star flipped down the sun visor and tossed on a pair of mirrored aviators that were too large for her. She revved the engine a little.

Sophie was quick to ask. "Star, why are the drones not attacking you?"

"Questions later," she replied while adjusting her glasses in the rearview mirror.

"Hey, maybe I should drive," Alex suggested, leaning forward.

She laughed "I think not. Lucy here is very particular

about who drives her, isn't that right, Meadow?"

She nodded in agreement. "Yeah, she won't let me drive."

Thomas gave Alex a confused expression.

Meadow adjusted the volume on the music that was beginning to seep out of the speakers. "Um, you think you can hurry it up?" Ryan said peering out, expecting the worst to happen as another drone flashed overhead.

"Wait for it," Star said, holding a finger in the air as a guitar kicked in, building slowly to a rising crescendo. It was the intro to "Thunderstruck" by AC/DC. Star tapped her fingers on the steering wheel, holding a smile, while Meadow placed her bare feet on the dashboard and was tapping out the beat of the tune on the ceiling. Alex looked at Sophie and both of them raised an eyebrow. What the hell was going on? It felt like he was trapped in a surreal nightmare.

"Thunderstruck!" both of them roared while banging their heads.

Star jammed the gearstick into drive and the Jeep tore

out, burst over a curb and veered onto First Avenue. Alex held on for dear life as they bounced in their seats, rocking back and forth as she drove like a maniac one moment then with all the precision of a professional street racer the next. "She tell you anything?" Sophie asked Thomas.

"Only a little about El Dorado, some ranch on the outskirts of the city not far from Golden."

Curious onlookers taking refuge in buildings watched in amazement as they drove the streets without one drone attacking, meanwhile they continued their barrage of assaults on survivors and buildings. Star glanced up at the rearview mirror and Alex could tell she was looking at him from behind those shades. What was going through her head? Who was this girl?

At no point throughout the thirty-five-minute journey did he think they were safe. He was waiting for a missile to drop and this girl to finally realize she wasn't untouchable. Rock music continued blaring from the speakers as the two of them acted like the world hadn't gone to shits. She reached over and turned it down ever so slightly as Alex leaned forward.

"This ranch. If your parents are dead, who owns it?"

"Abner."

"Who's that?"

"You'll see. He'll explain everything. I think you'll like the ranch."

"We won't stay long."

"That's what they all say," she muttered.

They? He frowned as he leaned back in his seat.

Meadow folded a piece of gum into her mouth. Star turned the music up again. Alex was beginning to wonder if the reason she was playing it so loud was to avoid questions more than for enjoyment.

As the Jeep glided through the streets and the four of them shifted uncomfortably in the small space, Alex looked over his shoulder into the rear storage space. It was filled with boxes and bags of canned food, some of it had blood splatter on it. He breathed a sigh of relief as he looked at the road as it wound out of the city and into the countryside.

Sophie leaned into him. "You okay about this?"

"We'll see. Maybe this Abner is her uncle or something. Perhaps he has horses or a vehicle."

"Horses?"

"Whatever it takes, right?"

She managed to summon a smile.

They soon saw signs for Golden as they drove on Highway 6 and headed farther out. Fifteen minutes north of Golden they took in the sights of expansive mountain meadows, and green lush landscape full of pine, spruce, and aspen that blanketed the region. Off to the right were heavily timbered land, undulating topography, streams, small lakes and rock outcroppings.

Somewhere between Golden Gate Canyon State Park and Ralston Creek State Wildlife Area, Star veered off onto an unpaved private road. They bounced around in the back as it hit a patch of rough ground then smoothed out.

The road seemed to go on forever, a winding path

cutting through a forest full of wildflowers. Snowcapped mountains that were common in Colorado even in the summer months could be seen looming over the rolling hills. It was peaceful, remote and mesmerizing.

Then, as they rounded a bend in the road, a vast valley opened up before them, naturally preserved, almost untouched by humans.

Trails fissured off in every direction.

Alex squinted as sunlight glistened off a spring-fed lake giving it a magical appearance as they were transported out of the horrors of the concrete city.

"Wow, this is something else," Ryan said, his eyes widening.

Even Sophie looked captivated.

It was like a forgotten country, God's country.

The way America was meant to be.

Rugged, natural, beautiful.

The closer they got, the more people they saw. Beyond that was an incredible log mansion set high up on a hill, the kind of structure that might have been used for weekend retreats.

Meadow shut off the music and turned as they passed under a pine archway with letters carved into the wood.

"Welcome to El Dorado."

Chapter 9

The fist to the side of his face blindsided him. Ken Fischer spat blood and a tooth rolled across his newly installed hardwood floor. His brain rattled in his skull as he looked up to see the living room full of tattooed Latinos. "Get him up," a strong and confident male voice said. He turned to see who it came from when a meaty paw grabbed him by the collar and hoisted him as if he was as light as a feather. They threw him into a chair across from Colleen. Black mascara from her tears covered her face, and her eyes were red and swollen. A rag was stuffed in her mouth and her ankles and wrists bound with her arms pulled behind her.

Ken instantly shot into survival mode. There was no courage here. Hand stretched out he began to grovel. "If this is to do with the state of the town, supplies or getting you guys a better cut, I'll just let you know right now, I'm not the mayor anymore."

"Not according to your council members. I mean, dead council members." A fearsome-looking individual, bald, tattooed, short and scruffy, the kind of man he'd seen arrested on TV shows, dragged over a chair from the dining table and flipped it around. He straddled it and blew smoke in Fischer's face, then tapped his cigarette ash onto his knee. Ken looked down at the ash and brushed it off.

"Dead?"

A grin spread on the man's face.

Ken looked nervously around the room. "Who are you?"

"I think you're asking the wrong question, homie."

"If this is about what happened at Hopper's Tavern, I never authorized the attack, okay? That was all Officer Garcia. And believe me I don't even like the guy."

"Hopper's Tavern?"

Puzzled, his brow furrowed. "You're Carlos' men, aren't you?"

He chuckled and looked at his guys who stared back

with blank expressions. Ken swallowed, feeling his nerves get the better of him. He needed to ratchet this up a notch, plead his case, find some way to get these men out of here. "Look, please, if it's money you want, I've got plenty of it," he said rising and pointing to the door. "It's in the truck, I can get it for you."

A shove and he fell back into the chair.

"Tell me about Garcia."

"Sure. What do you want to know?"

"Background, where he is?"

"Um." His eyes bounced between them as he tried to make sense of this. Obviously, Garcia had brought hell down on him and if it meant throwing him under the bus he would do it. "He was hired by the police department. Apparently had connections with the gangs. They thought it was a good thing to bring in someone who could reach… your kind."

"My kind?"

He cleared his throat. "I mean that most respectfully, Mr.…?" he fished for a name.

"Lopez."

The guy sucked on his cigarette causing it to burn bright orange.

"Mr. Lopez. Okay. Very good." Fischer bounced his head from side to side. He was gaining ground, maybe even controlling this. You got this. Four years of running this town, he'd learned a thing or two about human behavior. He'd pulled the wool over the eyes of some of the smartest. This guy before him didn't look as if he'd even graduated high school. I mean, who in their right mind would cover their face in all that ink? "Felix Garcia is his full name. He lives locally. He was behind the attack on a gang here in Petaluma. La Primera. Maybe you know them?" Every attempt at getting a response from them was met with a blank expression. The sound of the ticking grandfather clock in the room didn't help. It only added to his stress. A bead of sweat trickled down his back. "Okay. Maybe you don't. Well, that's it. What else do you want to know?"

"You missed out the part of where he is?"

"How would I know?"

Lopez chuckled and tapped more ash onto his leg before narrowing his gaze.

Ken shrugged. "The last time I spoke to him he rudely interrupted one of our meetings. He made some demands. I told him where to go. He left and the attack occurred. After, the killing here in Petaluma seemed to stop. It's not like we had a huddle every day. The few cops that are still alive have been gradually disappearing, whether that's because someone like yourself has put a bullet in them or they have decided to bail, who knows, and really… does it matter? If you had planned on setting up here, be my guest. I'm getting the hell out and I'm sure that's what Garcia did." He stopped and waited for a response. The imbecile looked back at him. No smile. No scowl, just a cold hard stare that made Ken fear for his life.

"Look, please, I have food, money, gold. Plenty of it. Hell, I have quite the stash, and it's all yours.… Just… please, let myself and my wife go."

Lopez closed his eyes and took another hard pull on his cigarette before he stood up and removed a handgun from his waistband. He walked over to Colleen and put the barrel on her kneecap. "Garcia's home address."

"Right. Uh. I can get that for you. I just need to go to…"

Crack.

He squeezed the trigger and Colleen let out a muffled scream.

Ken's hands shot out in front of him. "Please. Oh God. Please. No, no, no. I don't know it but I can get it. I just don't keep that kind of information at my home. And with the communication and internet down, I can't access it without going to the police department." Tears rolled down Colleen's face. Ken tried to reach for her but was pushed back into his seat. "You didn't need to do that."

"Let's go," he said nudging him toward the door with a jerk of the gun. Before leaving he turned to another guy. "Leo. You stay here. And Miguel, keep an eye on him."

Ken glanced back at his wife as he was strong-armed out the door. Four Latinos remained with her while the rest followed him out with Lopez. He could see the look of fear in Colleen's eyes. What else would they do? Would she be alive when he got back? Would he ever return? He berated himself inwardly, wishing he'd left in the first few days. He'd contemplated it. It would have been easy.

Still, these assholes were amateurs.

If they thought he was going to hand over Garcia without protecting his own ass, they were even more stupid than they looked. The whole spiel about the cops having all but gone was a lie. They were still only seven days into this.

Sure, in that time Petaluma had taken one hell of a beating. The bombs had destroyed the infrastructure, and half the buildings in town, and made their job hard, but this man was overlooking the resilience of the Petaluma people. With a dwindling police force and roughly ten officers left, Fischer had been smart enough to discuss with Chief Berryman recruiting those with a military or hunting background. The pitch went over well but the chief said the community wouldn't go for it.

They had already maxed out on the number of volunteers.

And with the drive-by shooting, morale had all but vanished.

That's why Fischer in a last-ditch effort before getting the hell out of Dodge had told the chief he would handle it. And handle it he did, with the assistance of his council members they'd showed up at the shelter in Lucchesi Park with new supplies. Supplies that had come from arrangements he'd made with store owners in the days after the bombings. To ensure that it all went according to plan, he needed the community to believe they had this under control. Did they? Like hell, that's why he was getting out but they didn't need to know that.

He'd given his best speech.

As his truck rumbled to life and he was forced into the passenger side by Lopez's men, he thought back to that day.

"Yes, the situation is dire, and yes there are no guarantees that a week, a month or even a year from now you will be able to go about your lives, but this downswing offers a host of opportunities, opportunities to have your name etched in history as those who didn't run but instead picked up the baton."

Oh, he laid it on thick. Hell, even William Wallace would have admired his speech as he walked before the crowd. They hung upon his every word because he had shown up with new supplies. Give. Take. The psychology worked. See, it was all a matter of control, and he was for the most part a master of that. Even now, as they drove to the police department, he was leading these tattooed fools to their death.

His thoughts drifted back to that glorious day.

Rallying together hunters, ex-military, anyone who knew how to fire a weapon.

"You don't need to know the law, you just need to follow orders. Those of you who are uncertain but have useful skills will be paired up with one of Petaluma's finest. You will

offer backup, support and assistance as we continue to search for survivors among the rubble, and rebuild this fine city."

After presenting before them boxes of food, he'd taken a can and stepped down into the crowd and placed it into the hands of a child clinging to her mother's leg. *"Here you go, hon. We are here for you. You understand. We won't let you go hungry."* Would they go hungry? Of course but it's what every politician did in times of crisis. By the time they caught on that things were getting worse he would be long gone.

It had worked.

That one small gesture caused the crowd to erupt in cheers.

The swell of pride as he walked back to the platform was second to none.

Immediately, he had his council members hand over the boxes to staff for distribution. It was a sign of strength, a message that they had this under control. He felt like a god among men as he watched person after person come up and sign their name to volunteer, listing their experience and skills.

It was like taking candy from a baby.

Later that day, he'd delivered that list to a grateful and wide-eyed chief.

"I don't know how you did it but it's much appreciated," *the chief said.*

In many ways he felt his job was done. Sure, it was all smoke and mirrors and eventually most of those good folk would die of starvation or be murdered as society returned to their primal instincts, but hey, at least he was going out with a bang.

Once the smoke cleared and society had begun to rebuild, he would reemerge and continue his position as mayor.

It was all going to plan until these assholes showed up on his doorstep.

Truth be told he had no idea where Garcia was.

A thorn in his side, it came as no surprise that he would abandon his post. He was weak. He'd never trusted him. Gang tattoos on the neck and arms. What kind of message did that send to the community?

As one of the gang members drove the truck, he glanced in the side mirror and saw a steady stream of vehicles following.

Would they keep him alive after this?

He had to think and fast.

A revolver was jammed into his rib cage.

"You know I can help you," Fischer said.

Lopez hadn't taken his eyes off him. He didn't reply so Fischer continued. "Sure, you can take what you want by force but if you want these people to listen, and I mean truly listen, I'm your man. I've already built up a rapport."

Lopez said nothing.

He had to dig deeper, try harder, get past that steely gaze.

"So… where you from?"

Nothing.

Time for some reverse psychology.

"You certainly know how to lead these guys. I admire

that. Not many can rise to the challenge. I imagine you have more followers back in the city, or wherever you come from? How many?"

"Enough," Lopez replied.

"And they all listen to you?"

Lopez looked ahead.

Damn it, it wasn't working.

Maybe he was going about this the wrong way. "You know with La Primera gone, it opens up the way for a new group to step in. Tell me, Mr. Lopez, do you have the support of the mayor where you come from? Or better still, the support of the local police?"

Lopez looked at him.

Ah, he'd got him — hook, line and sinker.

He'd seen that gaze before.

"You report to someone, don't you? Someone above you?"

"Keep your mouth closed."

He was pushing it by continuing but he had to try. His life depended on it.

"What if all this was yours? Free rein to run your enterprises, a guarantee that the cops would look the other way. Think about it. The infrastructure of this nation has collapsed, thousands of people have died, it will take months, even years to get back up and running again. Why settle for a sliver of the pie when you can have it all?"

Lopez lashed out, striking him across the face.

Ken leaned forward, blood dripping from his lip.

"That would imply it's not mine already. Fool!"

They continued for another five minutes before he guided them into the parking lot of the police station. How many armed volunteers were inside was unknown but he had to believe this was his one shot of getting away from these madmen.

Shoved out of the truck, he was led toward the main doors with the gun pressed into the small of his back. The rest of Lopez's crew followed, guns at the ready.

There was no hesitation on their part, no fear. Then it dawned on him. Keeping a firm grip on Ken, they were using him as a human shield. The second they were inside, gunfire unleashed as they took out those closest.

Three volunteers buckled under the barrage of gunfire before Lopez ordered the rest to lower their weapons or he would execute Ken in front of them.

Damn it, the plan had gone awry.

Chapter 10

The stockpile was something to behold. It took four of them to unload it from a trailer they'd borrowed from Harry. Fortunately, Liam's ties to the town of Willits, and his grandfather's friendship with Harry had earned them some leverage. For a short while after the spat between Garcia and Harry, Elisha figured they wouldn't receive anything but Liam worked his magic, told him a few stories about Theo and soon had Harry laughing.

Harry agreed to return an equal amount of supplies on one condition, that they swing by every day and help out at the shop. What he meant by that was watching over the business while he went out with Travis to hunt down whoever had killed his wife.

It was a little extreme but after seeing what they were given, she was more than willing. A huge blue tarp crackled in her hands as she folded it up while Liam took the bungee cords and tossed them into the trailer.

"Garcia, you got the keys?" he yelled. "I better get this trailer back to Harry before he thinks we've stolen it."

Garcia jogged out of the cabin, dangling them in his hand. "He's quite the character."

"He's got a good heart. His wife meant a lot to him. They'd known each other since they were seventeen. I think you can understand why he is the way he is. Anyway, maybe tonight you can tell us more about your background with the gangs."

"I don't know about that," Garcia said, leaning against the cruiser and regarding Elisha. "Not exactly something I want to remember. Look, I'll drop this off."

Liam grimaced. "That's not a good idea."

"Neither is letting you take the cruiser."

He shrugged. "What? I know how to drive."

"I'm sure you do but for now I don't want to lose it."

"So you think I'll let someone steal it?"

"You heard what Travis said. If Norteños are out there and they're carjacking people, better it be me they come across than you."

Liam groaned and gestured to the cruiser. "Go ahead then, just don't wind Harry up. The last thing we need is to have him on our back."

Elisha dropped the tarp in the trailer. "You want me to come with you?"

"No, I'll be there and back before you know it."

"Don't stop for anyone, okay?" Elisha said.

"You almost sound worried for me." Garcia smiled and got in the driver's side and pulled out.

Elisha stuffed her hands into her pockets and looked at the property. "So what can I do to help?"

Liam motioned with a wave. "A lot. Come, I'll show you."

As they walked around the side of the home, the sun shone through the trees spreading its warmth over them. "While I don't think the same people who broke in will be back, there's no telling if others will come so we need to focus on security." He reached for a roll of fishing line.

"What are you doing with that?"

"You'll sleep better knowing that there is a tripwire

alarm system surrounding the perimeter. The last thing we want is someone to shoot us in our sleep." He held up the line. "You can use this, or paracord, or snare wire. Just make sure if you use fishing wire that it's heavy-duty, nothing lighter than fifty pounds. There has to be some strength to it, otherwise, it snaps."

"You learned this from your grandfather?"

"Yep." Liam paused for a second and she could see him looking toward a weathered play structure in the yard. Was he remembering his childhood? "Theo was the father I should have had," he said as they walked through a grove of trees. The lake came into view, sunlight reflected off the surface. A gentle wind made the water lap against the shore. "Back when I was a kid I never really paid too much attention, I just thought he was kind of quirky. My mom would bring me up here and instead of taking me out to the movies, or that kind of stuff, he tried to instill in me the love of the outdoors."

"Did it work?" she asked.

He smiled. "Somewhat. Anyway, he had all these

acronyms for different things. He said it was the best way to remember."

Leaves and branches crunched beneath their feet, rays of golden light filtered through the canopy of green above. The sound of birds chirping made the whole place seem peaceful.

"Like what?"

"WESS for instance. W stands for water. When he bought this property he purposely chose it for two reasons: privacy but more importantly its proximity to a fresh water source." He pointed through the trees to Lake Ada Rose. "Not far from there is Willits Creek, and then about a mile east is a freshwater spring. A lot of people don't even know it exists but he did. He said it was good to know where freshwater springs were just in case the water shut off. Three days without water…"

"Yeah, I remember you saying when we were buried."

He gave a nod. "Learned it from him." Liam dropped to a knee and handed her the other end of the fishing line. "Take that for a second."

She gave a nod as she backed up. "So what's E stand for?"

"Elevation."

He pointed toward the cabin. "You don't need much elevation as you don't want your place to be silhouetted against the sky but it helps to have a place where you can eye potential threats. And of course there is the upside of being able to use gravity to filter water down from a high elevation into a bunker if you have one."

"Did he build one?"

"Nope. He had plans. I'll show you them later. It's quite something. He never got around to it."

"And S?"

"Safety. You don't want your bug-out location, tent or shelter to be in a spot where it could suffer from flash flooding. So canyons aren't good areas." He pulled out a pocket tool.

"What is that?"

"The Leatherman 300. Don't leave home without it, of course unless you're heading over to a girl's house to ask her out on a date."

Elisha stopped walking. "And where were you planning to take me?" She smiled.

"Wherever you wanted to go."

She continued walking back. He was quick to shift the topic. "The last S stands for security. Your location should have a perimeter — you know, some means of keeping you safe or at least alerting you to intruders. I don't like sleeping with one eye open, neither should you."

He used his knife to cut the wire.

"So if your grandfather was so into this, why didn't he have this all set up already?"

"My grandmother. She was quite a woman. Unless he wanted to sleep on the couch, he abided by her rules. Don't get me wrong. She was into survival and being prepared but there were some things she didn't want to have to deal with. Tripwire for instance." He smiled as he raised a finger at her. "Oh… uh… mind your step."

It was too late. She landed flat on her ass.

Elisha went red in the face.

"Nature's tripwire," he said before chuckling as she looked down to find a large tree root sticking out of the ground.

She summoned an embarrassed smile, shaking her head as she got back up. "I need to watch where I'm walking. Anyway, so how's this work?"

He stood up. "It's all about entry and exit points. For you, and anyone coming toward this cabin. You want to cut down the number of entry points for them and make it harder for them to approach without making a noise. There are natural plants, sticks, branches you can place on the ground that will create noise. If you don't have any palm tree leaves or saw palmetto plants, work with what you have. For us, there is a little trick my grandfather taught me. Stay right here, I'll be right back."

He jogged away leaving her basking in the beauty of the area.

A flock of birds landed in the trees just as a steady breeze made the leaves rustle.

A minute or two later he returned with some rolls of cooking foil.

"You planning on cooking?"

He smiled. "No. Look, branches and leaves and such are usually sufficient but if you take some of this and roll it out between trees and cover it with a thin layer of dirt and twigs, you'd be surprised at how much noise it makes in the dead of night. It's just one thing extra that you can add to your perimeter if you don't have enough to create what we are making. My grandfather said it was better to place the foil beneath a thin layer of sand or soil closer to the cabin, almost as a second and final means of alerting you to someone's presence. Of course if you have power, that's where floodlights come in but if you have no power, then you have to improvise, think outside the box."

Liam fished into his pocket and pulled out a small black device no bigger than his hand. Awkwardly he looped a plastic zip tie through one end of it, and tied it around a tree branch. Then he took the piece of wire that came from her and looped it through the other side of the alarm and tied that off.

"Damn arm," he said, struggling.

"You need a hand?"

"No, it's fine." He then worked his way back and reached for a stick, and told her to hold it while he grabbed a hatchet. He returned a moment later and made a few notches in the stick and fed the wire down from the tree and through the notches to stabilize it.

He then had her continue back and they tied it off before concealing the stick and the device attached to the tree. "Now someone would be hard-pressed to see that." Liam walked around it and looked at it from different angles. "Daylight, nighttime, it will do the trick. Now to test it."

"How's it work?"

"It's like a grenade. The wire pulls on the pin."

He took a stroll through the area, and seconds later, the alarm let out an ear-piercing wail. "Damn, that is loud," Elisha bellowed.

Liam turned it off.

"A hundred decibels. Been a while since I saw my grandfather test this." Liam set it up again.

"How many of those alarms do you have?"

"Not enough but that's okay. We'll use what we have on the major entry points and then go old school for the rest."

They crossed through the trees and he pointed to some of the open spaces people could enter through. "We'll need to cover that area and that one over there. Once we've made use of these alarms, we'll revert to deadfall traps and others."

They continued to work setting up traps around the perimeter while Andre watched from the porch, smoking a cigarette.

"Anything you guys need a hand with?" he asked.

"You want to dig a few holes?" Liam replied.

"What do you have in mind?"

Liam walked them through the process of creating punji stick traps. "They were made famous back in

Vietnam. A horrendous booby trap they used on American soldiers. Pretty straightforward. You create a pit in the ground and fill it with stakes then camouflage it."

"Sounds lovely," Elisha said jokingly. "What happens if you forget where you installed them?"

"They won't be in areas we will enter or exit. But you can be damn sure you'll appreciate them if they stop someone approaching in the middle of the night."

"And what if they're friendlies?" she asked as Andre came lumbering over with a shovel in hand.

"Oops, too bad," Liam said.

It was hard to imagine that it had come to this but it had. Seven days, that's all it had taken. Had it just been a simple power outage she didn't think people would lose their shit like this, but with the bombs destroying key facilities, desperation had taken hold. Whether people were approaching homes because they wanted to rob or worse, hurt someone, it was helpful to know that Liam knew what he was doing. Elisha touched the St. Christopher around her neck and thought of her parents again. Were they still alive?

* * *

Back in town, Garcia had just finished unhooking the trailer and pushing it back into a garage at the back of the store when gunfire erupted. He spun around, hand on his service weapon. He wasn't the only one who heard it. Harry appeared on the roof, rifle at the ready, scoping the road. He looked over at him and Garcia gave him the thumbs-up. Harry scowled. He brought the garage door down and locked it then took the key and tossed it up to Harry on the roof. "Much appreciated."

Another flurry of rounds and Harry spun like a spinning top straight off the roof. He landed hard. Garcia withdrew his weapon and dropped down beside him.

Blood was already blooming in his shirt. He'd taken a round to the back of the shoulder.

"You got the key for the rear door?"

"It's in my pocket," Harry said through gritted teeth.

He groaned as Garcia reached in and retrieved a huge set of keys. His first instinct was to protect him but Harry pushed him away. "Get my rifle," he said pointing to it a few feet away.

Garcia got it. "You'll be okay. Looks like…"

Harry was quick to cut him off. "Son, I was in Vietnam, you're damn right it will be okay." He groaned. He might have been as tough as nails at one time but his age was showing.

"Which key is it?"

"The red one."

He had them all color-coded with colored plastic around the top. He took it and opened the rear door, then helped Harry to his feet and took him inside. "Shut the door."

Garcia lowered him to the ground. He was bleeding pretty bad.

Another flurry of rounds, even closer now. Boots pounding the ground.

He quickly slammed the door shut just as he heard voices.

Harry was breathing hard, wincing in pain.

Garcia returned and dragged him into the main store area. "Medical supplies?" he barked.

"Behind the counter. You'll find a red container. Also grab the bottle of alcohol."

Garcia hurried even as he heard someone pounding on the rear door. A voice bellowed. "Open up, old man. You know we'll get in there eventually."

Harry bellowed back. "Screw you, assholes."

Someone fired rounds at the door. Harry laughed and looked over. "Don't worry, they won't get through that door. Trust me on that."

"What about the roof?"

For a moment, Harry frowned then a smile formed. "You've never been in the military, have you, son?"

"Nope," he replied as he hurried over with the first-aid kit.

He was going to tear his shirt open but Harry already had done it. The bullet had gone straight through. That wasn't what was surprising, it was what he could see all over his back — scars of bullet wounds that had healed over. "How long were you in?" Garcia asked.

"Not long enough." He reached down and pulled up his pant leg to reveal a prosthetic leg. He'd seen the limp but figured he was old and it was just life catching up with him. Nope, this old-timer had tasted the heat of war, no wonder he was taking this nightmare in stride.

Chapter 11

There was something strange and peaceful to El Dorado. No sense of panic, no fear of attack, no armed security roaming the perimeter. Sure, only seven days had passed since the bombings but the morale of people in cities was nothing like this. Groups of men tilling the ground nearby lifted their eyes as they stepped out of the Jeep. Star told them to wait while she went and got Abner from the mansion. Meadow walked over to a group of teens her age, said something to them and they all looked toward Thomas and Ryan. Several women attended to children, some hung up washing while others called out to kids playing.

Four pretty teen girls broke away from the group where Meadow was standing and walked past them. A girl with long dark hair looked Ryan up and down in a flirtatious manner. He followed her gaze with a smile.

It felt like they'd stepped back in time to a long-lost

era.

"I would love to meet the designer," Thomas said with a chuckle, noting their clothes were the same solid color, a modest potato brown. The whole place had a very Amish feel to it. Several large dogs barked and raced into the tall grass, only to leap out again as children chased them, giddy with excitement. Tiny kids no older than five sat on the steps of the cabin giggling and whispering to each other.

Their backs were turned when Abner emerged. "Greetings."

Sophie turned to face a broad-shouldered man with dark skin, five ten in stature. His dreadlocks flowed past his shoulders. His shirt was the same brown color yet he had some orange beads around his neck, and he was wearing loose white pants and sandals.

He beamed, flashing pearly whites that looked almost too bright.

Alex was the first to introduce them as Abner extended a hand and greeted them one by one. When he reached

Sophie, he held her hand a little longer and cupped it with his other hand as he stared into her eyes with a disarming smile. "The pain you feel. One day it will be gone," he said. And like that he let go of her hand and gestured for them to follow him.

Alex raised an eyebrow and she shrugged.

Abner stopped and lifted a finger. "Oh before we begin. We'll need your weapons. You'll get them back but while you are here we don't allow anyone to carry."

Alex stared at him. "Not happening."

Abner didn't appear to be offended. "That's fine, then you'll need to leave, I'm afraid. We don't condone violence here."

Thomas didn't hesitate, he was the first to remove his rifle and set it on the ground. Sophie followed suit with a handgun. Ryan wasn't carrying but he encouraged Alex to do the same, saying it was only for one night. Abner raised an eyebrow and locked his hands behind his back. "Your decision."

Alex didn't like it one bit but he followed suit.

"And the handgun," Abner said.

He reached into the small of his back and took that out.

"Very good. Come. Walk with me. Allow me to introduce you to our home." As they strolled past the children he placed a hand on each of their heads in a loving way. A couple of the kids said, "Hi, Papa."

"Are they all yours?" Sophie asked.

"Yes. Beautiful, aren't they?"

"What is this place?" Alex asked, his eyes roaming the flawless terrain.

"A haven. Long before the bombings I offered a retreat for people who were tired with day-to-day living. Weekends, month-long getaways, and for some permanent residence if they felt called."

"Called?" he asked.

Abner smiled. "To help."

"With?"

"Life."

"Why do you all wear the same clothes?" Thomas

asked.

"Modesty, practicality, and to avoid comparison."

"But what about individuality?" Sophie said.

He smiled as if none of these questions were foreign to him. "Is your individuality determined by the clothes you wear?"

"Not exactly, but it's an expression."

"And there are many ways to express." He shifted away from the topic and pointed out another large building. "That is the school over there. We grow all our crops, raise animals, and make clothes. We're pretty much self-sufficient."

"Then why did Star bring back boxes of canned food?" Sophie asked.

"So we can go above and beyond to help others."

"And by help, you mean risking your girls to help others?" Alex asked.

He found that amusing. "In times like these it's easy to think of the I and not the We, but there are many suffering, Alex. We aim to ease that suffering. Food, clothes, a shelter if need be," he said gesturing to the home. "Star is one of our most capable. She might be young but her mind is beyond her years."

"What about a vehicle?" Alex asked.

"For what purpose?"

"We are on our way to California. Our daughter is there," Sophie explained. Abner cast her a sideways glance and was quick to reply.

"Is she?" he asked in a way that seemed to bring into question the validity of that. "I'm sure we can accommodate, but first stay the night. Eat, rest, you all look very tired."

"If it's okay with you, we'd like to move on," Alex said.

"Alex," Sophie snapped.

Abner caught that. "It's one night, Alex. I'm sure the others would appreciate it."

"I certainly could use a meal," Thomas said.

Ryan was still staring at the girl with dark hair. He was listening but distracted. "Yeah, one night. It's just one night, right?"

Alex's brow furrowed as Abner continued to point out areas. "The lake over there is great for fishing and swimming."

"What about that building?" Ryan asked.

"Medical."

"You have supplies?"

He smiled. "Of course, Ryan. We have a lot of things here because we planned ahead."

Alex was quick to get to the question that was on all their minds. "In the city. How did Star avoid those drones?"

"That's a big question that can't be answered at this time." He gestured to another building, quickly changing the topic. "And that one—"

Alex cut him off. "What do you mean?"

He stopped walking and looked at them with a disarming smile. "You should be grateful that you're alive."

Sophie gave Alex a nudge. He looked at her then

Abner, who turned back toward the route they were heading in as Ryan and Thomas peppered him with questions, mostly about the females.

Sophie tapped Alex's arm.

"What?"

"Too soon."

"Is it? Don't you want to know?"

"Of course but later."

"I just want to get going."

"It's rude."

"No, it's survival," he said.

Abner led them inside the mansion that boasted over thirty rooms. There were cathedral ceilings in the main living room and a dining hall with ten huge tables that could seat up to a hundred people. As they walked the corridors, Sophie noticed that the women smiled but kept their heads low as if following some strange ritual. After they were given the full tour, Abner was called away so he left a woman by the name of Daisy to show them to their rooms. Alex and Sophie were put in the same room with one queen-sized bed.

Sophie raised a finger. "Oh, um…" Before she could get the words out, Daisy backed out, closing the doors behind her.

Alex tossed down his backpack on the bed, put a hand on his waist and ran the other hand over his jaw. "Well this is awkward."

"I'll speak to them later. See if they have another room."

"Or…" he said pointing to an uncomfortable-looking chair. "I could sleep in that."

"No. No, Alex, I wouldn't dream of it."

"Sophie, we've slept in a cramped truck for most of the way. I think this is a step up. It's fine. Besides, I don't like the idea of us being separated."

She smiled as she went over to a set of doors that led out to a balcony. It provided a breathtaking view of the lake, and the surrounding forest and hills. "Reminds me of our wedding night."

He took a seat. "Minus the two bottles of wine."

"What? I was nervous," she said.

He laughed.

"Man, I could use a cigarette." She had run out several days ago and was climbing the walls in her mind. Years ago she'd attempted to quit and it lasted all of three days before she caved in and bought a pack.

"Well maybe Holy Moses can heal you," Alex said leaning forward. "Seems to have everyone else in this place under his spell."

"Don't let him hear you say that."

Alex got up and ran his hands over a radio, then a painting on the wall. Were they watching, listening? "It's strange, isn't it?" he said.

"What?"

"This place."

"It's beautiful. Peaceful."

"Yeah, too peaceful." He joined her on the balcony. "It's like all these people are living in denial. Beyond this forest is a nation that has collapsed and they're all here playing happy families. You can't say there isn't something wrong with this picture. And what about Star? We have a thirteen-year-old who is capable of dodging drones that are wiping everyone else out, and then at the ranch we have a guy who looks like he's just stepped out of a New Age video."

She laughed. "One night. That's all. Half the day is already over with, Alex. What can happen?"

"That's what I'm worried about."

* * *

Leo was more uncomfortable with the situation with each passing minute. Since Ramiro had left, Miguel hadn't taken his eyes off him. The other three in the room stood around watching the lady as she bled out. "Let me at least bandage her leg," Leo said.

Miguel toyed with a handgun, drinking a beer at the same time.

"You're not in charge, Leo. She's fine."

"She's bleeding out."

Miguel smiled. "That she is."

The mistake they'd made was giving Leo a handgun.

They assumed that because there were more of them and he was under their watchful eye he wouldn't try anything. Maybe that was true. It certainly had prevented him from acting sooner.

The fact was gang members lived in fear of retribution, being jumped and beaten badly. Of course there was the fact that Alvaro had told him that if he didn't follow through with his orders, he would not only kill him but he would execute every single person in the church.

Leo leaned against the wall, looking at the woman. She hadn't stopped groaning since that bullet had entered her leg. Her face was a pasty white. Could she survive? Maybe, but there was a strong chance she would bleed out if he didn't get her some help soon.

Miguel put his feet up on an ottoman and tapped his fingers while keeping one hand on his gun. "Heard you had quite the reputation back in the day. What happened?"

"You don't want to know."

"C'mon, homie. You can tell us. You're among

friends."

"Friends?"

Miguel sucked air between his teeth and nodded.

"That why you have your finger on the trigger?" Leo asked.

He smiled as he leaned forward. "Alvaro told us about you. Like you were some kind of myth or legend. What was it?" he said clicking his fingers. "You killed sixty, maybe eighty gang members with that gun of yours. That right?"

Leo's eyes kept bouncing over to the woman who grimaced, her face a mask of pain and anguish. He couldn't do this any longer. He thought he could. He thought he could return, follow the law of calmado, but he wasn't going to kill an innocent man, someone who he didn't even know.

Miguel wiggled his fingers. "Come, let me have a look at that piece of yours."

He got up and walked over and Leo removed it from his waistband. Miguel ejected the magazine. It was loaded. He pulled back the slider and a round in the chamber ejected. He picked it up and put it in front of his face. "This is what we live and die by." He took the bullet and put it on the top of his tongue and swallowed it. He flashed a grin, two of his teeth pure gold. The other three in the room laughed. He palmed the magazine back in, and tucked it into the back of his waistband. "I have an idea. If you can get this off me, you can get a bandage for the lady. How's that sound?"

The others got this glint in their eye. They knew he was baiting him into a fight, a way to prove his manhood, a way to demonstrate to the others he had what it took to rise through the ranks. What better way than to give someone with a reputation a good licking? He backed up. "Make some room, guys. Drag her into the dining room."

Leo shook his head. "You think Ramiro would approve?"

"Ramiro isn't here. Let's see what you got."

Miguel handed off his piece to his pal and rolled up his sleeves, brought his fists up and baited him forward. Leo took a step forward and Miguel backed up, his nostrils flaring. "C'mon homie!"

When he saw Leo wouldn't do anything, he stepped forward and cracked him on the jaw. "You better use those fists of yours or you'll be spitting blood."

Leo opened and closed his jaw, working out the tension and releasing the pain.

Again, Miguel stepped forward to strike him but before he could fire off a punch, Leo kicked him in the nuts then cracked him with a hard punch that knocked him out cold. The other three looked on, their eyes widening.

"Any of you wanna try?"

He crouched down and removed his gun, making sure to load a round into the chamber. While he was on the ground, the thought went through his mind again. Three shots. That's all it would take. Ramiro would come after him. He'd have to live on the run. He glanced up at the three. It had been a few years since he'd fired. Was he rusty? As if perceiving what he was about to do, one of them reached for a handgun.

Worst mistake ever.

Three shots.

He took two of them out with rounds to the head and the last with one to the chest. He had to get up and walk over to him as he was writhing on the ground, still attempting to go for his piece. That was the thing about 18th Street, they weren't pussies, and they would fight to the death.

The guy's hand never made it.

Leo fired another round into the man's chest, then one more for good measure.

The woman in the next room cried out from behind her rag as he walked over to the window and looked out. They would be back soon and by then he needed to be gone.

Leo removed the woman's rag from her mouth, her cries echoed in the home as he tried to reassure her that he was going to help, that he wasn't like them and he would get her to safety. He untied her wrists and ankles, looped an arm around her waist and carried her out of the house toward her neighbor's.

He couldn't take her with him but he could hide her, ensure Ramiro didn't finish what he started because finishing the mission was always in the plans. If Ramiro had his way, neither this woman nor the mayor would live to see nightfall.

Chapter 12

As daylight gave way to night, Garcia watched the group of three through his rifle scope. They couldn't have been more than twenty-five years old, scrawny, meth heads by the look of their skin. Nearby, he noticed several new buildings were on fire. A hard wind blew the smell of smoke his way.

He'd waited a good ten minutes before heading up onto the roof. Harry was right, it was as secure as Fort Knox. The roof was made from steel, so no one could burrow in, and there was a reinforced steel hatch with multiple locks to prevent anyone from prying it open. Harry told him he'd had the store designed by a guy who created bunkers. There was even an area below the floor where he could retreat if faced with a biological weapon.

Harry said if the shit hit the fan and he couldn't get home from work he could hole up there for at least a good six months.

He'd thought of everything except this.

After he'd patched up his wound, Harry gave him a tour below the store. He'd lifted floorboards and revealed his huge stash of freeze-dried food, water bottles and enough ammunition to start a war.

It made sense. A man who had served his country for the better part of his life would go on to serve the community by offering them a means of surviving.

Staying low on the roof, Garcia shifted the rifle. He'd lost sight of the attackers behind a curtain of white smoke. When the wind cleared, his eyes widened. A good distance down the street he caught them heading over to a bank, there he caught sight of Travis. *Shit.* For a brief moment he thought they were in danger. He observed Travis slam one of the meth heads into a parked car and point back at the store. He looked pissed.

Had Travis seen what they'd done?

Would he kill them?

Garcia squinted.

Travis wagged a finger in the face of one of them, then

backed up and said something to Tate and Joe before breaking away from the group and heading for the store. No. It couldn't be. Why? Was he behind the attacks on the store? Had he known the two men that were lying dead outside? It sure as hell looked like he knew those tweakers. But that didn't make sense. If the goal was to get inside, he already had access. And why would he want to take what his grandfather had? Better still, why would he hurt him? He recalled what Travis had said when asked why he didn't have a key. And then he remembered Harry appearing on the roof before he opened the door. Was Harry aware of what Travis was up to?

Either way it was disturbing.

Garcia slid back. He turned and scaled down the ladder, closing the hatch behind him. As soon as he entered the store, Harry peppered him with questions. "So? Did you see them? What did they look like?"

"Um."

Harry narrowed his eyes as if trying to discern his reaction.

A knock at the rear door.

"That will be Travis," he said in a low voice. "You want to go up and check, to be sure."

Garcia frowned. "Why don't you open the rear if you know it's him?" Garcia asked. He kind of figured he knew why but he wanted to hear it from Harry.

"Can't be too careful, right?"

"Right," Garcia said nodding. "I'll, uh, be right back."

He could have told him he'd seen the three conversing with those tweakers but he didn't want to start accusing people, especially without Andre there to back him up. And with Harry still under the impression that a Norteño had killed his wife, he had to be careful. Who would he believe — Travis or a cop with gang tats? Climbing back up to the rooftop, he made his way over to the edge and peered over.

Travis had his hands in his pockets. "Hey, tell him to let us in."

"Will do." Garcia stared at him through new eyes. Had that been the reason they were in the police station that day? Were they the ones responsible for those officers lying dead? And if so, why hadn't they attacked them? *Liam.* Maybe he would know. Still confused, Garcia went back inside and let them in. If Travis was behind the attacks, surely he would have let the tweakers in. No, there was something more to this, something he was overlooking.

"Any luck out there?" Garcia asked as he held the door open.

Travis paused. "Nope."

"Huh! You never ran into anyone?"

Travis looked him square in the eyes. "No one. Everyone must be staying indoors, staying out of sight."

"Yeah, I guess. Dangerous out there. Never know who might stab you in the back."

Travis gave a nod and Harry looked at Garcia. They shared a look as if they each knew what the other was thinking. It didn't make sense though. If Harry knew that Travis was behind the attack, why hadn't he said anything? Done anything? Why was he still opening the door and letting him in? Was he living in denial or waiting for him to try something? And what connection did these tweakers have to him or the Norteños? Then it dawned on him. Had there been any gang members in Willits in the first place? Or was it all just a lie?

As soon as Travis saw his grandfather he acted all theatrical. "What the hell happened?"

"What's it look like, boy?"

His eyes darted to Garcia. "You bandaged him up?"

"As much as he would allow."

Harry got up waving him off. "I'm fine."

He was putting on a brave face but it didn't matter how strong a person was, being shot in the shoulder wasn't something you just brushed off. However, if there was a place to get shot, it was here at the store. He seemed to have more emergency medical supplies than a local hospital.

"Anyway, why are you here?" Travis asked Garcia.

"I returned the trailer."

"Oh. Right." Travis looked at Tate and Joe.

"You leaving now?" Harry asked.

On one hand, he needed to speak with Liam but on the other he didn't want to leave the old man alone. Could he handle himself? Possibly. That fool was as tough as nails. Anyone else might have broken a leg, shoulder or neck falling off that roof but he did it with all the finesse of a stuntman. Then again, landing on grass might have softened the blow. Still, for a man of his age it was something to behold.

"Yeah. You think you'll be okay?"

His eyes bounced between them.

"Survived this long, haven't I?"

Garcia gave a nod then turned to head out. As he was leaving, Travis caught up with him. "Hey, Garcia." He stopped at the door.

"Yeah?"

"Tell Liam I want to see him tonight. Maybe he could swing by."

"Why not come back with me now?"

He thumbed over his shoulder. "Ah, I have a few

things to do here. And with my grandfather's shoulder. Well…"

Garcia nodded. "Yeah, right, you want to help him."

"Exactly."

He didn't sound very convincing. "Anyway, just let him know I want to speak with him." He tapped Garcia on the arm. "And thanks, Garcia. For everything."

He feigned a smile as he let himself out. As Garcia jogged over to his vehicle, his eyes roamed the lot. He wasn't worried about coming face-to-face with those thugs. They didn't pose much of a threat, but Travis, well, whatever game he was playing, it was dangerous and it wasn't just Harry who might get hurt.

* * *

Elisha attached the last of the solar-powered, motion-sensor lights to the cabin while Liam held the rickety ladder. A task that wasn't easy with only one good arm. Andre had offered to help but she was determined to contribute. There was nothing worse than feeling useless. "What will you do about your parents?" he asked.

"What do you mean?"

"If they return, they won't know where you are."

"Yes they will. While a nurse was putting your arm in a cast, Garcia gave me a lift back to my mother's home, or what was left of it. I created a sign detailing where we are."

"What? Please tell me you didn't give this exact location."

She laughed. "No, of course not. I didn't know this location. I gave the name of the town. I figure it's small enough that we'd eventually cross paths."

The ladder shook and groaned beneath her as she descended.

At the bottom, Liam was grinning.

Elisha frowned, slowly bringing a hand up to her head. "What? Do I have something on my face?"

"No, it's not your face."

Her eyes widened. "My butt? Is there something on my…" Then she clued in. Her eyes narrowed and a smile appeared as she poked him. "Were you staring at my butt?"

"I can neither confirm or deny." He laughed.

She gave him a playful slap. "Get your mind out of the gutter. What's next?"

"We could install the burglar bars on the windows, but that will have to wait until tomorrow. The sun is almost gone. Which reminds me. Garcia hasn't returned. I hope he…"

He was in the middle of speaking when gravel crunched. They turned to see his cruiser winding up the driveway. After killing the engine Garcia got out and strolled over. "Nice work on the solar lights."

"Yeah, should alert us if someone is creeping around." He looked back at him. "So… how did it go?" Liam asked

Garcia stared at him with a pained expression. "How well do you know Travis?"

"We practically grew up together. He's like a brother. Why?"

"And his relationship with his grandfather?"

"Good."

"He wants to see you tonight. I think it would be worth going."

"Why? Garcia, what happened?"

He gave a nod toward the cabin. "We should go in. Have something to eat. I'll tell you all about it."

Chapter 13

Lopez loomed over the body of the chief and spat on him. "Rest in peace, asshole!" After the siege on the department, Lopez and his men bulldozed their way into the barricaded office of Chief Berryman. With a gun to his head, he had no option but to hand over Garcia's address. When asked where he'd gone, the chief couldn't answer other than to say he'd disappeared. Unsatisfied or simply thirsty for blood, he ended the chief's life. In less than ten minutes they had made quick work of the officers inside. Outnumbered, the few overseeing the department didn't stand a chance. Lopez had men posted at the main doors just in case others returned but the chances of that were slim. They were out patrolling the streets, searching through the rubble for survivors.

Now with Garcia's address in hand he had no reason to keep Ken around.

Shoved into the corridor and led toward the main

foyer, Ken fully expected to be shot in the back of the head, however, when they led him out of the building he wondered if Lopez was considering his offer.

"Are you going to kill me?"

"Get in the truck."

The unknown was crippling him.

Ken climbed in and Lopez pushed him over and slammed the door. He seemed to get off on keeping him in the dark. He drove in silence through Petaluma as Ken continued to try and make him think about how Petaluma could be a land of milk and honey. Lopez wasn't biting. His face was stoic and focused on the road ahead, even as he continued to hold a gun to his ribs. "Do you think that's necessary? It's not like I could overpower even one of you," he said, letting out a nervous chuckle.

No reply.

They drove to the northwest side of Petaluma to a quaint neighborhood just off Emerald Court. The road ended in a cul-de-sac. The homes were modest, Garcia's was a clapboard two-bedroom abode with an American flag out front, a common sight at many U.S. homes. There was no vehicle in the driveway but that didn't mean he wasn't there. Ken bounced in his seat as the truck went into the driveway and the other three vehicles parked outside. Like a SWAT team preparing to burst inside, they got out and removed rifles from the trunks of their vehicles and surrounded the building.

All he could do was watch as they unloaded a few rounds, breaking windows. They kicked open a door and entered. A moment later, Lopez stepped outside and motioned to the guy in the truck to bring in Ken.

Was Garcia alive?

Shoved through the main door, he was greeted by the sight of a pristine home, certainly not what he imagined. He'd always thought that Garcia was using his position with the police to cover up some shady business. He figured there would be drug paraphernalia on the table, lines of coke or a bag of cash sitting nearby. Nope. There wasn't one thing out of place. The carpets were immaculate. For a second he thought the chief had purposely given them the wrong address until he saw a photo on the wall, of Garcia with other cops from the department.

Lopez slumped into a chair, toying with his handgun. "You asked if I was planning on killing you. Where is he, mayor?"

Ken looked at the others, his heart speeding up with every passing second. This was it. The moment his life was over. All these years of toiling for the government only to die in an ex-gang member's home. The irony wasn't wasted. "You can't expect me to know that. You wanted his address; I gave you that. I'm not a mind reader."

Lopez raised his gun at him, and Ken put his hands out, tears forming in his eyes, the thought of being shot, being in pain, it was all too much to bear. Piss trickled down his leg pooling at his feet. "For all I know he could have left Petaluma," he spat out.

"That's not the answer I'm looking for, Ken."

Like a spark igniting in his brain, he suddenly came up

with a last-ditch effort at staying alive. He stabbed his finger forward. "Okay, okay, um. What was her name?" He clicked his fingers. "Reid. Reid. That's it! He was seen multiple times with the Reid girl."

"Who?"

"Um, a lady here in town who works for the hospital. Sophie Reid. She has a daughter. Elisha. Yeah. That's it. Word has it that Garcia was seeing her mother. And multiple times I saw him with her. She lives over on, uh…" He stumbled over his words, his mind barely managing to piece together a thought. "I know where she lives. That's what I'm trying to say. She helped in community events. If he's not here, they could have gone there."

Lopez uncocked his gun. "You better hope so. Let's go."

"Look, Mr. Lopez. I need to know. Are you going to kill me?"

"That depends."

"On?" he asked as he was pushed out of the door.

"Whether you outlive your usefulness."

"Oh, I see. Well, let me reassure you. I am very useful. I mean, they don't just make anyone the mayor. They chose me because I think outside the box. I…"

"Talk too much," Lopez said cutting him off. "Now shut the hell up and get in the truck before I change my mind."

Ken went silent, gulped and within a matter of a minute they'd left Garcia's residence behind. A wave of relief came over him. He was alive, but for how much longer?

Chapter 14

The supper that evening was outstanding. Lamb, mashed potatoes, fresh colorful salad followed by a dessert that could have been served in any five-star restaurant. Alex hadn't eaten food this good in over a week. Hell, they'd been living on a diet of food from smashed vending machines and anything they could scavenge from cafés, grocery stores or what was left of them.

Whether it was because they were guests or it was a tradition, they had laid out quite the spread that evening. As they ate, a group of three young women played music on a harp, a guitar and a violin. Nearby, two men engaged in an arm-wrestling match, while an artist painted a portrait of space by looking out through one of the many floor-to-ceiling windows that encircled the dining area.

Candles around the room provided a source of light, the flames causing shadows to dance upon the walls.

Alex looked at Ryan who appeared to be enjoying himself, surrounded by two young teen girls who were leaning into him, talking then laughing. Thomas on the other hand sat across the room, holding a glass of wine and offering an expression of skepticism.

They'd each been given seats, not together but apart. Alex was beginning to wonder if that was done on purpose, allowing them to share their beliefs.

He wasn't buying it.

All of them had been given silky white robes and treated like they were royalty.

The atmosphere in the room was like a busy restaurant with people coming and going, bringing in different food as if trying to impress them or fatten them up.

What was unusual was their host still hadn't appeared.

Meadow had explained that they didn't always do this and the meal that evening was in honor of them after risking their lives to help Star. Something that would have only made sense if the drones had been a danger. Meadow had still been very elusive when it came to asking why the drones hadn't fired upon them. "Answers. They will come in time, Alex. But first, eat," she'd said.

Distraction, it was another form of deception.

He caught Thomas' eye. Thomas rose and strolled over. He took a seat beside him. "Kind of wild, isn't it, Mr. Reid?"

"Fake you mean?"

He nodded slowly. "Yeah, something doesn't feel right but you have to admit, Abner sure knows how to throw one hell of a party. This place is off the hook."

"Is that what you call it?" Alex said, reaching for an apple and taking a bite. "Have you seen him?"

"Nope."

"I'm thinking we should leave early."

Thomas patted Alex on the shoulder. "Ah relax, tomorrow we'll head out. Until then, enjoy." He winked at a teen girl as she walked by him and followed after her.

A silver platter of what looked like fried frogs' legs was placed in front of him. The smell wasn't as bad as the look of them. "What are they?" he asked the server.

"Chicken wings."

Who were they kidding? He'd seen all manner of wings throughout New York State and even in the seediest of bars, none of them looked like that. "I think I'll pass."

Across the table, a woman in her sixties was holding Sophie's hand and talking to her. It was hard to tell what the conversation was about amid the ruckus of people talking, others laughing and music playing.

Every now and again he would catch Meadow staring at him, almost in an uncomfortable manner. He would just smile back and she would turn her head away, not returning the gesture. Alex gazed around the room searching for Star but hadn't seen her either. In fact, he hadn't seen her since their arrival.

Roughly thirty minutes into their meal, the room went silent and a door was opened at the far end and Abner walked in with multiple women, all of whom were now dressed in white. Abner himself had changed into new attire and was now sporting something that the Dalai

Lama might have worn — a three-piece outfit, an upper robe and an outer robe, the colors were white with a band of gold.

What was he, some kind of guru?

Everyone barring themselves dipped their head ever so slightly as if they were in the presence of royalty. Alex looked over at Sophie, and she acknowledged with a frown that something was amiss.

"Welcome. It's an honor to have you among us. We look forward to getting to know you all. To the rest of you. I want you to know that no matter what is happening out there, as long as you are here, you will know no fear, no sadness, no want. In return, we know you will give back."

Abner took a seat. Two servers hurried over and set a silver plate in front of him and removed the dome top to uncover his food. He thanked them.

A young woman with curly ginger hair, nineteen, twenty maybe, came around the table and asked if they wanted their glasses filled with wine. After what they'd gone through with Cowboy, his trust in people was at an all-time low.

Alex placed his hand over his glass as the woman went to pour. "No thank you."

"Drink," Abner said. "The night is still young."

"No, I need to get up early to get ready to leave."

"Right. Leave. And you, Sophie?"

"I will be going with him."

"In that case I wondered if you would care to join me tonight, Sophie. I give a talk to the people here. I would love to have you in attendance."

"We should probably get some sleep," Alex said rising from his chair.

"You won't join us?"

"I would love to but it's been a long day and…"

"That would be nice," Sophie added.

"Uh," Alex gestured toward the door.

"Then it's settled. We'll see you in the morning, Alex."

Alex stood there for a second, his gaze bouncing between Abner and Sophie. He looked for Ryan and

Thomas but they'd already left. He raised his eyebrows then walked out.

His room was on the second floor, two doors down from Ryan. As he was letting himself in, he saw several girls come out of Ryan's room, go over to Thomas' and knock. The door opened and they entered. Thomas looked out, grinned at Alex and gave him the thumbs-up before closing the door. So. That's how it was.

Inside, Alex slumped down on the bed and lay back. He sat up and looked around. The room was fairly basic. A queen-sized four-poster bed, a bathroom attached and a walk-out balcony. The floors and walls were all made from Douglas fir.

He couldn't help but get a sense that he was being watched.

Though it could have been his paranoia after seeing a show a few months back about cameras found in hotels. Still, it didn't hurt to check. He looked up at the fire alarm and stood on the bed to reach it. He opened it and checked inside.

Normal.

He went into the bathroom which used a small solar lamp that was positioned directly below a skylight to provide light.

No. Nothing was out of the usual. He ran his hand along the counter, looked behind the mirror, checked the outlets. If they were watching him he would have been hard-pressed to know for sure as cameras were becoming smaller and smaller with some no bigger than a screw.

As he was looking inside a cupboard, there was a knock at the door.

Startled, he banged his head. Alex rubbed the back of his head as he made his way to the door. When he opened it, Meadow stepped inside. "I brought you a hot tea."

"I'm fine."

"It's just a nightcap."

She closed the door behind her and set it on a counter.

"Meadow, look, I appreciate it but I'm really tired. I should turn in."

She brought a finger up to her lips and directed him

toward the balcony. His brow furrowed as he followed her out, wondering what was going on. As soon as they were outside, she closed the doors behind her. "They're listening. We have to be careful."

"What? Who's listening?"

She swallowed hard. "I wanted to say something earlier but she was there and though I've tried to speak to her she's besotted with him."

"Star?"

She nodded. "I uh…" She had a pained expression. "A week ago, I arrived here with my family, my brother and my uncle. Within a day they had vanished and I was told they left without me but I know that's not true. My brother would never leave me behind. We grew up in Denver. Our building was destroyed in the fires and we lost both of our parents. At some point we came across Star, and she offered us canned food, and said there was more at the ranch, a lot more. At first my uncle didn't want to go but then…"

"She eluded the drones."

Meadow nodded.

There was a sound like someone had dropped something. It spooked her and she looked scared. "Look, I don't know fully what's happening here but I know my uncle and brother didn't leave without me. I know they didn't. And your family aren't the only ones. There have been others over the last week, every few days. It's like clockwork. The last time I went out to Denver that was the second time."

"What were you told?"

"To find survivors, offer them food, then offer shelter."

"So you weren't collecting those cans."

"No. We gave them out."

Alex frowned as he gazed at the lake which was lit up by a crescent moon.

"So she didn't run into us."

"No, she saw you earlier." Meadow breathed in deeply. "Look, I don't want to stay here anymore but they watch me like a hawk. When you leave in the morning. Please, take me with you."

He nodded. "Meadow. How is she avoiding the drones?"

She shook her head. "I don't know. I haven't seen all of this property. Some areas are off-limits like the barn at the far side of the lake. No one is allowed there except Abner. Sometimes he takes women out there and they aren't seen again and anyone that returns is different."

"In what way?"

"Like Star, besotted with him. It's like they're afraid." She shook her head. "I'm meant to go there in a couple of days and… look, please. When you leave tomorrow. Take me with you."

He nodded. "You have my word."

And like that she went back into the room, picked up the tea, poured the contents into a sink in the bathroom and exited the room but not before giving him a pained smile.

What the hell was going on here?

* * *

"No way, I don't believe it," Liam said, rising from the table and taking his plate over to the sink. He let it slide into the water and stood there looking out, trying to make sense of it.

"I'm telling you what I saw. Now I don't know what his angle is but he knew those guys."

"You must be mistaken. You said there was a lot of smoke drifting across the town, maybe you mistook them for the same guys."

Garcia leaned back in his seat. "Liam, I've been a cop long enough to remember a face. My job relies on specifics not generalities. He knew them."

"His grandparents were always good to him. Travis wouldn't do that."

"There's a lot of things people wouldn't do if society was the way it used to be. This whole event has changed the nation."

Liam slammed his fist against the counter. "It's been seven days. I hardly think Travis would attempt to kill his grandfather or kill the police. The next thing you'll say is that he was responsible for his grandmother's carjacking and death."

Garcia shrugged.

"You are joking?"

"All I'm telling you is what I saw. I'm not saying for you to call him out or believe it. But we need to be careful. Think about this for a second. Usually when a home gets broken into on a remote stretch of road like this, other homes are also affected. I stopped by six of the homes along this street on the way back tonight and spoke with some of the residents. No one has had a break-in. No one saw any gang members. So ask yourself. Who else knew about your grandfather's cabin? Who knew about all the gear he had inside?"

There was a pause.

"But he said that Theo gave it to Harry."

"Did he? Did Harry speak to Theo?"

Liam leaned against the counter with a confused expression.

"No. No, I know what you're trying to do here."

"What?"

"Turn me against him."

Garcia looked at Andre and Elisha. "What reason would I have to do that?"

"Think about it, Liam. Has he lied to us yet?" Elisha asked.

Liam balled his fists. Travis had been his closest friend growing up. Everything Garcia had told him went against the grain of who he was. Travis loved his grandparents. He would have done anything for them. If he wanted Harry dead, why wouldn't he do it himself? Or why not open the store when his grandfather was asleep? Something about this didn't ring true.

The very notion that Travis would break into Theo's cabin and take his supplies, then lie, only angered him. He didn't need this hassle. Not now.

Liam scooped up the keys to the cruiser.

He stood by the door, gripping the handle, ready to leave. "I'll speak with him but you're wrong, Garcia."

"I hope so for your sake," he replied.

Chapter 15

He was going to die. There was no doubt about it. After locating the Reid residence and finding a sign in the front yard with a message from Elisha to her parents, Ramiro now had the general location of where they were. Whether Garcia was with them or had simply given them a ride, that didn't matter.

He'd expected to be shot in the head and left in a puddle of his blood outside her home but instead they took him back to his house.

Of course.

He probably wanted to kill Colleen in front of him before snuffing his light out.

That's how these gang members got off.

Pushed toward the front door, Ken noticed it was ajar.

Stumbling into the house, his eyes widened at the sight of four dead bodies.

"No. No!" Ramiro yelled. He hurried outside and

looked around the darkened streets. "Leo!" he bellowed, raising his gun and firing a round. He had this look of death in his eyes. There was no mercy. He wasn't a man that could be reasoned with. Ken knew this was his only chance to escape. In the commotion, as Ramiro yelled at his men to search the streets, he was distracted, overwhelmed, no longer focused on Ken.

The one and only guy standing by the door had his back turned.

Ken took a few steps back, casting a glance over his shoulder.

If he could reach the kitchen, there was a possibility he could duck out the rear and escape through his neighbor's yard. There was coverage. Even if they saw him. He could zigzag, weave his way around trees, scale over fences and hole up inside someone's home if a door was open.

His heart slammed in his chest as he took one last look to make sure the coast was clear. He took off, his mind focused on that rear door. It was already wide open.

Had Colleen opened it? Had she escaped? Where was

Leo?

He pushed the thoughts from his mind as he leaped into action, bursting out of the house, still hearing Ramiro shouting at his men.

He glanced back momentarily to see if anyone was following.

They weren't.

Perfect. He had a head start.

His lungs felt like they were on fire as he inhaled deeply.

Just as he was scaling over the fence into his neighbor's yard, he heard his name.

"The mayor. Fischer. Where is he?"

His heartbeat faster as his knees pumped like pistons. He sprinted down the side of one house, scaled over another fence. All the while he was thinking that at any moment a bullet would strike him in the back.

He could hear the sound of blood rushing in his ears as he darted through the back of a home that was empty and out the front door. Sweat streamed down his back, his cheeks flushed as he put everything he had into escaping. He hadn't run like this since he was a kid. Colleen had bought a treadmill a few years back, trying to get him to use it, but the idea of walking on the spot seemed worse than death.

Stumbling forward, Ken tripped a few times.

His knees drove into the dirt, his hands gripped weeds.

Each time his mind raced with thoughts of death or worse, being stomped.

He'd managed to make it two streets over, to Valley Oak Court, when it happened.

Ken had looked over his shoulder to see if anyone was coming when a meaty paw grabbed his collar and dragged him back into a house. He would have cried for help but a hand was clamped over his mouth.

The door slammed and he turned to find Leo glaring at him.

"Whoa, whoa, please don't shoot."

"Where are the others?" Leo asked.

"They're... back at the house. I escaped out the back."

"Did anyone see?"

"No. At least I don't think so."

The guy forced him up the stairs and into a cramped bedroom.

"Oh God you're not going to…"

"Just take a seat and shut up."

"You're Leo, right? The one they're after."

He gave a nod as he pulled back a curtain and looked out.

"Where's my wife. Colleen? What have you done with her?"

"She's safe. Okay? She's with one of your neighbors."

Ken offered back a puzzled look. "You helped her escape?"

"Couldn't exactly leave her there. They would have executed her."

Ken nodded. His hands were shaking. Sweat was streaming off him. He pulled at his tie to loosen it, then reached into his pocket for a pack of cigarettes. "Damn it."

"What?"

"No cigarettes."

"That stuff will kill you."

Ken broke into laughter, stress getting the better of him. "Why did you help her?"

"Because I was as much a captive as you and she were," he said, squinting and looking out. "I don't think they'll find us but we should probably get moving. Knowing Ramiro he'll go house to house."

"No. He won't," Ken said confidently. "He has the location for Garcia. Willits. He got it from the Reid residence. Stupid girl left behind a message for her parents."

"And you led him over there?"

"What did you expect me to do? He had a gun pressed into my ribs." Ken got up to go and Leo raised a hand.

"I need to get a towel. Is that okay?"

He nodded and Ken went into an adjoining room and returned wiping his face. "I don't get it. You arrived with them. Why would you bring this heat down on yourself?"

"Long story."

"Well it doesn't look like we are going anywhere, so I'm all ears." He removed his jacket and unbuttoned his shirt which was soaking wet. Leo continued looking out the window.

"Several years ago I used to run with 18th Street. I was what they classed as a triggerman, one of the top guys. At some point I decided to leave. Had enough. The problem is you don't just walk away from gang life. You end up in prison, dead or in service to the church."

"You? The church?" Ken laughed.

"Anyway, there is an agreement in place called calmado. It means you can walk away but you never really walk away. You're no longer under obligation to kill or work for them but if push comes to shove and they need you back, you have to return."

"Have to?"

"Unless you want a bullet in the head."

He stabbed a finger at him as he continued to dry himself off. "Got it!"

"What's the situation in this town?" Leo asked.

"Dire. Desperate. Destroyed. Does that answer your question?"

"You were planning on getting out, weren't you?"

"Colleen told you that?"

"In no uncertain words, yeah."

"Do you blame me?"

"Mayor, I don't even know you. I don't care either way. My only goal is to survive this."

"If you want to do that you might want to find Garcia. Anyway, why are they after him?"

Leo ran a hand over his face. "Long story. Gangs united."

"So you were made to go with them."

"I was meant to kill Garcia."

"You?"

He nodded, rolling his bottom lip into his mouth. "According to Ramiro, word reached us that they needed additional support to deal with a problem. You said this guy was an ex-gang member? A cop?"

"I know. Strange, isn't it? That's what I tried to tell the chief but he wouldn't listen. Said he could make an impact, keep the gangs at bay and… well… look at the way things turned out. He started a war in our backyard and at the worst time."

"You know what he looks like?"

Ken ran a hand over his pant leg in front of him. "Regrettably, yes. The man was a thorn in my side. No offense but I kind of think that gangs should stay with gangs, and police stay with the police. Mixing the two is a recipe for disaster. Like a chemical reaction. I was right as well. But no one listened to me. No, we must have diversity. We must have someone who represents the gang community." He chuckled shaking his head.

"Willits. Where is that?"

"North of here, almost two hours' drive. In cottage country."

Leo nodded then patted him on the leg as he got up. "We'll obtain a vehicle and I want you to take me there."

"Uh. Hold on a second. I'm not going. My wife is

here."

"You wanted to get out of town, yes?"

"Yes but…"

"Then you'll take me to Willits. After we find Garcia, you can do whatever you want."

"I don't get it. We are facing a collapse of society and you want to find this man? Why? Why not just leave like me?"

Leo stopped at the door and looked back at him. "A seventeen-year-old boy fled 18th Street back when I was in the gang. He changed his name, moved across the country, even started a family. The gang tracked him down. He now works for the gang earning money to prevent them from killing his kid. You don't walk away. Whether a nation is in ruins or not, loyalty is the only thing we have and once that's gone — you're gone."

He stepped out of the room and didn't need to explain any further.

Chapter 16

Liam waited in the cruiser outside Forest City Surplus, contemplating what Garcia had shared. Before arriving he'd cruised around the streets looking for anyone, or anything that might have looked out of place. Were there gangs here? Had Travis lied to them? It seemed ludicrous. Why would he do that? He'd known him since they were nine years old. They'd stayed over at each other's house, hung out together. He'd seen the way he was around his grandfather. Harry doted on him, as did his grandmother Arlene. There was nothing he couldn't have had if he'd asked.

No, Garcia had this wrong.

He shut off the engine and made his way to the rear door. He gave it a few hard thumps and stood back waiting for Travis or Harry to appear on the roof but they didn't. The door opened and Travis smiled at him. "Liam Carter, come on in."

"Why did you open the door?"

He shrugged. "I knew you were coming."

"But you didn't know who was out here."

Travis chuckled patting him on the shoulder. "Just get inside before real trouble shows up."

It struck him as odd especially after his grandfather had been shot. If he believed gangs were in the neighborhood he would have taken extra precautions, of course unless it was just another lie and he was the one responsible.

He would have to be tactful in his line of questioning.

While he didn't feel threatened by Travis, he'd seen the way things could turn on a dime. "Here, you want a beer?"

"Sure."

"Tate, grab Liam a brewski and get me one too."

As they entered the guts of the store, he glanced around looking for Harry. "Where's Harry?"

"Down below. Resting."

Which meant in the bunker.

"Sorry to hear what happened to him. You find out who did it?"

"No, but I'm sure it's the same guys who killed my grandmother and took out those cops."

Tate returned with three Budweisers. He tossed each of them a can. Travis cracked his open and took a seat in a camping chair. They'd set the chairs in a circle near a display area for camping gear. They were in the middle of playing a game of cards. Liam gave a nod to Joe who was peering at him through a set of binoculars with a big grin while he puffed away on a Cohiba.

"Here, you've got to try one of these," Travis said, crossing the room and returning with a portable humidor. It was made of rosewood. He cracked it open and inside was a line of fat cigars. "One hundred percent Cuban."

Travis clipped the end and gave him one, then brought a flame to it as Liam turned it in his fingers, and smoke billowed around him.

"Good, right?"

"Not bad," Liam said with a smile, leaning back in his

chair.

Travis closed the case then sat across from him. "Man, it's good to see you again. It was getting a little boring around here without you. So… that bit of ass you're with. You banging her?"

Liam blew out smoke. "Don't be crude."

Travis cracked up. "Ah man, I'm screwing with you." He smiled. "Seriously though, you hooked up?" He burst out laughing and tapped him on the knee. "I'm just messing with you."

Tate peered over his beer can, amused.

"So what did you want to see me about?" Liam asked.

"Huh? Can't old friends have a drink together?"

"It's just Garcia made it sound like you had a reason."

Travis leaned forward in his seat and cast a glance over his shoulder as if making sure Harry wasn't listening. "I do but we'll get to that. All in good time, Liam. So you guys set up the cabin?"

"Yeah."

"And what's the deal with this Garcia fella?"

"What about him?"

"Seems a little odd. When's he heading back to Petaluma?"

"Why? You have a problem with him?"

"Me? No. Of course not. Just think it's odd. What about you, Tate?"

"Real peculiar."

"Joe?"

He sat up and removed a pair of dark shades that still had a price tag dangling from the corner. "Strange."

Travis rose from his seat and took a swig of his beer. "Come with me for a minute. I want to show you something." Liam went to put his beer down and he told him to bring it with him. "Guys. No looking at my hand. You got it! That means you, Joe."

Joe rolled his eyes. "Like I would do that."

As Travis led him up onto the roof, he kept talking. "You remember when we were kids we used to come up here and pretend we owned the town?"

Many a fond memory came back to him. "Yeah."

"Seems like a world ago. Who would have imagined that it would come to this?" Travis unlocked the hatch and pushed up. Once on the roof, he extended a hand down and helped Liam up. They strolled over to their spot at the front of the building and Travis sat down, his legs dangling off the edge. "Sit."

Liam sat beside him and Travis pointed to some tar they'd engraved their names into one summer, a few days after his grandfather had put the new roof on. When they were youngsters they would sit there for hours, eating food and watching bicyclists, dog walkers, and people driving by or visiting Harry's place or the convenience store across the road. "Remember getting that old guy to go in and buy us our first pack of cigarettes and a pack of Budweisers?"

Liam smiled. Those were better days. Summers that seemed to last forever. There was no sense of danger or panic like what they'd gone through. As they stared out at the empty street it felt very different, cold, even though they were in the midst of summer. Memories rolled through his mind.

Travis took another hard swig of his beer and set it down. He inhaled his cigar then spoke as wafts of gray smoke came out of his mouth. "You remember what I said to you back when we were fourteen?"

"You said a lot of things."

"No, I mean about this town. That one day I would run it," he said glancing down the street.

"Yep!" He took another swig.

There was a pause and without Travis looking at him he replied.

"What if we could, Liam?"

"What?"

"The population here is 4,875, give or take. Nothing but a speck on the map to most, but to me, it's my entire world. This is my America. My patch."

"What are you talking about?"

"1862. President Lincoln signed the Homestead Act. You know — to allow settlers to claim lots up to 160 acres as long as they lived there and improved the land.

What a time that must have been. No one telling you how much you needed to pay. No one telling you what you needed to do. You just showed up in an area and as long as it wasn't claimed, you could put your roots down and create a life, a real life." He looked at him. "That was the way it was meant to be. Not today. You know I tried to get an apartment in this town. You know how much they wanted?"

"Nine hundred?"

"And the rest," Travis said, chuckling.

"C'mon, even if it's fifteen hundred. That's not bad."

"Not bad?" He nearly spat out his beer. "Yeah, maybe on your salary but not on mine."

"Your grandfather pays you well."

He laughed. "My grandfather pays me what he thinks I deserve. Big difference." Travis shook his head. "No, there was a time it would have cost nothing. Nothing to build over there," he said pointing to a lot that was in the early stages of development. It looked as if they had laid the foundations for an apartment block. "I mean of course you would have had to find your building material but…" he trailed off. "If the bombings hadn't happened where would we be?"

Travis shook his head and took another swig of his beer.

"Everything okay, Travis?" Liam asked, sensing that something was amiss.

"Yeah. Yeah. Drink up," he said slapping his back. "How's that arm of yours?"

"Painful but I'm managing."

"I thought you got it to match Long Legs."

"Travis."

"I'm messing with you, man. Geesh, when did you lose your sense of humor? So serious." He blew out more smoke then tossed his cigar.

There was a long pause as they sat there.

"I need to tell you something," Travis said. "I'm not proud of it but…" he trailed off. He breathed in deeply. "The shootings at the police department. It wasn't a gang. I lied."

"What?"

He looked at him. "Those cops. It wasn't a gang, at least not the kind you had in mind. Like Garcia I mean."

"Travis."

"Listen to me. Hear me out. You know me, right."

"What have you done?"

His hand started shaking ever so slightly and he closed his eyes. Travis then got up and drained the remainder of his beer and tossed the bottle. It smashed as it hit the ground near one of the dead bodies. "You were always going to do something with your life. Me? No. I would be stuck here forever."

"That's not true. Your grandfather would pass on the store and —"

Travis cut him off. "No. Liam. He was planning on selling it."

"Oh." There was a long pause. "Well, I'm sure he needed the money for his retirement."

He snorted. "That old coot has more money in his account than he knows what to do with. He didn't need the money. I tried to get him to change his mind. You know, even sell it to me, of course for a discount price that I would pay back over time, but he wouldn't listen. Said he wanted top dollar, upfront. A businessman through and through." He looked resentful. "You know I put hours and hours of my time into this store, working for chump change in the hope that one day when it came time to sell he would…" He trailed off and shook his head. "No. He wants to leave me out of the loop. I mean I could run this store with my eyes closed, couldn't I?"

Liam nodded.

"What have you done, Travis?"

He'd never seen Travis this shaken up. Travis brought a hand up to his face and ran it over his head. "When the bombings happened I figured he would want to get out of town, you know, get away. I saw an opportunity. I told him I would look after the store. Sell out what was there but he wouldn't do it. He wanted to close up, shut it down and…" He paused for a second. "I just wanted to scare him, Liam. That's all."

Liam stared at him. "Garcia was right."

Travis shot him a look. "About?"

Liam moved away from the edge. "He saw you with a group. The same ones that shot up this place. He knows you're behind it."

An expression crossed his face, undisguisable. "Who else knows?"

Liam stared back at him. "All of them."

Travis looked despondent.

"And your grandmother?" Liam asked.

"It was an accident. Things got out of hand."

"Out of hand?" Liam backed up, squinting at him. "You killed her?"

"No. God no. It was them." Travis dropped down to a crouch, bringing both of his hands up to his face. The realization set in. He might not have been the one who pulled the trigger but he'd put them up to it. "The cops hadn't figured it out but there was a witness. We umm…"

Liam shook his head. "Took care of the witness."

"Yeah but she wasn't the only one and…"

"So you had to deal with the cops."

"Not exactly. It's complicated." Travis groaned. "After the bombings their resources were strained. There were only a few holding down the fort so…"

Liam approached him and gave him a shove. "Damn you. Damn you!"

"I didn't mean for anyone to get hurt. You've got to believe me, man. I just…"

"You let them do this. Harry could have died because of you."

"I… I know. They weren't meant to go that far. I reamed them out but it was too late."

Liam shook his head. "You need to tell him."

"I can't. I just can't."

"Then I will."

Liam went to walk by him but Travis quickly got in front of him, hands extended. "Liam. Please. I will do it but not now. Not while he's in that state."

"You know I used to look up to you, man." He shook

his head. "We are done."

"Liam." He grabbed his arm but he shrugged it off.

"Tell him tonight or I will."

As he went to leave, he stopped at the opening of the roof and looked back at him. "What did you hope to achieve? Huh? It wasn't like you would have taken over the business. Look around you, Travis. The town is in ruins. The people are scared. Scared of people like you. You!" he said. "You call this town your everything. Your America. If this is what you think America is, I don't want any part of it."

With that said he climbed down. On the way out, Joe called out to him. "Hey, dude, you want another beer?"

"Keep it."

He marched out, shouldering the door.

He had been both right and wrong.

Garcia was right about his involvement but wrong to believe that he did this. Travis didn't have the nerve to do it. He was a coward who relied on others to do his dirty work.

As he went to get back in the cruiser, he looked up at the roof and saw Travis crouched, his head in his hands. He couldn't believe the same kid he'd grown up with had spiraled down this far. Sure, chaos could bring out the worst in people but there was always a line that should never be crossed. In times like this, family was everything and he had just lit a fuse and let it burn.

Chapter 17

Meadow was absent from breakfast the following morning. After he inquired, one of the servers told him she'd gone into Denver with Star. As he drank a cup of coffee he looked at the others roaming the room. Were they like Meadow? Were they being held here against their will? Did they know what Meadow knew? Why hadn't anyone done anything?

Alex hadn't got much sleep that night. It was a combination of things: the disturbing conversation with Meadow, the uncomfortable chair with a spring that stuck into his upper back, and then Sophie who'd returned to the room at a late hour.

She'd entered sometime after midnight.

Surely Abner couldn't have talked that long?

He'd pretended he was asleep when she crept in, stripped down to her underwear and slipped beneath the covers. It had been a long time since he'd seen her without clothes on, even longer since they'd slept together. Under a faint band of moonlight seeping through the drapes Alex gazed at her, questions roiling in his mind. The past, the present, the future. At some point he'd drifted off, managing to get a few hours. It was certainly more than he got on the road.

Later, he'd exited the room and roamed the grounds in hopes of seeing something unusual, anything that might give him an indication of what was really going on. Meadow's words came back to him. What was in the barn on the far side of the lake? He'd made a beeline for it, however, before he got halfway around, a golf cart rolled up beside him with Abner and one of his followers. That's what Alex was calling them now — followers. Like a cult, placing a man on a pedestal as if he was somehow closer to God, they seemed to hang on his every word, and gaze at him, as if he possessed some kind of unknown power.

Abner sat casually in the passenger side, his arm resting on his thigh as a long-haired follower with a gaunt face leaned against the steering wheel. "Morning, Alex.

Beautiful day, isn't it?" Was this guy out of his mind? He acted like the world was fine. It wasn't. It wouldn't ever be fine. "Jump in, I'll give you a ride back to the house."

Alex waved him off. "I'm good."

"You're not hungry?"

"Not yet."

"Then let's talk. Sophie told me a lot about you."

"She's…"

"Divorcing you." He nodded. "I know. Jump in." He jerked his head to the rear where there were two more seats.

Alex looked off toward the barn. "What's that used for?" he asked before getting in the cart. Abner followed his gaze across a glistening lake that reflected the blue sky.

"Horses, hay. General essentials for the animals. C'mon, hop in."

Reluctantly he took a seat.

The cart lurched forward and he gripped a railing as they swung around, away from the barn and onto a winding path that led into the forest. "I know you have questions, Alex, everyone does when they come here and I'm here to answer them. However for this place to function efficiently it requires that we all make sacrifices."

"And by that you mean?"

He turned in his seat. "Sophie wants to stay longer."

"No, we're leaving."

"It's not forever, just a few days. I think it would be good for both of you."

"Yeah, well, I appreciate that but we'll be heading out this morning."

"And how do you expect to leave?"

Alex raised an eyebrow.

"You'll need a ride, I mean."

"Right."

"As much as we would like to give you one, the need here is great. Now, if you stayed a while longer and contributed, we might be inclined to gift you a vehicle."

"Or I could search the back roads and homes and take one."

"You could," Abner said, nodding. "But let me ask you

this, Alex. Where is this all heading? This race to get back to California?"

"My daughter."

"You think you'll find her?"

His questions were irritating him. "I expect to."

"And if you don't?"

He paused for a second. "Listen, Abner. I can see you affect the people here. I don't know how or who you are to them — a friend, a leader, a guru or a god, but I will make it home and I will find my daughter."

"I'm not saying you won't. But if she's not alive. How will you cope? Surely you've considered this?"

"That's between me and Sophie."

"Then that's a conversation you will need to have as she's made up her mind."

"And we will on our way out."

He nodded and chuckled as if finding something amusing. The cart weaved its way up through a forest of spruce and fir, then continued until it reached a clearing at the top of a hill that overlooked the entire property.

The driver stopped the vehicle and Abner got out. "Come, I want to show you something."

He led Alex to an outcropping of rock that provided a breathtaking view of the valley below. A blanket of green spread for miles around, highlighted by the rising sun. Abner clasped his hands behind his back. "What do you see, Alex?"

From their vantage point he had a clear view of the ranch, the surrounding forest, and the city of Denver in the distance or what was left of it. "What do you want me to see?" he said in a way that made it clear he was frustrated.

"Hope. Despair," Abner said. "People are lost without a shepherd to lead them."

Alex scoffed. "And let me guess, you're this shepherd?"

"I'm whatever you choose me to be. You asked how Star was able to elude the drones. Do you still wish to know?"

Alex looked at him. "I think it's obvious."

"Is it?"

"You control them or someone you know controls them."

He smiled with quiet confidence. "Are you a God-fearing man, Alex?" He didn't give him the chance to reply. "There is an account in the Old Testament where God sends an angel of death to kill the firstborn sons of Egypt. God tells Moses to sacrifice a lamb and smear the blood on the doors of the homes of the Jewish people. On those that had it, the angel would pass over the houses and leave them alive."

Alex laughed as he shifted from one foot to the next. "You expect me to believe you or God is preventing those drones from touching people?"

"Believe what you will."

"So you control these drones?"

"Not exactly."

"Then who are you working for? Huh?"

"They asked the same thing the last time I was here."

Alex's brow wrinkled, his mind made the connection, then he laughed. "Oh man, there is always one."

"I am here to do my father's work, Alex, nothing more."

"I'm sure you are. And this father of yours. Who is he? Iran? Russia? What are you, part of a terrorist cell?"

"Far from it."

"Then what are you talking about, man, as you really are making no sense."

"I'm here to protect and lead."

Alex groaned and slapped him on the back before heading back to the cart. "Well, Abner, best of luck with that, pal."

As he walked back, Abner spoke again,

"What happened to Michael was not your fault, Alex."

He stopped walking and cast a glance over his shoulder. "What did you say?"

Abner turned toward him. "You blame yourself. You blame Sophie but neither of you are to blame. Death is a natural part of life."

Alex raised a finger. "You don't know the first thing about me or Sophie — and you sure as hell don't know

Michael."

"I know you're in pain."

Alex scoffed and shook his head walking back toward him. He jabbed his finger in his face. "I don't know what crap you are telling these people, or what you've made Sophie believe, or even what she told you, but it doesn't matter. We are leaving this morning and whatever you're doing here, whoever you are working for, I don't give a crap. All I care about is my daughter and getting back to her." With that said he got back into the cart. Abner stood there looking at him, seemingly unaffected. No reaction either way. He got back in and told his guy to take them back to the ranch.

* * *

After finishing breakfast, Alex retreated to his room to collect his belongings and get the others ready to leave. On his way up, he passed Ryan who was wearing a black hoodie and looked bleary-eyed. He was holding the hand of some blond girl, looking as if he was on a country walk.

"We're leaving in twenty. Get your shit together."

Ryan balked. "What?"

Alex didn't stop to explain. He pressed on down the hallway and banged on Thomas' door until he answered. He too looked like he'd just rolled out of bed. His hair was a mess, and he was squinting at him. "Hey, wassup?"

Alex heard some girl in the background ask Thomas who it was. *What the hell was going on?* "We're leaving. If you're coming, get your bag."

"But I haven't even had breakfast yet."

Alex charged off leaving him with his mouth agape.

Back in his room, Sophie was sitting on the bed, leaning forward and tying the shoelaces on her boots. "Oh hey."

"At least one of you looks ready to go."

"Go? What?"

Alex grabbed up his bag. "Yeah. Leave. Head out. Back to California. Elisha. Or have you forgotten?" He headed into the bathroom and snagged up a towel and his toothbrush.

She took a few steps toward him. "Alex. I've been meaning to talk to you."

"No need. Abner already filled me in. Doesn't matter. We're going."

He ignored her as he gathered together what few things they'd taken out of his backpack.

"What if I don't want to?"

He whirled around. "What?"

"I mean. Of course, we'll leave but… not immediately."

Alex dropped his bag on a chair, a scowl forming. "This is about last night, isn't it? What did he put in your head?"

"Alex, look, we don't know if Elisha is alive. Look around you. The world is in ruins. The odds are slim and look how long it's taken for us to get halfway across America and that's with a vehicle. It could take us weeks if we don't find transportation and Abner isn't exactly handing out rides to anyone who asks."

He shifted his weight from one foot to the next. "So

that's it?"

She stepped toward him and placed a hand on his arm. "Even if she did survive, she's probably not in Petaluma. Then what? We're stuck in a ruined city. No food. No shelter. No one to rely on. But here..."

He took a step back. "Huh! I can't believe this. So all that talk before about getting back to Elisha. What was that about?" Sophie lowered her eyes. "What's the deal with this guy? Huh? What kind of control does he have?"

She dipped her head. "It's not like that."

"No? Because it sure as hell looks like it." He crossed the room. "People following him like he's some guru, listening to him talk until the early hours of the morning. What's all that about?"

"Hard to explain, you need to listen."

"I'm done listening. Meadow visited me last night. You know what she told me?"

Sophie frowned.

"She said she came here a week ago with her uncle and brother. Within a couple of days she was told they left without her. And you know what else? Apparently he takes women out to that barn and they go missing," he said crossing the room and pointing outside. "I asked him today, what that place was. He said it was for the horses. Now you tell me. Why would Meadow make this up?"

"I don't know. Maybe she's a troubled girl."

"What did he talk about last night, Sophie?"

She shrugged as if it was nothing. "Life, the universe, our place in it. This whole event. Peace. Safety. He reassured us that as long as we stayed here we would be protected from whatever came our way."

Alex laughed. "And you believe him?"

"Alex, since we left Elizabeth City have you seen any other place like this? His people can go into the city and those drones don't touch them."

"Maybe you should ask why because I did today and you know what he said? Some mumbo jumbo about how his people wouldn't get touched and that he was here doing his father's work. This guy thinks he's some kind of Christ figure."

"How do you explain those drones not touching them?"

"Are you seriously asking me that?"

"Answer the question."

"Oh my God. I thought you were smarter than this, Sophie."

"Don't talk down to me."

"Think about it. They don't touch his people. Do you think he has some mind control technique? That the big guy upstairs, his father, is preventing them from touching these people? Oh that's quite something, except it's all bullshit. Either this guy is controlling them or someone he knows is, and he has some deal in place. Either way, he's dangerous and the longer we stick around, the higher the odds are of us not getting out."

"His people say that…"

"His people?" Alex shot back.

"You know what I mean."

"Sophie. I can't believe you are so gullible."

"What?"

"Of course. One night. That's all it took. But you know what, I kind of figured this would happen. You did the same with Michael. Just brushed it all under the carpet and moved on to Ryan, as if he could replace our son."

"How dare you."

He took a step forward and jabbed his finger at the ground. "How dare I? How dare you!" Alex pointed west. "We have a daughter out there. I don't know if she's alive or dead but I am not leaving her there. I'm going to find out what happened to her."

Sophie was quick to retort. "Because that's what you do, right? Save people. You've got to be pulling people out. Saving the day. But where has it gotten you, Alex? You pulled Michael out of the water and are you any better for it?" She got closer to him. "Abner was right. You. Me. We are both still in pain. Covering it up with excuses. We need to deal with this. I need to deal with this before I go out and…" She looked away. "A few more days. That's all I'm asking. A moment to breathe. I just want to breathe. We haven't stopped to get our bearings since this happened. I don't care what you say. These are good people. He's helping them and…"

"Yeah, why?"

"Why what?"

"Did you stop to ask him why his people don't get touched by drones when they go into the city? Do all of them go or just teenage girls!?"

"I'm not doing this. You're escalating and…" she said walking toward the door. "I'm going to have breakfast. We'll talk about this later."

"The only reason you agreed to come with me was because Ryan was there. You didn't want to look bad. You never want to look bad."

"I'm not listening."

"That's right, go on. Walk. You've always done that. You don't want to face it. That's why you don't want to go back. You don't want to have to face the possibility that we've lost our daughter and son."

She turned back to him in an instant, all red-faced. "If

that was so, I wouldn't have come," she spat.

"No, you questioned me as I was getting ready to leave. Three thousand miles, you said. You had doubts and don't deny it!"

"And so do you!" she shot back.

"Yeah, I do, but at least I haven't given up."

"Maybe that's your problem, Alex. You want to stay in that moment, in the past. Well, I have news. Michael is gone! He's gone! We're never getting him back, and it doesn't matter how many times you go into that ocean and save people, you will never bring back Michael!"

He shook his head, looking at her, and then in a steady voice replied. "No. No, I won't, but at least I never tried to replace him."

Sophie lashed out and slapped him across the face.

"You bastard." She went to slap him again but he caught her wrist, so she tried to slap with the other. He held both until the fight went out of her. "Let me go!" She wriggled out of his grip and stormed out, slamming the door behind her.

Chapter 18

Elisha peered through the scope on the AR-15 and breathed out as she squeezed the trigger. A brown bottle resting on a line of rocks exploded. "That's it," Garcia said enthusiastically, standing just off to the side. "Remember, keep a good shoulder-width stance, and lean forward, and keep those knees bent." That morning before the rest had risen, Garcia had offered to show her how to use a weapon. He'd already shown her the right way to fire a handgun and had moved on to a rifle. Over several hours, he had her shooting from standing, kneeling and cover. At first the eruption of the gun scared the hell out of her but the more she stayed with it, the more comfortable it became.

"I think you're getting the hang of it. Just remember, if you are ever in an exchange, control your breathing. Don't panic. The number of accidents that happen from people panicking is high."

She nodded, lowered the weapon and handed it off to him.

"When was the last time you dated a woman besides my mother?"

"A long time ago," he replied. He slung the rifle over his shoulder and they made their way up from the lake.

"What is it about her you like?"

He smiled; his head lowered. "She's got a good sense of humor."

"She has one?" Elisha shot back.

He looked at her and he laughed. "I can see you take after your mother."

"But you must have connected over something."

"My mother was a nurse," he replied.

"Ah, well, that makes sense."

She breathed in the warm morning air as birds broke away from the trees.

"So, what was it like growing up in the gangs?"

"Strangely normal. I know that sounds odd but I didn't know any different. My father was gone a lot. Was often out selling drugs. He ended up doing time inside."

"So your mother wanted something better for you?"

"They always do. Sophie's the same."

Elisha nodded, lips pursed. "Did my mother tell you she was planning on fostering a kid?"

He nodded. "Yeah."

"Or that we lost my brother in an accident?"

"She told me everything."

"So you know about my father."

"A little. She made him sound like he was a good man."

Elisha squinted into the sun. "Was? He is. A little preoccupied with his work but after going through Coast Guard training, I can see why now."

Liam emerged from the cabin, a gray cotton blanket wrapped around him.

"Hey. How did it go last night?" Garcia asked, slinging off his back some fish on a line. They'd caught some overnight using automatic fishing reels called YOYOs. It used a spring-loaded reel with some line and a hook attached. Garcia had set them up the night before down by the dock. While they slept, the reels had caught four, allowing them to be more productive throughout the day.

Liam took a seat on the steps and cocked his head from side to side.

"You were right about everything."

Garcia placed a foot on the first step and nodded. "I'm sorry, Liam. I know he's your friend."

"Not much of a friend."

"What did he say?" Elisha asked.

Liam brought them up to speed on the conversation they'd had. Upon finishing, his shoulders sank.

"You think he will tell him?" Elisha asked.

"Would you?" Liam replied. "I'm heading into town this morning to find out."

"Be careful," Garcia said. "When people are pushed into a corner they often react and I've seen friends turn on friends and that was before this."

Liam noticed the fish. "Damn. That makes life easy."

"Sure does." Garcia lifted the fish in front of him so he

could see. "Well, let me get these on and see if that lazy ass is awake." He went over to a propane BBQ and fired it up and then set the fish on the side.

Elisha took a seat beside Liam on the steps and they looked down toward the lake. "You want to take a walk?"

"Sure."

They got up and strolled off.

"Don't be long," Garcia yelled coming out with some herbs and spices. "Breakfast will be ready soon." Despite the power grid going down and the ongoing challenges that the nation now presented, it felt good to know she was with a group that knew how to survive. As they walked in the silence of the morning, birds chirped around them.

"Have you thought of speaking with Harry?" she asked.

"It's not my place. Can you imagine me telling him that his grandson was behind his wife's death, the attack on the department and the men who shot him in the shoulder?" He snorted. "Yeah, that would go over well.

No, out of courtesy to him as my friend, I gave him twenty-four hours to tell him. If he hasn't by then, I will."

"What do you think he'll do… Harry, I mean?"

Liam blew out his cheeks and wrapped the blanket tightly around him. "No idea. The man is a wild card. But I wouldn't want to be there when he tells him." He shook his head. "You know, growing up with someone, you think you know them but then you wonder if you really ever did."

They reached the shore full of sand, dirt and small rocks. Elisha reached down and picked out a few smooth ones and tossed them across the surface of the water. Each one skipped a few times before disappearing into the deep. "You think it's safe here?" she asked.

"It's not safe anywhere."

"But here?"

"Moderately. Anything can happen though. Why?"

"I've been thinking about Carlos. What happened in the cellar. Garcia said that he'd told him he had connections to some group, the 18th Street, a huge gang out of L.A."

"L.A. is a long way away."

"But it's possible they could head this way. I think that's why Garcia was showing me how to shoot this morning."

He smiled. "Oh really?" He looked out across the lake and shouted. "Sorry!"

"For what?"

"The fishermen you shot."

She patted him on the arm, chuckled and directed his attention to what remained of the bottles that she used for target practice.

* * *

Leo was in uncharted territory. He always knew it would come down to this — pitted against his kind. In the early hours of the morning before the sun spread its light over Petaluma, he and Ken had ducked out of the house on Valley Oak Court and had managed to make it halfway across the city. They arrived at an abandoned home and found a set of keys to a vehicle in a two-car garage.

Ken told him that he knew the owners. They were close friends of his. A week before the bombings they had gone on an Alaskan cruise and weren't expected back for two weeks.

As Leo gathered together food, clothes, candles, matches, and a flashlight, Ken rambled on about his future or lack thereof.

"I was supposed to retire wealthy. I had this big dream in my head. You know, the big house, all the toys, multiple vacations a year. And then all this happened." He sat at the foot of the stairs, shaking his head. "I've made a lot of wrong choices but you understand that right?" he asked looking to Leo for sympathy.

"Yeah. Bad choices. Whatever. Give me a hand trying to find the keys to this. We might need it." He'd come across a gun cabinet in the closet on the main landing.

"He keeps the key upstairs in a drawer beside his bed," Ken said raising his eyes. Leo furrowed his brow. "What?" Ken asked. "They invited my wife and me over for dinner several nights a month. He showed it to me. We're good friends. Oh, and while you're up there you might as well grab his bag of weed. I could use a smoke."

Leo chuckled. "Mayor? And there was me thinking you were a pillar of the community."

"Everyone has their vices and in this town, you need a little something to keep yourself from losing it."

Leo gestured for him to go up with a nudge of the gun.

Ken frowned. "I just told you where it is."

"And leave you alone down here? If I turn my back for a second you'll be gone."

Ken grumbled as he trudged upstairs. He came out of the room a moment later dangling a pair of keys and a clear bag of weed. "Satisfied?"

After getting in the truck, they veered out of the garage, leaving it open, and made their way out of Petaluma heading northwest on Highway 101. With the city behind them, Leo breathed a sigh of relief, though he was still scanning his mirrors every few seconds to check that they weren't being followed. The journey would take them through the heart of Santa Rosa, a city known to belong to the Norteños, rivals to 18th Street. If he got caught crossing through their territory, the repercussions would be far greater than if he ran into Ramiro.

However, they never made it that far.

Somewhere along that stretch of lone road, minutes outside of Petaluma, he saw them. Leo eased off the gas pedal as the four black vehicles with dark-tinted windows came into view at the edge of the road. The men were outside their vehicles, some smoking cigarettes, others leaning against their rides. They hadn't blocked the road. Still. Driving past them would only lead to a chase. He applied the brake. Had they seen them? No, they were too far away. Ramiro wouldn't know they were heading this way unless… he turned to find Ken pointing a gun at him.

"Sorry, I have to."

Leo shook his head. "When?"

Ken kept staring at him. "In the same drawer with the

keys to the gun cabinet. My friend always kept a piece beside his bed just in case anyone broke in."

Leo clenched his fist.

"Kill the engine, hand me the keys and get out."

"You are killing yourself," Leo replied.

"No, I'm saving myself and my wife. And if Ramiro comes back to Petaluma, I've earned a favor."

Leo smiled as he slowed the vehicle.

"Does he know?"

"He will."

"You stupid man. He'll kill you."

"I'll take my chances," Ken said.

"Were you planning on doing this all along?"

"No. But I figured if the worst happened, and it has, I would be ready."

Leo brought the vehicle to a standstill. Up ahead, they'd attracted their attention. If they turned now, it would be a clear giveaway. Ken was directing him to get out. If he did that, they were as good as dead. That weasel of a man. "Turn off the engine," Ken said firmly. "Hurry up."

"If I do that, you are dead."

"I don't think so."

Leo slowly moved his hand back toward his waistband where his handgun was.

Ken made a tutting noise. "Nope. You don't want to do that."

"Okay. Just be cool." Leo nodded as he reached for the keys and switched off the engine.

"Now hand them over."

Leo pulled them out, and went to hand them to him but at the last second, he dropped the keys on the floor. A small distraction but that's all he needed.

As Ken's eyes diverted down, Leo sprang into action, wrestling for control of the gun. A moment of struggle and then the gun went off. Both of them sat there, eyes wide open, mouths agape.

* * *

As they arrived in Willits that morning, Andre drove, veering the cruiser up off the main road into the parking lot around the back of Forest City Surplus. There were a few from the community on the streets but not many. The brave ones were checking stores to see if anyone was open. No sooner had they rounded the corner than Liam saw it.

The back door to the store was wide open.

There was no way Harry would have allowed that.

"Whoa, whoa, stop the vehicle," he said. He opened his door and jogged over, handgun at the ready.

"Liam. Wait," Garcia said. It didn't take long to catch up even as Liam reached the door and called out. "Harry? Travis!"

There was no response.

"Let me go in first," Garcia said.

Liam backed up and followed. Inside it was dark but beyond the open door the only sign of trouble was empty boxes left in the hallway. They had to step over some and kick others out of the way. When they finally made into the main store it was empty, completely stripped bare. Not one item remained on a shelf, rack or behind the counter. Steel shelves that had once been upright were on the ground, a rack had been used to smash the glass counter. Shards were everywhere.

His eyes shifted to the bunker, the one place Harry would have retreated to if he felt under threat. The hatch looked closed and for a second he thought that was where they'd gone.

That all ended when he found it unlocked. Liam pulled it back and climbed down into the guts of the bunker.

His stomach sank.

There before him was the lifeless, cold body of Harry, a bullet through his head.

He'd expected to find Travis, Tate or Joe nearby but it was just Harry.

"Oh God," Liam said. He ran a hand over his face as he crouched down beside the old-timer and placed a hand on his back. Garcia took a look.

"This was him. This was Travis."

"You don't know that," Garcia said.

"C'mon, man. Of course it was. A gun to the back of the head? He didn't want to face him."

He stepped over Harry and pulled up some of the flooring. It was all empty.

"Bastard. He took everything. Damn it!" Liam swiped at a bowl on the table and it flew across the room. It shattered against a steel wall. He slumped into a chair, placing his head in his hands. "I could have stopped this. I should have told Harry. I should have."

"Liam," Garcia said placing a hand on his shoulder.

He lifted his eyes.

"Blaming yourself won't change this."

It was at that moment the realization hit him.

If Travis had taken what was at the cabin before, would he do it again? Liam's eyes widened as he burst back up the steps into the store, eager to get back to the cabin.

Chapter 19

The bullet grazed his upper arm.

In an instant, Leo grappled and twisted the handgun out of Ken's hand. Enraged, he smashed the butt end into his nose, bursting it like a fire hydrant. Not wasting a second, Leo scooped up the keys and started the vehicle just as one of Ramiro's vehicles did a U-turn to head their way.

"You idiot!" Leo bellowed.

"You… you… you broke my nose." Ken cupped hands over his face as blood gushed over his mouth and chin.

"You're lucky I didn't kill you," he said. He jammed the gearstick in reverse, then yanked hard on the steering wheel to spin the truck around. As soon as they were facing the other way he crushed the gas pedal and fishtailed out of there with Ramiro's crew in pursuit. "Thanks to you we now have these assholes after us. I'm starting to think you didn't escape and you and Ramiro arranged this."

"No. No, it was all me."

"Yeah? Then how do you explain them stopped at the edge of the road back there?" The truck growled as it reached a speed of over a hundred. He held the pedal to the floor.

"He was probably heading for Willits."

"Yeah, and he stopped to read the map? Please. You aren't convincing anyone."

"I thought I could…"

"Could what? Huh? These aren't men that can be reasoned with, don't you understand that? They are born killers."

"All right. All right. I didn't know. I just wanted to protect myself."

"Protect yourself? More like you wanted to benefit. You are all the same. It's all about money. All about prestige. You don't care who you throw under the bus to get where you need to go. Who cares about anyone else.

All that talk about leaving the city, fraud and then you have the nerve to look down on someone like Garcia because of his previous gang association?"

Ken didn't respond. He was too busy nursing his face. He coughed blood over the dashboard. Leo reached over and slapped him around the back of the head. "Fuck. Put a hand over your mouth."

Leo scanned his mirrors. A frown formed. For some reason they'd stopped following. Did they know it was them? They were a fair distance away. He eased off the gas and brought the truck over to the shoulder of the road, squinting at his mirror. "You know another way around?" Leo winced as he gripped his bleeding arm.

Ken spat red into a tissue and balled it up, then kept his head tipped back holding a hand over his face. "Yeah. But what about gas?"

There was half a tank. "Which way?" Leo demanded.

"Two miles up, hang a left. It will take us longer but you'll avoid the main vein." He groaned. "Look, Leo, I'm sorry, man."

"I don't want to hear it. You're not sorry. You're sorry I wrestled that gun out of your hands. For now, don't talk to me unless it's to give directions."

* * *

Back in Willits, they'd returned to the cabin to find it exactly the way they'd left it. The tripwires were undisturbed. No one had broken in. Nothing had been taken. While Liam was relieved he was still concerned that Travis might double back, so they left Andre there to watch over the place while they headed for Travis' family home on the south side.

Grove Street was a new subdivision behind Howard Memorial Hospital. Originally, Travis lived only five minutes from where his grandfather was, but as Forest City Surplus became a hit, not just in the county but online, his mother who had worked for his grandfather had ended up buying a place in a more desirable neighborhood.

"You sure it's around here?" Garcia asked as they slowed and scanned doors numbers.

The cruiser veered around another bend in the road and then Liam pointed. "There. That one."

It was a one-story abode, red brick foundation, sandy brown siding, and black shingles. It had an attached garage in matching brown. In the driveway was Travis' red truck, the same one he'd seen outside Harry's. They parked five houses down, taking in the sight of neighbors who were out talking.

Hurrying toward the house, they drew the attention of neighbors. One glance at Garcia's uniform and weapons at the ready and curious onlookers were quick to get inside. Upon reaching the house, Liam glanced in the back of the red truck. He lifted a blue tarp. Beneath it was a shovel, and some paracord.

Garcia sidled up to a window and peered through. He shook his head. No movement. Elisha stayed with Garcia at the front, while Liam went around back and tried the rear door. It opened. He cocked his head and listened before entering.

No sound.

Inside the kitchen nothing was out of the ordinary.

Boxes of cereal on the table, unwashed dishes, but no garbage. That was just like Travis' mother.

In many ways they'd bonded not just because of their grandfathers but because Travis came from a divorced family much like him.

Where was his mother?

He kept moving down the hallway, rifle at the ready, clearing each of the lower rooms before opening the front door and letting Garcia inside. Liam pressed his back to the wall and ventured up the stairs while Garcia did another sweep of the main floor.

It was a two-bedroom, one room for him, the other for his mother.

As Liam stepped into his bedroom he noticed something odd.

It looked identical to when they were kids. "What the heck?"

Posters on the wall from bands they used to like, a bass guitar in one corner of the room, magazines from years gone by in a pile on the side table.

"Liam!" Garcia yelled.

He hurried out of the room to the top of the stairs.

"What is it?" Garcia's head dipped. "Garcia, what is it?" he asked again in a firmer tone as he came down the stairs. Garcia put a hand to his chest as he looked to where Elisha was standing. The doorway to the attached garage was open. Liam shrugged Garcia off and made a beeline for the door. As he stepped inside the darkened room, he expected to see Travis' mother but instead he stumbled back, hand gripping a wooden railing.

Hanging from the rafters was Travis.

Below his dangling feet, a suicide note.

Chapter 20

Four black sedans with dark-tinted windows prowled the streets of Willits that morning. While Ramiro was searching for any sign of Garcia, he knew the odds of finding him were slim. His thoughts returned to that interaction on the highway. Was that Leo? They were too far away to tell who the occupants were and he was in no mood to go on a high-speed pursuit all over the county only to come up empty-handed, so he'd called it off.

If only that worm of a mayor hadn't escaped.

They pulled into a large parking lot outside a grocery store and waited.

Unlike Petaluma, Willits looked as if it had breezed through the heart of the bombings. The stores weren't open and shutters were down on most.

"So what's the plan?" Diego, one of his men asked while gazing out.

"We separate, search every street. If we see anyone, and

I mean anyone. Grab them. Ask them what they've seen, who they've seen. He has to be around here somewhere."

"But that could take forever!"

Ramiro scowled at him. Diego gave a nod and got out and went to each of the three vehicles and told the others. The sedans rolled out and Diego returned, sighing as he got into the driver's side.

"Do you think he would come here?" Diego asked. "Leo, I mean."

"Would you?"

"No, I would get as far away from California as possible."

He nodded. He had no way of knowing if Leo would return to L.A. but it was doubtful. It would be like signing his death sentence. "Alvaro will deal with him later. Right now, we handle Garcia then head back."

Diego nodded, took a blunt and lit it.

Smoke filled the inside.

Ramiro growled. "Open the damn window."

He brought it down and a gust of fresh warm air blew

in.

"You know, Ramiro. Don't you find this a little strange? The nation is at its breaking point and we're here risking our asses while Alvaro isn't."

Ramiro cast him a glance. "You been listening to Leo?"

He shrugged and blew smoke out the corner of his mouth. "I'm just asking."

"No, you're repeating what he said like a damn parrot."

"I just think that…"

"Don't! I think, you listen. Okay, homie?"

He frowned and looked away.

Ramiro balled his fists. He had to keep them in check as Leo had already got into these guys' heads.

Call it mutiny, testing him, whatever, there wasn't a day that went by that he didn't have one of them push their luck. Of course he didn't fault them for it. He would have done the same in their shoes.

There was silence for what felt like an hour as they waited. A few times Diego and the others got out and approached a few people on the street. There weren't many. Anyone with a lick of sense had holed up in their home or left in search of safer communities. Two hours in, the group of sedans reappeared, swerving in front of Ramiro's vehicle. Juan got out of one and opened the rear door, yanking out a shaggy-haired guy. He shoved him forward, the gun jammed into his back. The guy looked petrified; all the color drained from his skin.

Ramiro brought his window down.

"Says he knows." Juan gave him a shove. "Tell him what you told me."

The kid hunched up his shoulders, his eyes darting between them, the same nervous look their victims got before they assaulted or shot them. "Garcia. He's at a cabin north of here. It belongs to a friend of mine."

"Yeah? Describe him."

The kid went on to describe Garcia, and some of the others. He told them there were four staying at a cabin, three guys and a female.

"Good. Get in the back. You can take us there."

"But I…" He stopped talking when they gave him a hard stare. He squeezed in beside the other two guys. The door slammed shut and they rolled out.

"What's your name, kid?"

The shaggy-haired guy leaned forward. "Tate."

Along the way, the kid filled him in on his association with some guy named Liam.

"So why's Garcia here?"

"Something to do with the girl. Dating her mother or something like that."

Ramiro brought a hand up to his chin. "Huh. What's her name?"

"No idea."

"She live around here?"

"Nope."

Ramiro looked out, his eyes washing over some of the buildings that were in ruins. Black smoke spiraled up drifting across the road. "Look, I have no problem with you guys. My friends and I are already in enough shit as it is."

Ramiro ignored him. He had every intention of killing him, especially once he led them to Garcia, but after losing the mayor, he wouldn't let this guy out of his sight until then.

"Just sit back and enjoy the ride."

The road wound around going deeper into a heavily wooded area. Through the trees, he could see a lake coming into view. It wasn't the first time Alvaro had sent him to drag someone back and it wouldn't be the last. He glanced at Diego out of the corner of his eye. What these young guys didn't understand was that an event like this provided an unparalleled opportunity. There was no telling how many casualties there were. There had never been a time in history when they could take what they wanted without fear of repercussion. It would take years for America to bounce back.

* * *

Andre was installing the last of the burglar bars on the windows when he heard gravel crunch beneath tires. He couldn't have finished at a better time. At first he figured it was Garcia returning. Had he not turned at that exact moment he might not have made it inside.

He wiped sweat from his brow and tossed a screwdriver down.

Through the forest he saw black cars with dark-tinted windows and pimped-out rims.

He wiped his hands with a rag from his back pocket and squinted. Would they drive past? A moment or two and he saw them veer into the driveway.

Andre grabbed up his AR-15 and dashed into the house to collect more ammo.

He could have run, hidden, but letting them take the recent supplies was not an option. Although he hadn't seen the occupants, he already had a good idea who they were. He and Garcia had discussed what might happen if and when 18th Street showed up. He just didn't figure it would be this soon. How had they found them?

None of that mattered now. He locked the door and placed boxes of ammo beside each of the windows. He already had a magazine in. He chambered a round and set the rifle down, then shifted a heavy dresser drawer behind the door and took up a spot near a window out of sight.

A minute or two passed.

Doors slammed.

"Garcia. You in there?" a voice cried out.

There was no point in staying quiet as they would only force their way in.

"He's not here!" Andre bellowed out. He peered through the pane of glass and watched as the crew spread out, all heavily armed.

"Where is he?"

"No idea."

"Then we'll wait until he returns."

"You're trespassing. Get back in your vehicles and get off my property."

The guy who was doing all the talking turned and a kid appeared at his side. "Tate," Andre said under his breath. "Bastard." The guy forced Tate forward to let him speak.

"Hey, uh, Liam. Can I talk to you?"

Rats. How had they got their hands on him?

Did he want to tell them that Liam wasn't here? No. The less they knew, the better. If they learned that he was alone, that would only work to his detriment. "Get off this property now. I won't warn you again."

The group feathered out, some crossing the threshold and getting dangerously close to… He'd barely had the thought when one of the guys fell into a hole they'd dug in the ground. Impaled on upright, sharpened sticks, he let out an excruciating cry followed by cursing. Then a barrage of gunfire erupted, peppering the walls and showering him with glass, and splinters of wood. He stayed low until it was over.

But it wouldn't be over, at least not until he was dead.

Chapter 21

There was no sign of her.

Ready to leave, Alex waited outside for Sophie and Ryan. Thomas sat on the steps, picking at the wood and looking depressed. While he hadn't questioned his reasons for leaving, it was clear he didn't want to go. Who would? They had everything here. Food, fresh water, shelter, beauty, privacy and the word of a man who had yet to fail them. In many ways it was the perfect settlement to ride out this shitstorm, but for Alex, too many things weren't adding up.

While they were waiting, a plume of dust billowed up behind a Jeep as Star returned.

"Finally. I thought for a moment we'd have to leave Meadow behind."

Thomas shook his head. "I still think that she's playing you."

"We'll see." Alex stepped away from the steps and

adjusted his backpack on his shoulder. The Jeep slowed down and veered in front. Star hopped out with three other people but Meadow wasn't one of them.

"Where is she?"

Star was unloading a box of cans from the trunk when he asked.

"Who?"

"Meadow."

She shrugged. "I don't know. She didn't go with us."

He raised a finger. "No. One of the women told me she saw her leave with you this morning."

Star shook her head as she juggled the box over to a young guy who took it inside. "No. It was only me. I brought a few people back but that's it."

"What room is she in?"

"Twelve but you can't go up there. That's…"

Alex turned and ignored her as he hurried into the mansion and made his way past the winding wooden staircase. He went to room twelve and banged on the door. Star wasn't far behind him. "Alex."

"Meadow. You in there?"

A few other girls came out of their rooms to see what all the fuss was about.

"She might be working in the fields."

"Can you find her?"

"Why?"

"That's between me and her."

Star frowned raising a hand. "Okay. I'll go and see."

As Alex turned to head back to the main foyer, several of Abner's followers lingered in the doorway of rooms, staring at him. The longer he was there, the stranger it felt. There was something very off about them but he couldn't put his finger on it. Maybe the clothes, the adoration for one man. If he wasn't mistaken, it had a very David Koresh feel to it. Back outside, he noticed Ryan and Sophie still hadn't come out.

"Have you seen them?" he asked Thomas.

"Nope."

He was losing his patience and fast. Making his way up to the second level he went down to Ryan's room only to find him inside schmoozing with some girl on the bed. "What part of we are leaving did you not understand?"

"Sophie said she's staying. I thought she told you."

"She did. I didn't expect her to follow through. Where is she?"

Ryan swung his legs off the bed. The girl beneath the sheets covered herself up, she was partially nude. "The last time I saw her she said she was heading to Abner's office."

"Which is where?"

He shrugged. "I don't know."

"Get your shit together. We are leaving."

"Alex."

"Now or I'm leaving you here."

Back on the main floor he asked a woman where the office was and she pointed to a small cabin perched up on a hill overlooking the valley. He could see several ATVs parked out front. He left his backpack with Thomas and jogged up. As he was getting closer, two hulking guys sitting on a porch rocker rose and blocked his entrance.

"I'm here to get my wife."

"She's busy right now. Abner doesn't want any interruptions."

"Really?" He went to move past them but they put out a hand to stop him.

"So that's how it is?" he asked.

They stared blankly back at him. Alex nodded slowly a few times then turned as if he was about to leave. The second they turned their backs to return to the rocker, he burst past them and entered the cabin. There was Sophie, lying on a brown leather couch, while Abner was seated in an armchair nearby, his legs crossed and a pad of paper in hand. It looked like a therapy session. The cabin wasn't large. There was a mahogany desk in the corner, a rifle and a deer's head on the wall, multiple photos of Abner and his followers and a library of books against the wall. Startled by the intrusion, both of them looked at him.

"Sorry, Abner, we tried to stop him."

"That's fine, Eric. Come on in, Alex."

Alex looked back at the two guys as they closed the door behind him.

"I was just working with Sophie here."

"Yeah? With what?"

"Healing through hypnosis."

"Hypnosis? Huh. Well that explains a lot. Is that what you did for a living before this event?"

Abner smiled. "Come, take a seat. Can I get you some coffee?"

"No, we're leaving."

Sophie slung her feet off the edge of the couch and placed them firmly on the floor. "I'm staying, Alex. At least for a few days."

Abner remained quiet as he continued to fill his cup with coffee.

Alex took hold of Sophie's arm. "How about we have this conversation outside?"

"Anything you need to say can be said here. It's a safe place," Abner said turning toward them. He took a sip of his drink.

"I appreciate that but this is between us."

"Sophie?" Abner asked.

She looked back at Alex and pulled her arm back. "I'm staying."

"Yeah? What about Elisha?"

"It's been a week, Alex. I'm sure if she survived a week, she can hold out for a few more days. It's not like we'll be there tomorrow."

"We might if we get on the road. There are roughly twelve hundred miles remaining. Nineteen hours tops. If we don't stop we could get there within a day's drive."

"What's an extra seventy-two hours then?" Abner asked, taking a seat and crossing his legs looking all smug.

"It's not your daughter."

"No it's not but doesn't Sophie have a say in the matter? She's making such good progress here, aren't you, Sophie?"

She offered back a strained smile.

Alex wasn't sure what niggled him more — that smug expression on Abner's face or the fact that so many had bought into his shit.

His thoughts shifted to Meadow, and that barn. What

was he hiding? Perhaps staying one more night might allow him a chance to see what was really going on here, maybe he could expose this man for who he was — a cult leader, a manipulator. Arrogant. Haughty. A real piece of work.

"A few more days then we'll leave. I promise," Sophie said.

Alex balled his fists. "Fine. Two days but that's it."

Chapter 22

Guilt. Travis had been unable to live with what he'd done. If his suicide note was to be believed, he hadn't killed his grandfather. Hell, by the sounds of it he'd already hung himself before his grandfather died. A line in the note was made out to Harry, explaining his role in his grandmother's death, and apologizing.

His only crime was getting involved with a sordid group of meth heads, desperate people who would have done anything for their next hit. After cutting Travis down and burying him in the backyard, Elisha returned to find Liam sitting at the table with his head in his hands. The note in front of him was drenched in tears. She placed a hand on his shoulder, and squeezed it.

"I should have stayed," Liam said. "I didn't listen. I…"

"Liam, you did what anyone would have done. You didn't know this would happen any more than America knew it would come under attack."

"It was all there. The signs. The way he was before I headed off to join the Coast Guard. The depression. The lack of purpose. The inability to think he could do better than this." He shook his head and wiped his red eyes. "I should have stayed." He sighed.

Garcia entered the kitchen.

"If he didn't take Harry's supplies, who did?" Elisha asked.

Liam lifted his eyes. "Probably the same meth heads Travis was involved with."

"What about Tate and Joe?" Garcia asked.

"No. They wouldn't do it. They hung on Travis' every word. Followed him around like puppies."

"Then how did he end up here without them?"

Elisha took a seat. "Maybe they knew something. Maybe they screwed him over?"

Liam looked up, a frown forming. "Joe doesn't live far from here."

"Well, we have two choices," Garcia said. "We can go back to the cabin, stay there and ride this out, or we can go and find who took the supplies and get them back. We sure as hell could use them. If this event lasts longer than six months we'll need more."

Liam rose and scooped up the suicide note and slipped it into his pocket. He slung his AR-15 over his shoulder and led them out.

"What about his mother?" Garcia asked. "We should leave a note."

"She's away. Vacation I think. There was a phone number of a resort in Florida on the fridge," Liam replied.

As they climbed into the cruiser and peeled out, Elisha piped up, "Makes you wonder, doesn't it?"

Garcia looked at her. "What?"

"How many will come home from vacations and find their loved ones dead?"

"I imagine most won't get that opportunity," Garcia muttered.

Liam remained quiet, only speaking to give directions.

It didn't take long. Joe's home was in an area of town called Holly Heights. A quaint neighborhood just off the main stretch. According to Liam, Joe's mother ran a convenience store in town, a store that had been looted and burned to the ground. If anyone was in dire need of supplies, it was him. That was soon confirmed as they pulled onto Holly Street and slowed down outside his home. Liam got out, looked up at the two-story house and was just about to tell them to wait when Garcia burst out of the vehicle.

"Garcia?"

"There he goes!"

Liam glanced off toward a house one block over and sprinted after him. Joe had obviously seen them outside and had opted to flee through his neighbor's yard. Liam and Garcia were far ahead of Elisha as she scaled over a fence and ran around a swimming pool, squeezed between two posts, and ducked down an alley full of overturned trash cans. An Alsatian barked loudly behind a chain-link fence as she hurried to catch up with them. Curious neighbors watched from behind windows. As she came hurtling around a bend, she found Garcia on top of Joe, holding him down with a knee against his shoulder and his hands bent behind him as if he was about to slap cuffs on his wrists.

"C'mon man. Get off me. I can't breathe."

"Why did you run, Joe, huh?" Liam asked. "Wouldn't have anything to do with Harry lying dead with a bullet in the back of his head, would it?"

"No, I thought you were someone else."

"In a cop car?"

"Yeah. Now those cops are dead people are driving around in cop cars. You don't know who to trust."

"Don't bullshit me!"

"I'm telling you the truth."

"Are you?" Liam said as he crouched down beside him. "What about the fact that Travis is dead now?"

"I didn't have anything to do with that."

Liam glanced at Garcia. Something in his reply caught him by surprise. "But you knew about it." He didn't reply so Liam pressed the barrel of his gun against his face. "Did you hear me?"

"Yes. It was Tate. Okay! Tate screwed him over."

"Keep talking."

"I would talk a lot better if you let me up."

"Not happening," Garcia said pressing his knee down harder.

Joe groaned through gritted teeth. "After you had that conversation with Travis, he told us he was going to come clean with Harry, that it was the right thing to do. Tate convinced him to hold off, to sleep on it and if he felt the same way the next morning then he would go with him."

"And?"

Joe frowned. "Didn't Travis tell you?"

"Tell me what?" Liam bellowed.

"C'mon, let me up. I won't run. I promise."

"Joe, you better come clean now or I will squeeze this fucking trigger. You hear me?"

"All right. All right." He breathed hard and Garcia eased off his back a little but kept his hands pulled back in a painful pose. "Travis' mother was dating a local meth dealer named Jethro Nash. When the shit hit the fan, he, like many others, wanted a piece of Harry's store. Survival, right? Well, that's not as easy as it looks. That old coot might have been old but he was smart. Hell, he didn't give his own grandson a key to that place."

"But he let you in."

"Sure he did. But he never once turned his back. It wasn't that he didn't trust Travis, it was us. Anyway, Travis probably told you that he tried to scare off his grandparents so he could have the place for himself. That wasn't the truth. Jethro told him he had a week to get Harry out of there or he would deal with it himself."

It was all beginning to make sense. Travis didn't want to tell him the truth. He didn't want him to think less of him. The fact was he'd been pushed into a corner.

"Why did he agree?" Liam asked.

"He didn't. I mean, not exactly. At first he spoke with Harry and asked him to sell the business to him. He tried to do it the right way, but that old man wouldn't have any of it. He was gonna ride this out and then sell it off when America got back on its feet. Harry said the store was more valuable than gold. Anyway, that's when Jethro sent some of his guys over to apply pressure. When you came back, Travis started to think differently. I don't know, maybe because of you. After you found out what was happening he gave you the vanilla version. It was the truth but not entirely."

"Why?"

"Why? Because he didn't want you to think less of him, and he didn't have the balls to stand up to Jethro."

"What about Travis' mother?"

"She left. Got the hell out."

"So she never went on vacation."

"No. God no. That was her cover story. You've got to understand something. Jethro used to beat her up. That whole spiel that Travis told you about his grandmother being hijacked was a lie. Arlene tried to intervene, get the police involved, so Jethro took her out, made it look like a carjacking. Then after the bombs hit, he dealt with the cops who threw him in jail for the night while they were processing him for abuse. His guys got him out. They shot the cops. After that he wanted Harry's place and he was going to get it one way or another."

"Huh!" Liam nodded. "That's why you were running. You thought we were Jethro."

"Like I said, I was telling the truth."

Liam took a few steps back as Joe continued, "Anyway, last night Tate went to Jethro, mostly to save his own ass and mine, though I didn't go with him. I promise you that."

"And Travis?"

"Jethro."

"He didn't commit suicide?"

"No," Joe said.

"But there was a suicide note there."

"He was suicidal. Said he was going to shoot himself. He wrote that note last night but he couldn't go through with it. Said he was too much of a coward. Tate told Jethro and well…" He took a deep breath. "I'm sorry, Liam. I really am. It's just a fucked up situation that spiraled out of control."

"I knew it. Travis wouldn't have hurt his grandparents. He sure as hell wouldn't have had the nerve to kill himself." Liam stumbled back a little coming to grips with the news. Garcia took over.

"So the supplies?" Garcia asked.

"Jethro has them. All of them."

"And where is this guy?"

"No idea, and you don't want to get close to that. He's bad news."

"What about Tate?" Liam asked with a look of rage.

"He um… he was waiting outside my house. I went in to grab some smokes and as I came out, I saw some Latino guys talking to him. The next moment they grabbed him and threw him in the back of a black sedan and tore away."

"Latino?"

"Yeah, one had a tattoo on his chest. Eighteen in Roman numerals."

Garcia looked at Liam. "18th Street. What did they want with him?" Garcia asked.

"I didn't hear the conversation."

Garcia got off Joe but kept a firm grip on him as he rose. "You better not be lying."

"I'm not. Anything Travis told you that wasn't true was because he looked up to you, Liam. That's all. He didn't want you to think less of him."

Garcia paced, his handgun out, eyes roaming the street. "We need to get back to the cabin and fast."

Chapter 23

As night swallowed the ranch of El Dorado, Alex was no closer to finding Meadow. Star told him that her closet was empty, her belongings gone, and no note had been left behind. No one had seen her leave which to him was suspicious. He'd seen the fear in her eyes. If she had planned on leaving without them, why ask for a ride out? If she could have left, why hadn't she done so sooner?

Well, that evening he planned on finding out the truth.

After the rest of the followers headed to the communal area to listen to Abner give another one of his life-altering speeches, he made a beeline for his room.

Outside, it was nearly pitch dark, barely a star in sight. Alex eased himself over the balcony and carefully set his foot on a ledge that would take him across to a thick black drainpipe. A quick shuffle, a fast descent and he was soon on the ground, taking cover behind a large collection of rocks and tall grass. He darted across the hilly landscape, hidden by the night. Dashing toward the barn, he circled the lake, staying in the shadows to avoid being seen under the moon's light.

The barn was forty feet high by around a hundred and fifty feet in length, a deep red with a white door at the front, and brown shingles. In and out of trees, he crossed over a hill and pitched sideways down a slope as he drew closer. He dropped behind a collection of boulders and squinted at the sight of a guard coming out of the barn with an AR-15 slung over his shoulder. Guns not allowed? Yeah, right. The guard lit a cigarette, it glowed brightly. Alex waited then made his way down after the man was out of sight. Just about to dart out of the maze of undulating bushes, the guard returned and looked his way.

Alex dropped and held his breath at the sound of boots approaching.

Quickly, he took out a knife and prepared for the worst.

The footsteps stopped a few feet away. He peered through brambles and underbrush and could see the guard looking around. The guy turned away from Alex, so he got up and followed, staying low, keeping out of sight. He darted behind a tree as the guard looked over his shoulder. A moment of panic before the guard sucked on his cigarette and continued walking up a path toward the mansion.

Reaching the barn, Alex tugged at the handle.

It was locked. He'd seen it open earlier.

He went around the barn and made his way along, hoping to find another way in. That's when two chained pit bulls darted out barking at him. They got within inches but were held back by the thick chains. Alex moved fast hearing someone approach. Taking cover in a grove of nearby trees, he waited as another guard came into view and stopped by the dogs. The guard surveyed the area. What were they protecting? And why the lies?

The guard moved on and he sprinted out, making his way to the far end. He was about to approach the door when another guard came out of the barn. He pulled back and held his breath as footsteps got closer. He would have run back the other way but the dogs were there and the chances of making it to the tree line before the guard came around were slim. Sliding the knife back into his jacket, he opted for a different approach.

The short man came around but before he could register, Alex grabbed him and lifted him off the ground, hanging him in midair in a sleeper chokehold. In a matter of seconds his body went limp. Alex dragged him out of sight then went on, this time entering the barn.

A diesel generator churned nearby. A small strip of yellow light lit up the interior. There were two levels. On the lower floor there were horse pens that stretched from one end to the other. Coarse tails whipped around in a couple, and a few horses looked out. Loose hay covered the floor. Staying in the shadows he made his way along peering into each stall. Everything looked normal. He lifted his eyes and saw lots of haystacks on the upper level.

Voices caught his attention, Alex ducked into one of

the stalls. The horse looked at him. He stayed low. Between the planks of wood he observed two men exit. Where did they come from? He slipped out and made his way to the far end. The door was locked. He climbed a ladder to the second level but there was nothing but hay. As he was crouching and trying to make sense of it, the voices returned, this time the two men walked back in and went to the far end and entered a stall. Out of sight, he expected them to emerge but they didn't. Alex made his way down and when he entered the stall, there was no one there.

What the hell?

A gust of air created movement on the floor. He crouched and placed his hand against the wood. That's when he saw it. The hay moved ever so slightly, and a faint glimmer of light emanated from a crack. Alex ran his hand around and found a handle. He pulled it and his face was instantly bathed in a warm glow. A metal staircase led down to a steel enclosure. He glanced over his shoulder one last time before venturing down.

Chapter 24

As the cruiser careened around a bend, the tires barely remained on the ground. In the distance they could see thick smoke and fire flickering between the trees.

Across the water, an orange glow arched over the property. Initially when they saw the smoke they thought someone had set the surrounding forest ablaze. Since the power had gone out, residents were using fire pits in their yards so it was possible one of them had got out of control but its location to the cabin and news of the 18th Street gang in Willits made them think otherwise.

"Be ready," Garcia said.

They had no idea how many there were.

For all they knew there could be ten, twenty, fifty.

An ever-present sense of impending doom hung over them.

Garcia gunned the engine and it growled loudly as

they veered around the lake on Primrose Drive. Joe was in the back sandwiched between Liam and Elisha. He hadn't stopped complaining since they bundled him inside.

By the time they made it onto Lilac Drive the tension in the car could have been cut with a knife. Two hundred yards from the property, Garcia swerved, cutting off the road, and hopped out. He went around to the trunk and pulled out his Bushmaster M4. He donned a bulletproof vest and had this steely look in his eyes, the kind that was seen in every cop when they were running into chaos while others ran the other way.

"Elisha, stay here. If we don't return or you see any gang member you take this vehicle and get as far away as possible."

"Really? So teaching me how to shoot a gun was for nothing? One arm or not, I'll be damned if I'm staying here babysitting this asshole," she said glancing at Joe then taking out a handgun from her holster.

"You sound like your mother," he replied. "Okay, but please, stay back. And I mean it. If this gets…"

Rounds erupted, a torrential onslaught of gunfire was deafening. All of them ducked thinking they were under fire but it wasn't directed at them. It was coming from the property. "Liam. Follow my lead, okay?"

"You bet."

"What about him?" Elisha asked.

"Let me help," Joe said. "Cut me loose and give me a gun."

"Fuck that! After all that's happened?" Liam said. "You're lucky I haven't shot you."

"Liam. It was Tate not me."

"Yeah, maybe, but for now you can stay put." Garcia pushed him back into the vehicle and locked the doors.

Joe yelled on the other side of the window, his voice muted. "C'mon man! Let me out. I can help."

As they ran at a crouch toward the cabin, they could hear Joe kicking the window.

"Can he get out?"

"No. Trust me, that cruiser has taken one hell of a beating. It's not the first time someone has tried to kick their way out."

Moving through the surrounding forest, Elisha stumbled over roots. Branches raked her skin. Flickering flames licked up into the night sky while others crept up the side of the cabin.

Armed silhouettes darted in and out of trees.

They stopped thirty yards away and could see numerous bodies on the ground. How many? Four, six, maybe eight.

Muzzle flashes lit up the night.

"Andre," Garcia said under his breath, a smile flickering. Garcia lifted his rifle and began to engage, releasing a burst of rounds. Silhouettes crumpled. Everything seemed to slow at that moment. The air filled with the sounds of gunfire, yelling and rounds chewing up the earth and tree bark. Liam went right as Garcia darted left, leaving her in the middle, crouched behind a tree gripping a Glock 19. Frozen by panic, her hands were trembling. Garcia's words came back, his instructions as clear as day.

Where she found the courage to lift that gun at that moment was unknown. Maybe it was the fear of getting shot or the worry that the ones who'd kept her alive so far could die in these gloomy woods. Either way, she twisted, brought up the gun and saw one of the thugs dart across. She squeezed the trigger. A flash. The target kept moving but now changed direction heading her way. Panic rose in her chest, her eyes bouncing between Liam and Garcia. Even if she cried out, they wouldn't hear her over the chorus of gunfire.

Faced with certain death, she fired again, and again. Each time missing because the strapping fella kept zigzagging. *C'mon. C'mon.* As she leaned forward to take another shot, her St. Christopher dangled from her neck. She touched it for a second before resuming her grip.

God help me.

This time she took a deep breath and forced herself to relax with a few more deep breaths. The hulking figure darted out, this time firing rounds at her and getting closer.

Any second now and he'd be upon her.

She pulled back, fear now gripping her at the snap of bullets.

Rage soon replaced panic. On her knees, she leaned back and changed position, turning sideways. Whether it was luck, fate or St. Christopher watching over her, she squeezed the trigger, once, twice, four times.

The guy's legs buckled and he went face-first into the ground only twenty feet from her. She didn't wait to see whether he was still alive. Elisha bounced up, darted over and fired another round into him before moving into another position and continuing to provide cover to both Liam and Garcia.

* * *

The fight continued for what felt like half an hour but was probably no more than fifteen minutes. Eventually the noise ceased, and the remaining gang members pulled back behind the safety of their sedans.

"Andre," Garcia yelled

"I'm here, brother."

"You okay?"

"I'm hit."

Over the noise of a few more rounds, another voice called out.

"Officer Garcia. If you want your friends to live, come with us."

"Who are you?"

"I think you know."

"I'm afraid I can't do that."

"Then you will die out here with the rest of them."

"Seems like you've lost your fair share. How about we call it a day?"

He heard laughter. "How about you stop being a bitch and come with us or do you want their blood on your hands?"

Garcia couldn't clearly see any faces. It was too dark. The only light came from the moon but that was partially hidden by the canopy of leaves. If he could just figure out how many were still alive.

"How many, Andre?"

"There were roughly fifteen by my headcount. I took out at least six of them."

Garcia moved as another explosion of gunfire took hold, lighting up the forest, each muzzle flashing on and off like fireflies. "C'mon homie, come with us and it all ends now," the voice cried out again.

He kept moving, nothing more than a dark figure strafing through the trees. This time though he tried to get around the cabin so he could get a better look.

As he rounded a tree he nearly fell over a dead body on the ground. He reached down and scooped up a handgun, then continued on. Every so often he saw a head peek out from behind the sedans.

Then, just as he was getting closer, two of the vehicles started up and headlights were turned on, sending a burst of bright light through the trees revealing his location. Before he had a chance to react, two rounds exploded and he was struck in the chest sending him down.

Chapter 25

A huge underground bunker existed below the barn. Abner wasn't lying, but he wasn't telling the whole truth. Why? What was he hiding? What was this place being used for? Alex navigated a steel catwalk that wrapped around a storage area reserved for thousands of canned goods, barrels of water, medical supplies and animal feed. He worked his way down a second ladder and quickly ducked behind stacks of boxes as two followers packing AR-15s strolled by. For someone who was adamant about having them turn over their weapons, Abner certainly had a double standard.

When he no longer could hear footsteps, he peered into the maze of corridors. A lot of work had gone into creating it. It was akin to what he imagined a small version of Cheyenne Mountain was like. The vast arched network of tunnels was illuminated every few feet by overhead fluorescent lights. The tunnel was wide enough that two golf carts could have passed each other while providing plenty of room for those on foot.

Alex darted out and kept his back to the wall as he went in the opposite direction of the men. He didn't have to travel far to find the first area of interest. As he rounded a bend he had to pull back as he nearly walked into an open area with ten or more people. Alex looked over his shoulder to make sure no one was coming. He couldn't remain there as he was exposed, out in the open. Peering around the bend he noticed a host of bright computer screens and Abner's followers. On a large overhead screen there was an aerial view of Denver and it was split up into segments.

Most of it was seen through the green hue of night vision.

Alex squinted as he leaned forward trying to make sense of it. Of course Abner was involved but to what extent? It was nighttime and if Star was telling the truth, no drones would have been in operation. But from what he could see that wasn't true. Playing out on different screens were moving images, FLIR showing areas of orange heat throughout the city below. Were they mapping and selecting targets? Did it take all of them involved to control those drones or just one? Were they part of a hacking network, a terrorist organization that was in charge of the second wave of attacks? Or was this even more nefarious?

Heavy footsteps put him on alert. His eyes darted, searching for anywhere to hide, but he was caught in a tight spot. Back along the tunnel there had been multiple doors but he figured they led into offices or bunks for staff.

He had no choice. Alex raced back expecting at any moment to see one or more of Abner's followers. He reached for the first door and pushed it open. Expecting to see someone inside, he was stunned to find himself in another storage area full of metal crates full of weapons. He crouched down and looked at the words on the side. It was from the U.S. military. Had someone higher up in the government provided them with this? Or were these smuggled in after being sold to Iran by the U.S.? He remembered reading about the U.S. selling arms to Iran. It would be crazy if the country they had sold to attacked them with their own weapons. He unbuckled the latches and looked inside. Inserted into foam cushioning were rocket launchers. Case after case, his eyes feasted on a wide array of weapons: M4s, AR-15s, machine guns, grenades, landmines and what appeared to be small missiles. This wasn't your run-of-the-mill collection used for anything less than fighting a war.

The handle turned and Alex bounced back.

"Yeah, I've got to bring a case up. I'll get to that after."

Standing behind the door, his heart caught in his throat. Alex waited for the guy to walk in. As soon as the door swung closed, he pounced, grabbing the guy around the neck and choking him out. Once the guy was unconscious, he fished through his pockets looking for anything of use. It was then he found a card, the kind used by hotels. What did this unlock? The guy wouldn't be out long. Alex relieved him of his Beretta and magazines and pocketed them, then grabbed up a rifle and made sure it was loaded before he cracked the door open and looked out.

A golf cart shot by with two men inside.

As soon as they were out of sight he burst out and hurried in the opposite direction, this time going where the first two guys he'd seen went. Mentally he kept a note of the turns he took out of fear of getting lost in the winding passages.

Making it about two hundred yards down a long tunnel, he came upon an area with multiple doors, all of which had slots for a card. Alex fished into his pocket and was about to try it when he looked up and saw a camera pivoting. *Shit.*

He pressed his back to the wall.

That had been the first one he'd seen. Why did they need them here?

Against the tiled wall, he waited for it to turn away before hurrying out.

Each door had no window. It was just steel with a

handle and a card lock. A small red light above the handle was solid. He slid the card through the reader and heard it unlock. He pushed it open and his eyes widened.

There was a young girl, late teens, tucked into a bed.

Nothing else in the room.

At the sound of the door opening she looked at him.

Something wasn't right. Her eyes. Her eyelids looked heavy.

She'd been drugged. "Who are you?" Alex asked. She couldn't even respond. He moved back to the door and she didn't seem too bothered. Curious to see who was in the other rooms, he went from one room to the next, all the while avoiding the camera that kept dipping and turning. In the next was a male, older, mid-twenties, in the same drugged-out state. A third room revealed another woman, older, late forties, the same condition. Who were these people? Why were they drugged and locked up?

One after the other, he entered seven rooms, all the same.

It was on the eighth that his jaw dropped. Alex rushed to the side of the girl's bed.

"Meadow."

She was in a fetal position buried beneath the blankets and wearing nothing more than a thin nightgown. He noticed marks on the inside of her arm. She managed to open her eyelids but couldn't recognize him. "I'll get you out of here," he said flipping back the covers. He slung the rifle around his back and then scooped her up in his arms and carried her out. No sooner had he exited than the lights started flashing red and a siren wailed. He'd been spotted. He glanced at the rooms. He wanted to free them all but it wasn't like they could run.

Alex hurried, making his way back to the steps that led up to the catwalk. He hoisted Meadow over his shoulder in a fireman's hold and ascended. Even though she couldn't have weighed more than a buck twenty wet, his legs were burning as he scaled up, trying desperately not to lose his grip.

He'd made it to the catwalk when suddenly a bright

light shone on him.

"There's our little mouse," Abner said, strolling out into the opening below him and looking up. Right then several guys appeared on either end of the catwalk; rifles aimed at him. "And I had such high hopes for you, Alex. Still, there is Sophie and the others. I'm sure they will learn to accept you leaving just like others before you."

"What sick game are you playing?"

"A game? Oh, this is not a game, Alex. No, this is deadly serious."

Alex scowled. "You have all these people believing you are some kind of god but you are nothing more than a terrorist, a murderer." He glanced at Meadow. "How could you do this? She's just a teen."

"A teen that was asking too many questions, like her uncle and brother. But, she'll be given another chance. But you, I'm afraid this is the end of the road for you."

Alex reached for his handgun but those on the catwalk thrust their guns at him.

"Yeah, I wouldn't do that," Abner said. "However, you

wouldn't be the first to have tried."

Quickly the men moved in on him, removed Meadow and then led him down. Abner got close to him and smiled. "Don't worry. Sophie is in good hands." Alex lunged at him but was held back by two armed guards. Abner tutted. "Take him down. Give him his own room and a little something to keep him relaxed."

Alex cursed as he was dragged away at gunpoint.

Chapter 26

It felt like he'd been hit in the chest with a sledgehammer. When the initial shock wore off, he expected them to be on him but they weren't. Garcia heard the staccato of gunfire and figured Andre, Liam and Elisha were covering him. He rolled to his side, groaned then got right back into it, delivering a three-round burst before rolling out.

Pain still emanated from beneath his bulletproof vest as he crawled to his feet. In all his years in service he'd yet to be shot but if it was anything close to this, he didn't want to know. Dropping down to his belly, he brought the rifle up and set the barrel on a tree root and peered through the scope. His eyes frantically scanned the terrain.

"Garcia," Andre yelled.

"Still here," he replied.

Silhouettes darted in and out, rounds tearing up the

dirt near him.

Then again it stopped.

"Hey Garcia. This only ends one way."

He tried to get a bead on who was doing all the talking. They were behind one of the sedans. "You're right about that." He engaged, peppering the vehicle, taking out the tires, a side mirror and the windshield. After, he removed a magazine and palmed another in, making sure a round was in the chamber before moving into a new position.

"Andre. How bad is it?"

"Bad."

Thick smoke filled the air from where one side of the cabin was on fire.

"There's medical supplies in the cupboard below the counter."

"No good, man. I'm not gonna make it, brother."

"Don't you talk like that," he muttered to himself as he darted at a crouch into a new position to fire off two more rounds. One of them took out a guy who stuck his head out from behind a tree.

His mind flashed back to the past. Having gangs roll up and open fire was a way of life in the ghetto. The constant threat of death lingered but was rarely talked about. It was a given that most would die on a street corner dealing drugs. It was accepted. That's why these assholes hadn't turned tail and run, that and they must have figured they had them outnumbered. But it wasn't about numbers as much as it was about skill, precision and a refusal to flee. If he didn't end it here, others would come.

Under fire, Garcia reached the main door of the cabin, coughing hard because of the smoke. "Andre."

He burst in as rounds splintered the door, and another round hit his bulletproof vest in the back and sent him down. Andre kicked the door closed. Garcia groaned and rolled. There was minimal light inside, mostly coming from hand-crank lanterns. "You son of a bitch. Why the hell would you come back here?"

"And leave you to have all the fun?" Garcia said. "We

need to get you out of here. The smoke is getting worse." He could feel the heat of the flames.

"No man, just go." Andre coughed hard, then a smile started forming.

Garcia shuffled over to his friend. "Where are you hit?"

Andre pulled at his jacket and showed one round had struck him in the gut, and another in the upper leg. He'd used a tourniquet on his leg but his pant leg was covered with blood. It was bad. Even if he could have gotten him to a hospital the chances of surviving were getting smaller by the minute. Most of the color was gone from his face.

"Hang in there," he said. He moved over to a window and stuck his gun out as Andre did the same on the other side. They continued to empty magazines, one after the other until Andre fell back gripping his stomach.

Garcia shifted over to him and applied pressure to the already covered wound.

"Hang in there, man."

Hands gloved in blood, he wrapped a hand around

Andre's neck and placed his forehead against his friend's.

"Been one hell of a ride, hasn't it?" Andre said.

"That it has," Garcia replied.

More gunfire erupted, and yelling came from Liam. It sounded as if they were trying to get closer to the cabin.

"The kids?" Andre asked.

"Yep."

Andre gripped his hand tight.

"Give him hell," Andre said. He coughed a few more times, blood trickling from the corners of his mouth before his eyes glazed over and Garcia heard his final breath leave his body. Garcia teared up, coughing even harder.

"See you on the other side, brother."

His nostrils flared, rage filling his being.

He stared at Andre for but a few seconds then scooped up his rifle, palmed another magazine in. He went over to a box of items they'd brought in and fished through it. Taking out a flare gun, he loaded it and headed over to the window. As the continual barrage of gunfire assaulted the cabin, he set the barrel on the edge of the opening and aimed for one of the sedans.

Click.

A burst of red shot out and exploded upon impact, lighting them up.

He swung the rifle around and one after another, he squeezed off rounds. Then he loaded another flare and switched out, this time it missed the car and flew up into the sky, exploding above them.

Under a barrage of gunfire, bodies dropped, but was it enough?

Taking hold of the door handle, he glanced over at Andre one last time before darting out, firing as he went while sprinting for the cover of trees. "Elisha. Liam!" He heard their voices for but a second as he came around the cabin, then out of nowhere he felt the full brunt of a rifle to the side of his head.

Then his world turned to black.

Chapter 27

"His bag is gone," Sophie said to Thomas.

After returning later that evening to her room she'd noticed Alex wasn't there. After checking in with Ryan, who said he hadn't seen him, she went over to Thomas' room.

"Everything's gone?" he replied.

She nodded, arms folded, an expression of concern.

Perched on the edge of his bed he shrugged. "He did say he wanted to leave."

She raised an eyebrow at him.

"That was Asheville."

"C'mon Sophie, you saw how fired up he was this morning."

She shook her head. "No, he said he would stay a few more days."

"Maybe he changed his mind."

She turned to exit.

"Where are you going?"

"To speak with Abner."

Call it a gut instinct, and years of being married to him, but she could tell something was off. Sure, there was a possibility he could have left, and maybe she could have believed that except after her therapy session with Abner she'd spoken with Alex. His concern for Meadow's whereabouts was what had given her pause for thought, that and the conversation with him the previous night.

Had he gone looking for her?

On her way down, she passed Star who had a magazine in her hand.

"Everything okay?" Star asked.

"You haven't seen Alex, have you?"

"Earlier this morning. He asked about Meadow."

"And?"

"I said I would look for her but I didn't have any luck."

"So she's gone?"

"Appears so."

"Okay, thanks, Star. Look, if you see Alex tell him I want to speak with him."

"Will do."

It was a little after nine, and most had retreated to their rooms, or were conversing in the common room, a huge area of the mansion that had six white sofas, colorful bean bags and recliners. People sat around drinking tea and chatting. It had a very hippie feel to it.

Making her way out into the night, a light breeze brushed against her cheeks as she headed up to Abner's office on the hill. A warm yellow glow emanated from the windows. Outside, Pete and Eric, Abner's security, rose to greet her.

"I'm here to see him."

"Hold tight," Eric said. He walked to the door and gave a knock. A moment later Eric opened the door, muttered something, then waved her on in. Inside, Abner sat behind his desk. He closed a large book in front of him and removed spectacles from his nose. He'd changed out his regular attire and was wearing what looked like navy silk pajamas with a thin white stripe around the collar. "Sophie. What can I do for you?"

"It's Alex. I can't find him. His belongings are not here."

He offered an expression of concern and gestured to the couch. "Take a seat."

"I'd prefer to stand."

"Fine. Can I get you a drink? I was about to have warm water with lemon."

"No, I'm good."

He crossed to a large wooden cabinet where he prepared his drink.

"I'm worried."

"Of course you are. However, you must have expected he might leave after his outburst this morning." A spoon clinked inside the cup as he poured steaming hot water into it and stirred.

He took a seat in a comfy chair as if he was ready to dish out therapy again. His monotone voice was consistent, almost hypnotic.

"Well certainly but he…"

"I'm afraid Alex left this afternoon, Sophie."

"What? Why didn't you say anything?"

"Sorry. I assumed he would have told you."

"No. No he didn't," she said taking a seat, letting it sink in.

"Yeah, I guess after this morning he must have given it some more thought and decided to head out. I imagine he didn't want to start another argument. I mean, you had mentioned arguing."

"Yes but…"

Abner leaned forward and placed a hand on her leg. Sophie looked him in the eye and she could tell it was more than just a reassuring pat. She stood up and paced, stopping by a window as her eye caught sight of a fire glowing in the darkness. "It doesn't make sense."

"What doesn't?" he asked.

"Alex was concerned about Meadow. He said she wanted to leave with us in the morning. He said…" she hesitated but felt it was important to continue. "Meadow told him that you take people to the barn and they're never seen again. She was scared."

"And what do you think, Sophie?"

"I don't know what to think. I don't get that impression."

He gave a confident smile. "A few things you should know about Meadow," he replied as he set his drink down and crossed the room to where she was. "She has a wild imagination and tends to blame. Ever since she arrived here she's struggled to fit in."

"Really? Because she seemed quite relaxed around Star."

Abner clasped his hands behind his back and looked out the window at a bonfire that had been lit. Roughly ten people were sitting on logs surrounding it. "Let me guess. She blames me for her uncle and brother leaving?"

"Yes."

He nodded, a smile forming. "Her uncle came to me the day before he left to ask if I would look after Meadow while he went to collect the rest of his family. He took her brother with him for support because as you know, not everywhere is as safe as this place."

"Then why did she think they went missing?"

"Because they didn't tell her. Her uncle knew that she would react and so he left in the night with his nephew. The next morning, Meadow was of course upset and was looking for someone to blame. Since then she's refused to help around the ranch and concocted a story that she tells everyone who shows up here. We had Star take her out on trips into the city with the hope she would rub off on her. Even though Star is young, she's ahead of her years."

"Star's parents. What happened to them?"

"They're dead. Star has been with us for several years, long before this event. Anyway, I imagine Meadow followed through with her plans to leave and took off. I mean, we're not going to stop her. No one is a prisoner here," he said.

Sophie nodded and gazed out, past the bonfire, across the lake to the barn.

She pointed. "So what goes on in there?"

He laughed. "Even after what I just told you, you still have your doubts."

"No. I…" she trailed off. "Yes."

"Okay. Fine. Let's go."

"Where?"

He crossed the room and paused at the door. "To the barn of course. You want to see it, right? I mean, I could be holding people prisoner there. Unless of course you're worried you won't come back." He laughed and she gave a nervous chuckle. "Come on, we'll chat on the way down."

They stepped out. Abner locked up, and told Eric where they were going before they made their way down the steep hillside. She breathed in the aroma of burning wood. Along the way, Sophie continued. "This place is beautiful, Abner, but eventually I'll need to leave and head back to California. Alex was right. Our daughter could be alive and if she is, she'll need us."

"Of course. Whenever you are ready."

Maybe it was his disarming manner but she never got

the impression that he was anything more than a kind, genuine person. Sure there were a few things that were odd about the ranch but no more than some of the spiritual retreats that were offered before the bombings. If offering spiritual help was a crime, thousands of spiritual teachers would have been guilty. In her mind it was no different than that. As for why they looked up to him, it was simple — in times of desperation and questioning, those who provided answers and a sense of security were seen as a strong anchor. "The drones. Alex said that you were involved."

"Not in the manner he was alluding to. I'm not a terrorist, Sophie."

"Then how is it that those drones don't touch your people or that Jeep?"

He sighed. "Do you believe the world has mysteries, things that we can't understand? That makes no sense and defies logic?"

"Of course."

"Do you have faith?"

"I do."

"Even though you can't see?"

"Of course."

"And would you agree that what I have built here is helping people?"

"Seems so."

He looked deep in thought. "Do you recall Moses leading the Israelites through the Red Sea?"

She nodded.

"Do you believe that happened?"

She didn't answer right away. Her upbringing had been one grounded in faith but in her mind they were all just stories, perspectives told by a different culture, open to interpretation, certainly not to be taken as fact. But she would have been a fool to deny that she hadn't witnessed remarkable things in her own life that made her believe. Before she could reply, he answered.

"This event is like the Red Sea, and I am safely leading people through it. I don't know how or why me, but I know those who come in contact with me are protected.

Call it what you will, a divine intervention, the hand of God or a calling. That includes you, Sophie." He stopped and took her hand. "I hope over the coming weeks to get to know you more." He ran his thumb over her hand. It could have been taken in any number of ways. "I believe you have a great calling on your life."

As they continued, she mulled it over.

"I'm not sure about weeks."

"Right," he said. "I forgot."

Her bullshit meter was flashing red and yet her heart was telling her different.

He seemed to have an answer for everything, whether it made logical sense was neither here nor there. Most, if not all matters of spirituality were up for debate but something about his talks in the evenings, his charm, it was magnetic. She could see how people might be attracted to his persona and the ranch. It was like a calm ocean in a storm, an oasis in a barren place.

Still, she wasn't a fool and understood Alex's reservations.

When they made it to the barn, he pulled back the large red door and beckoned her inside. As soon as she entered, she smiled and let out a chuckle. "What beautiful horses."

"Equine-assisted therapy. Have you heard of it?"

"Experiential therapy that involves interactions between patients and horses. Yes."

"Before the bombings, when I was running the retreat, it was something Angelica wanted to include."

"Angelica?"

"My previous wife. She died many years ago along with my son."

"You never told me about that."

"Like I said, hopefully over the coming days I can share some of my life with you. Anyway, we created the barn and brought in some of the finest horses in America as well as a trainer. It became a staple part of our retreats." He walked over to one of the stalls which held a beautiful black horse. "Years of trauma, disorders, addiction, compulsions and grief, among other things, can be treated with these magnificent animals." He brought her hand up and placed it on the horse. "Every animal has an energy. Can you feel it?"

She smiled.

He gave her a guided tour and led her up into the second level where all the stacks of hay were. "See. Nothing. Just horses and hay. Unfortunately to protect the horses we have limited the number of people who can come over. And of course when you place limitations on things, people question. All it takes is a few people like Meadow to stain the waters of the mind and you have people thinking we are up to no good. Come, take a seat," he said, perching on a stack of hay. Sophie sat down. "Just as animals have energy so do humans," he said turning toward her. "Close your eyes."

Reluctant but feeling foolish for having believed Alex, she closed them. He took her hands and placed them between his. "Do you feel that warmth?" he said.

She nodded as he released her hands. "Energy is just like water, it flows and can get stuck. When this happens it causes all manner of problems. But there are ways to unblock it. Do you trust me, Sophie?"

She swallowed hard. "Maybe we should head back."

He clasped her hand. "Letting go of your fears is the first step to liberation. Close your eyes." Frustrated but not wanting to be rude, she complied. That's when she felt his hands run up her leg, then felt his lips touch hers.

Instantly she lashed out, slapping him and rising to her feet. "What the hell are you doing? How dare you."

He looked back at her with a smile, rubbing the side of his cheek.

"I think I should leave," she said.

"And go where?"

"Alex was right. We should…"

A siren blared. It was muted, hard to pinpoint.

She peered over the edge. It was coming from below the barn. "That's coming from…" As she turned and pointed, she felt a hard strike to the side of her head. On the floor, she groaned as Abner loomed over her with a pitchfork in hand.

Chapter 28

The fight for survival began the second they dragged him into the room.

Alex knew that once he was pinned down, he'd be injected and any hope of getting out would be lost. Under a cocktail of chemicals his mind would turn to mush just like Meadow, just like the rest of those poor bastards locked away.

As they dragged him through the maze of corridors, his mind was firing, coming up with a way to escape. Both of them were armed. It was beyond risky. However, he'd made up his mind. He would rather die than be imprisoned. As soon as he entered the room he began to struggle and just as he expected they resisted, locked hard onto his arms, giving him the exact leverage he needed for what came next.

Forcing him across the room, Alex shoved back, slamming them into the wall. Again they dragged him forward but this time he used the opposite wall to his advantage.

With their arms securely locked around his, he bounced up using them as leverage and pushed off from the wall with his feet, causing them to fall back, knocking the wind out of them and releasing their grip. In an instant, Alex reached across and yanked a knife out of one guy's sheath and stabbed him in the throat.

It all happened in a flash.

Before his buddy could react, Alex was on him fighting for control of the rifle. The guy below held on to the barrel and buttstock, pushing up as Alex forced his weight down until he got under his chin. The man's eyes bulged as Alex used brute force to crush his windpipe.

His face went red.

Shock.

Pain.

C'mon. C'mon.

Then it happened.

The man released his grip on the rifle, Alex stood and

fired two rounds, one into each of them. He scooped up additional magazines from both and exited. Cradling the AR-15, he swiftly moved down the corridor and unleashed a flurry of rounds at anyone he saw.

Within minutes the siren wailed; lights flashed red and the war began.

* * *

Pain shot through Sophie's skull but the blow hadn't knocked her unconscious. Still looming over her, Abner sounded garbled. Something about Alex. Something about Meadow. *They're as good as dead.* That she heard clearly. "And you're joining them."

"The fuck I am!" she muttered under her breath. Still having the wherewithal to fight back, and with him not expecting it, she swept his legs and took his feet out from beneath him. He landed hard as she clawed at a stack of hay to get up.

Abner cried out in anger, a barrage of cursing.

Sophie stumbled forward, away, trying to reach the ladder but she didn't make it.

Abner tackled her from behind, slamming her shoulder into the floor then grasping a clump of her hair. She screamed in pain. He dragged her across the floor as if he was about to throw her off the second level. As he lifted his foot to move forward one more time, she grasped the other and pulled it out, almost sending him over the edge.

Scrambling up, she went for the ladder but he was too fast.

This time he slammed into her, driving her head into a pile of hay where he collapsed on top. Abner flipped her over and she swiped at his face with her nails, enraging him. He fought back, with a jab to the face then wrapped his hands around her neck and began to squeeze.

Through gritted teeth he said, "You bitch!"

She grasped his wrists, trying to pry them loose, but he was too strong.

Using any means of defense she could, she plowed a fist into his side but that only angered him more. He stared at her consumed with a desire to kill. Darkness slowly crept in at her peripherals. Any second now she would lose consciousness. With him choking her, he'd forgotten one thing. Using every ounce of strength she had, she drove her knee into his nutsack and his eyes widened, the shock hit him like a lightning bolt as she did it again followed by a hard crack to the ribs. Abner rolled off, clutching his privates and groaning in agony.

Breathing hard and gasping for air, Sophie struggled to rise to her feet.

She managed to get one knee up but before she could lift the second, Abner latched on to her ankle, tugging her back. She let out a cry and fell forward, her knee driving into the floor, but instead of writhing in pain, she rolled and smashed her one free foot into his face. In pain, seething and cursing at her, the second time she tried to kick him, he slapped her foot out of the way and began tugging her toward him.

He was like a rabid dog that wouldn't let go.

There was no way in hell she would let him get the advantage again.

With him straddling her legs, she thrust her fingers at

his eyes, screaming, releasing her fury as the sirens continued to wail. It was pure chaos. Abner kept his head low but that was his mistake, as he clawed his way over her, she thrust her knee up under his chin. It must have caused him to bite his tongue as he howled, revealing a mouth full of blood. A bulbous chunk of bloodied flesh hung from his mouth.

But she didn't stop there.

Sophie threw a right hook catching him under the jaw, then a jab to the side of his face until he rolled off moaning in pain. She didn't catch what he said as she got up and staggered toward the pitchfork. Realizing what she was about to do, Abner was now the one trying to escape.

She scooped up the heavy fork and wailed as she ran at him full force.

Abner turned; his eyes widened and his hands went up but it was too late.

She thrust into his gut, pinning him against the wall of the barn. Sophie stared at him as blood streamed out of his lips and off his chin.

Chapter 29

The ceasefire was sudden. One moment they were engaged, the next it was quiet. Through darkened trees, Elisha saw them drag Garcia's limp body into an open area under the glow of the sedans' headlights. They dumped him on his face and a man placed a foot on Garcia's back, holding a rifle to his head.

"Lay your weapons down and come out or I'll execute him right now."

Elisha scanned the terrain, doing a quick headcount.

There were four remaining or at least that's all she could see.

The firefight had been brutal, had it not been for the cover of trees, she was sure they would have died. The group could have charged them, except they couldn't be sure how many they were up against, at least that's what Liam said. Movement was key, shifting from one position to the next. Under the canopy of darkness it was hard to tell where anyone was, which provided an advantage but also made it hard to tell who was who.

There was a slim possibility they could take out the remaining opposition but chances were if they opened fire, Garcia would be shot and right now he was the one person that had kept them alive.

Liam darted over to her, staying low, twigs crunching beneath his boots.

"What do you think?" she asked.

"If we stay they'll kill us."

"And if we leave they'll kill him," she replied.

"He took that risk coming in. We all did."

"So we engage," she shot back.

A bald guy with lots of tattoos on his head, wearing baggy pants and a dark T-shirt, came into view, though partially hidden by the trees. A rifle was in his hand, and he was wearing a bulletproof vest similar to Garcia's.

"I know there are only two of you out there."

"Well there goes our advantage," Liam muttered.

Garcia looked up and the man above him forced his

head down.

"C'mon now. He's not worth it," Baldy shouted.

"Shoot him!" Garcia cried out. The one above him reacted by striking him in the face with the barrel of his gun.

Elisha looked at Liam. He shook his head.

She remembered what Garcia said and yet the thought of turning tail and getting out of there seemed wrong, especially after he'd risked his life for them at the tavern. And yet she knew the second they engaged, Garcia would be killed.

"What if I take out the one closest to him? Maybe it would give him a fighting chance, then we unleash on the others and hope to God they focus on us not him," she said.

Liam nodded. "Let me do it. You focus on the other guy off to his right."

Her heart was hammering in her chest as she took up position and waited for the thumbs-up.

"Come on out and he'll live."

Liam glanced over as he raised three fingers. He dropped one, then the second and was about to drop the last to indicate to engage when someone beat them to the punch.

A single round erupted, except it didn't strike the one looming over Garcia but the bald guy. His head jerked and his body collapsed to one side, alerting them to a shooter nearer the sedans.

A few seconds of surprise.

A glance back at Garcia.

And that was their moment.

Liam squeezed off the round and took out the one above Garcia while Elisha neutralized her target.

The fourth had the good sense to drop his gun and fall to his knees, thinking that would save his life. It didn't. Garcia rose up behind him, rifle in hand, and ended him execution-style from behind.

When the dust settled, and they were certain there were no more, they made their way into the clearing to join Garcia.

The ground was covered in bodies and brass casings. It was a massacre.

As she was wrapping her arm around Garcia, two men stepped out of the shadows.

"Fischer?" Garcia said.

The other looked like a gang member.

All of them reacted by raising their guns but Fischer got in front of the man.

"He's okay. He's not with them."

"Those tattoos would say different," Garcia said. "Who are you?"

The man slung a rifle over his shoulder. "The name's Leo Henriquez. I used to be with them. Not anymore."

"How did you find us?"

"We saw the flare and then the fire from across the lake," Ken said motioning to the cabin which was a smoldering charred mess. Fortunately the flames had only destroyed two sides of the home. Elisha later learned it was because of the way his grandfather had built the cabin. The roof was made of tin, and behind all that wood siding were sheets of steel.

"Yeah, how can I be sure?" Garcia asked, still not taking his finger off the trigger.

Leo motioned to Baldy. "He's dead, isn't that proof?"

"He's telling the truth," Ken added.

Garcia lowered his rifle and the man extended a hand.

"Well if this isn't strange," Garcia said, shaking it.

Two rival gangs, both working together.

"There's a first for everything, right?" Leo said.

"Maybe."

Chapter 30

Alex struggled to carry Meadow as he emerged from the underground to the distant sound of chopping. What was that? His mind was still reeling from what he'd done, his eyes transfixed in a state of shock. He'd lost count of how many he'd killed down there, six, nine, twelve, maybe more, most hadn't seen him until it was too late. He wasn't sure what scared him more, his lack of hesitation or lack of remorse.

He stumbled out of the stall and collapsed, exhausted, his knees driving into the dirt, his left arm bloodied and limp from a round. Meadow rolled out of his arms, drugged, still hazy. He took a second to catch his breath, feel the dirt beneath his nails before his senses went on high alert expecting trouble.

"It's okay. It's okay," he reassured Meadow in a soft voice. "I'll get you out."

At the whoosh of helicopter blades he raised his eyes

toward the nearest doors, toward the night sky between.

Black Hawks?

"Alex?"

Sophie.

His eyes shifted to the right then up to the floor above at the sight of movement. Sophie hurried to climb down a ladder, her hands gloved in blood. She raced forward, wrapping her arms around him and holding him tight.

He winced, pain coursing through him.

She pulled back his bloodied shirt and saw the wound. "You're…"

"Yeah, look, just give me a hand taking her out."

With a jerk of the head toward the stall he said, "There are others."

She got up to go over. "No. No. Sophie."

He wanted to save her the gruesome sight. "Where is he? Abner."

"Dead." She glanced at her hands that were trembling, then raised her eyes.

Suddenly, at the far end of the barn, one of Abner's

followers burst in. They locked eyes for but a second before Alex reacted. Adrenaline still surging through him, he raised his handgun and took out the threat with two squeezes of the trigger.

The man buckled, falling forward.

Sophie rushed to collect his rifle.

"Come on," Alex said, as he struggled to lift Meadow over his good shoulder. He ground his teeth and dug down deep into the grit formed from years of being thrown into deadly waters, wild oceans that had hardened him to adversity.

Carrying Meadow out of the barn, it was hard to believe what they were seeing. Three Black Hawks in the sky zipped overhead sending down a wash of air that kicked up dirt. Turning their eyes to the mansion in the distance, they observed women and men emerging, rifles in hand, lifting them to the sky. Some taking potshots. Others looked on bewildered, some fanning out, many running for the hills.

Alex squinted as the thump of helicopter blades got

louder and the air became thick with dust. More followers caught their attention as they sprinted their way. Alex dropped and used his body to cover Meadow as he engaged. After emptying a magazine, he palmed in another and lifted it again. One squeeze of the trigger and a guy went down as two more raced for the cover of trees. One even dropped his rifle, panic getting the better of him.

These weren't soldiers, militia or professionals.

They were ordinary folk deceived by a man dangling salvation like a carrot.

Across the lake gunfire echoed loudly.

Alex moved briskly along a dirt path leading around the lake. Several pickup trucks and motorcycles swerved away from the mansion trying to escape the repercussion of government.

Loyalty vanished in the face of prison or death.

For others, this was it, the battle that no doubt Abner had said would one day come, a face-off between light and darkness, good and evil, freedom and captivity.

Chaos erupted as followers opened up with automatic rifles and the Black Hawks circling overhead drew fire only to have door gunners push them back, tearing up the dirt before them. The closer they got to the mansion, the louder the bark of a machine gun became. Bodies dropped; rifles fell out of hands only to be scooped up by another follower. A dirt bike raced toward them, its muffler coughing smoke into the sky. The two passengers, a man, and a woman, looked at them for but a second before tearing up the hill and buzzing into the woods.

Some had the good sense to flee while others defended the ranch until death.

Parents scooped up children and piled them into a truck, taking off in the opposite direction. Alex's mind was on full alert, his senses heightened as he returned fire on any that raised a gun at them.

Ryan and Thomas raced out of the mansion, turning their heads, surprise and shock spreading as if unable to process the chaos unfolding around them.

"Ryan!" Sophie cried out.

Their heads turned and they bolted toward them, Thomas stumbling as panic took over. As soon as Alex handed off Meadow to them, he went to assist the soldiers in the helicopters who were being attacked from the ground. "Alex." He heard Sophie's voice but kept running forward. He dropped to a knee, scooped up a rifle from a dead follower and unloaded on two guys standing in the doorway with an M134 gun, a modern-day Gatling gun. For a split second his mind went back to that room, those metal boxes full of ammo and weapons of all kinds. They had been preparing for this, maybe for a long time.

Not expecting fire from the ground, they didn't see it coming, but the soldiers in the Black Hawk did. He was sure he caught one of them giving him a thumbs-up before the helicopter circled overhead. The sharp pain in his arm was now worse, he was losing blood fast and could feel himself becoming faint.

He stumbled forward, grasping a railing a second before Sophie appeared at his side, drawing him back, away from the heat of battle.

Shots continued to ring out from every direction until those on the ground were neutralized. Within seconds the pilots had the helicopters on the ground and fire teams of Rangers broke away running at a crouch, rifles ready, scanning for threats as some entered the mansion and others continued to kill followers crouched in the tree line.

To avoid being mistaken for threats, all of them got on their knees. Alex dropped his weapon and kept his hands up. Three Rangers came toward them. "Don't shoot. We're not with them," Alex said.

Surrounded, they listened as Rangers communicated with one another, alerting each other to friendlies, and threats that had been eliminated.

One of the rangers turned toward them. "Ryan Valez?"

They all turned to look at him.

In a slow, measured way, he replied, "That's me." He raised a hand.

"We have orders to bring you with us," a Ranger said coming around and strong-arming him away.

Sophie got up and instantly the other two Rangers pointed their rifles at her. "Wait. He's my son. Where are you taking him?"

"Peterson Air Force Base."

"Then I'm coming with you."

"I'm afraid we only have…"

"Fuck your orders. That's my son."

Alex rose to intervene. "Sophie."

The Ranger got back on his comms and walked a short distance away. He turned his head. "Sophie Reid?"

"That's right."

"Okay, come with us."

She pointed at Alex. "I'm not leaving without them. My husband is injured."

They took one look at him and made a gesture with his head. "All right. Let's go."

"There are others, injured, drugged, far below the barn. You'll find the entrance in the floor of the stall at the end," Alex said as they were led to the helicopters.

The Ranger yelled over the whooshing blades. "We'll

handle it. For now, get in."

No sooner had they got inside than the Black Hawk lifted in a plume of grit, revealing a gruesome bird's-eye view of El Dorado. A ranch meant for peace.

It now looked like a war zone.

Chapter 31

The full extent of Ryan's involvement with the U.S. bombings soon came to light over the next three days, as did Abner's role in the wave of attacks in Denver. After being flown into Peterson Air Force Base, they were met by Assistant Director Danielle Gardner of Homeland Security. Few words were exchanged except to say that after receiving medical attention they would be escorted to Cheyenne Mountain where Ryan would be held. Sophie wanted to go with him but was denied. Unbeknownst to them, Homeland Security had placed a tracking device inside his jacket so they could keep tabs on his whereabouts and monitor conversation.

That whole confession he'd given outside of Asheville had been exactly what they wanted in the beginning. It seemed they knew he wasn't telling the truth the first time around but instead of forcing it out of him, or holding him, they figured the best way was to cut him loose with the hope he would inadvertently reveal more.

He did.

Now they hoped to use him to not only shut down the flaws in their code but catch the same people who he'd sold the flaws to on the black market.

Iranian hackers.

At least that's what they were told.

In no uncertain terms they were informed that the event was believed to be retaliation for killing the head of Iran's elite Quds Force unit. To the U.S. government, he was a terrorist and a war criminal but to Iran, he was a hero whose popularity extended beyond those who supported the regime.

They were given no timeline of when he would be released or if he would, only that his work was important to national security and that took precedence over any fostering agreement she had in place. Sophie protested, demanding to speak with someone higher up, but her words fell on deaf ears. Fortunately, she was allowed one last meeting with Ryan before they were given a ride back to California.

In Alex's mind that was the only upside to it all.

As for that weasel, Abner, it came to light that he was an Iranian sympathizer, leading one of many terrorist cells throughout the U.S. The same group who were responsible for the second wave of attacks. However, unlike the other cells, he'd used his newfound position and past work with inner healing to convince people to join him, mostly for his own sexual pleasure. Like many of the other sickos, Abner joined a long line of cult leaders, people who had convinced many to do horrific things under the guise of spirituality.

They were informed that Meadow, Star and anyone else who was a victim of Abner would be taken into custody, questioned and then released to a FEMA camp.

That was the last they saw of them.

After a tearful goodbye, with no idea of when they would see Ryan again, Thomas, Sophie, and Alex boarded the belly of a V-22 Osprey and took to the skies.

Their arrival in Petaluma was as they expected, full of

fear and worry as they took in the aftermath. That soon changed when they found a message from Elisha scrawled on a sign outside Sophie's home.

The pilot was kind enough to take them on from Petaluma to Willits.

From his window, Alex eyed the cattle in pastures, rolling hills and creeks snaking their way through the terrain before the V-22 set down in a wide, expansive high school field.

They exited and the pilot gave a thumbs-up as they watched it take off. The whoosh of the blades whipped the air, sending a gust up and filling their eyes with grit.

Their arrival was filled with mixed emotions.

Sophie's heart was heavy and her mind filled with worry.

Thomas was quiet, and Alex filled with a sense of gratefulness to be alive.

"Well. Let's go find our girl."

* * *

Warm rays of sunshine speared through the canopy of

trees as Elisha returned to the cabin with a five-gallon jug of fresh spring water. After the attack, they had loaded the bodies of Ramiro and his crew onto the back of a truck and disposed of them in a quarry just on the outskirts of town rather than bury them in a shallow grave.

Tate was not among the dead. Although Liam searched the town over the next few days, he never found him.

Steps were taken to rebuild what was destroyed though talk in the evenings circled around finding a new place, somewhere that was more secure, remote, possibly even a larger group who were riding out the shitstorm together.

Strolling up the hill, Elisha saw Garcia crouched near the grave of Andre.

He'd been quiet, more reserved since losing him.

Elisha set the water jug down at the cabin and made her way over. A cross was stuck into a mound of dirt surrounded by rocks. A few wildflowers protruded from the earth. "Hey. You okay?"

Garcia glanced over his shoulder. "Just taking a

moment."

She nodded looking thoughtful. "He'll be missed."

"Yeah."

"How long did you know him?"

"Since I was a kid. Grew up in the same neighborhood, had the same interests."

She took a deep breath and stuck her fingers into her jean pockets. "When I lost Michael, I didn't think I would smile again but eventually I did. The pain is still there and I can get back to it if I think about him but it doesn't sting as much anymore."

Garcia gave a nod as he rose and they walked away from the grave. "Where's Liam?"

"Went into town with Leo to see what they could scavenge."

In almost two weeks since the event the situation hadn't got better. With so many towns and cities in ruins, and many forced out of homes and work, it had created a different world. One filled with fear and suspicion.

While food wasn't scarce yet, and there was plenty of

game to hunt in the area, they were already beginning to talk about moving, if only to avoid any future trouble from outsiders. Ken Fischer had offered to have them come and stay at his cabin but the animosity between him and Garcia was palpable, so they declined.

"You showed a lot of heart that night. Your parents would be proud."

"I appreciate that," Elisha said as they took a seat at a picnic table outside the cabin. Garcia brought out smoked meat, and bread they'd made from a batch of flour. They'd taken to searching homes and businesses that were no longer occupied. Although it wasn't the safest method, the need to survive made everyone think differently, including Garcia who had for the longest time been a man of the law. "Do you think others will come?" Elisha asked as she chewed a piece of meat.

Garcia sliced into the bread. "No. Even gangs know when to throw in the cards."

"Do you think it's true about the safe zones?"

A few days earlier, they'd used a hand-crank AM/FM

radio and had come across a message being broadcast mentioning safe zones throughout the USA.

"If it is then maybe there is hope for the country."

"I'd like to believe that," she said before stuffing her mouth with bread.

The sound of a vehicle approaching caught their attention. Instinctively, they both reached for their rifles. Fortunately it wasn't trouble, just Liam and Leo returning. The cruiser wound into the driveway and Elisha laid her rifle down and turned her back to continue eating.

A few seconds later, doors were slammed, and Liam called out.

"Hey Elisha. Take a look at what we found?"

"Later, I'm eating."

"I think you'd be interested."

"If it's another case of beer…"

Before she could turn, she felt hands on her shoulders, then a cheek pressed against hers. Garcia had this big smile on his face. As Elisha turned, she dropped the food in her hand. "Mom?"

"Hey darling."

Rising, she saw that she wasn't alone.

Her brow furrowed. "Dad!"

"Hey beautiful." His arm was in a sling as he walked from the car over to her.

Tears welled in all their eyes as they took a moment to embrace.

"Came across them in town," Liam said perching on the edge of the table, a grin forming. Another guy came into view behind her father, a ginger-haired short guy who couldn't have been much older than her.

"Ryan?" She asked.

"No. That's Thomas. Ryan is..." Sophie trailed off. "He'll join us later. I hope."

Elisha briefly caught the look her mother gave Garcia, a smile that faded fast as her eyes bounced back to her father.

They hugged and over the next few hours swapped stories of how they'd managed to survive, what they'd learned from Homeland Security, and all they'd been through in different towns and cities across America. All of it confirmed what she believed — the nation had fallen, and it wasn't rising again anytime soon.

Still, with Ryan working with Homeland Security there was a sense of hope on the horizon.

The conversation soon turned to the future, to the challenges that lay ahead over the coming days and weeks. Ruined communities meant desperation, and desperation meant trouble. Elisha looked around the table at the faces of survivors, each one different in age, background and experience. It was a strange dynamic but one that had served them well. They'd come through a lot, and with it gained a new strength that would carry them through the coming days as they fought to survive.

And survive they would, together, against all odds.

* * *

THANK YOU FOR READING

As Our World Burns #3 is out

If you enjoyed that, please take a second now to leave a review. Even a few words is really appreciated. Thanks kindly, Jack.

About the Author

Jack Hunt is the International Bestselling Author of over forty books published. Jack lives on the East coast of North America. If you haven't joined Jack Hunt's Private Facebook Group you can request to join by going here. https://www.facebook.com/groups/1620726054688731/ This gives readers a way to chat with Jack, see cover reveals, and stay updated on upcoming releases. There is also his main Facebook page if you want to browse that.

www.jackhuntbooks.com
jhuntauthor@gmail.com

Printed in Great Britain
by Amazon

BRADFORD
Butcher

Sheridan Anne
Bradford Butcher: Bradford Bastard #3

Copyright © 2022 Sheridan Anne
All rights reserved
First Published in 2022
Anne, Sheridan
Bradford Butcher: Bradford Bastard #3

This book is a work of fiction. Names, characters, places, and incidents are products of the author's imagination. Any resemblance to actual events or persons, living or dead, is entirely coincidental.

No part of this book may be reproduced, stored in a retrieval system or transmitted in any form or by any means, without prior permission in writing of the publisher, nor be otherwise circulated in any form of the binding or cover other than in which it is published, and without a similar condition, including this condition, being imposed on the subsequent purchaser.

Cover Design: Sheridan Anne
Photographer: FXQuadro
Editing: Heather Fox
Formatting: Sheridan Anne

BUTCHER!

This book is for all the psycho bitches who play bullshit games and make the stories I write about seem plausible! Keep doing your thing, ladies! Mumma needs that content!

Also… Stay away from me. I don't need that kind of drama in my life!

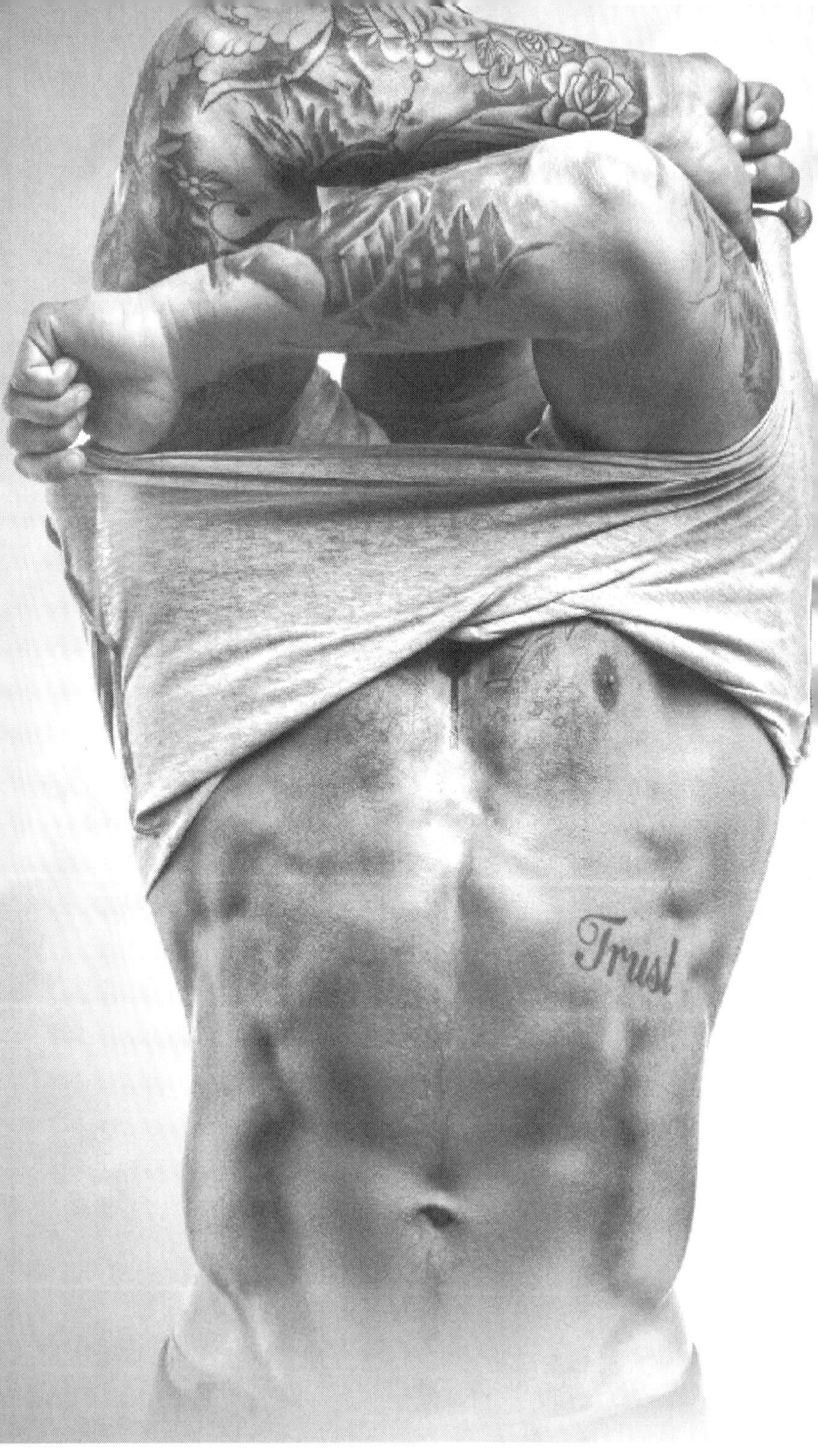
Trust

CHAPTER 1
TANNER

Sirens sound in the distance, cutting through Arizona's terrified wails, as the bright headlights of scattering cars creates an eerie glow over the darkened racetrack. My knees crash into the grass beside Bri, fear like I've never known blasting through my chest as my panicked stare sails over her body.

Blood coats the front of her tank, quickly spreading and pooling beneath her waist, making it nearly im-fucking-possible to breathe. My eyes flash to hers, seeing nothing but terror, and my heart races faster. This can't be real. This can't be happening.

She can't fucking die here tonight. I won't allow it.

"No, no, no, no, no," I chant, tearing her shirt up to find a nasty stab wound threatening her precious life. My hands slam down over it, applying pressure as she silently weeps, knowing this is the end.

There's no fucking way I'm about to let her go without a fight.

Her eyes are glassy and she's losing color fast. "Please, Killer," I beg, unable to even think, resisting the desperate need to shake her. "Please don't go. Stay with me. I can't lose you. I love you. You hear me? I fucking love you, Brielle. Don't you dare die."

Those gorgeous blue eyes stare up at me, her brows furrowed with fear as a perfectly round tear falls down the side of her cheek. "I'm sorry," she murmurs, her voice breaking over the lump in her throat. "I … I can't. I'm not going to make it."

"Over my dead fucking body. You're not dying on me today. This isn't how we end."

Blood pools over my hands as the ambulances speed across the property, desperate to get to us. One after another until it looks like a scene out of *Fast and Furious*.

Riley drops onto the grass by Bri's other side, his panicked stare sailing over her body. "Fucking hell," he breathes, quickly adjusting himself and cradling her head in his lap. "You're gonna be okay," he tells her, wiping the tears off her face. The raw fear in his eyes doesn't match the soothing words coming from his mouth. "You're gonna be okay."

Logan's pained cry sounds through the night, and my head snaps up, watching as he hovers over his twin brother, tears brimming in his dark eyes. "I'll never fucking forgive you if you die, asshole. Keep your goddamn eyes open."

My chest aches watching the scene as Arizona shakes Jax's shoulder, heavy sobs tearing from her chest. "JAX! Fuck. Wake up. Please wake up."

Her head shoots toward the paramedics quickly approaching. "They're not going to make it in time," she cries in sheer desperation. "He's going to die."

"Either shut up or fuck off," Logan hisses at her, too fearful to realize she's just as scared as he is. "You're not helping, all you're fucking good for is messing with his head."

Arizona shakes her head, not believing him for one moment as she drops her gaze back to Jax's limp body in her arms. "He's going to die," she cries. "He's going to fucking die."

Fear ripples through me before Riley forces my stare back to his. "Jax is gonna be alright," he murmurs, trying to calm me, somehow able to keep his head on straight and be the voice of reason I need during this shitstorm. "Logan won't let anything happen to him. Arizona doesn't know what the fuck she's talking about. She's just scared."

I shake my head, looking back down at my girl, her eyes growing heavy as soft tears continue falling down her cheeks, the heaviness weighing on my chest and making this whole moment nearly impossible to get through. "I don't know, man," I tell him, watching the way Brielle's eyes flutter, straining to keep herself awake. "I don't know how any of us are supposed to get through this."

Riley doesn't respond, knowing how fucking right I could be, but my mind is already somewhere else. "Talk to me, Hudson," I call over my shoulder, hoping he can hear me from the bottom of the hill as my gaze snaps across to Colby's lifeless body, his chest still not moving up and down. "Tell me Addison's alright."

Hudson's agonized grunt rumbles across the hill, and I glance back to find him dropping to his knees with Addie tucked tightly against his blood-soaked chest. "I don't know," he says, his voice filled with the worst kind of pain that destroys something deep in my soul. "I don't know how to help her."

Ilaria and Chanel barrel in beside him, looking over Addison's face as Hudson falls apart, his whole world flashing before his eyes. "She's still breathing," Ilaria calls back, desperately searching over her. "But she's lost a lot of blood. I … I think she's going to be alright."

Clenching my jaw, I close my eyes for a brief moment, trying to force myself to take a calming breath as I press harder against Bri's wound. "Her clothes?" I ask Ilaria, not sure if I'm ready for her answer. "Are they … did he hurt her again?"

"I … I don't know. It's hard to say," she calls back up the hill, trying to wrestle her out of Hudson's arms, needing to apply pressure to her wounds. "They're torn, but they're intact. I think maybe he tried but didn't get what he wanted."

Hudson lays her down, barely holding himself together at the thought of losing the girl he loves. Ilaria and Chanel dive for her at the same time, pulling at her clothes and searching for her injuries until they find a deep stab wound just below her chest. Chanel gasps as Ilaria shoves her hands against Addie's body to stop the bleeding. Hudson takes Addie's face in his hands and begs her to wake up.

I can't watch any longer and look back at Bri, sending silent prayers to anyone who will listen.

The sirens drown out Addison's familiar cry, but it's all I need to keep breathing. She's going to be alright. Addie has been through worse and overcome the impossible. But if that fucker raped her again … I don't know what version of my sister I'll get back after this.

I don't know what the fuck I'm doing or how I will get through this. All I know is, if Addie, Bri, or Jax die here tonight, I'll never forgive myself. Addison left to go to the bathroom, and I should have insisted on walking her, but I was too fucking busy getting my dick wet with my girl. And Jax … he shouldn't have been anywhere near Colby. That was my fight, my business, and now my cousin has suffered the consequences of my mistakes.

I should have kept my cool. I should have known something like this would happen, especially after dropping Colby's ass at the courthouse. He was not a forgiving man, and I knew that. Colby was reckless and out for blood, just as I was, and now because of my actions, the people I love are dropping like flies.

I lost control—the one thing I promised Bri I wouldn't do.

I gave her my word that she'd never have to see that side of me again and now here we are. She's hurt because I couldn't stop the rage, couldn't keep myself from making irrational decisions. Colby swung his knife over and over again while Bri stood at my back trying to pull me away, and instead of listening to her and seeing the danger I was putting her in, I was thinking of myself. I needed to see the life fade from his eyes, needed to get justice for what he did to my sister, for what he did to Bri.

And now … fuck.

I've killed a man.

My hands shake, and the only thing keeping me calm is the way Bri's hand shifts from the blood-soaked grass and curls around my wrist, her grip barely tight enough to hold on. I meet her teary expression, and the overwhelming bullshit circling my mind begins to ease, just as it always does whenever those blue eyes are locked on mine. The world fades away, and all I see is her.

"It hurts," she whispers as Riley wipes another tear off the side of her face.

"I know, baby," I murmur, swallowing hard over the lump in my throat, doing everything I can to appear strong for her. "That's a good thing. If you can still feel it, that means you can fight through it. You're going to be alright. I promise I'm not letting you go."

Her fingers tighten around my wrist, and I see nothing but fear shining through her stare. "You're scared," she tells me.

"You're damn fucking right, I am," I admit. "I'm terrified, but I gave you my word, Killer. I just need you to meet me halfway. You gotta keep fighting, okay? I lean, you lean, remember? I'll give you anything you want, just stay with me."

"Anything?" she questions, those beautiful full lips pulling at the corners into a soft smirk. "Even butt stuff?"

I can't help but grin at her as I shake my head. "Fucking hell, babe. This isn't the time to be joking," I tell her, not surprised one fucking bit that even on her fucking death bed, her blood pooling over my fingers, she's cracking jokes about getting railed in the ass.

"Wait," Riley says, his gaze lifting to mine. "You haven't fucked this sweet ass yet? Dude, lacking. I'm not impressed." He glances at my girl before I get the chance to curse him out. "Just say the word, babe. If you want me to pop that ass cherry, it'll be my honor. Any time, any day, any place. You bring the ass, I'll bring the equipment."

If my hands weren't currently keeping my girl from bleeding out on the grass, I'd fucking beat his ass black and blue. "Watch your fucking mouth, man," I spit, the harshness in my words more than enough warning. "I've already put one asshole in the ground. Don't make it two."

Riley grins back at me, and I realize too late what the two assholes have been doing—distracting me enough to calm me down and keep my mind off the bullshit that's out of my control.

Letting out a sigh, I look back at my girl and, while keeping my hands on her wound, I lean down and brush my lips over hers. "I love you, Brielle," I tell her. "You're my whole fucking world, and if you fight to keep yourself alive now, then I promise you in return, I'll fight for us every day for the rest of our lives. I'll make you so goddamn happy, you'll want to pulverize me. You got that? You have to live because I don't want to face a world where you're not doing everything in your fucking power to make me want to hate fuck you until you scream."

"Swear it?" she questions, her lips moving against mine, her voice barely audible.

"I fucking swear it, Killer. You and me … maybe Riley too, but really, we should probably find him some other poor girl to sink his claws into before he starts thinking this is a group project."

"Wouldn't have it any other way."

Her eyes flutter again, and a wave of panic soars through my chest, nearly crippling me. If it weren't for the fact that my position here is what's keeping her alive, I would have succumbed to the horror ages ago.

With the first responders getting closer by the minute, Chanel scrambles to her feet and races toward them, waving her hands and screaming for them to hurry, probably feeling just as helpless as I do. But the fact they're close enough for Chanel to reach has relief pulsing through my veins.

They're so close. We're gonna make it. Everyone is going to be okay.

The cops come blasting in behind the paramedics, covering the property like a plague of red and blue flashing lights. I can't help but glance back at Colby's lifeless body, unease and fear gripping my chest and squeezing impossibly tight.

There's no way the cops are going to let me walk away from this. Not now. Not after ending his life with my bare hands.

Catching my stare, Riley shakes his head. "Don't fucking go there, man," he tells me. "Bri, Addie, and Jax are what's important. They need you more than anything. Go to the hospital. I'll stay here and deal with Colby."

"But the cops—"

"No," Riley says. "The cops don't know shit. They don't know it was you or what went down. Just get in the fucking ambulance with Bri. I'll stay here. Besides, their first priority is to try and save him."

"There were too many witnesses," I say. "They'll fucking know."

The first ambulance comes to a screeching halt, stealing my attention away from my best friend as Hudson's patience wears thin. He scoops Addie off the ground as Ilaria curses him out. "HELP!" he hollers as the paramedics bail from the rig. He races toward them, Ilaria barreling after him, her hands soaked with Addison's blood.

They tear open the back of the ambulance, and I watch Hudson all but toss her inside. Two paramedics immediately get to work, surrounding Addie as Ilaria drops to her knees in the grass, letting out a heart-wrenching sob of despair.

Hudson clambers into the back of the ambulance, refusing to leave her side, gripping Addie's hand as the paramedics do their thing. Before I know it, the other ambulances and cop cars are coming to a stop too.

Relief pounds through my chest, but Riley isn't done with me yet. He grips my chin tight and forces my stare back to him. "Listen here, there were plenty of witnesses, each one of them able to clarify that Colby came here looking for trouble. It was self-defense. Nothing else. You saved Jax and protected Bri by keeping him down. You did what you had to do to preserve the lives of the people you love. You got that? This wasn't cold-blooded murder, Tanner, it was self-defense."

My gaze shoots back across to Colby's lifeless body, and an ache squeezes my gut. Either way Riley looks at it, I killed a man, and that will forever live on my conscience.

A hand lands on my shoulder, and I whip around to find a paramedic standing over me. "Let me take over, son. You've done well."

I scramble out of the way as the paramedic moves in, assessing Bri with a skilled gaze. "Stab wound to the lower abdomen," he says as another paramedic moves in on her other side. They get to work, taking her vitals, and before I can ask how she is, they place her onto a gurney.

"Tanner?" Bri panics, her eyes wide and terrified.

"I'm right here." I rush in, gripping onto her outstretched hand with everything I have. Up ahead, I notice the door of another ambulance closing on Jax, leaving Arizona and Logan behind.

"Hey," the guy saving Bri's life says, catching my attention. "The lights are on. That's a good sign."

I swallow hard and nod. "None of this is a fucking good sign."

"Too right," he responds as Bri's gurney lifts off the ground, finally stable enough to move. We hurry down the hill as others run in the opposite direction, heading for Colby's body, but I keep my mind locked and loaded on Bri.

She's loaded into the back of the ambulance, and I scramble in beside her, trying to keep out of the way as I watch Riley race in beside Ilaria and scoop her off the dirty ground. He pulls her into his arms, holding her tight and letting her use his shoulder to cry on. Chanel weeps beside them, all of our friends just as terrified as I am.

Bri refuses to release my hand, and I'm fucking grateful, needing her touch more than I need to breathe. As they close the back doors, I watch Addison's ambulance take off at top speed, the sirens and lights blasting through the night.

Letting out a shaky breath, I give Brielle a warm, encouraging smile. At some point, I will have to call my mom and tell her, for the second time, that her baby girl's life is hanging in the balance.

CHAPTER 2
Brielle

Pieces of a murmured conversation trickle through the foggy images in my mind, and I let out a pained groan, refusing to open my eyes as reality comes crashing back to me.

The races, Jax, Addison, the knife … Colby.

Fuck.

Tanner.

Desperation to check on him courses through my body, and I strain to open my eyes, but the fogginess keeps me locked down. I must be on some pretty intense painkillers, maybe morphine. I'm not going to lie, it kinda feels good.

At some point, Colby's knife slashed through my abdomen, and I know it must have hurt, but the adrenaline kept me going. All that mattered was Tanner, until I was laying in the bloodied grass with his hands pressed against my wound. That fucking hurt. I'd prefer to have my ass rammed at a million miles per hour with no lube than to experience the sheer agony of that stab wound again. Right now, I feel perfectly fine, though I'm not foolish enough to think this is going to last. The pain meds will wear off and when they do, it's going to suck … a lot.

Despite my pain and blood loss, it was the devastation in Tanner's eyes that nearly killed me. After watching Jax go down and seeing his sister in Hudson's arms, he thought he was going to lose me too. I could see the fear in his eyes, but he did what he could to save my life, all while relentlessly promising that he wasn't going to let me die.

He's so strong. He's everything a girl could ever want or need. He's my whole world, and I owe him my life. Fuck, I love him so much it hurts sometimes. I just don't know how he's going to get through this. If Tanner did end Colby's life, it's justified, but the toll it would take on him mentally … I don't know. That's a lot for anybody to handle. I'd just hate to see him suffer like that, after everything he's already been through.

My heart breaks for him. I want him to be happy and have the life he's always deserved, but this might just have the power to destroy him. I'm not going to let that happen though. I will prove to him just how amazing he is. No matter what I have to do.

A warm hand curls around mine and gently squeezes before I hear his soft murmur in my ear. "Killer?" he says, his voice breaking with despair. "Are you awake?"

Squeezing his hand in return, I try to open my eyes again, but they feel too heavy. "Mmmm," I grumble, certain that my face is doing that ugly morning scrunch thing that makes me look like an overweight rodent.

"Oh, fuck," Tanner sighs, the relief in his tone clear as day. He leans forward and rests his forehead against my wrist, and I pull my hand from his before curling it around the back of his neck, needing to feel him as close as humanly possible.

"I'm okay," I whisper, finally able to open my eyes, if only just a little.

The clinical light of the hospital room floods my vision, and I squint against it as my eyes adjust enough to see him. He's sitting beside my hospital bed, the chair pulled in close enough that his long legs are bound to be cramped beneath the bed. We're alone in the room, but I could have sworn there was someone else in here.

"Hey," I say over the lump in my throat, my fingers tightening around the back of his strong neck. "Look at me."

His head pulls up, and the moment those dark eyes come to mine, everything feels okay in the world. All the bullshit and chaos fade away, and I'm left with nothing but the pure love shining between us. He watches me for a moment as if unable to believe this is real, and after what feels like a lifetime, he leans in close and brushes his lips over mine. "You have no fucking idea how happy I am to see you awake."

"You're telling me," I murmur. "I would have been pissed if I didn't make it and missed out on a lifetime of kinky fuckery and ass ramming."

Tanner laughs and curls his arm around me, snaking his arms around the back of my neck just so he can wrap me in his warm embrace without jostling me. "I swear, I don't know whether to hate or love your smart fucking mouth," he tells me. "Do you have any idea how frustrating it is to hear you joking about butt stuff while you're bleeding out?"

"Probably just as frustrating as watching you panic over situations that are out of your control."

"Fair point," he tells me, dropping a kiss on my forehead and pulling back just enough to see my face. When his eyes come back to mine, there's something much deeper there, a hollowness that tears at my chest. "I'm so sorry, Killer. I never should have taken you to the races so soon after what happened in court, both you and Addie. I knew Colby was going to retaliate, and I wasn't thinking."

"Don't," I tell him, reaching up and cupping the side of his face, my thumb gently stroking over his warm skin. "I'm not somebody you can keep caged because some asshole might lose his fucking mind. The world is always going to keep turning, there's always going to be a new threat, but I'm not going to hide at home because there's other shit going on in the world. That's not how I'm going to live my life, and I'm sure Addison would say the same thing."

"Babe—"

"No," I tell him. "What happened at the track, that's not on you. Colby decided to retaliate, and he came at us with a knife. You protected us. You did what you had to do."

Tanner presses his lips into a hard line, and I hate the denial plaguing his stare. "Yeah," he mutters, but the conviction is absent from his deep tone, telling me what he thinks I need to hear just so we don't have to discuss it anymore.

"Tanner," I whisper, my gaze sweeping over his face. "If Colby's knife didn't kill me, your inability to see just how amazing and good you are, will. I love you, and it kills me to see you doubting yourself like this."

"I'm sorry, Killer. It's just … it's my job to protect both you and Addie, and I let you both down. I was too fucking consumed by rage to notice you'd been hurt when I promised you—*I fucking promised you*—I would learn to control myself."

His head falls again, his forehead dropping to my hip as he unintentionally crushes every last remaining part of my soul.

"I swear to God, Tanner Morgan. If you start giving me this self-pitying bullshit, I'm going to whoop your ass into next week. If you're to blame for Addison getting hurt again, then I'm responsible as well."

His head shoots straight back up, his brows furrowed with distaste. "The fuck are you talking about?"

"I was with you out in the woods, Tanner. I watched your sister walk away, and I happily left with you. I could have told you to go after her or I could have gone, but I didn't. I'm just as much to blame. The same could be said for Hudson. Is he gonna cop the same heat you're giving yourself? He didn't race after her. What about Riley or the twins?"

"That's not fair."

"Isn't it? You're blaming yourself for Colby's actions, so why the hell can't I do the same?"

"You got stabbed right in front of me, and I didn't fucking notice."

"*I didn't even notice,*" I throw back at him. "Yes, you were consumed by rage but, given the situation, it was justified. At that point, Jax and Addie had already been hurt. There was nothing you could have done to change that, and if you didn't go after him, he would have come for me, and this stab wound could have been a lot worse."

"I never would have let that happen."

Everything softens inside my chest, and I brush my fingers across his jaw. "I know that," I tell him. "Just promise me you're not going to carry the burden of this."

He glances away, his hand coming up and curling around mine, bringing them both down to the bed. "I think I killed him."

The pain in his voice tears me apart, and I squeeze his hand a little tighter. "Have you heard anything?" I ask. "How long have I been out?"

Tanner shakes his head. "It's just after five in the morning, so six-ish hours maybe," he explains. "Riley's been going from room to room, trying to keep everyone updated. As far as I know, both Addie and Jax are out of surgery. We're just waiting for them to wake up. As for Colby—nothing."

"I could be wrong, but I'm sure if he were actually dead, the cops would have dragged you out of here for questioning ages ago."

"The fucker wasn't breathing."

Pressing my lips into a hard line, I pull our joined hands up to my chest and hold them to my body. "I'm sorry," I murmur. "I wish

I could do or say something to make this all go away, but I think it's gonna get worse before it gets better."

"Yeah," he says, his gaze dropping once again. "You don't need to worry about me. All I want is to see you better."

My gaze sails down my body and I lift my gown, peering through the neck hole to assess the damage. "How bad is it?"

"Not as bad as it looks," he tells me. "You'll be back on your feet soon. The knife didn't hit any vital organs, but it was close. Just a little bit lower and you would have been taking laxatives for at least six to eight weeks."

My brows shoot up, horror rocking through my body at the thought of having to take laxatives for weeks on end. "Fuck. Really?" I gasp. Nobody wants to see me on laxatives. I had an unfortunate incident with a gummy once, and I turned into a human squirt machine. And not in a good way.

"Yeah," he says as a stupid grin cuts across his face. "That would have been a fun conversation."

"Oh, I'm so glad my misery amuses you," I say, though we both know the smile on his face would have made it all worth it … kind of. Okay, not really, but at least it helps.

"I'm sorry," he says, his eyes sparkling with laughter as he tries to control his face. Though if I'm honest, I'd take that smile a million times over the hopelessness from a moment ago. "I really don't mean to laugh, it's just the look on your face. Laxatives don't agree with you?"

"We are so not talking about this."

"Call it market research. After all, I plan on spending the rest of my life with you, and at some point, something will happen, and you'll have to take them. Don't you think it's best to get it all out in the open now?"

"Trust me, if I was on laxatives, everything would already be out in the open, and it wouldn't be pretty."

Tanner laughs and leans forward to press his lips to mine. "I fucking love you," he tells me, "but please don't ever put that mental image in my head again."

I grin right back at him, loving the warmth I feel from him. "And risk never grossing you out ever again?" I gasp, feigning outrage. "What kind of life would that be?"

Tanner rolls his eyes and settles back into his chair, his brow arching with curiosity. "So I suppose this isn't the time to remind you about all the butt stuff you so desperately want?"

My cheeks flush with embarrassment, despite Tanner being the one person I don't need to be embarrassed in front of. Though, I'm more humiliated that I let a comment like that slip out in front of Riley. I can only imagine what that idiot is going to do with it. "You're an asshole," I tell Tanner, just in case he forgot. After all, it's been a while since I reminded him.

Tanner laughs and shakes his head. "Seriously, Killer? You make it too easy."

I love the way his eyes sparkle as he laughs, and it pains me to burden him with the questions I've been holding back. Unfortunately, my desperation can't wait any longer. "How are Jax and Addie?" I ask, watching as all the happiness seems to drain from his face the moment I mention his sister.

"They were lucky," he tells me. "Well … not as lucky as you, but considering the alternative, they're lucky," he says. "The knife tore straight through Jax's liver. He only got out of surgery an hour ago, so I don't have more details than that, but from what I can find on google, he'll be out for a while. A few months maybe. Enough to end the football season for him."

"Shit," I mutter, my lips pressing into a hard line. "That's gonna destroy him."

"Understatement of the fucking year," he tells me. "That's not a conversation any of us wanna be around for."

"At least he's still breathing," I say. "That's all that matters."

"Try telling that to Addie," Tanner says, darkness swarming his deep tone.

My brows furrow, watching the array of emotions crossing his face. "What's that supposed to mean?" I question, a hint of desperation seeping through my tone.

"Colby punctured her right lung," he explains. "The knife slipped off her rib and went straight through the lung. She's lucky to be alive."

"Holy shit," I breathe, the thought of losing her wreaking havoc on my mind. "Is she alright though?"

"Physically she'll be alright, but mentally? I don't know. She was messed up after the first attack, and now this? I don't know if I'll ever see the carefree version of Addison she was before Colby got his hands on her. I'm just …" He pauses as his hands ball into tight fists, his tone lowering to a soft whisper. "I'm just glad it's over. He's gone and we can just focus on getting her the help she needs."

"How long until she's out of here?"

He shrugs his shoulders. "Mom's been in with the doctors, so I'll know more after that, but I suppose it really depends on the severity of it and what kind of damage Colby did. Google can't help me with that shit. All I know is that Addie won't be dancing for a while, and that's gonna kill her. She's already been off since the first attack."

"Shit, well you know I'm here if she wants—"

A soft knock sounds at the door and not a moment later, it's pushed open and Arizona's head pokes through the small gap. "Can I come—oh, shit! You're awake," she squeaks, her puffy, red-rimmed eyes lighting up with relief.

Arizona barges through the door, flinging it open and storming into my room. She cuts across the end of my bed and all but climbs over Tanner's lap to get to me. Her arms fly out wide before she crashes into me, and within seconds, she's sobbing into the crook of my neck.

Tanner gapes at me over Arizona's shoulder before awkwardly climbing out from beneath her and moving to the far corner of the room. Arizona wails against my neck, releasing all her pent-up frustrations and fears, and all I can do is hold her. "Are you okay?" I murmur, trying to crane my neck to get her hair out of my face.

"I tho—I thought I was," sob, "going to," sniff, "lose you."

My heart breaks for her. I can't even imagine how everyone must be feeling right now, watching their best friends being taken away by paramedics, their hands and clothes soaked in blood, not knowing if we were going to survive. It would have been the scariest thing they've ever been through. "You think you can get rid of me that easily?" I tease. "I'm like a bad rash that won't go away, no matter how hard you try."

"You're gross."

"Yeah, well, you had Riley's junk in and around your mouth at the lake, so technically, that makes you grosser."

Arizona laughs and pulls back, dropping her ass into Tanner's vacated chair before blowing her cheek out with a heavy breath and wiping her tears on the back of her sleeves. "Holy shit," she mutters under her breath before finally raising her chin and meeting my stare again. "Okay. I think I'm alright."

"You sure?" I ask. "If you need to cry some more, I can kick Tanner out. It's no problem."

"Over my dead body," Tanner mutters from the back of the room, leaning against the wall and crossing his strong arms over his chest, his biceps on full display with those damn tattoos that make my mouth water.

Arizona shakes her head. "No, really. I'm okay," she says. "It's a freaking sob-fest out there. I've already gotten most of it out. I was just so relieved to see you awake and alright. I swear, between me, Chanel, and Ilaria, I'm surprised the waiting area isn't flooded with tears."

My bottom lip drops, hating to hear they're not doing so well. "They can come in here if they need somewhere to break down."

"I'm sure they will," she says. "We've been fighting over who gets to go and check on you first, and of course, I lost. So I told them I was going to pee instead and jumped the line."

A soft laugh bubbles up my throat as I shake my head, not surprised by her tactics. "How are you really though? Have you heard anything more about Jax?"

Arizona shakes her head and the pain in her eyes nearly destroys me. "I wouldn't know," she says with a nasty bite in her tone. "Logan is refusing to let me see him or even tell me how he's doing. Apparently, all I'm good for is messing him up and I don't need to mess him up any more than I already have."

"That's bullshit and you know it," I tell her. "Logan is just scared for his brother and you're the perfect target for him to lash out at. Once Jax wakes up and Logan relaxes, he'll be able to think with a clear head and then you'll be able to see him."

"Yeah, well …," she says, glancing at her hands. "I don't know if I want to see him."

My brows furrow and I search her eyes but see nothing but the agony his rejection at the track caused, still burning so bright despite everything else that's happened over the past six hours. "Ari …" I breathe.

"Don't get me wrong," she cuts in. "I'll hang around and check in on you and Addie when she wakes up, but I can't bring myself to face him yet. It's too hard. I'll just creep in the corridors, hoping I hear some kind of update."

I take her hand and give it a tight squeeze, hating how much she's hurting. "I'm sorry," I whisper. "He just needs some time to realize what he's missing. I'm sure he'll—"

Three short raps at the open door have my head craning around Arizona's shoulder to find two policemen crowding my doorway. "Brielle, is it?" the one on the right questions as they welcome themselves into my room.

My gaze briefly flicks toward Tanner before returning to the cop. "Yes," I say, the hesitation clear in my voice. "Can I help you?"

"You can," he says. "However, not right at this moment. We'll be back to take your statement in a little while. You've only just woken up from surgery. I'm sure the last thing you want to be doing is talking to us."

"Okay," I say slowly, noticing the way the other cop watches Tanner with a close eye. "Then what can I do for you?"

"Nothing," he says, turning his sharp stare toward Tanner. "It's what he can do for us. Are you Tanner Morgan?"

Tanner pushes off the wall, not liking the harsh bite in the cop's tone. "Why do you need to know?"

"Come on, Tanner," the second cop says. "Let's not make this harder than it needs to be. It's after five in the morning and the last thing we want to be doing is dragging you out of here in cuffs. We have multiple witnesses who claim you were involved with the assault of Colby Jacobs. We just need to have a chat. That's all."

Tanner glances back at me, holding my stare a moment longer before pursing his lips and letting out a deep breath. "I'll just be out in the hallway," he tells me. "If you need anything, just call out and I'll come right back in."

"I'll be okay," I tell him, holding his stare and sending a silent message, reminding him that he did nothing wrong. "I love you."

"You too," he says, giving me a tight smile before following the policemen out of the room.

The moment he disappears out the door, nerves break through the surface, and I grip onto the bed sheets, bunching them in tight fists as I turn my terrified stare to Arizona. "It's going to be okay," she says, reaching out and taking my hand, forcing me to release my hold on the sheets. "There were hundreds of people there. They know Colby was in the wrong. Tanner's going to be okay, and like they said, they just want to talk. They're probably just taking his statement and getting a clear picture of what happened."

Knowing she's right, I try to breathe, but it doesn't stop the panic from overwhelming my every thought. Despite everything that's happened over the past few months, I feel like a lost child, way in over her head, needing her mom to hold her and tell her everything will be okay.

"Do you think …" I pull myself up short as a cringe settles across my face, not sure if this is what I really want.

"What's wrong?" Arizona asks. "What do you need?"

"I was going to ask if maybe you could ask my mom to come in, but I … I don't know. Things are still weird between us, and she'll probably only start ranting at me about making shitty decisions and then probably blame the whole thing on me, but …" I pause again, indecision plaguing me. "You know that feeling when you're having a really awful time and all you need is your mom to hold you and tell you that everything is going to be alright?"

"Yeah, I know the feeling," she tells me, her lips pressing into a hard line as her eyes flicker with a strange guilt, holding something back.

"What?" I ask. "What is it?"

"I'm sorry, Bri," she says, gripping my hand a little tighter. "Tanner called your mom, but she never showed up."

"She didn't come?" I ask, disbelief hitting me like a fucking freight train. I know things are messed up right now, but surely she'd still show up for me. Surely the past eighteen years have meant more to her than this. "Are you sure?"

Arizona gives me a broken stare. "Girl, I'm sorry," she says, pushing up from the chair and dropping her ass to the mattress. "Your mom doesn't know how lucky she is to have you. One of these days, she'll realize exactly what it is she's been pushing away. Until then, you've got me. Now scoot your bitch-ass over so I can snuggle with you until you pass out."

Without another second of warning, Arizona pushes in beside me, under the blankets and all. Her arm slips beneath my neck the same way Tanner's does, and she pulls me into her, holding me close, not giving two shits about the stab wound that's all too close to my nether regions for my liking.

Letting out a broken sigh, I cry into her shoulder, wishing desperately that things could be different.

CHAPTER 3
TANNER

The door of the hospital conference room closes behind me as the cop with the staring issue indicates for me to take a seat. It's a far cry from the corridor I told Bri I'd be in, and it makes me wonder if these assholes plan on having a little more than just a friendly chat. Why else would they bring me into a private room? The cops of Bradford aren't exactly known for being the forgiving type.

Taking my seat, I watch the two cops as they strategically place themselves around me, blocking the exits while also keeping a firm eye on me. Though I can't blame them. They know what I did. Why else would I be here? They have a right to treat me like a fucking criminal. That's exactly what I am.

The bigger of the two—the one who looks like he's running the show—pulls out a chair and takes a seat. He silently watches me, and I can only imagine the bullshit running through his head. I'm nothing more than a delinquent teenager who's had everything handed to him. Why the fuck should he take it easy on me? I'm probably the next bastard in a long line of assholes he plans to make an example out of.

"This doesn't need to be any harder than it already is, Tanner," he starts in a gruff, dismissive tone, placing a recording device in the center of the table. "If you're up front and honest with us, then this will be quick, and you can get back to caring for your girlfriend." He pauses a moment, waiting for me to acknowledge him, but I remain silent. "I'm Detective Daniels and this is Officer Kennedy. We will be conducting this interview and it will be recorded. Do you understand?"

"Yes." I press my lips into a hard line, not liking this one bit, but I fucking killed a guy. This was never going to be easy. "What do you want to know?" I ask, wanting to get back to Bri. "I've got nothing to hide."

"We have witnesses who place you at the scene," Daniels says. "Others who claim you're responsible for putting Colby Jacobs in a coma."

My back stiffens, and my eyes widen in shock. "Coma?" I question, my heart racing a million miles an hour, a strange hope blasting through my veins—the kind of hope Colby doesn't deserve. "I thought he was dead."

"It was close," he says as his partner hovers nearby, watching me like a hawk. "Colby sustained significant injuries to the brain. He's been put into a medically induced coma until the swelling on his brain can recede and the doctors can assess him properly. However, there is a very good chance that he is brain dead."

"So, what you're telling me is, whether he's breathing or not, I fucking killed him."

Officer Kennedy leans forward against the conference table, getting closer. "So you admit you did it?"

"What did you want me to say?" I question, resisting the urge to lunge forward and knock the fucker out. "You already told me there were witnesses who placed me at the scene. You know damn well I was involved. Would you have preferred I lied? What's the fucking point? You have statements from hundreds of witnesses, and it's their words against mine."

Daniels clears his throat and forces my attention back to him. "No, I appreciate your honesty," he says, trying to keep control of what could potentially turn into an ugly situation. "Don't be fooled, we know exactly who you are, Tanner, and we know all about your connection to Colby Jacobs. We're just trying to get a sound understanding of what happened last night."

"Okay," I say slowly, not wanting to trust this false sense of security. "What do you want to know?"

"Start from the beginning. What were you doing there last night?"

"It's my cousin's property," I explain. "We go there every Friday night to let off steam. Fuck around and have a few drinks. Shit like that. Everybody comes. It's always a big party."

"Oh, we are well aware of your Friday night parties at the Morgan property, and we are more than aware of what actually goes on there," he says, a disapproving darkness in his eyes. "However, that seems irrelevant right now. Can you recall where you were when Colby showed up? Time? Location? Any kind of details."

"My girl and I," I say, remembering exactly what happened in those woods in fine detail, "were talking on the outskirts of the property. A few of my friends had an argument and everyone needed a moment to chill out. It was maybe eleven when we started walking back and heard everyone screaming. I thought someone must have been shot or something. Everyone was running, not watching where they were going. I've never seen anything like it. Bri got body slammed and I was barely able to hold on to her, but I needed to get back to my friends and my sister to make sure they were okay."

"You didn't run for your car to get out of there?"

My brows furrow, not understanding his train of thought. "Like I said, my sister and friends were there. I wasn't about to leave without making sure they were safe. They're the only family I've got."

"Very honorable," he says, though the lack of conviction in his tone suggests he thinks I'm full of shit. "What happened next?"

"Bri and I ran through the crowd and we were just making our way back up the hill when we found Colby. He had a knife in his right hand, and it was already coated in blood. He was talking shit to my cousins, Jax and Logan, and they were trying to calm the situation, but Colby wasn't having it. His back was to us, and at this stage, he didn't know Bri and I were there. He was too busy making demands."

Officer Kennedy crosses his arms over his chest. "What kind of demands?"

I shrug my shoulders. "The usual bullshit," I say. "He was saying he wasn't leaving until my friends told him where *'she'* was."

"She?"

"Yeah. He said *she,* and I assumed he meant my sister, Addison. Colby made plenty of promises that he was going to come for her after the rape charges were dismissed. We've been walking on eggshells every fucking day, just waiting for that bastard to step out of the shadows. So when he said *she,* I figured he was looking for her, and so did Riley because he told Colby that he'll never give Addison up to him. That's when Colby laughed and was taunting him that he'd already dealt with Addison and was saying how fucking easy it'd been."

My hands ball into tight fists at the memory, but Daniels' sharp tone cuts through the room like Colby's knife slicing through Jax's stomach. "What were his exact words?"

My nails dig into the palm of my hand, and I try to control the rage just to get through this fucked-up interrogation. "When Riley said he'll never give up Addison, Colby laughed and said *'That bitch? Oh, I'm already through with her. She was easy then, and easy now.'*"

The cops glance at one another, their expressions impossible to read. "Right," Daniels says. "And when Colby referred to a *'she',* who was he looking for?"

"My girlfriend, Brielle," I say. "They used to date when she went to Hope Falls. He's had it out for her since the second she dumped his ass. In some fucked-up way, he blames Bri for pushing Erica to go to the cops about him raping my sister. Not that she went to the cops with the fucking truth."

"Colby Jacobs was cleared of the rape of your sister."

I scoff. "Only because his lawyer is a dirty piece of shit who messed with the rape kit."

"Do you have evidence of this?" he questions.

I press my lips into a hard line and shake my head. "No, sir."

He stares back at me, his dark eyes like a mask concealing the demons inside. "That's a very serious accusation, Mr. Morgan."

I stare right back at him, letting him see just how far I'll go for this. "I know."

The silence in the room could fucking kill me as we remain locked in each other's feral stares. "You're speaking of Orlando Channing. The top criminal defense lawyer in the country, your neighbor, and your girlfriend's new stepfather," he says. "Are you sure you're not acting out due to personal differences? Perhaps he doesn't approve of your relationship with his daughter."

"Stepdaughter," I clarify. "And you're damn right it's personal. The guy is the dirtiest fucking lawyer I've ever met. He allowed my sister's rapist to walk free for the purpose of his own fucking ego, the little girl next door who he's watched grow and mature into a beautiful young woman. It's because of him that last night even happened. If he hadn't stood in the way of true justice, Colby would have been behind bars, awaiting trial while my sister, girlfriend, and cousin wouldn't be suffering in this goddamn hospital—"

"And Colby wouldn't have been beaten to a pulp, suffering severe brain injuries and in an induced coma," Officer Kennedy says.

"And if Colby hadn't come onto private property with a fucking knife, he wouldn't be in his current situation either," I throw right back at him.

"Okay, okay," Daniels says, holding out his hands. "We're getting off track. Let's rewind and take this back to last night. You were saying how Colby was looking for Brielle and had just alluded to the fact that he'd hurt your sister."

"Yes."

"Are there other witnesses who can confirm what Colby said?"

"Yes. There were a bunch of people. Jaxon, Logan. My friend Hudson, and Brielle's friends were there too. They all heard it."

"Okay," he says. "Go on. What happened after that?"

"It's a bit of a blur after that. All I could think about was my sister. If she was alive, where she was, and if he'd really hurt her like he'd done before. I think I yelled or said something because Colby turned around and saw me with Bri and he started running at us—at her—and I couldn't let him hurt another person I loved. I was ready to take him out, but Jax was closer and lunged at him. He tried to drag him back, but Colby took him down. It happened so fast. One minute he was there trying to save everybody, and the next thing I know, everyone was screaming and blood was covering Jax's shirt.

"Bri was pulling on my arm, and I think I pushed her away. Maybe that was later, I don't know. All I know is, Colby was coming for us, and I had to protect her. I took him to the ground, and at some point, Hudson went to find Addison, but it's all a blur. Colby was still swinging his knife, trying to get me off him and I think he nicked me.

It wasn't until he'd stopped moving and I was running back down the hill to check on my sister that I realized Brielle had been hurt as well. She fell into the grass and I ... I couldn't help everybody. They were all dying and there was nothing I could do to help them."

"Everybody survived," Detective Daniels says, watching as the trauma of the night plays on my mind. "You did what you had to do."

I stare at the table, wishing to be anywhere but here. "What's going to happen from here?"

"At this stage, it's too early to give you any definite answers. Statements and evidence need to be collected. However, from where I'm sitting, it is a self-defense case. With so many people on the property, I'm sure there are enough witnesses to corroborate your story, and I wouldn't be surprised if video footage showed up."

"And if Colby dies?"

"That complicates things," he says, pushing back out of his seat and standing. "For now, sit tight. This is a very messy situation you've gotten yourself into, and I don't think I need to tell you the implications if you were to run from this."

"I'm not going anywhere."

"See to it that you don't," he says, nodding to Officer Kennedy, who reaches across the table and scoops up the recording device. "I'm sure we'll be seeing a lot of each other. In the meantime, let's hope this doesn't turn into a murder case."

And with that, Daniels and Kennedy walk out the door, leaving me staring after them, unsure what to make of everything that just happened. Though one thing is for sure—Colby Jacobs still lives, and until his heart stops beating, I won't stop fighting for justice. And if that justice never comes, the whole world will feel my wrath.

CHAPTER 4
Brielle

Gripping my stomach and my drip, I try to pull myself up off the toilet for the tenth time in the last fifteen minutes.

It's useless. I'm going to die on this toilet. I've been bursting to pee all morning, but apparently getting onto the toilet isn't nearly as hard as trying to pull myself off it again. Who would have known getting stabbed isn't nearly as bad as caring for it the next twenty-four hours after?

The hospital kicked Tanner out twenty minutes ago when he started to look like the walking dead, insisting he get some rest, and as much as I love the idiot, I couldn't wait for him to go. Pretending I didn't need to pee all morning is a crap load harder than it ought to be. It's stupid, I know, but Tanner still thinks I'm a sexy, deviant goddess.

I don't want him witnessing my toilet habits quite so soon, and I know damn well he would have demanded to take me.

If only I weren't so stubborn. A normal person in my predicament would have pressed the big, red *for-the-love-of-God-someone-please-help-me* button that's conveniently placed on the wall right next to the toilet paper.

Fuck my life. How did I get here?

I've been out of my bed for long enough, and at some point, I'm either going to tear my stitches or somebody will walk in to witness my humiliation, and knowing my luck, it'll probably be Riley. The asshole has been non-stop messaging me all day, wondering what the deal is with my ass cherry. It's his messed-up little way to let me know he's thinking of me, but the joke's on him. My ass cherry was popped long ago, I just wish it wasn't. The whole ordeal wasn't pretty, and I was way too underprepared for a monster like that. It only happened once, but my ass never forgave me. I said it at the track as a joke to help calm Tanner down, but now the more it's mentioned, the more my curiosity is piqued.

Shit. I shouldn't be thinking about ass stuff while stuck on the toilet.

Giving it another try, I suck in a breath and prepare myself for toilet domination … fuck, no. That doesn't sound right. Unless someone feels like shoving laxatives down my throat, there will be no toilet domination today.

Planting my feet firmly on either side of the bowl and gripping the drip, I clench my eyes and give it one last try, hauling myself up and feeling as though all my guts and insides are about to come falling out of my stab wound. "Holy fuck," I breathe, wobbling on my feet and using the wall to keep me upright.

Maybe it's time for more painkillers.

After struggling through washing my hands, I finally get out of the bathroom, only for my whole world to crash and burn once again. My mom and Orlando crowd my room as though they have every right to be here, and the irritation I feel at seeing both their faces is like nothing I've ever known.

I should have let the toilet end me.

My jaw clenches as their heavy stares fall on me. "Now you decide to show up?" I mutter, gripping tighter onto the pole of the drip, wondering what kind of weapon it could make as I studiously ignore the way my mom wears her despair on her sleeve. I mean, damn. If she wanted to care about me, the time for that has passed.

"You honestly think anything in the world is going to keep me from seeing my daughter?" Mom questions, as if horrified by the very thought of not being able to see me in the flesh.

Dropping my ass to the edge of my bed, I try to scoot back into my spot and get comfortable. "Well, the sun certainly did. Tanner said he called you hours ago. I was looking for you and you weren't here," I tell her, unable to hide the pain in my voice. "The one time I really needed you, and you weren't here."

"Oh, honey," Mom says, walking around the side of my bed to perch her ass beside me. She finds my hands and scoops them into hers, holding them tight. "It's not like that at all. You know I would have dropped everything to be here with you. I've never been so scared in my life. I thought I was losing you."

Pulling my hands out of hers, I look away, unable to handle the pain in her eyes. It's so fake, so forced, and it only makes it hurt that much more. "Talk all you want, Mom. You can tell me how you would have dropped everything to be here until you're blue in the face, but the fact is, you didn't. You weren't here."

"Bri—"

"No," I say, hating how obvious I am about how much her absence has hurt me. "Have you ever been stabbed, Mom? Have you ever laid in the grass bleeding out? I thought I was going to die. I've never been so scared in my life, and all I needed was to wake up and have you here, but you let me down. Again. You were supposed to be my family, but that means nothing to you now, does it? You've got the fancy husband and the fancy car. Money, mansion, designer clothes—nothing else matters to you anymore."

Mom stands, gaping at me as though she can't believe the words coming out of my mouth. "How dare you say that," she whispers, her hand pressing to her lips as she tries to hide just how horrified she is. But hell, actions speak so much louder than words.

"Where were you when Colby wrapped my car around that tree, huh?" I ask. "I sure as hell didn't see you by my hospital bed then. Or what about when Erica and Colby had me arrested on rape charges? *Rape, Mom.* I didn't see you in the precinct demanding my release. Hell, all I saw was your palm across my face. You believed every one of their lies. How could you do that to me? You believed the word of a rapist over your own daughter. You've remained with a man who would rather help a rapist walk free than defend your daughter."

Mom shakes her head, tears welling in her eyes. "You don't understand."

"I understand perfectly well," I tell her, the remaining shards of my shattered heart turning black with poison. "You made your decision, and it wasn't me."

"That's enough out of you," Orlando says, stepping closer to my mother. "How dare you speak to your mother like that. Can you not see how much she's hurting over all of this?"

I groan, my sharp gaze slicing toward Orlando. "Oh, fuck off, leech. Get out of my room. You're not welcome here."

"Considering I'm the one paying your hospital bills, I dare say I am. Now, apologize to your mother this minute."

"Or what?" I question, my voice lowering and filling with venom, a clear warning not to fucking cross me. "You'll cut me off? Kick me out of your stupid mansion? News flash, I don't need that shit to survive. I'm not my mother. I don't need cars and a fucking mansion to feel validated. I already have everything I need."

Orlando laughs. "You mean the boy next door? Tanner Morgan?" he questions. "He's a delinquent child with an aversion to authority. Do you honestly think he's going to stick around? I've watched that boy go from girl to girl. You're nothing but a whore keeping his bed warm until the next one comes along."

My jaw clenches, but instead of falling victim to his bait, I turn my gaze back toward my mother. "I guess we have something in common after all."

Mom gasps and stumbles back a few steps as though my words physically assaulted her. "What did you just call me?"

"Nothing that your husband didn't call me first, but that wasn't a big deal, was it?" I ask her before glancing back at Orlando. "For what it's worth, that delinquent child is the only reason I'm alive right now. Without him, I'd be rotting in the morgue. If you insult him again, I'll take it as a personal attack against me. And next time, I won't be so forgiving."

Orlando throws his hands up in frustration. "How blind are you, girl? Tanner Morgan is the reason you're in this mess in the first place. He and his whore of a sister. If he hadn't retaliated at the courthouse, none of this would have happened. Colby would not have felt the need to take matters into his own hands. Your blood is on his hands."

My eyes bug out of my head. "Excuse me?" I spit, pushing myself up in my bed, not giving two shits about the pain coursing through my body. "You want to blame Tanner for the fact Colby couldn't control his need to pick up a knife and slaughter anyone in his way? Do you even hear yourself speak?" I gape at my mother, unable to fathom how she can stand by his side through all of this. "Honestly, Mom? You're throwing away the last eighteen years to be with *that*? What is wrong with you?"

"Honey, I—"

"No, I don't want to hear your bullshit excuses. I'm done with you. You've had chance after chance, and I'm not hanging out to watch you fuck it up again. You're on your own," I say, looking back at Orlando, not nearly done with his bitch-ass. "But if you want to play the blame game, then let's go ahead and blame the asshole who let Colby walk free in the first place. If it weren't for you, Colby would be locked up, right where he belongs. Your fucked-up ego is the reason two of my best friends spent the night fighting for their lives, one of them being a fucking minor. *A child.*"

"Colby was cleared of all charges."

I scoff. "No, you messed with the rape kit and forced the judge's hand. Colby is not an innocent man, and if his parents don't pull the fucking plug, I sure as fuck will."

"Brielle," my mother spits. "Don't you talk like that."

"Just get out," I tell them both. "I don't want you here."

"No," Mom says, giving a firm shake of her head, tears streaming down her face. "I'm not going anywhere. You're my daughter, and I will stay as long as it takes."

"You misunderstood me, Mother. There's no amount of time you can stand at my bedside—pretending you give a shit—that's going to fix this. I'm done. I don't want anything to do with you. You've chosen him one too many times. Congratulations, I'm officially broken, now please leave. I'm not asking again."

Orlando steps closer, his eyes filled with a sickening venom. "Watch your mouth, girl," he says. "I pay for your whole lifestyle. Your school, your hospital fees, the food you eat. With just a click of my fingers, it could all be gone."

I grin back at the fucker, more than ready to take him up on his offer when my door swings open with a ferocious *BANG*, the handle slamming against the drywall. "She asked you to leave," Addie spits, the anger in her eyes like nothing I've ever seen as she clutches onto the pole for her drip, barely able to stand. "Now get the fuck out before I'm forced to call security."

My eyes widen, horror rocking through my body. She shouldn't be out of bed, not even for a moment, and especially not after suffering a punctured lung. Is she out of her goddamn mind? My mouth drops as I prepare to bitch her ass out, but the scathing stare she sends me is a warning to keep my mouth shut.

"I'm waiting," she says, glancing between Mom and Orlando, her brow raising with impatience as she steps out of the doorway, making space.

Seeing Orlando's indecision as he looks back at my mother, a smug as fuck grin cuts across my face. "Come, Cora. We will deal with this when your daughter returns home."

Like hell.

Mom looks between me and Addie before turning back to Orlando. "But—"

"NOW," he demands, that one syllable turning his face red with anger.

Mom whimpers and walks out of the room, unaware of how much easier it is to breathe without her here. Orlando spares me one last scathing stare before finally following Mom out the door, and I don't miss the way Addison shrinks back, trying to keep as far away from the asshole as possible.

Once he steps through the doorway, Addison turns and steps out behind him, her voice echoing up the hospital corridor. "Oh, and go ahead and cut her off, asshole. You know damn well my family has the means to support her. Brielle doesn't need you and neither does the rest of the world. Go and drown yourself. The world would be a better place without you in it."

Without waiting for a reply, she steps back into my room and slams the door shut before immediately collapsing against it. Panic soars through my chest as I prepare to throw myself out of my bed, but she holds up a hand, letting me know she's okay. "Oh. My. God. You're an idiot. What the hell are you doing?" I demand.

"What does it look like I'm doing?" she grumbles, taking a few calming breaths through the pain. "You clearly weren't getting the job done on your own."

"You should be in bed."

Addison grips her drip tighter before finally pushing off the door and walking across my room, trying to keep the grimace off her face. "Yeah … I'm not going to make it all the way back to my room," she says, reaching the end of my bed and falling against it. "Shove over."

Gripping the side of my bed, I heave myself over, the pain in my abdomen almost enough to make me wish I were dead. "Sure thing," Addie mutters. "Take your time, why don't you? Just suffering a punctured lung here, but it's fine. I'll wait."

Rolling my eyes, I pull the blankets back and she slides in beside me. I help as much as I can, but between the two of us, we're pretty much useless.

After what feels like a lifetime, she finally settles beside me and we're both as comfortable as we're ever going to get, only the heavy silence in the room is going to kill us both. "Addie," I say, my gaze slowly meeting hers. I swallow hard, the haunting knowledge of what she's been through crushing my chest from the inside out. "Are you okay?"

Her lips flinch and move as she tries to figure out how to word her response, and after a short pause, she finally shakes her head. "I don't think so," she whispers, the hollowness in her gaze killing me. "Up until last night, I thought I was going to be okay. The nightmares were going away, and that dirty, unclean feeling was starting to fade. I think maybe that has something to do with Hudson, but when I saw Colby last night … I just … I don't think I'm ever going to be okay."

Tears well in her eyes, and I pull her closer. "Whatever you need, I've got your back."

"Will you go into his room and finish what Tanner started?"

"If that's what you need," I tell her. "But you know we're gonna get caught, right? Even the best ski masks aren't going to disguise our gimpy asses crawling down the hall. I don't know about you, but I won't be able to pull off a jumpsuit."

"Speak for yourself," she says. "I'd look bomb in a jumpsuit."

I laugh and she relaxes again, up until broken, pained words fall from her lips. "Tanner hasn't been brave enough to ask, and I … I don't really want to talk to him about it, but will you tell him that Colby didn't, you know … rape me again."

Relief pounds through my body and my eyes close for a moment. "Oh, thank God," I say. "I know they said your clothes had been torn, but I wasn't sure. I've been so worried about you, and yes, of course I'll let Tanner know."

"Thank you," she whispers, and a tear falls and splashes against my arm. "It happened so fast. One second I was coming out of the bathroom, and the next, he was there. He pushed me back in, and when I saw the knife, I just ... I froze. I didn't know what to do. He started grabbing at me and saying something, but I was too scared to make out the words. I think I fought back. He was getting so angry and then he panicked when someone walked in. He stabbed me right through the chest and took off."

"I'm so sorry, Addie," I say, tears hot on my cheeks. "I hate that you're hurt again. It should never have happened. I should have gone to the bathroom with you, or ... I don't know. I just wish I'd done something more to protect you."

"It's not your job to protect me, Bri," she says. "I knew the risks of walking away, and I did it anyway. I thought I would be fine and that's on me. Besides, Colby is just a dumb jock and clearly knows nothing about the human body. He took swipes at you, me, and Jax, and couldn't take a single one of us out."

"Addie," I say, not approving of her *shrug-it-off* attitude.

"What?" she says. "I'm fine. It's barely a scratch."

"You and I both know it's not just a scratch, just like me nearly not being able to shit isn't just a scratch. It's okay to be scared, and it's okay to acknowledge that he hurt you. He hurt me too."

Addie lets out a heavy sigh and glances toward the door, gripping my hand like it's her only lifeline. "Does it make me a bad person for hoping he dies?"

I shake my head. "If it does, then that makes me a bad person too."

CHAPTER 5

TANNER

Pushing through the door of Jax's room, I come to a stop, finding it completely empty, bed and all. "What the fuck?" I mutter, stepping back out and double-checking the numbers on the door.

I'm definitely in the right room, so where the fuck is he, and why is his whole-ass bed missing?

Pulling my phone out of my pocket, I check that I haven't missed any updates from Logan and start to panic that he's been taken into surgery again. If that were the case, Logan would have said something, and he'd be in this room right now, pacing like crazy.

Moving back out into the corridor, I unlock the screen and click on Logan's name. As it rings, I make my way to the nurses' station, ready to hit them with a million and one questions about the whereabouts of my cousin, but when I get there, the desk is empty.

The phone rings in my ear, and as I wait impatiently for Logan to accept my call, I let out an exhausted huff. It's barely been eighteen hours since Colby's attack, and despite my mother's objections, I haven't had a wink of sleep. I know everybody is safe and healing, but it does nothing to stop the fear from rattling through my empty chest. Every time I close my eyes, all I see is Addison hanging limp in Hudson's arms or Brielle falling onto the grass, begging me not to let her die. And then there's Jax, my cousin and one of my best friends since the day he was born. I'll never be able to forget the image of Logan hovering over him, his hands pressed to his twin brother's torso as blood escaped between his fingers. I can still hear the agony in his voice as he screamed for his brother to make it.

Colby deserved so much worse than what he got.

A moral part of me is relieved I didn't kill the asshole, but the part of me that so fiercely loves my sister, Jax, and Bri, desperately wishes I'd finished the job.

Logan accepts my call. "Yo, what's up?" he groans into the phone.

"Were you sleeping?"

"Trying to."

"Shit. Sorry, man," I mutter, scanning up and down the hallways, positive Jax probably slipped into some girl's room and is trying to get laid, even while on his deathbed.

"It's fine. What's up?"

"Do you know where your bro—" I cut myself off, seeing a

familiar bare ass hurrying down the corridor, pushing his bed and trying to navigate around the obstacles lining the hall. Letting out a sigh, I shake my head, unable to grin at his ridiculous performance. "Don't worry. Found him."

"Found him?" Logan questions. "What do you mean, *found him*? Where the fuck did he go, and why is he not in his room?"

"Good fucking question," I mutter, following Jax down the hall, my curiosity piqued. "I'll let you know when I figure it out."

Logan sighs, knowing his brother all too well. "Yeah, alright. Just don't let him do anything stupid. He only woke up from surgery six hours ago. Knowing him, the idiot will bust open his stitches and end up with a fatal infection. Besides, Dad's flight will be here soon, and that's exactly the type of shit Jax would pull when he's there. Fucking idiot," Logan continues, almost as if talking to himself now. "Always pulling fucked-up stunts at the worst possible times. It's shit like this that'll get my Camaro confiscated."

I laugh, watching as Jax pauses at the corner, peering around it to make sure the coast is clear before forging ahead. The way he sidesteps gives me a clear view of his dick and balls hanging between his legs through the back of his open hospital gown.

Logan is right. He really is a fucking idiot.

"Fucking hell, man. You planning on coming down here with your dad?"

"Yeah, why?"

"Bring the fucker a pair of boxers why don't you?"

"Ahhh, fucking hell," Logan mutters. "Don't tell me he's swinging his dick around for that hot nurse again? He already asked her for a sponge bath."

"Why am I not fucking surprised?" I say, rolling my eyes. "I'll let you know what's going on when I figure this shit out."

"Alright, man," Logan says before ending the call, hopefully to have a few more hours of sleep before coming back here again.

Concentrating on the mystery before me, I follow Jax around the corner, wishing I could look away from the train wreck before me, but I just can't. It's like I've been hypnotized by his swinging dick. Left. Right. Left. Right.

When will this torture end?

By the time he gets around the next two corners, I know exactly where he's going. When he darts in front of his bed to open Brielle's door, I almost step in, but my curiosity wins out, and I sit back to watch the show.

He's clearly taken one too many hits on the field because he doesn't think to open both doors, just tries to ram his bed through the tight gap like he's going in raw with no preparation, a lesson I figured Jax would have learned a long time ago. The side of his bed catches on the door, but despite all the noise he's making, not a single nurse has come to check what the hell is going on.

Figuring I better help him before he gets us all thrown out of the hospital, I stride over while shaking my head. "The fuck are you doing?" I mutter, walking around him and the bed to unlock the second door.

"Oh, hey man. How long have you been there?"

"Long enough to watch your dick swing from left to right the whole way down four separate corridors. I mean, fuck. You know your hospital gown is open at the back, right? I can see your whole ass and junk right through your legs."

"No fucking way," Jax laughs, moving through the open door only to spin around and show my girl exactly what he's working with. "Yo, Bri, can you really see my ass back here?"

"Awwww fuck, Jax," Bri groans in disgust. "I can see a shitload more than just your ass. Cover yourself up or get back in your bed. I don't want to see that."

"I second that," another voice says, making my brows furrow in confusion.

"What the fuck?" I mutter, pushing right through the door and squeezing past Jax to find Addison kicked back and chilling in her bed that's been squished up next to Bri's. "What are you doing in here?" I question, scanning over her quickly to double-check she's doing alright.

"Ummm, well …" she starts. "I kinda came for a little stroll down here earlier, you know, for the sole purpose of bitching out Orlando fucking Channing, which has obviously been the highlight of my year by the way. And when the nurses told me to go back to my room, I kinda put up a fight until they realized it was just easier for us to room together."

"And Jax?" I question, shaking my head, kinda wanting to know more about this bitching out Orlando thing.

Bri shrugs her shoulders. "Jax is Jax," she explains. "We Facetimed him to check in, and when he realized we were rooming together, he got a little jealous."

"Hey," Jax grunts, trying to navigate his bed around Bri's to get it in the corner, only to keep getting it stuck on the edge, "I'm a real fucking man. I don't get jealous."

"Uh-huh," I say, going to help the idiot before he really ends up in surgery again. "Get out of the way before you break something, and while you're at it, close your fucking gown."

"What's the matter?" he quips. "Afraid your girl is gonna like it?"

Bri scoffs. "Don't get me wrong, you have a cute ass. It's nice and ... squishy, but Tanner's ass. Fuck, I could just sink my teeth into that one."

"Ummm, hello," Addison says, all but waving her hands to get our attention. "Do you guys not even see me here? This is not a conversation I want to be involved in. First off, whorebag," she says to Bri, "if we're rooming together, then any of my brother's body parts and what you want to do to them are a no-go zone. You hear me? I will bitch slap your ass into next week, and I won't even feel bad about it. And as for you, Jaxon Morgan," she says, turning her gaze on our cousin, "if you can't keep your goddamn gown closed, I'm going to make you a pair of pants out of your own goddamn skin."

Jax grins back at her. "I'd like to see you try," he says before narrowing his gaze on my girl and making his way toward his bed. "And for the record, my ass is not squishy. It's delightful. It's perfectly plump, like a nice juicy peach."

Jax walks the few steps to his bed, his exhaustion quickly closing in, and the moment his face is hidden from the girls, he drops the mask and I see just how much pain he's really in. It fucking kills me. He's never been one to let on how much pain he's in, even as a kid when he broke his leg. He was always smiling, always making jokes to ease everyone else's concerns, but he can't fool me. I won't stand for it.

"Get your ass in bed," I tell him, keeping my voice low and walking around to him, ready to help him up, though I doubt he'll let me. "You're moving too much. You're going to pop your stitches."

He leans against the edge of the bed, but as the door opens and he twists to see who it is, he doubles over in pain, mooning every last one of us. "Holy fuck," Riley says from the door, getting an eye full of not just Jax's asshole, but his junk too. "I wish someone would have warned me this was a full moon party. I would have come better prepared."

Hudson follows him in, and I'm not surprised to see Ilaria striding in a moment later. Ilaria goes straight to the girls as Hudson slinks across the room to check on Jax. But not Riley. That asshole has other plans.

He bypasses the chairs for visitors and heads straight for Bri's bed, making himself comfortable right beside her. "So, speaking of full moon parties," he says, hooking his arm over her shoulders and leaning back. "Given any extra thought to me popping that ass cherry?"

Bri stares up at him with complete adoration. At least, that's what it'll look like to him. To me, it's the face she gives me right before she's about to fuck with my day. "Actually, I have," she tells him, making his whole body tense beside her, unease flashing in his usually bright eyes. "And I think you're right. We should just do it and get it over with.

Otherwise, this desperate need I've had for you since the moment we met is never going to go away. Just one reckless, passionate night is all I need."

Riley's arm pulls back off her shoulder and he scoots just a fraction away, his gaze awkwardly swinging to me before landing back on Bri, her big, wide eyes staring up at him as though she's terrified he will break her heart. "Babe, I … I don't know what to say. I'm sorry, I … I've just been messing around to get under Tanner's skin. I wasn't intentionally leading you on. I … I thought you knew that."

Bri's face falls and for a second, the heartache in her eyes kills me. I'd give everything I have to never have her look at me like that. "What … what do you mean?" she questions, reaching out and taking his hand in hers. "I thought you wanted this. All the comments and secret glances. Don't tell me this isn't real. Can't you feel this pull between us?"

"I'm sorry, Bri. I don't," he says, pulling his hand from hers before pulling himself off the side of her bed and turning toward me, looking as though he's about ready to receive the biggest ass-whooping of all time. His hands go up, more than ready to start groveling. "Hey, man. I didn't—"

Riley cuts himself off as a wide grin cuts across my face, and as if on cue, Bri breaks out into a loud, booming laugh that has her clutching her stomach in agony.

"Wait," Riley says, looking back at Bri. "You're fucking with me?"

"How could you not tell? I'm a terrible actress."

Ilaria scoffs as she shoves Riley out of her way to take his space beside Bri on her bed. "Are you kidding?" she says, rolling her eyes. "Riley's ego is so big, he wouldn't even think to question someone confessing their need for his cock. Why do you think I work so hard at trying to knock his ego down a few pegs? It's not for my own pleasure, it's for the greater good."

The girls have barely finished laughing at Riley's expense when Chanel and Logan walk in with the twins' dad in tow. He takes one look around the room, and after eighteen years of dealing with the boys' bullshit, he thankfully doesn't bother asking what the fuck is going on. Instead, just walks over to Jax's bedside to drill him about his surgery and what's to come next. Despite how much he genuinely loves his sons, we all know he'll be back on a plane come morning, leaving the boys to figure it out themselves.

The girls talk among themselves, and when Jax's doctor strolls past the open door, he glances in and shakes his head, as though the few hours treating him is already enough to know he shouldn't have been surprised by this shit. He comes in and decides it's probably best to speak with Jax's father out in the hallway. The moment he's gone, Jax's head snaps toward the girls, a strange hesitation in his eyes. "Where's Ari?" he questions, making Bri press her lips into a hard line.

"She said she had something to do today," Bri lies, averting her gaze.

Jax's stare falls into his lap. "In other words, she didn't want to see me."

"No," Bri cuts in to save him from the heartbreak. "That's not it at all."

Chanel scoffs. "That's totally it."

Bri glares at her friend. "Really? The guy just got stabbed and nearly bled out. You couldn't just break it to him softly?"

"It's Jax," Chanel throws back at her. "He doesn't take anything softly. Hell, I don't think he even understands what softly means. He's a literal guy. You have to give it to him straight or don't give it to him at all."

I can't fault Chanel, she's right. Jax doesn't play games … Well, technically, he plays a lot of games. He loves that shit, but when it comes to something as serious as this, he needs the cold, hard truth. Tiptoeing around it isn't going to help anybody.

"You think she'll come around eventually?" Jax questions.

Chanel shakes her head. "Not unless getting stabbed has made you see the errors of your ways, and now you're ready to pull your finger out of your ass and truly be with her. She's done being nothing but a hook-up to you, and every time you treat her like one, you're breaking her just a little bit more."

"That's not fair," Jax says. "She's one of my best friends. She knows she means more to me than that."

Chanel shrugs her shoulders as I make my way to Bri's side, indicating for Ilaria to get out of my spot. "I don't know what to tell you," Chanel says. "She's hurting and needs time to heal before facing you again."

Jax sighs, and Logan takes pity on the guy and goes to sit by his side as I move to pull Bri against me carefully. "You okay?" I ask, hating seeing her stuck in this bed. Though from what I can see, having

Addison and Jax rooming with her seems to be helping them all.

"I should be asking you the same thing," she says. "Did you sleep?"

I scoff and she rolls her eyes, putting an end to that topic, each of us knowing exactly what's going through each other's heads. She lets out a frustrated sigh and pulls back to better meet my eye. "Have you heard anything more about Colby?"

I shake my head, seeing the messed up, confused emotions flickering through her bright blue eyes. She doesn't know how she's supposed to feel about this. Our whole lives, society has told us how terrible someone would be for wishing another was dead, but right now, that's all any of us want.

"I'm scared for you," she tells me.

My brows furrow and I press a kiss to her forehead. "Why?"

"You know why," she says, raising her brows to give me a pointed stare. "If he dies … it's going to mess you up."

"That's where you're wrong," I lie, knowing damn well just how right she is. "I want him gone."

"I know," she says. "But you're not a killer, Tanner. You're kind and sweet, and yes, you would do absolutely anything it takes to protect the people you love, but you're not a killer."

I nod, pulling her back in and keeping my lips on her warm skin. "It's all going to be okay," I promise her. "I swear, Bri. We'll find a way through this, and if he does die … we'll find a way through that too."

"You don't sound so sure," she says, her hand falling into mine.

"Would I make you a promise I couldn't keep?"

"I don't know," she teases "You have been known to talk shit from time to time."

Bri laughs at her own wit as I shake my head, but when a seriousness comes over her again, I glance down, meeting those eyes I'm so completely in love with. "You know at the track … when we were walking back?" she starts, nervousness flickering through her gaze. "You said there was something you wanted to talk to me about, but when everything happened, we never got a chance to talk."

Blood rushes through my veins, my heart racing with the thought of having to discuss this now. My stomach clenches and I try to give her an encouraging smile. "It's okay," I tell her. "We can talk about it once I get you home."

"Are you sure?" she questions, the heaviness of the situation reflected in her eyes, and while she has no idea what this is about, I know she's felt a difference in me ever since the courthouse. "It seemed … important."

"It is," I agree. "But nothing is more important than the people in this room and getting you all better. I swear, it's nothing that can't wait a few more days."

"Okay," she finally relents, a nervous grin pulling at the corner of her lips. "But ummm … speaking of when we get home. You and I are about to jump ahead a few years in our relationship because I'm moving in with you."

I stare down at Bri, not understanding how we got here. "Okay," I tell her. "But first, you need to explain what the fuck is going on."

Bri laughs and glances across at Addison. "Ask your sister," she says as Addie glances up and looks back at us with an awkward cringe, knowing damn well what we're talking about. "She's the one who got me cut off."

Well, shit.

CHAPTER 6
Brielle

Tanner strides into my hospital room looking like a new man, freshly showered and somewhat rested. At least that makes one of us. Addison and Jax got to go home two days ago while I've been stuck here, staring at the wall with nothing to do.

It's been a little over a week since Colby's attack at the track. To be fair, Addison and Jax only got to go home because they were able to shit … I, on the other hand, have not.

"You shit yet?" Tanner questions, giving me a stupid ass grin.

"I'm going to smack you."

Tanner laughs, and I cross my arms over my chest to sulk. Who would have known having internal trauma would have caused such a pain in my ass … literally. I've got no one to blame but myself … and

Colby, of course.

Addison and Jax had no problem shitting with everyone in the adjoining room, but apparently, I'm a little shy in that department. Jax certainly wasn't shy though. I don't know what was worse, the smell that wafted out after him, or the sounds Addison and I had to endure during it. The whole thing only got worse when I refused to take laxatives, and now, I'm regretting that decision.

Tanner sits in the chair beside my bed. "How's the pain going? Getting any better?"

"Yeah, I can move around a lot easier now, but it still sucks. Last night, I was drinking some water and it went down the wrong way. When I started coughing up my lungs, it hurt so bad I had to force myself to choke in silence."

Tanner stares at me, his face twisting with indecision. "What?" I question, my gaze narrowing on him.

"I don't know if I should laugh at you or say something to make you feel better."

Letting out a sigh, I reach for his hand and glance off toward the window. "To be honest, I'm kind of sick of people trying to say things to make me feel better. There's literally nothing anyone can say to make me feel better about my situation."

"Yeah, I know," he murmurs. "But if it helps, Logan was in charge of looking after Jax for only one night before he came knocking at my door and dumped us with Jax, so now he's moved in temporarily too."

"What?" I laugh. "How did he pull that shit with your mom?"

"Oh, he didn't," Tanner says. "Mom's always been able to see through the twins' shit, but for some reason, she has a soft spot for them. All Logan had to do was hit her with the puppy-dog-eyes. He fed her some bullshit about not being responsible enough for such a big job. Pretty sure the fucker even pinched himself just to put a tear in his eye. My mom has never caved so fast."

"Ahhh, so that's where you get it from," I tease.

Tanner rolls his eyes, but as he watches me, his brows furrow, making me hate just how easily he can see through my bullshit. "What's wrong?" he questions, those dark eyes gazing into mine as he sits forward, concern marring his face.

"Nothing," I murmur. "I'm just … done. I want to get out of here and start moving on, but every day is always the same, and since Jax and Addie left, it's just been worse. I feel like I'm trapped here with nothing but my thoughts. I mean, if I don't get discharged today, be prepared to break me out of here."

A grin pulls at the corner of Tanner's lips, and he leans nice and close, so fucking close that his lips brush over mine as he speaks. "Then take a dump, babe. It's that fucking easy. I swear, I'll wear noise canceling headphones if it'll help."

My mood plummets all over again and I shove him away. "I can't," I mutter, glancing away, knowing one little grin from him is going to send a wave of humiliation washing over me. "It's just … everything down there hurts, and what if like … I try and then the stitches break, or I accidentally move funny and the wound gets deeper and cuts right through my intestines?"

"I, uhh …" Tanner says, leaning back and running his fingers through his hair, trying to hide the smirk tearing across his face. "I don't think it works like that."

The humiliation is real. "Go away," I groan, dropping my face into my hands as my cheeks flame with embarrassment. "You're never going to think I'm sexy ever again."

Tanner outright laughs and reaches for me, attempting to pull my hands away from my face. "On the contrary," he says. "Seeing you vulnerable and needing me, while also holding tight to that smart-ass mouth of yours is the sexiest thing I've ever seen."

"Oh really?" I question. "If you have a nurse kink, just say the word. I'm sure we can find one of those sexy nurse outfits for you to wear somewhere around here. Though we might have to adjust the skirt, otherwise, your dick is going to hang out the bottom."

"And so it should be," he says. "Every nurse should have easy access to their oral thermometer."

"That's true," Nurse Kelly says, striding through the door, making my cheeks flush for a whole new reason while Tanner just sits back in his seat, looking far too proud of himself. I've become friendly with Kelly over the last few days, and it's no surprise why Jax had a ridiculous crush on the woman. She's hot as hell with a personality that could start wars between men. She's down to earth and happy to talk to me during the long-ass nights where I can't sleep, but hearing about Tanner's thermometer isn't exactly something I'd hoped she'd overhear, let alone agree with the idiot.

"So, what's going on?" she says, picking up my chart off the end of the bed and scanning over it while clicking her pen. "Do I get to send you home today?"

I cringe before giving her a guilty smirk. "Ahhhh … yes."

Kelly watches me with a narrowed stare, not believing me for one minute. "Don't you lie to me, Brielle Ashford. I have my ways of finding out, and trust me, you're not going to like it. Your boyfriend's thermometer might, though."

My cheeks flush again and I roll my eyes. "Fine," I mutter. "It's still a no-go on the evacuation."

Kelly shakes her head, not impressed with me one bit. "Do you know what these are?" she questions, pulling out a piece of paper and holding it up. She waits for me to shake my head before continuing. "They're your discharge papers. All it needs is my signature and you'll be free to go home."

I give her a blank stare as she crosses the room, shoves the papers against the wall, and uses a blob of blutack from her scrubs to pin the papers where I can see them. Kelly steps back to survey her handiwork with a proud smile. "Your ass is the only thing standing between a thorough probing and freedom. So what's it going to be, Brielle? Am I signing those papers or are we spending another long night together?"

I clench my jaw and throw my blankets back.

Fuck. My. Life.

"Atta girl," Kelly says, giving me a fake-ass grin and two thumbs up. "Unclench that asshole and the rest will be history. You'll feel like a brand-new woman."

Muttering to myself, I stop at the bathroom door and glance back at the two banes of my existence. "Are you just going to sit there and wait?"

Tanner knows better and keeps his mouth shut while Kelly grins a little more. "Damn straight we are," she says. "And for the record, it's in your best interest to make it quick. The longer you spend in there, the longer I get to ogle your man."

I send her a scathing glare before letting it slide across to Tanner. I don't need to say a damn word, he knows what's up, and being the smart man he is, he stands and rolls his eyes. "Fine. I'll go to the cafeteria and get us something to eat, but if you're not out by the time I get back, I'm coming in there and squeezing it out of you like the last drop in a tube of toothpaste."

My glare hardens and his eyes widen just a fraction before he scrambles out of his chair. A cocky smirk cuts across his face, and just before he steps out of my room, he glances back at me, laughter roaring in his dark eyes. "Go get 'em, tiger."

The bastard narrowly escapes with his life.

Ten minutes later, I stride out of the bathroom with a bounce in my step, and my gaze circles back to Kelly. Before she gets a chance to even question me, I grip the discharge papers, yank them off the wall, and shove them toward her. "Hope you got a pen hidden in those scrubs because as of this very minute, I'm a free agent."

"A free agent with clean pipes," she congratulates me.

Taking the discharge papers from me, Kelly strides around to the small wheely table beside my bed and gets busy signing for my freedom. Then just as I tear off the ridiculous hospital gown and start pulling on a pair of comfy sweatpants, Tanner comes walking back into my room, his brows furrowed, staring at the ground.

Unease settles into my stomach, and I step toward him. "What's wrong?" I question, pulling my tank over my head and searching his face.

"I was just scrolling through …" Tanner pauses and looks up at me, his whole face marred by a strange emotion I've never seen from him before, something that makes my stomach ache with anxiety. "Have you ever heard a turtle come?"

Kelly's hand stops moving over my discharge papers as we both look up at him. "What?" I breathe, the corner of my lip tugging into a crooked grin. "What the fuck have you been searching?"

Kelly finishes with my papers and hands me a copy. "Okay, I was cool with the shit talk, but turtle porn is where I draw the line," she says. "You're free to go. Just remember to keep the wound clean. I've written my personal number on the back of your papers if you have any questions. Just whatever you do, don't give it to your friend. The last thing I need is to unlock my phone and see his turtle rearing its ugly head in the middle of the night."

"Alright, deal," I laugh.

Kelly gives me a fond smile before reaching out and squeezing my shoulder. "As much as I loved having you here, try to keep away from knives in the future. They're sharp."

"Thanks," I laugh, and with that, she strides out of the room, leaving me and Tanner to finally bust out of here.

When we get to the parking lot, Tanner helps me into his Mustang, despite my attempts to do everything on my own. After finally getting my ass into the seat, we're on the road. Every tiny bump in the asphalt makes my life a living hell, and I blow my cheeks out, trying to focus on anything but the pain. Not to mention my ribs that are still causing me a bit of hell after Colby's earlier attack, though compared to this stab wound, it's barely a blip on my radar.

"You good?" Tanner asks, glancing at me from the driver's side, making everything down south ache for a whole new reason. I mean, damn, the way he works that stick shift with his opposite elbow propped on the window. Goddamn!

"Mmhmm," I say, trying to clear my throat while also not drooling on myself. "Do you know how to go around the potholes or do you get bonus points for every one you hit?"

Tanner rolls his eyes, and just to be an ass, he makes sure to hit another. Though, I don't doubt he'll be making up for it later.

Despite only being a fifteen-minute drive, it feels like a lifetime before he's finally pulling into his driveway, and my brows furrow when I see all our friends' cars parked out on the curb. "What's going on? Is there some kind of party?"

Tanner scoffs, pushing his door open. "Something like that," he says, hurrying around the front of the car to help me out. "Since Addie is here, Hudson has to be here, and with Jax claiming the downstairs living room, Logan's always here, and wherever Logan goes, Chanel follows. And you know Ilaria and Riley don't like the thought of missing out, so they've been chilling too. The only one who hasn't been taking up residence in my living room is Arizona because, well, you know why."

I nod as we make our way toward the front door, realizing the next week stuck in bed could be a little more interesting than I anticipated, but the thought of walking into Tanner's home to stay has me glancing across to the mansion next door.

My heart trembles and contracts, feeling like someone has tied a rope around it and is pulling it as tight as it can go. "Have … have you seen my mom?" I ask, trying not to let my pain show.

"Yeah," he murmurs, his hand slipping into mine. "She was there while we were packing a few of your things. I let her know you were staying with me, but she didn't respond, just walked back out."

"Oh," I sigh, my gaze falling to the ground. "I shouldn't be surpri—wait. *We?* Who's we?"

"Huh?"

"You said when *we* were packing your things."

"Oh," he says, looking all too proud of himself. "Me and Riley. He wanted to help, though come to think of it, he wasn't much help at all. He was more interested in snooping through your underwear drawer."

My eyes bug out of my head. "Tell me he didn't."

"Wish I could, babe. That asshole was strutting around in your thongs like he was preparing to walk the Victoria's Secret runway. And just for future reference, that was the exact moment your mom decided to walk in."

A long groan tears from deep in my chest, and I try to put the thought of Riley wearing my thongs to the back of my mind as we make our way inside. The noise hits me straight away, and Tanner was right, while it's just our friends here, it sounds like a raging party.

Music flows from the back room as loud chanting, shouts, and laughter attempt to drown it out.

"What the hell?" I breathe as we weave through the mansion, Tanner rolling his eyes, all too accustomed to the guys' usual bullshit.

"Welcome home," he mutters, his voice so velvety smooth as he curls his strong arm around my waist, prompting me to glance up into those dark, stormy eyes I love so much.

God, I could keep this man forever, and if he dares deny me, I'll have no choice but to lock his ass in my basement just so no other dick-stealing whore can have him.

We make our way past the kitchen to the living room when I bring myself to a stop, staring in at the chaos. "Hoooooly shit," I mutter to myself. The couches have been shoved back against the walls as three massive beds take over the room, creating some kind of temporary hospital. Addison sits cross-legged in the bed on the far left, making eyes at Hudson across the room as Jax claims residence of the middle bed, sprawled across it like he didn't just suffer a near-fatal stab wound. The third bed, the one I assume is supposed to be mine, currently has Riley standing on top of it wearing nothing but my red lace thong, his dick and balls spilling out the sides as he beats his chest like a fucking gorilla.

"Hey, if it isn't my new best friend," Riley cheers, seeing me at the door with Tanner.

He jumps from my bed and strides toward me, moving too fast for this to be comfortable. He wraps me in his big arms and thankfully doesn't squeeze. "I take it this means you finally took a dump?"

I gasp and shove him off me before glaring up at Tanner, who looks as though he doesn't know what the hell Riley's talking about. Lucky for him, Riley grabs me and starts pulling me into what will be my new shared room for the next few weeks … or until things with my mom start to improve. "Check it out, mother-fuckers, our girl is back."

Everyone cheers as I roll my eyes, but before I even have a chance to sit, Logan strides in wearing the very nurses' outfit I'd imagined for Tanner while back at the hospital. Bottles of painkillers and medications line the silver platter he holds in one hand. "Never fear," he announces, putting his other hand on his hip and posing like Superman. "Nurse Logan is here."

Riley laughs, the booming sound way too close to my ear as Chanel follows Logan in, holding a few bottles of water for the patients. They visit Addison first and start sorting out her medications, and as I perch on the edge of my bed, Riley grins at me. "I plucked a few pubes and hid them under your pillow for you," he says with a wink as my jaw drops, more than ready to burn this bed to the ground. "You know, for those long nights where Tanner just ain't doing it for you. We'll always have each other, babe."

"Thanks, Riley," I say, giving him a stupid grin as I place my hand on my chest. "You're honestly the most thoughtful person I've ever met. How would I ever survive if you weren't around?"

"I know," he says, placing a hand to my shoulder, his dick way too close to my arm. "It's a shame, but you have to learn to live without me. This fine piece of man-meat can't be held down. I'm a ladies' man, Bri. You're gonna have to learn to let go."

"It's hard," I tell him. "But I think I can do it."

"That's the spirit. You've got Tanner, and I know he's no match for the mighty dicking powers of my schlong, but he'll have to do."

"The fuck is going on over here?" Tanner questions.

Riley looks back at his best friend and gives him a tight smile. "You're a lucky man, Tanner. You've got yourself a good girl, but it's a shame you'll never be able to fuck her as deep as I could. Just remember when she's screaming your name, she's really wishing it was mine."

And with that, Riley struts away, the back of my thong long lost between his ass cheeks.

CHAPTER 7

TANNER

Don't ask me how the fuck I ended up sleeping on the couch in my own damn house when there's a perfectly good—and empty—bed right upstairs, but apparently Jax makes the rules here now, and when Bri insisted on coming upstairs with me, the fucker put his foot down. I mean, shit. He's an eighteen-year-old manwhore. He shouldn't be so worked up about wanting a fucking slumber party.

I shouldn't have been surprised. The moment this shit even had the possibility of turning into a party, Jax was all over it. I thought it was bad enough when he demanded I couldn't take Bri up to my room for the night, but when he said I couldn't even share the bed she's got down here, I was about ready to explode. The only thing I don't understand is how the fuck I ended up caving to this bullshit.

It's probably got something to do with the giant hole through his guts.

It's well past one in the morning and everyone is out cold from taking their pain meds. So, I suppose the joke is on me. There's nothing and no one stopping me from going up to my room and sleeping in my bed like a normal fucking person, yet I find myself chilling out on the couch, watching Brielle sleep.

Fuck, that kinda made me sound like a creepy stalker, but hell, it wouldn't be the first time I've stood by to watch her sleep. Only this time, it's different. I nearly lost her. I nearly lost them all. I can't even describe how grateful I am to see them all okay. Having them in the same room like this, right where I can watch over them, eases something in my chest. I know Colby is out for the count, at least for now, and I don't have to protect them like I did before, but the memories of what happened last week keep me close.

Staring up at the ceiling, I try to convince myself to go to bed upstairs when Addison starts fretting in her sleep. She kicks her legs and screams, trying to push some invisible force away. I sit up, my eyes wide as I watch her for a moment. "No, no," she cries, her head whipping from side to side. "Don't touch me. No, stop. Don't touch me."

Fuck.

She's dreaming about Colby.

"Help," she cries. "Help. Somebody, please help me."

The moment my feet hit the floor, I notice Hudson stumble off his couch from a dead sleep to get to her. He's by her side in seconds, and I freeze as he takes her hand and gently shakes her awake. The fear in his eyes is like nothing I've ever seen. It's been a week of this, every night watching her relive the worst moment of her life over and over again, and it's been slowly destroying us all.

The moment Addison was discharged from the hospital, Hudson has been here, refusing to leave her side, and I'm grateful for it. As much as I want to be her protector, it's not me she needs. But that doesn't mean I'm going to stop trying. I'll never stop.

Addison wakes a moment later, and I'm unable to tear my eyes off the two of them. Hudson wraps her in his arms, holding her tight as she nuzzles her face into his neck, and he whispers something into her ear. His hand slowly moves up and down her back and having seen enough, I take a step back and avert my gaze. As much as I want to help her, this is a private moment, and with everyone else still asleep, I can't help but feel as though I'm intruding.

Wanting to give Addie some space, I walk out of the living room and through the kitchen, but with every step I take, my control slips just a little bit more. I hate that she's going through this, and I hate it even more that no matter what I do, I can't save her from the demons inside her head. I could end Colby's miserable life a million times over, but that won't do anything to change the memories that relentlessly haunt her.

Needing some fresh air, I take off through the front door and find myself pacing the lawn, my control slipping further with each passing second. I try to rein it in, try to calm myself with slow, deep breaths, but the sound of Addison's fear circles my head, making it impossible to find peace.

I pace across the lawn until it becomes too much, and I force myself to drop down onto the grass. My elbows rest against my knees as my head falls forward. I close my eyes, doing what I can to listen to the soft sounds of the night—the leaves rustling in the breeze, the rumbling of an engine a few streets away, the sound of an owl in the distance. It goes a long way in allowing me to calm myself, or at least I thought it had until Hudson steps through the door.

My head whips around, wide-eyed and panicked. "Is she okay?"

He shrugs his shoulders as he joins me in the grass. "I don't fucking know," he mutters, his jaw clenched tight. "She won't talk to me. She allowed me to stay just long enough to calm down, but then she pushed me away. Said she wanted to be alone."

I shake my head, digging my nails into my palm. "She's so fucking stubborn," I murmur. "She needs to let us in. We can't help her like this."

"She'll come around," he tells me, his words sounding like a plea of desperation. "She has to."

"I don't know," I say, shaking my head. "She's too far gone. We barely just got her back after the first attack, and now this? Before she was only living with the memories, but now she has physical scars as well. Every time she looks in the mirror and sees it staring back at her, she'll be reminded of him. Every time her fingers brush over her scar and feel it, she'll think of him. Every fucking time, man. I can't fix this for her. I can't make it go away."

"You think you're the only one feeling like this?" Hudson throws back at me. "She's the goddamn love of my life, and I can't even make her smile. Every fucking night she dreams about what he did to her, and it kills me. I just wish … I wish she could just let me in."

My head falls forward again, and I let out a heavy breath. "I never should have let her walk away at the track. I should have gone after her."

"Why'd you even let her go, man?" he pleads. "You should have told her to stay home. I would have stayed with her. I could have protected her here."

My head snaps up, my brows furrowed with anger. "The fuck? She's my goddamn sister, not a fucking animal. I don't let her do anything. She doesn't need my approval to leave the house if she wants to go out. I'm not her fucking keeper. If you didn't want her at the track, maybe you should have asked her to fucking stay home."

"I … no," he says, shaking his head. "It's not my position to be telling her what she can and can't be doing."

"And you think it's mine?" I demand. "You know damn well had I told her to stay home, she would have found a way to be at that track and made a point of rubbing it in my face."

He continues shaking his head. "You should have tried."

"What's the matter with you? Too fucking scared she'll push you away if you tell her no? Look at you, Hudson. You're sitting out here in the fucking grass instead of comforting her inside. She's already pushing you away, and all you've done is cater to her like a fucking love-sick puppy. Grow a pair of fucking balls and stop trying to be her best friend. She's already got enough of those. She needs a fucking man who's going to protect her, not a fucking child."

Anger bursts across his face, and I see the exact moment he decides he's had enough. His jaw clenches, and he balls his hands into fists. I almost dare him to come at me faster. I fucking need this just as much as he does, and I'll be damned if I let an opportunity like this slip through my fingers.

Hudson lunges at me, and I almost welcome him with open arms. He may be one of my closest friends, but I'm not above kicking his ass, especially if he wants to start blaming me for the shit Addie is going through. This is on him just as much as it is on me. He could have gone after her when she took off at the track. He could have asked her to stay home. He could have grown a pair and asked to take her out somewhere just the two of them. Yes, I failed to protect her, but so did he.

His fist slams across my jaw, and the momentum throws me back against the grass. Before I can right myself, Hudson is on top of me. His fist comes down again, splitting my brow, and I revel in the sweet punishment, finally able to feel something. "That's all you've got?" I mock, bringing my knee up and slamming it right into the center of his back.

He roars in pain and arches back, leaving me the perfect opportunity to throw him down into the grass. I scramble to my knees and lunge for the fucker, giving him everything I've got as he fights back just as hard. Our knuckles bleed just as much as our faces do, but neither of us dares to stop, both desperate for the release this relentless punishment can offer.

It goes on and on, trading punches for punishment, only stopping when a wave of freezing water slams against our backs. "Stop fucking around and pull yourselves together," Jax says, holding the garden hose at full blast, more than disgusted by our performance. "You're gonna wake up the girls."

Hudson and I fall apart, me on my back while Hudson kneels on his hands and knees, trying to catch his breath, but Jax doesn't dare relent with the hose, holding it on us like some kind of messed up joke. He flicks it between us, hitting us both in the face and watching as we try to squirm away from it, spluttering against the cold water. "The fuck is wrong with you?" I demand, dragging my hand over my face, wiping away the water and blood while making a point of not cringing at the pain.

Jax turns the hose on Hudson's ass as he remains on his hands and knees. "What's wrong with me?" Jax questions, raising a brow. "You two are out here fucking-up each other's faces in some bullshit attempt to feel like a goddamn hero defending Addie's honor, while I've been inside, lying awake for the past four hours with a raging hard-on because I can't get off without Ari. I'm so fucking horny, even Hudson's ass looks pretty good right now."

"The fuck?" Hudson says, pushing to his feet and having to brace himself against his knees, still catching his breath.

I shake my head, sitting up as I look at Jax and see the raging hard-on he's referring to, his bullshit dilemma somehow making our fight seem so trivial now. "Turn the fucking hose off and go jerk off somewhere."

"You don't think I've tried?" he spits, aiming the hose to the ground as he twists the top, turning it off. "I've been in there trying to grab it for the past twenty minutes but all I can hear is you two bitches going at each other."

"Wait," Hudson says, turning to look at him, water dripping from his hair. "You've been trying to jerk off while lying in the bed right beside Addie? The fuck, man?"

Jax scoffs. "Don't be so fucking stupid," he says. "She's my cousin. It's not like I'm thinking about her or anything. I was looking at Bri."

"The fuck did you just say?" I demand, shooting to my feet.

"What the hell is wrong with you two? You're acting like I've been in there violating them or something. All I need is to fucking come. Weren't you listening?" he demands, his frustration getting the best of him. "I can't. No matter how much I try. I can't fucking hold it without feeling like I'm going to pass out. I'm getting to the point where it feels like it's about to fall off. I mean, fuck. Please, one of you just get on your fucking knees and suck it. I'll close my eyes. I don't even need to know which one of you did it. It's just a couple of friends having each other's backs, right? No big deal."

Hudson laughs, watching Jax as I get to my feet. "You know damn well I'm not about to put that thing in my mouth," I tell him, walking past him and pausing to grip his shoulder. "Put yourself out of your misery and call Arizona already."

"Oh yeah," Jax mocks, "because that's going to go down well. *Hey babe, I know you hate my fucking guts right now because you think I treat you like some B-grade whore, but just wondering if you could pop around to suck my dick really quick, maybe bounce on it for a minute? Mmkay, thanks."*

Hudson chokes on a laugh. "You're on your own," he says, pausing by the door just to shoot me one last venomous glare before striding back into the house and leaving us out in the wet grass.

Jax stares at me hopefully, and I shake my head, hoping like fuck he's not actually serious, but desperate men make desperate decisions. He pouts as I turn and head back inside, letting out a sigh as I go. I wish Jax's hard-on was my biggest problem right now. "Just call one of those bitches you're always fucking."

He shakes his head. "Can't," he mutters, his voice lowering as we get closer to the back room. "They don't do it for me anymore. Not since I found out how Ari feels at the lake. She's the only one I can get off with now. But I swear, if you fucking tell anyone, I'll end you."

A grin kicks up the corner of my lips, and I try not to laugh at the fucker as he follows me back into the make-shift hospital room, only to find both Addison and Brielle sitting up in their beds, glaring at me like I'm some kind of rabid animal. "What the hell did you do?" Addison screeches, grabbing a pillow and trying to launch it at me, only it falls flat with her lack of strength.

"Me?" I demand, glancing at Hudson. "He's the one who came at me. Get on his ass, not mine."

"Wait," Brielle says, looking between Hudson and me before narrowing her suspicious gaze. "You didn't start this?"

"No," I scoff. "But I sure as fuck finished it."

Hudson rolls his eyes and moves toward Addison, letting her look over him as though he's too precious to take a beating. Bri just gives me a hard stare. "Really?" she questions, not impressed at all. "Can't we just have a few days where no one gets hurt?"

Jax steps around me. "Speaking of hurt," he says, and the hint of desperation in his tone makes me want to clobber him. "I need you to call Ari and let her know I'm not going to make it through the night."

Bri gapes at him, not understanding, but I think I already know where this is going. "What the fuck are you talking about? The doctor said you were going to be fine." Her eyes cut to mine like bullets in the night. "What the hell did you do to him?"

I'm about ready to argue my innocence when Jax lets out a heavy sigh and indicates down to his junk. Bri's gaze drops and the look of disgust almost makes it worth it. "Eww, Jax. I don't want to see that shit. Go take a cold shower or something."

He lets out a heavy sigh. "I take it you're not going to call Ari then?"

Bri rolls her eyes and throws back her blankets as she looks at me. "You, come with me. I need to clean you up before you bleed all over the house."

"No, don't get up," I tell her. "I'll be fine. I can do it myself."

"Don't tell me what to do, Tanner Morgan," she says, her brow raising with the challenge. "If I want to clean your stupid ass up, then that's exactly what I'm going to do, and there's nothing you can do or say that's going to stop me."

I groan and make my way toward her, taking her hand and helping her out of bed as Hudson does the same with Addie. We start making our way toward the bathroom, but Addie cuts in front of us and shoots me a nasty glare as she blocks the entrance. "Find your own bathroom, asshole. And while you're at it, figure out how you're going to apologize to Hudson."

"Excuse me?" Bri spits, stepping in front of me and glaring daggers at my sister. "He doesn't owe anyone an apology. But Hudson sure as fuck does."

"Okay," I say, taking Bri by the shoulders and pulling her away from Addie, knowing the two of them could go at each other like this for hours. "No one owes anyone anything. We were both letting off steam. He said shit. I said shit. We beat the fuck out of each other and now we're cool." I catch Brielle's stare and hold it as she glares back at me, waiting for her anger to pass. "Alright?" I demand.

She relents for a minute before finally letting out a breath and relaxing. "Fine," she says with a huff, allowing me to take her hand and pull her away, just as Hudson does the same with Addie.

CHAPTER 8
TANNER

Brielle trails up the stairs behind me as I lead her to my private bathroom, holding her hand in case she needs me. When I open the door for her, she storms past me in search of the first aid kit. Bri opens the cupboards beneath the sink, and I step into her, taking her hips as she bends down, her firm ass pressed against my dick.

She finds the first aid kit and straightens up before turning to face me, trying to hide the cringe of pain the movement has caused. Her hand brushes against my chest as I reach down and grip her ass, lifting her to sit on the edge of the vanity. She places the first aid kit down beside her as I step in between her legs, needing to be as close as humanly possible.

Her soft gaze searches my face, looking over every little mark and bruise on my skin before dropping her stare down my body. She looks over my chest and arms before moving all the way down to my hands. Brielle takes my hand and lifts it to her lips before pressing a gentle kiss on my swollen knuckles. "You're an idiot," she tells me, lifting her gaze back to mine as her thumb gently brushes over the back of my hand.

"An irresistible idiot?" I question, the corner of my lips pulling into a dazzling smirk that she usually can't resist.

Her stare hardens and she shakes her head. "No. Just an idiot."

Well, shit. That didn't go how I'd hoped, but it doesn't stop my smile from widening. "Come on," I tell her, watching as she opens the kit and digs for what she needs. "Don't be mad at me. We were just letting off some steam."

"What were you even doing out there in the first place? It's the middle of the night."

Letting out a sigh, everything softens inside me, and I lift my hand to her cheek, gently sliding it around the back of her neck and roaming my thumb over her warm skin. "Addie was having another nightmare about Colby, so Hudson sat with her while I went outside for some fresh air, but then she wanted some space, so he came outside too. We were just frustrated. He was getting at me, so I threw it back at him. The next thing I know, his fist is in my face, and we were beating the shit out of each other."

She gives me another hard stare. "Like I said, you're an idiot. You both are. All you've achieved is giving each other black eyes."

I shrug my shoulders. "To be fair, I feel better now that I've let it all out. So, it wasn't a complete waste."

"If you needed to let off steam, you should have gone to the gym and taken it out on a punching bag."

"Nah," I say, my grin returning. "A punching bag doesn't hit back."

Bri rolls her eyes and just to make a point, she dabs antiseptic cream on my jaw and watches with delight as I squirm like a little bitch.

"Fuck, Killer. That hurts."

"Hmmm, peculiar," she says to herself. "And here I was thinking you got off on the pain. I wonder where I would have gotten that idea. Oh well." Then just like that, she dabs the damn cream on my skin again, a wicked grin cutting across her gorgeous face.

Fucking hell. This girl is going to be the end of me.

She gets me cleaned up quickly, and I have to admit, after only a few months of being together, she's become a professional at patching me up. Bri begins scrunching up the trash into a tight ball before tossing it into the empty sink and looking back at me, waiting for me to move so she can jump down, only I'm not ready to move away from her, not even close.

My hands drop to her thighs, and I push my hips in closer, her warm cunt pressed right up against my dick. "Thank you," I murmur, leaning in and dropping my lips to her neck.

A soft moan slips from between her full lips, and as if on cue, she tilts her head to the side, opening up and giving me more space to play. My tongue flicks out, roaming over her neck, moving up toward the sensitive space below her ear. She reaches up and hooks her hand around the back of my neck before sliding her fingers through my hair, her nails gently moving across my scalp. "We shouldn't," she whispers as her leg hooks around mine, becoming tangled and pulling me in closer.

My hands slowly inch up her perfect thighs as I grind against her pussy. "Why the hell not?" I question, my thick tone rumbling deep through the private bathroom.

"Everybody is downstairs. They might come looking."

"Then I hope they enjoy the show."

A soft chuckle vibrates through her chest, but as my lips continue working her neck, it quickly turns into a needy moan. "You're bad news, Tanner Morgan."

A grin pulls at the corners of my lips as my hands continue sliding higher, her body twitching and squirming with anticipation. "Then tell me to stop."

Bri groans, reaching up and gripping my face, lifting my chin to her. "Hell no." Her lips fuse to mine with erratic desperation, and I meet her there with a fiery need of my own. I kiss her deeply, my tongue plunging into her mouth as my hands finally reach the promised land. One cups her pussy to give her just the slightest bit of relief, while the other hooks into the side of her underwear and tears them down her legs, doing what I can not to jostle her too much. I know she'll tell me she's fine, but I see the way she cringes when she thinks no one is watching.

Brielle kicks her panties off her feet, her legs spreading wide as she reaches for the front of my sweatpants, her cool hand dipping inside and curling around my thick shaft. A groan rumbles through my throat, and I kiss her deeper, my hunger for her like nothing I've ever known.

Bri inches my sweatpants down past my hips, refusing to release my cock as she does. Her tight fist works up and down, her thumb curling over my tip and circling the bead of moisture waiting for her.

She pulls back from my kiss and meets my stare, making a show of releasing my cock and sucking her thumb into her mouth. She moans, and after her thumb falls from between her lips, her eyes flame with hunger as I become mesmerized by her tongue rolling over her bottom lip.

Bri reaches for my cock as I dive for her, crushing my lips against hers once again. "Fuck, Killer," I mumble against her warm mouth, gliding my fingers over her clit and making her jolt against me. I do it again and she gasps into my mouth, and I can't help but need her more.

She's like putty in my hand, willing to take anything I give her, just the way I like it.

Her grip tightens on my cock, stroking up and down as I circle her clit with my thumb. When I stretch my fingers down, she's soaking wet for me, and I don't hesitate to push two thick fingers inside, deep and fast, curling them just the way she likes.

"Oh, fuck," she grunts, tipping her head back, opening that gorgeous throat for me again. I give it to her again, watching the way her eyes roll to the back of her head, and just to be the perfect gentleman, I flick my tongue over her warm skin once more.

My fingers plunge deeper, and I swirl them around inside her, feeling her walls tighten as my thumb works her clit. I've got the perfect rhythm, driving her crazy with need, only when she reaches lower with her other hand and takes my balls firmly, I just about lose it.

"Shit, Killer. I need to fuck you."

"Shirt," she pants. "Take my shirt off. I need to feel you against me."

A chance to get those perfect tits in my mouth? Fuck, yeah.

Without a moment of hesitation, I grip the fabric and pull it over her head, throwing it toward the shower. I can't help the way my gaze drops to her toned body, seeing the bandages still across her lower stomach, reminding me that while I'm railing her into oblivion, I need to be careful.

She's fucking perfect, every man's wet dream, and those fucking tits—I could fuck them every day for the rest of my life and never get enough. God, what I wouldn't give to spurt hot cum all over them.

My fingers trail over the soft curve of her tits, but my desperation is too great, turning my gentle touch into a firm grasp as my thumb rolls over her pebbled nipple.

"Tanner, fuck," she cries, her head tilted back as my fingers plunge deep inside her again, working her just right. She draws me closer with her legs, panting with desperation. "I need you inside me," Killer begs. "Now. Please."

Fuck me. Who am I to say no?

Pulling my fingers from her throbbing cunt, I line myself up with her entrance before gripping the back of her neck. Her stare locks onto mine, both of us lost in one another's gaze, the intensity quickly building. I don't dare look away, and as I push into her, stretching her walls, she crushes her lips to mine.

Bri groans into my mouth, and I swallow the sound with a fierce eagerness.

I keep pushing, keep sinking deeper until there's nowhere left for me to go, and only then do I pause, completely succumbing to her warmth. She clenches around me and I tremble. It's like Christmas fucking morning.

"Fuck," I groan, meeting her stare. "If this is hurting, if it's too much, you need to fucking tell me now."

Bri pulls back, the wild rise and fall of her chest moving against mine. "I'm okay. It's not hurting," she promises. "But you need to start moving. I can't take it anymore."

My cock twitches inside her and I grin, more than ready to give her exactly what she's asking for.

I grab her thighs, pull her right to the edge of the counter, and push her shoulders back against the mirror, giving me the perfect view of my cock buried deep inside her cunt, while she's in a much easier position to relax. I pull back, unable to tear my stare away from the way my cock glistens with her wetness.

Bri groans at the movement and I reach between us, pressing my thumb to her clit, gently circling and preparing her for what's to come. "You ready?" I mutter, my voice deeper than usual.

She lets out a heavy breath. "Fuck me, Tanner."

Goddamn.

I slam back into her, my balls pressing against her as she gasps, her hand flying out and gripping the edge of the sink. "Oh, fuck. Yes," she pants, not a hint of pain in her raspy tone. "Again."

I give it to her again, pushing deep inside her slick heat over and over again, my cock just about ready to fucking explode. I work her harder, rubbing her clit as my thighs push her legs wider, the perfect view of her sweet cunt. Fuck, if I weren't already buried deep inside her, I'd be on my knees eating her out like a fucking buffet.

In. Out. Rub. In. Out.

It's a torturous cycle, but it's fucking everything.

Bri's walls tighten around me, and I know she's close. So, I give her more, pushing her to her limits as my fingers curl around her breast, gently pinching and watching as her whole body jolts. "Holy fuck," she cries out. "Again."

I give her exactly what she needs, watching as her eyes clench and her grip on the sink tightens. My lips kick up into a cocky grin, watching her come apart under my touch.

"You okay?" I ask with a deep grunt.

She nods, panting heavily. "I'm gonna come."

"Let me see you, Killer," I demand, my balls itching for release. "Come for me."

Her whole body spasms as her orgasm rocks through her. "Oh, fuck," she breathes, her head tipping back against the mirror as she clenches her eyes. Her walls convulse around me, squeezing me so damn tight, and it's the best fucking feeling known to man.

Her sweet cunt pushes me to my limits, but I hold on, not daring to stop until she comes down from her high, and only then do I tear out of her and shoot hot spurts of cum across her chest. She looks back at me like a fucking vixen, taking it all just as I knew she would.

My knees go fucking weak, and I catch myself against the counter, my hands falling on either side of her thighs. "Holy fuck," I breathe, unable to take my eyes off my load across her tits, slowly dripping over her nipples and down the curve of her breast. "You look good enough to eat."

"Oh yeah?" she questions, bringing her finger up and trailing it over her tits, sliding it through my cum. Her hooded gaze lifts back to mine, full of fire. "Then come and get me."

My tongue flicks out and rolls over my bottom lip, hunger already burning through my gut. I lift my hand, brushing my thumb over the soft curve of her tit, dragging it through my cum before lifting it to her mouth. She opens wide, eagerly sucking it into her mouth. "You hungry, Killer?"

"Starving," she says, her eyes burning for more.

Curling my arm around her waist, I lift her off the vanity, her body pressed firmly against mine as I walk us into the shower. Pinning her against the tiles, I kiss her deeply, then reach around her to turn on the shower.

She gasps at the cold water on her skin, and I put her down before taking her hips and spinning her around, keeping the majority of her bandages away from the water. Though let's be honest, I'm going to have to replace them after this. My chest presses to her back and I take her hands, placing them on the cool tiles as she looks back over her shoulder, watching me closely.

Taking her hips, I pull her back, bending her over until that sweet ass is up in the air. And just when I have her exactly where I want her, I drop to my knees behind her, more than ready for dessert.

Leaning in, I close my mouth over her cunt, my tongue flicking out and working her clit as my hands come to her ass cheeks, firmly squeezing before inching toward the center and pressing against her hole. She pushes back against me, and just like that, I go to fucking town, giving her exactly what she wants.

CHAPTER 9
Brielle

Two weeks.

Two long-ass, painful weeks of having my bed next to Jaxon Morgan's bed while he whines about Arizona ruining his dick.

I never thought I'd be excited to go back to school, but the second the doctor cleared us all, I couldn't have been happier. Not because that meant I was healing, but because I get to spend hours at a time without hearing about Jax's dick.

Don't get me wrong, I bet there are plenty of thirsty hoes at school who would love to hang off every word Jax says, especially when he's talking about his dick. Hell, I bet the majority of them have already spread their legs for him a time or two, but that won't be happening anymore. At least not until he can get this shit with Ari sorted. But it appears that'll never happen because she's been avoiding him like the plague.

Today should be interesting though. She can run, but she can't hide. If Jax gets her in his sights, she's screwed. Even with a hole stabbed through his liver, there's nothing she can do to evade him now. It's been torture. She blocked him on all her socials, even blocked me and Addison after he was caught stealing our phones to try and contact her. Hell, Tanner even caught him trying to steal his bike, and if it weren't for the fact he accidentally set off the alarm while trying to start it, he would have gotten away with it.

At least now things can start to go back to normal. Well, mostly.

As long as Tanner's mom will let me, I'll be staying at her place. I haven't seen or heard from my mom since she walked out of my hospital room nearly three weeks ago. Not even a quick text asking me if I was alright or checking up on how I've been healing.

I miss her, and fuck, I hate that I miss her. It makes me feel like I'm holding on to a piece of my childhood that doesn't deserve to have me. She's not the same woman I lived with in Hope Falls. She's a stranger now, and what's worse is that I don't know if the mother I love and miss even exists anymore.

Tanner drives through the student parking lot of Bradford Private and reaches across to hold my hand, feeling the eyes of the whole student body already on us. I let out a shaky breath and drop my gaze to our joined hands. I don't know why I feel so nervous about this. It's been three weeks since I was at school, plenty of time for talk to die down. Besides, Riley and Ilaria told me that most of the talk centers around Tanner and Addison. While people know most of what happened, no one has heard the story directly from any of us. There are questions that haven't been answered, and their curiosity must be killing them. I just know today is going to be hell, and it won't stop until the masses get what they want. Though they'll have to get used to disappointment, because this is something none of us will be sharing with the outside world anytime soon.

Tanner pulls his Mustang into his parking spot and cuts the engine before turning to me. "You sure you're ready for this?" he questions, knowing just how bad it's been. After all, he's been in and out of school over the past few weeks, attending just enough to keep his spot on the team and not be benched for any of the games. Though to be fair, his coach knows most of everything that's happened, and if he were to come down hard on Tanner for needing a day or two at home, I'd beat his ass into the next century.

"Not really," I admit, looking up into those deep, dark eyes. "But I have to face it at some point. Besides, all I got was a little stab wound. I doubt anyone will even notice me when Addison will be walking the halls."

Tanner's lips press into a hard line, knowing just how right I am. This isn't just Addison's first day back after being stabbed, it's her first day since Colby raped her months ago. Sure, there might be heat on me and Tanner today with questions flying left, right, and center, but it will be nothing compared to the speculation, rumors, and whispers Addison will have to face.

The very thought of what Addison will have to go through has me glancing out the window to Hudson's car, watching as she climbs out of his passenger seat. There's fear in her eyes, but there's also a strong determination. Hell, if she can survive Colby, she can survive high school. She's going to be okay. She's got both Hudson and Tanner at her back. If someone even looks at her the wrong way, the boys will be there to protect her.

"Come on," I tell him. "Let's just get it over and done with."

Tanner nods, and as we climb out of the Mustang, we find Arizona, Chanel, and Ilaria already making their way toward us. Arizona barrels into me, flinging her arms around my shoulders and locking me in her embrace. "How are you?" she questions, refusing to let me go. "Are you doing okay? Ilaria said you were healing really well, and I swear, I wanted to see you but I just … freaking Tanner. It's all his fault. If he didn't kidnap you and keep you holed up in his house for the past few weeks, I would have been able to see you."

"What?" Tanner butts in. "How the hell is this my fault? If you wanted to see her, you could have. It's not on me that you're too chicken shit to be in the same room as Jax."

Arizona's hand whips out, poking Tanner hard in the ribs. "Mind ya business, asswipe."

Tanner rolls his eyes and shakes his head before taking off toward the front gates of the school, leaving us to trail behind and continue our conversation in peace. "I'm fine," I tell her, lifting the hem of my shirt and showing off my scar. "See, it's barely even a scratch."

Tanner scoffs up ahead, but luckily he decides to keep his

comments to himself.

The girls roll their eyes at his back, and I try not to laugh at his expense. "Really though, I'm just happy to have my freedom back. Don't get me wrong, being holed up with Tanner for weeks on end, using him as my personal sex slave and butler isn't so bad, but I'm ready for life to get back to normal. Besides, if I have to spend one more day sleeping in the same room as Jax, I'm going to go insane. I don't know how you ever spent so much time with him. The guy is a basket case."

Arizona smirks before remembering she's supposed to hate him right now and presses her lips into a hard line. "How, umm … how is he?" she asks, hesitation strong in her tone. "I mean like, he's not dying or anything?"

"He'll live," I tell her. "He's healing fine, but he's super irritable. You know what he's like. He can't handle sitting around and doing nothing. It was a win being cleared to come back to school, but his doctor hasn't cleared him for exercise yet. That could still be a while. He has to take it easy, and hoooooly shit, he's pissed. It basically puts him out for the rest of the season. I heard about it all night."

Arizona cringes as Ilaria just laughs. "I do not envy you," she says. "I got locked in the closet with him in seventh grade after playing seven minutes in heaven. This was back when he was a frigid little bitch and was too scared to say the word pussy, let alone eat one, and instead of rocking my world for seven minutes straight, the idiot just talked, like non-stop to the point I had to bail early. He was literally sucking all the oxygen out of the closet, and I swore that I'd never be locked in the same room alone with him ever again. Like seriously, girl," she says, turning to Arizona. "It's not too late to reconsider this whole *wanting to be with him* thing. Honestly, I don't know how he doesn't drive you insane."

Arizona gives her a forced smile, clearly trying to hide just how much it hurts, but she won't be getting away with it that easily. After all, in her attempt to avoid Jax, she's also been avoiding me, and I won't stop until I know she's okay.

We walk up the steps and into the school before making our way down the hall and stopping at Chanel's locker. "So, how are you doing?" I ask Ari as we watch Chanel riffle through her things, looking for who the hell knows what. "You know ... after everything went down at the track?"

Ari shrugs her shoulders, her lips pulling into a sad smile. "I'm fine," she tells me. "Really. I've had a few weeks to process. As bad as it sounds, you guys getting hurt has distracted me from the whole *Jax doesn't want to be with me* thing, so it's made it a little easier. But now that you're all back, I don't think I can avoid it any longer."

"There's no way in hell," I say. "That idiot has been moping for three weeks straight. Every day he'd ask me if you were coming to visit or if I'd heard from you. I know you needed space from him to figure yourself out, but he's really missing his friend."

Ari scoffs. "He's missing getting his dick sucked."

"That too," I laugh before leaning in. "Haven't you heard?" I question, lowering my voice and watching as the idea of gossip has her eyes widening with excitement. She leans in to hear me better and a wide grin cuts across my face. "He can't get off. He hasn't been able to come since the last time you two were together. He's tried everything. At first, he was trying to rub one out, but couldn't bend or move that way because it hurt, which honestly sounds like shit to me because all he had to do was lay there and grab it. I mean, there's not that much movement involved for a guy, so I think he was trying but just couldn't, you know … finish."

Her brows shoot up and she gapes at me. "You're lying."

"Cross my heart and hope to die," I say as the girls continue up the hallway, me and Ari trailing behind. "He was desperate. I bet everything I have that his dick is red raw from going at it for days straight without a happy ending. He's been so snappy and frustrated, but I would be too if I couldn't come."

"Holy fuck."

"Yeah, the guys suggested he just find some random chick and fuck her like he always does, but he couldn't do it. The only person he wants to fuck is you. You're the chosen one, Ari. You've got the magic vag."

She rolls her eyes, her cheeks flushing the softest shade of red. "Shut up."

"No can do. It's a done deal, from here on out, you shall be known as Mag—magic vag."

We reach Ilaria's locker, and Arizona falls back against the one beside it, letting out a heavy breath. "This isn't good," she says, glancing down the hallway just in time to watch Logan and Jax walk through the doors together. Jax's eyes are already on Ari. "So, not only is he desperate to talk, but he's also horny as fuck?"

"Yep."

"I'm fucked."

"So fucked," I agree.

We cross the hall to my locker next, and I can't help but notice the way Ari hides behind us, peeking out to keep an eye on Jax as they make their way down the hall. The twins stop to meet the boys, but Jax has his sights firmly on Ari and won't be letting her escape so easily.

Hudson and Addie come from the opposite direction, stopping when they reach us, and the moment they do, I notice the whispers that follow them. Questions about why they're standing so close, what happened at the track, why she's been away so long. Hell, there are even comments from assholes suggesting she faked the whole thing.

Addie keeps her head down but, for the most part, she seems okay. "Are you okay?" I murmur, moving in closer after shutting my locker.

She shrugs her shoulders, not really wanting to talk about it. But the longer I hold her stare, the more I can read her and damn it, she's not okay at all.

"Just say the word and we can get you out of here," I tell her. "If you're not ready, we can try again next week or the week after. There's no pressure to be here."

"Yes there is," she says. "I can't keep hiding, pretending everything is fine. I need to face it to put it all behind me, otherwise, I'll never be able to move on. Even in a fucking coma, Colby still has a chokehold on me, and I'm over it. I'm sick of him having this control over my life. I'm taking it back, and if I have to beat every fucking person in this school to make it happen, I'll do it."

"Damn straight you will," I say as we shuffle along to Ari's locker, only for her to tear it open, shove her bag inside, and bolt down the hall without another word, or glance over her shoulder.

"Fuck," Jax mutters from right behind me, the guys at his back.

I let out a frustrated sigh and pin him with a hard stare. "Seriously? You couldn't just give her ten minutes of peace?"

"Please," he scoffs. "I've given her three fucking weeks of peace. How much more time does she need? We're not getting anywhere while she's avoiding me. No conversation means no progress. We're just sitting still in this awkward mess and I'm over it. I need to know what's going on in her head."

"Do you even know what's going on in your head? If she comes to you right now and says she's still crazy in love with you and wants to be together, do you know what you're going to say?"

"I … umm." He trails off as he shakes his head, having no fucking idea.

"Then leave her alone. If you can't give her a definite answer, then you have no business demanding the same from her."

Jax clenches his jaw and stares down the hallway after her. "It's not that easy, Bri."

"Put yourself in her shoes," I tell him. "She's stood by, giving you everything you wanted from her while watching from the sidelines as you've fucked around with other girls, not giving a shit about how it might affect her. Then when she finally has the courage to tell you how she feels, you shoot her down like the last few years have meant nothing, but yet you still expect her to want to fuck? You're killing her inside, Jax. If she said she needs space, then give her that space, and hope that when she's ready to come back to you, the damage you've caused to her heart wasn't bad enough to destroy the friendship."

Jax swallows hard and turns on his heel, anger bursting in his eyes. He stalks back down the corridor, whipping his hand out to slam an open locker, the loud BANG echoing through the crowded hallway.

"What was that about?" Tanner says, stepping into me, his hands taking my waist and pulling me in close.

My chin lifts and I meet his soft stare, everything inside of me melting as I sink into him, his warm body pressed right up against mine. "I think Jax just realized that Arizona's feelings matter just as much as his do."

"Shit," Tanner mutters, dipping his head to brush his lips over mine. He presses me back against the cool locker as I kiss him back, listening to the way Addison pretends to gag.

Tanner grins against my lips, and just to be an ass to his sister, he deepens the kiss, giving me exactly what I want. My hands wind up his body and curl around the back of his strong neck, holding him close, but nothing is better than when his thigh pushes between my legs and grinds against my clit.

"Get a room." Riley's booming laugh sounds through the hallway just moments before his hand flies up and smacks Tanner on the back of his head.

Tanner laughs against my lips before regrettably stepping back and taking my hand. His eyes sparkle with happiness as he looks down at me, and my whole body warms. This right here is home. I haven't seen him happy like this for a while. There's always something weighing him down, but at this very moment, nothing else matters to him.

Tanner loops our joined hands over my shoulder and pulls me in tight beside him, positioning us in a way that Addison is blocked from the students passing us in the hall. Considering what she said earlier, I really can't tell if Tanner is trying to protect Addison from their whispers or protect them from her wrath.

Logan and Chanel start bickering, and just as I roll my eyes at their performance, the bell sounds and as one, we sigh. "Come on," Tanner says, stroking his thumb over my wrist. "I'll walk you to homeroom."

Ilaria falls in beside me as everybody takes off in different directions. We follow Addison and Logan down the hall, and just as Tanner releases my hand outside the door of my homeroom, a passing comment has venom pulsing through my veins.

"Fucking whore," a guy I recognize from Tanner's team says, turning around to look back at Addison as she passes him. "I bet you wanted it, didn't you? You filthy little slut. You were frothing at the mouth. Bitches like you are always begging for it." He laughs at his own comments, clearly not having enough sense to shut his mouth. "Probably cried rape because you got caught, but we all know you were bouncing on his cock like a fucking pornstar."

Tanner tenses beside me, and my eyes widen with fear. "Tanner don't," I rush out, reaching for him in a panic, but it's already too late.

He rushes him, grabbing the fucker with ease and tossing him around like a fucking ragdoll. His back slams up against the wall before he even knows what hit him. "The fuck did you say about my sister?" Tanner growls, the sound so icy-cold it sends shivers down my spine.

Fear flashes in his eyes, knowing damn well what Tanner did to the last guy who got in his way, but the cockiness quickly comes rushing back. "Come on, man." The asshole laughs, trying to shrug it off. "I was just playing around with her. Chill out."

"Oh yeah?" he questions as Logan barrels back down the hallway, wanting to defuse what could be a really bad situation if someone doesn't intervene. "If you're just playing around, you wouldn't mind saying it to my face then."

The guy swallows hard, realizing just how much trouble he's in, and I push in beside Tanner, gripping his arm that's pressing against this asshole's throat. "Tanner, let's go," I urge him. "You're already in enough trouble."

His jaw clenches and those dark eyes flash down to me before he turns and glances down the hallway, finding Addison standing at the other end, tears streaming down her face. Agony twists in the pit of my stomach, but before I can run after her, she disappears into the crowd.

"Shit," I sigh, watching as Logan pauses, knowing damn well he needs to double back and find her, and the moment he does, a new resolve comes over me. Fuck football, fuck the cops. Addison is hurting right now, and the longer we allow assholes to get away with talking shit like this, the more it's going to hurt her.

Reaching up, I grip Tanner's chin and force his stare down to mine. He's visibly shaking with rage, barely holding on, but because I asked him not to, he's doing everything he can to hold that rage inside. "Take a breath," I tell him, keeping my stare locked on his and watching as he calms before my very eyes. "You good?"

He nods, more than ready to release the asshole back into the wild, but I shake my head, trusting him to be in control. "Now, teach him a fucking lesson," I tell him. "Let him have it."

Without another word, I take a step back, narrowly avoiding Tanner's elbow as it pulls back past my ribs. He doesn't hesitate, and like lightning, his strong fist slams into the asshole's stomach, instantly winding him.

The guy drops to the ground, groaning and gasping for air as Tanner calmly steps back and glances at me, the asshole already long forgotten as Tanner refuses to lose control. "Love you," he says, ducking his head to press a feather-soft kiss to my lips before dropping his hand to my lower back, the moment so melodic and peaceful.

He walks me right to homeroom, leaving me gaping in the doorway as he walks backward, his eyes lingering on mine and sparkling with a heat that I can only describe as animalistic. His lips kick up into a cocky smirk, and just before he turns away, the fucker winks, leaving my knees weak.

I've never been so turned on in my life. I clench my thighs while panting like a needy bitch in heat, itching to take this new, controlled version of Tanner Morgan for a wild ride.

CHAPTER 10

TANNER

The school library usually empties with the final bell, but my girl is still hard at work. I lean into a bookshelf as I watch her across the room. She's been working her ass off to finish all her missed assignments. "You ready?" I question, noticing she's the last person here apart from the librarian, Mrs. Greene, with whom I have a love-hate relationship.

Bri's head snaps up, her eyes widening in shock. "Holy crap," she says. "I didn't hear you come in. Have you been standing there long?"

I shake my head. "Nah," I tell her. "Only just came in, but had I known you were so oblivious to the world around you, I could have snuck up on you instead, maybe bent you over the desk and fucked you while Mrs. Greene went about her business, completely unaware of the filthy things I was doing to you."

A wide grin stretches across her face as she looks back at me, her brow raising, though it's not exactly the response I was expecting. She doesn't say a word but holds my gaze, her cheeks flushing as she tries to hold back a laugh.

I'm just a second from interrogating her on it when a throat clears behind me, and I whip around to find Mrs. Greene standing at my back. "I'm curious, Mr. Morgan. What exactly are these filthy things you intend to do in my library?"

My eyes bug out of my head. "I, uhmm …"

"That's what I thought," she says with a blank stare, clearly not impressed. "I suggest you get out of here before I'm forced to call your mother, and you know how that usually goes. She and I haven't had a good chat in a while."

"Yes, Mrs. Greene," I say, glancing back over my shoulder at Bri who's silently shaking with laughter as she scrambles to clean up her things. Letting out a defeated sigh, I cross to Bri's table and grab her bag before slinging it over my shoulder and taking her hand. "You got everything?"

Bri double-checks under her table and nods, allowing me to drag her away before I get my ass put back on Mrs. Greene's shit list. Trust me, it's nowhere anybody wants to be. She made completing my tenth-grade science experiment way harder than it needed to be—but to be fair, I did light her trash can on fire. There's been an odd smell in the library ever since.

Taking Bri down to the student parking lot, I fling her bag into the back of my Mustang and drop into the driver's seat as she gets in. "How was training?" she asks, looking back up at the school to where a few of my teammates are still lingering around.

Shrugging my shoulders, I put the Mustang in reverse and start backing out. "Fine," I tell her, not wanting to go into details about how I may or may not have kicked Daniel Carter's ass after his comments toward Addie in the hall this morning. "Nothing special, but Jax wasn't happy. Coach had him sitting on the bench the whole time, just watching. The fucker couldn't handle it."

"I bet," she laughs. "After Arizona avoided him the whole day, I'm sure he was already on edge."

"Damn right," I tell her, laughing at the way his whole body was vibrating with restlessness on that damn bench, but I feel for him. I've been in his exact position. There have been too many bad days where I've gotten myself benched and had to sit through training, needing to work off the excess energy. Unfortunately for Jax, this won't just be a one-off. He's going to be benched for weeks. I wouldn't be surprised if he ends up sneaking in a gym session and fucking up his progress.

We get halfway home before I turn to her, watching as she looks out the window. "You know, you didn't have to wait for me. You could have driven home, and I would have hitched a ride with one of the boys."

Bri gives me a dazzling smile. "I wouldn't have left you stranded like that. Besides, when the doctor told me I was cleared for school and light duties, I doubt he meant I could drive."

"I'm sure you're fine to drive."

She shrugs it off. "It gave me a chance to get through a bunch of schoolwork anyway. I'm so far behind."

"Didn't you speak to your teachers?" I question, glancing at her again. "The school is aware of what's been going on. Mom's been keeping them updated. So I'm sure they'd give you some leeway on your missed work. There's no need to be pushing yourself so hard to catch up."

"I want to," she says. "I don't want them taking it easy on me because of what happened. They didn't want to help me when I was accused of being an accessory to rape, so I won't accept their pity now. Besides, I didn't miss too much. Just a few essays and a handful of assignments. Nothing I can't handle."

"Sounds like you're punishing yourself," I mutter, focusing on the road as I turn down our street, purposefully glancing away to avoid the eye roll I know is coming. We've been arguing about it for the past week. I think she should ease back into it, but Brielle has a go-hard-or-go-home mentality, and usually, I love that about her. Only in this particular situation, it's the most frustrating thing she's ever done.

Approaching my driveway, I can't help but notice the black Aston Martin sitting in the neighboring drive, and a chill sails down my spine. Just as it does every time I see Channing. He's got me in a fucking chokehold and he knows it. One wrong move from me, and my world will implode, and I don't doubt he'll come through on his threat.

He knows too much, and there's not a damn thing I can do about it.

My hand tightens around the steering wheel, my knuckles paling as I turn into my driveway, only as I come to a stop, the door of the Aston Martin swings open. Channing steps out of his car with his phone glued to his ear.

My heart races as anger burns through my veins, singeing me from the inside out as my stomach somersaults, making me hold back a gag. He walks around the side of his car, his gaze lifting to mine, and the second our eyes connect, the oxygen is sucked out of the car. Tension builds, and I feel my whole body vibrating with uncontrollable rage.

As Channing holds my stare, I clench my jaw so fucking tight, my teeth could shatter. A smirk kicks up the corner of his lips, looking at me like I'm a pathetic piece of shit who's at his complete mercy, and he's fucking right. That's exactly what I am.

Those photographs ... they're something I thought I'd never see again, never have to be reminded of the horrendous things I did that night. It's my darkest secret, my greatest regret, and every day that passes, I feel it creeping up on me, constricting my chest, making it impossible to breathe.

"Tanner?" Bri questions, her voice filled with concern, but I tune her out, unable to look away from Channing as he finally drops his gaze and turns his back. He walks toward his front door, but I watch every fucking step, my whole body beginning to close down.

I'm out of time. My world is imploding, and I don't know how to make it stop.

"TANNER?" Bri demands, grabbing my shoulder and pushing it back against the seat, forcing me to look at her. "What the fuck is wrong with you?"

I shake my head and reach for the door handle. "It's nothing, don't worry."

"No," she snaps, grabbing my arm and yanking me back. "Fucking talk already. I'm done with this bullshit. I know something is going on, something you're refusing to tell me, and every time I ask, you shrug it off like it doesn't matter. I see what it's doing to you. What does he have on you that could be so bad? Why won't you just talk to me? I've tried to give you space. I knew something was going on after the wedding, then we were going to talk at the track, and again when I got out of the hospital, but you've been avoiding it. I've been trying to give you space, hoping you would come to me when you were ready, but it's been weeks, Tanner. Weeks."

Guilt tears at my chest, and I can't even meet her eye, the shame overwhelming me like never before. "I'm sorry, Bri," I tell her, my hands shaking in my lap. "I can't … I can't tell you. I thought I could, and I want to. I don't want to keep things from you, but what I did … you'll never look at me the same again."

Bri reaches for me, but I pull out of her reach and her shoulders sag with defeat. "Tanner," she whispers, balling her hands into fists to keep from trying again. "*You lean, I lean,* remember? I thought we were in this together. You put Colby in a fucking coma, and I didn't walk away. I thought we were stronger than that."

"We are," I say, finally looking up and meeting her broken stare. "You're my whole fucking world, but what I did … what happened … that's bigger than us."

Brielle reaches for me again, but this time, she doesn't let me pull away. She holds my hand tight, pulling it into her lap. "Tanner, talk to me. Whatever it is, we'll get through it."

"Can't you see how fucking sick this makes me? You don't understand, you're not hearing me," I tell her. "You will never look at me the same again. You will never love me as you do now. Everything is going to change. You'll walk away from me, and I won't even blame you."

Bri shakes her head, her eyes filling with tears. "No," she whispers, swallowing hard before climbing across the front seat and straddling my lap. She takes my face in both her hands, forcing her stare on mine. "That's not possible, Tanner. The way I love you … this is forever. In the courthouse, when you asked me not to walk away if you ended Colby's life, I promised you that I'd never walk away, and I fully intend to stand by that."

My gaze drops as my world closes in on me, leaving no way out. I reach up and curl my hand around the back of her neck, and she drops her forehead to mine. "The way I see it," she whispers, "is that this is haunting you right to your core. Whatever you did, it will destroy you if you don't learn how to move forward. The only way to do that is to lay it all out in front of you and deal with it." She pauses, her words weighing on both of us. "Talk to me, Tanner. I want to be here for you. I want to help you through … whatever this is, but I can't do that if I don't know what's going on, and we can't learn how to move past it until that happens."

I meet her eyes again, and the unbreakable trust staring back is killing me. "Swear to me, Killer. Swear you won't write me off. I'll give you the time you need to come to terms with it, but swear that when you're ready, you'll come and talk to me, give me a chance to earn your trust," I beg of her. "I don't want to do life without you."

Brielle leans in, her lips gently brushing over mine. "I swear," she whispers. "I lean, you lean."

My heart breaks knowing what I have to tell her will destroy everything we've built. I just hope we're strong enough to come back from this.

Silence fills the car as I cling to her, not knowing the next time I'll be able to hold her. A minute passes before I find the courage to say the words I'd locked away a long time ago. "After the courthouse, when I was locked up," I start, "I think I told you that Channing came to see me?"

Bri nods slowly, her eyes locked and loaded on mine like a fucking missile ready to strike.

Letting out a breath, I continue before I convince myself to bitch out and bail. "Channing wasn't there just to threaten me with assault charges. He wanted to permanently gain my obedience by blackmailing me with photographs from my past."

"What kind of photographs?" she questions, her tone wary and uncertain.

"They were still shots from a security feed," I explain, having to look away, unable to meet her blue gaze as the horrendous shame fills every part of my body. "When I was fourteen, I was involved with some guys from Hope Falls. They were older, maybe eighteen or nineteen, and saw me as the little rich kid they could exploit. They—"

"The Hardin brothers?" she questions, taking a guess as she cuts me off. I nod and she pulls back just a bit, her hands pulling into her stomach to put space between us, clearly knowing who these assholes are. "They're part of the reason crime was so bad in Hope Falls. People were terrified of them. They would torment everyone."

I nod, my stare locked on her hands. "I was a punk kid. My dad was away, and I guess I was acting out to get his attention. Hell, the Hardin brothers were the people who first introduced me to Colby. Though, back then, he was nothing but a stupid kid too."

"What happened?"

"They said we were going out to have fun, put some hairs on my fucking chest. I figured it was a party or some shit like that, but when we got there, the house was dark. No lights were on, no music, and there weren't any people around. I knew something was going on, but I had no clue. They promised me a good night, so I blindly followed them."

"Tanner," she breathes, heartache strong in her voice.

"We broke into the house, which is when they pulled their guns and started ransacking the place. I just stood in the doorway dumbfounded until one of them shoved a bag into my hand and told me to start picking up shit, anything that looked expensive, and I fucking did it. I thought we'd just get what they wanted and leave, but then I heard a woman screaming, and the next thing I know, one of the brothers was dragging her out of her room by her hair. He threw her down in the kitchen and held a gun to her head while the other two were trashing her home.

"She was weeping the whole time, trying to keep as quiet as possible, but she was fucking terrified. Then out of nowhere, this kid, maybe nine or ten, only a few years younger than I was, screamed for his mom and came running from his room with a baseball bat. All he wanted to do was protect his mother, but the brothers weren't having it. It happened so fucking fast. One second he was there, the next—BANG."

I shake my head, needing to take a breath as the images rush through my mind, the blood splatter across the room, the mother's horrified screams, the broken sobbing.

"The bullet went straight through his skull, killing him instantly. I'll never forget it. I see it every time I close my eyes. The blood … It was the first time I'd seen anything like it, and I just froze, watching as the mother reached out to hold his hand. She just sobbed. She was so numb, she barely even fought him off when he tore her night dress up and raped her."

Brielle gasps, and I drop my head, so fucking ashamed of everything I was involved in that night. "The second they heard the sirens, they got out of there, but I took off on foot before then. I didn't want anything to do with them."

"Did you report it?" Bri whispers, her voice broken and almost sounding like a plea, hoping for at least some good news to come out of this story, but she won't find any here.

I shake my head. "I ran all the way back to Bradford, but the brothers were already here waiting for me. They warned me to keep my mouth shut, otherwise, my family would be next, and I fucking believed them. Then instead of just fucking off, they beat the shit out of me and left me for dead in the gutter. I called Riley and stayed at his place for a few weeks, making up some bullshit story about going away with his family. I couldn't let my mom know what happened. It'd break her. It fucking broke me."

Bri leans even further back, looking at me as though I'm some kind of stranger, and the heartbreak in her eyes kills me. "That was the last of it. The case went cold, and the Hardin brothers walked free, just like Colby did. I never uttered a word until now."

"And Orlando has images of you in that house, being involved in … the cold-blooded murder of a child and the rape of his grieving mother?"

I nod, sick to my fucking stomach as Bri tries to keep her hands from shaking. A tear falls from her gorgeous blue eye, trailing down her cheek and dropping to her collar. I try to reach up and wipe it away, but she flinches from my touch, fear brimming in her eyes.

"Do you hate me?" I ask in a small voice.

She just gives me a blank stare, still trying to process everything I told her, but I see it there just as I knew I would. Things will never be the same. How could it? I was involved in a home invasion where a child was murdered, and his mother was raped as she clung to his lifeless hand.

I truly am a monster. No better than Colby Jacobs.

Brielle deserves better. So much better. Hell, I should have fucking told her why Channing is blackmailing me with the photographs. I know she's probably going to think it has something to do with guaranteeing my silence when it comes to fighting for Addison, but in reality, it's much more sinister than that.

Without a word, she reaches for the door, pulls the lever, and pushes it wide before climbing off my lap. I watch as she stands at my open door, her face marred with pain. "I, umm … I just need a few days. You know, to process."

I nod, and with that, she walks back to Channing's home, opens the door, and slips inside.

CHAPTER 11
Brielle

The afternoon sun beams down over Bradford as I lay out by the pool with my textbooks surrounding me and my wobbling laptop balanced on my knees. I have so much schoolwork to catch up on, but concentrating over the past few days has been harder than I ever thought possible.

The past few days … they've sucked. There's no other way to put it. I haven't spoken to Tanner, needing the time to wrap my head around the horrendous things he was involved in as a kid. Fuck, does being a kid even count? He was fourteen. That was only four years ago. Sure, he was an adolescent teen, and I could see the regret and shame he's been living with, but the fact he still hasn't reported it … He still hasn't done what he can to make this right.

I have questions. A lot of fucking questions.

A child was murdered, an innocent life ended, and as his mother sobbed in grief, she was raped by one of the Hardin brothers, men who are widely known in Hope Falls for the way they terrorize the community. The second Tanner finished explaining what happened, I ran up to my room and threw up. The fact that I'd walked back into Orlando's home didn't mean anything in comparison.

Tanner walked into that house willingly, but the second he did, he became a victim of their crimes, and while I know deep down he was innocent in this, I'm still struggling to wrap my head around it.

After Damien left for boot camp, Mom and I had to be even more cautious while we were home alone, and the Hardin brothers were the very reason. They made a mockery of Hope Falls, the streets being their own personal playground, the residents their toys to fuck with. Just knowing Tanner had anything to do with them haunts me. Surely he couldn't have been stupid enough to trust them.

Tanner was forced to be a pawn in their games. He was just doing what he was told out of fear, and the moment he truly understood what was happening and got the chance, he ran as far as he could. And yet he was still beaten by the brothers, just for knowing what went down. I'm struggling to figure out if he's an innocent party in all of this or if I need to hold him accountable, but every time I think about it, my stomach twists with nausea and my world starts to crumble.

I don't want to lose him. I gave him my word I wouldn't walk away, and I don't want to, but how the hell are we supposed to work past this? He warned me it was bad, and yet I still trusted that everything was going to be okay. I know his heart, know the man he is today, and the regret he holds for what happened that night has been slowly killing him.

Tanner Morgan is a good man, and I believe that with every fiber of my being.

It's been three days since we sat in his Mustang, and he broke himself just to let me in, but I haven't spoken a word to him since. It's been weird between us. He's given me the space I needed while at school, but every day, I see his resolve beginning to fail. He needs to know where we stand, but I don't have the answers he's looking for. At least … not yet.

Shrill laughter comes from the house just moments before the back doors swing open. Arizona, Chanel, and Ilaria come waltzing outside, more than happy to have let themselves in. The moment they see the spread of books before me, they each shake their head. "Oh, hell no, Marjorie," Arizona says, stepping up beside me and pushing the laptop closed. "You've been buried in books for days. It's time you remember you're only young once and enjoy yourself. Besides, I didn't come all the way here to be your study buddy."

"Damn straight," Chanel says, dropping down on the sun lounger beside me and reaching for one of my books. "Eww, advanced math. What the hell is wrong with you? We only have a few hours of sunshine left to soak up. You can study after dinner."

"But—"

"But what?" Ilaria says, a cocky smirk across her face. "Don't act like we haven't noticed you've been avoiding Tanner like the plague.

You're living in the sugar daddy's house despite not having made up with your mom yet, which can only mean Tanner accidentally called you another girl's name while banging."

I roll my eyes. "He did not."

"Well, whatever it is, you guys will figure it out," Ilaria adds. "But the point I'm getting at is, in those wee hours after dinner, I don't think you'll be busy practicing baby-making with your boyfriend, so you'll have plenty of time to study then. Right now, you're chilling with us because we miss your bitch ass."

"I literally just saw you at school," I remind them, watching as Arizona strips off her tank and shorts before bombing into the pool, splashing Chanel and making her squeal.

She flies up off the sun lounger beside me, water dripping from her body, and immediately starts ripping into Ari while Ilaria sees her chance and swoops into Chanel's vacated seat. "That's more like it," Ilaria says, tearing off her tank and leaning back to sunbathe in her black string bikini.

Realizing I have absolutely no say in the matter, I collect all my books before Arizona decides to drown them in the pool and slink away to the kitchen. I dump my work on the island table before rummaging through the fridge. After grabbing the lemonade and fruit juice, I reach up to the higher cabinets and grab the bottle of vodka. If we're doing a pool day, then we're doing it right.

Balancing everything—plus cocktail glasses and fancy straws—I make my way back out to the pool and Chanel hurries to help me before I accidentally trip and ruin it for everyone. We get busy mixing drinks, and I hand one to Ari as she stands at the pool's edge. "Here you go, Mag."

She winks as she takes the drink from me, her tongue poking out to try and catch the straw as it circles the rim of the glass. "Thanks, Marge," she says, her tone full of laughter. "Kinda has a nice ring to it, don't you think? Mag and Marge."

I drop down beside Ilaria as she scrolls through her socials, already sipping on her drink. "Please," she scoffs. "Mag and Marge? Those names make you sound like the knock-off version of *Kath and Kim* in your matching tracksuits, muttering under your breath about the punk kids running amuck in the streets because, back in your day, the children were disciplined and knew that when the streetlights came on, it was time to head home."

Arizona holds her glass up toward Ilaria. "Jealousy doesn't suit you, Illy. If you wanted a cool name, all you had to do was say so," she says. "But unfortunately for you, that ship has sailed and all you're left with are the rejected names."

"Dare I ask what they are?" Ilaria says, rolling her eyes as Chanel drops down beside the pool, playing on her phone as her feet dangle in the cool water.

Ari grins and I can only imagine what's about to come spurting out of her mouth. "Your choices are Whack-A-Mole, Cuntasaurus, or Pussy Juice. Take your pick."

Ilaria thinks hard and long about it, her lips pressing into a firm line. "If I go with Pussy Juice, can I be PJ for short?"

"Absolutely."

Ilaria grins wide. "PJ it is then."

A laugh bursts from between my lips. "Cheers to that."

"Wait," Chanel says, holding up a hand. "I'm claiming Cuntasaurus before that gets taken. I can't be Whack-A-Mole, that doesn't fit my aesthetic. But Cuntasaurus, now that's what I'm talking about. Besides, Logan would agree that my lady tunnel deserves a strong, dominant name."

Ari chokes back a laugh. "You mean, you want to name your pussy after an old, dusty dinosaur that's been dead for millions of years … sounds about right to me."

Chanel's mouth drops as her eyes widen, realizing exactly where she went wrong. "No, no, no, that's not what I meant. I changed my mind. I wanna be Whack-A-Mole."

"Too late, Cunty. Addison is Whack-A-Mole from here on out. You made your decision and now you have to live with it," Ari laughs. "Though, just between us girls, you better spruce up that dinosaur love muffin of yours before Logan decides he needs to find one with a pulse."

"Oh, trust me," Chanel says. "It's got a pulse."

"Speaking of Whack-A-Mole," Ilaria says. "Where is Addison?"

I shrug my shoulders. "I don't know, but at school today, I heard Hudson say something about wanting to talk to her about the way their relationship is progressing, so if anything, she's probably locked in her bathroom, trying to avoid an awkward conversation."

Arizona laughs. "Don't worry, I've got this," she says before walking to the very edge of the pool, closest to the boundary line between the two houses. Her hands circle her mouth and not a moment later, the loudest squawk comes tearing from deep in her chest. "ADDISON MORGAN," she hollers. "GET YOUR FINE ASS OVER HERE AND BRING A BIKINI. WE'RE HAVING COCKTAILS."

I roll my eyes, unable to tear the grin off my face. "You could have just texted her."

"Now what fun would that have be—"

"Ari?" a familiar voice calls from over the fence, cutting her off and making her eyes bug out of her head in fear. "Is that you?"

"Oh, fuck," Arizona panics, desperately searching for an escape just as Jax's head pops up over the fence, zoning in on her like a target, locked and loaded. "Oh, no, no, no, no, no," she starts chanting, trying to rush through the water to get her ass out of there.

"Don't even think about it," Jax says, a cocky grin across his stupid face. "You're not getting away from me this time." Without another word, he grips the top of the fence and hauls himself up before swinging his legs over and jumping down on our side. He tears his shirt off and tosses it on the ground before throwing himself into the pool, something I'm sure he'll regret later when that stab wound through his liver is giving him hell.

Chanel, Ilaria, and I watch with wide eyes as his head surfaces right in front of Arizona, his hands slamming against the edge of the pool, caging her between his arms and body. "We need to talk," he tells her. "It's been weeks, babe. I'm sick of you cutting and running the second I walk into a room."

"Jax, don't do this," she begs, gently shaking her head, real fear in her eyes of being pushed too soon and having to face the haunting reality that he'll never love her the way she needs. "I … I can't—"

He moves in even closer, his strong body pressed right up against hers as their eyes lock and she becomes mesmerized by his stare. "You and Logan saved my life, Ari," he mutters. "I know there are other things we need to talk about, and I'm not going to force you to do that, but I can't go another fucking day without holding you. I saw the way you looked at me when I was down, the way you cried—"

Her hand falls to his chest, her fingers shaking. "You were dying in my arms. I thought I was going to lose you."

Jax takes her waist and drops his forehead against hers, and just seeing the raw emotion in both of their eyes has tears welling in mine. "You know I love you, right? You're my best friend."

"But you're not *in* love with me, Jax."

"I can learn," he tells her. "It'll come. I promise, I just … I can't stand to see you walk away from me."

"It's not enough," she tells him. "I don't want empty promises of a future you don't know if you can give me." Silence falls between them, and he pulls her into his chest, holding her close and refusing to let go. Though truth be told, I don't think she wants him to. A moment passes before I see her tears splash against the water's surface. "You broke my heart, Jax."

Jax's arms tighten around her, pulling her hard against his chest, and I watch with despair as she nuzzles her face into his chest. "God, Ari. You have to know that was never my intention. I'd never knowingly hurt you."

Chanel glances toward me and Ilaria as Jax and Ari's conversation falls quiet. "I feel like we're intruding," she says with a cringe. "Should we have like … disappeared already?"

Reaching for my glass, I slowly stand, trying to be discreet before slowly walking back toward the house. "I think yes."

Ilaria and Chanel snicker before choking on their laughs and doing the same, making a point of not forgetting their drinks. We get through the back door when I walk straight into a hard body, his familiar scent wrapping around me.

Uh-oh.

His hand drops to my hip, steadying me before I make a complete ass of myself, and as Chanel and Ilaria turn around, their eyes go wide. "ABORT! ABORT!" Ilaria shouts, knowing damn well I haven't spoken to Tanner in days.

Having just enough vodka in my system to make me stupid, I take off at a sprint, my feet slamming against the tiles as Chanel and Ilaria bolt too, only Tanner's reflexes are like nothing I've ever encountered. "Not so fucking fast," he says, his hand snapping out and catching me around my elbow before I've even gotten two steps away.

Chanel and Ilaria howl in laughter as they take off out the front door, most likely to go and bug Addison and Hudson, having no idea what kind of fresh hell they just left me to deal with. I mean, sure, they're not blind. They know something has been going on and that it has to be big to drive a wedge between us. But there is no way in hell I'm about to betray his trust and tell them what's truly going on.

Letting out a heavy sigh, I move back in front of Tanner and pull my elbow free of his strong grasp. "Tanner, I—"

"You swore you wouldn't walk away from me," he cuts in, the pain radiating from his dark gaze.

"And I meant that," I tell him. "I'm not walking away, but that doesn't mean I don't reserve the right to want to strangle you."

"Killer," he begs, reaching for me again, only I evade his touch. "I can't stand having you hating me like this. The way you're looking at me right now … it's like you don't even know me … like you're scared of me."

"Maybe I am," I scoff, glancing back at the pool to make sure Jax and Ari can't overhear our conversation. "What you did … I never thought you'd be capable of something like that, let alone not coming clean about it after. It's been years, Tanner. That mother is still grieving, and those assholes are still roaming the streets, tormenting the families of Hope Falls. Who knows how many other women have been attacked."

"Babe—"

"No," I cut him off. "All the blood they've spilled since that night is on your hands too."

"That's not fair," he says, grabbing my arms and pulling me away from the door, hiding us around the corner for a little more privacy. "I told you what they did to me, what they said. What kind of choice is that? Keep my family safe, or risk it all trying to put them away?"

"Or," I say, stepping back from him again, anger burning through my veins. "You could have been a fucking man and owned your shit. You were a kid. You could have spoken to your parents or the police and ensured your family was protected while they worked on putting the Hardin brothers away. Worst case scenario, you would have done a few months in juvie, so don't go acting like you were backed into a corner. You weren't, and you never have been. That mother is still out there, still waiting for justice for her little boy, and you're the reason she hasn't gotten it."

"It's not that simple," he spits through a clenched jaw, desperation in his eyes. "I can't just walk down to the police station and tell them all about it. I have people I need to protect, people who are relying on me to keep them safe."

"Oh, please," I scoff, already having made my opinion on that quite clear.

"What about Addie?" he questions. "What do you think they'll do to her if I confess and nothing comes from it? Or what about you? You're the most important person in my whole fucking world. If I report this, I'm hand-painting a fucking target on your back. Do you really think you'll be safe? You know these assholes. You've feared them for years and know exactly what they're capable of. Do you honestly think the cops aren't aware of who they are? That they haven't tried locking them behind bars a million times, only to watch them slip right out of their grasp?" Tanner pauses, shaking his head in frustration before looking back at me, that pain in his eyes shredding me to pieces. "I get it, okay. I do. I know you want to do the right thing and protect those who can't do it for themselves. It's one of the reasons I love you so fucking much, but I'm begging you, don't push this. It's a death sentence, Bri. I won't be the reason why someone I love ends up in the ground."

My whole body shakes as tears well in my eyes, not knowing what to do or what to even say. All I can do is stare up into those eyes I thought I trusted. "Tanner—"

He steps into me, his hands dropping low and curling around my ass, and in one quick movement, he lifts me off the ground and presses my back against the wall. Tanner's lips come down on mine in a gentle, longing kiss. It only lasts a few moments, but when he pulls back, his eyes are overwhelmed with emotion.

Tanner drops his forehead against mine, both of us breathing heavily. "Just tell me you don't hate me," he whispers, the words lingering between us like a heavy paperweight.

My hand curls around the back of his neck, needing to hold him closer, terrified that he'll pull away before I'm ready. "I could never."

And just like that, Tanner nods and lowers me back to my feet before brushing his knuckles down the side of my cheek. His eyes linger on mine, and then all too soon, he turns on his heel and walks out, leaving me with the burden of what he did still weighing down on my shoulders.

CHAPTER 12
Brielle

Stepping through the doors of the cafeteria, I'm immediately faced with a crowd of bodies. Apparently it's pizza day, and if you don't get in quick, you don't get any at all. Considering I got held up talking to my English teacher about my latest essay, I can only assume the good shit is gone.

"Over here, Marge," I hear Ari call over the chaos of the cafeteria. My head snaps up, and I find the girls huddled around our usual table, watching as Ari points to a spare plate beside her. "We saved you some."

Fuck, I love them.

A grin tears across my face as I cut through the cafeteria, but my gaze sweeps to the boys' table out of habit. Tanner's intense stare locks on mine, making my heart race as the tension builds around us. I hate this weirdness between us, but here and now isn't the place to have this out.

I'm ready though … I think. The second he's home from football training this afternoon, I'll be right there, knocking on his door and demanding answers to the questions I'm not sure I want to hear … or maybe I do. Who knows? All that matters is that Tanner and I make it through this, though I know we will. We're stronger than that. I may have needed time to come to terms with his past, but I can't forget about what he needs, and right now, that's me.

Hell, Tanner has enough going on with his sister's recovery and with Colby still in a coma. He pretends it doesn't get to him, but I see the fear in his eyes. When he took Colby down, he was acting in desperation. He was doing what he had to do to save the people he loved, and while he definitely lost control, he's no murderer. I don't know if he'll be able to live with himself knowing he took someone's life. Though I'm not going to lie, the fact it's Colby sure as hell makes it easier.

Tanner refuses to look away as I come to a stop in the middle of the cafeteria. I want to go to him, and a lump forms in my throat as I linger in hesitation. Sensing my dilemma, Tanner stands, ignoring his rowdy friends as he walks around the table, each step bringing him just that bit closer.

My heart pumps erratically as my palms grow sweaty, the tension burning between us like never before.

Tanner walks straight into me, and my arms instinctively fly around his neck. He locks me in a tight embrace, lifting my feet off the ground as he holds me against his warm chest, our hearts beating as one. "I fucking love you, Killer," he mutters in my ear. "I can't stand the way you're looking at me."

"I'm sorry," I murmur, trying to hold myself together. "I just … I hate feeling this way. I hate how things are between us."

"I know," he whispers, gently lowering me to my feet but refusing to release me. "It's okay. I get it. You needed time."

I pull back just a bit, needing to lock onto those dark eyes that consume my heart and soul. "I swear, I'm not doing this to punish you. What you told me … I—" I stop abruptly, glancing around at the number of people crammed into the cafeteria. "Maybe we shouldn't talk about this here."

Tanner presses his lips into a hard line. "Maybe not," he murmurs, glancing around. "You wanna get out of here? We can go somewhere to talk, somewhere we can be alone."

The need to be with him pulses through my veins. I'd do anything to ditch school right now, but I shake my head, reality being a fucking bitch. "We can't," I say, clinging to his biceps as his hands claim my waist. "If you miss any more of your classes, Coach will have no choice but to bench you for this week's game, and with everything else going on, you don't need to take another hit like that. Besides, I'm still trying to catch up on schoolwork. The last thing I need is to have even more piling up."

Tanner nods, trying to give me an encouraging smile, but I see the hurt in his eyes, and it almost brings me to my knees. "I hate it, but you're right," he mutters, clearly not pleased with the situation. "Just tell me we're okay."

"We're okay," I promise him. "Maybe I can come over after training? Avoid Mom and Orlando and stay the night at your place? We'll have all night to talk."

Relief flickers in his eyes. "Wouldn't have it any other way," he tells me before leaning in and pressing a gentle kiss to my lips, lingering there before reluctantly pulling away. Tanner steps back and my hands fall heavily to my side, his stare locked and loaded on mine.

The weight still rests between us, and damn it's fucking heavy, but I see the light flickering between us, demanding to ignite the wild, reckless flames once again. I feel us coming back, coming out of this darkness to thrive. But we have to talk first, and he knows that just as well as I do.

I watch as Tanner makes his way back to his table, having to stop when some of the guys from his team demand his attention, but it's clear he's not into it. The only good that comes from it is the moment his stare falls away from mine, the spell between us breaks and I'm finally able to keep walking.

I join the girls a moment later, and as I sit down, I can't help but notice how twitchy Addison seems. She's staring off across the room in the same direction I'd just been staring, only it's not her brother who has her messed up—it's Hudson. She watches him, worrying her bottom lip as she drums her fingers against the table, her lunch forgotten.

"What's up with her?" I ask Ari as I take my seat beside her, my stomach growling at the sight of the warm pizza just waiting for me to annihilate it.

Ari shrugs. "I don't know. She's been like this since she sat down. She stares at Hudson for a while, starts pumping herself up for something, stands up, and goes to storm over there before gasping and sitting her ass back down again like a little bitch-ass chicken."

A wide smile stretches across my face as I shake my head, understanding Addison more than she'll ever know. After taking a bite of my pizza, I lean across and place a hand on Addie's arm. "You good?" I ask, way too amused by all of this.

"I'm fine," she snaps, frustration thick in her tone as her stare remains locked across the room. "Though, be a darling and tell Arizona if she ever calls me a bitch-ass chicken again, I'm going to fuck her up."

Ari and I laugh, realizing this could be a long break, though at least we have some form of entertainment that doesn't have anything to do with our own messed-up problems. I get back to my pizza while it's still warm as Chanel whines to Ilaria about something Logan said, even though Ilaria isn't even remotely paying attention, too heavily focused on the endless reel of social media she's scrolling through.

"—idiot thinks he's king fucking shit with the way he talks himself up," Chanel goes on. "I swear, if I have to hear how he's the star of the school and holding the team together with his fucking superior football skills, I'm going to scream. I mean, do you have any idea how hard it is to smile and nod at the fucker when he's being like that? He needs a giant dildo rammed up his ass to knock his ego back a bit."

"He can't be that bad," I laugh.

"Have you met the guy?" she mutters. "Everyone knows he wouldn't be able to score without Tanner making it happen. Don't get me wrong, he is kinda amazing on the field, like so amazing that I've given him way more blow jobs after a game than he's ever deserved, but the ego! It's only gotten worse since Jax has been off because now all the attention is solely on Logan, and I swear, he eats that shit up. Maybe it's a twin thing."

"What's a twin thing?" Addie asks, clearly not paying attention as she continues staring at Hudson.

"Logan and—"

"OH, FUCK NO," Ilaria booms, her face buried deep in her phone as she cuts Chanel off. Ilaria whoops with big, heaving laughs, unable to catch her breath, let alone explain what the fuck is going on. Tears well in her eyes as she grips her stomach, losing control.

"The fuck is going on?" Chanel demands, yanking Ilaria's phone out of her hand and immediately starting her investigation. "Oh no. What an idiot," Chanel chuckles, her lips stretching into a wide grin as she shakes her head.

"Okay, what gives?" I question, needing to know what the hell is going on. Chanel whips the phone around and our eyes are assaulted by Riley's latest thirst trap. "Oh no," I groan, taking in the image of the dude, butt naked at some party, holding his junk with one hand and holding up the other to flex his muscles.

The girls laugh as Ari reaches across and takes the phone from Chanel before zooming in on all the good parts, and when it comes to Riley Sullivan, it's a damn guarantee that it's all going to be good.

What can I say? The kid has a certain appeal and he knows it. Doesn't help that he's a complete flirt with the kind of charm that has women dropping their panties.

Ilaria wipes a stray tear before leaning in and pointing to her phone. "Look at the hashtag."

Every eye drops to the screen as Ari presses on the information at the bottom, expanding the text. "Tell me he didn't," Addison laughs, shaking her head as the secondhand embarrassment becomes all too real while we each read over the single hashtag at the bottom. *#Beastmode*

"Oh, he did," I laugh, unable to resist glancing up across the room to find the idiot in question only to see the pride shining through his eyes, probably certain his latest thirst trap will go viral. I wouldn't be surprised if it did though. They usually do.

Ari continues zooming and frothing over the image when something in the background has her mood souring. "Uggghhhhh," she groans, looking down at Jax who stands in the background in nothing but a pair of swim shorts with his hair all messed up and dripping from the water. She pushes the phone away and drops her head to the table. "I can't get away from him. Everywhere I look, Jax is right there, practically rubbing it in my face."

My hand falls to her back as Ilaria swoops in and steals her phone back off the table. "But you guys talked yesterday. I figured things were better after that."

"No," she mutters. "All he did was undo all the progress I made over the last few weeks while he was healing and remind me how badly

I want to be with him. You saw that shit in the pool, right? You saw just how sweet and nice and caring he can be. It's like he knows just how easily he can reel me in and then BAM, he hits me with the *you're my best friend bullshit*. Like, fuck. I don't want to be your goddamn friend, dude. Love me, already!" She lets out a heavy huff, her cheeks blowing out as she props her chin up on her hand. "I swear, all he's good for is twisting the knife that's already buried in my spine."

"It'll get better," Ilaria promises.

Ari shoots her a blank stare. "If you honestly think that, you're fucked in the head."

"Yeah, maybe, but I just—"

Addison flies up off her seat, determination in her eyes as Ilaria stops talking, all four of us looking up at her with anticipation. Her hands shake as she stares across the room. Hell, she looks like she's about to throw up, but she shouldn't be nervous. If she's wanting to do what I think she's wanting to do, then she'll be perfectly fine. Though, I can't pretend to know how she's feeling. What she went through with Colby would make moving forward with any relationship scary as hell.

She hovers by our table, standing motionless as she tries to remember where the hell she left her balls, and then just like that, she steps out from behind the table and storms across the cafeteria.

I suck in a breath, watching with wide eyes as Arizona gasps and clutches my arm, her nails digging into my skin. "Holy shit, she's actually going to do it."

Ilaria shakes her head, positive she's about to bitch out while we watch with bated breath as she marches all the way over to the boys' table. Hudson's head shoots up first, almost as though he can sense her there. He stands as she walks around to his side of the table, all the guys finally noticing her presence.

Seeing the terrified look on her face, Hudson steps toward her, his brows furrowed, more than ready to beat down every last fucker who even looked at her wrong. He reaches her, taking hold of her shoulders as the boys watch with wide eyes, ready to back him up.

Hudson searches her face but before he even gets a chance to demand answers, she pushes up onto her tippy toes and crushes her lips against his. Addison doesn't touch him anywhere else, just kisses him deeply as he freezes, too scared to make a fucking move.

A second passes and Hudson relaxes, but just as Jax and Riley start cheering them on, Addie's whole body tenses. Her hands come up and she slams them against Hudson's chest, shoving him back with a force none of us were prepared for. He stumbles back into the table and the cheering immediately stops.

Addison just stares at him, horrified, and as Hudson straightens himself up, she bolts toward the exit. I stand, ready to go after her, but Hudson already has it under control, flying out the door in her wake as Tanner remains standing by their table.

Tanner glances back at me, anger and hurt burning in his eyes. It's one thing for an older brother to see his sister making out with one of his best friends, but it's another to watch her suffering while she's trying to find her happiness.

His gaze falls back to the table, and as he drops into his seat, Logan claps his hand over Tanner's shoulder, murmuring something I couldn't even dream of hearing from across the room. Tanner nods and just like that, leans back in his seat, ready to get on with his afternoon.

"Hey," Ilaria says, claiming my attention. "She'll be okay."

I shrug my shoulders and press my lips into a hard line, not really sure anymore.

"She will be," Ilaria says, determination thick in her tone. "I know it sucked and she's probably out there bawling her eyes out and refusing to let him even touch her, but whether she knows it or not, she took a huge step today. It's only going to get easier from here."

"I hope so," I say, knowing she's right, but nothing on this green earth will stop it from sucking. Addie tried, she took a leap, and I'm sure for a moment it felt amazing. She was bold and courageous and went after what she wanted, but despite everything, she wasn't ready. Lifting my head, I give the girls an encouraging smile, one I don't feel in my soul. "Let's just hope she gets her justice along the way."

"Speaking of," Chanel says, reaching across to take the remaining slice of pizza off my plate. "What's going on with Colby? Is he still a dead man, or will the asshole magically revive himself?"

"No idea," I say. "I haven't spoken to Tanner much this week, but last I heard, there was no change. I've tried ringing the hospital a few times, but because I'm not family, they won't give me any updates. And the cops aren't really forthcoming with information to Tanner, so it's like walking on eggshells with him, always waiting for the other shoe to drop and our lives to spiral out of control again."

Ilaria's face scrunches up. "Hypothetical question that has absolutely nothing to do with the current conversation at hand. Does it make me an asshole for not wanting someone to wake from a coma?"

Arizona snorts an ugly laugh, sounding like a bulldog getting a rectal exam. "Classy."

Ilaria rolls her eyes as a smirk pulls at her lips. "What's classy is the fact I haven't asked Bri about her brother despite how thoroughly he rocked my world after her mom's wedding."

I send a sharp glare her way while shaking my head. "You just had to go and ruin my appetite."

"Oh, please," she scoffs. "You could be sitting in a pile of rotting corpses, using some dude's grubby toenails to pick shit out of your teeth, and you'd still have a rock-solid appetite." I grin. She's not wrong, but damn, there's something seriously messed up in her head. "Now," she continues, "answer my goddamn question. When the hell is Damien getting back and do you think he'd be down to bend me over like a freaking pretzel?"

Dragging my hands over my face, I groan. "Ughhhhh." Not thrilled to be having this conversation, I give her what she wants just for the sake of being able to move on. "He'll be back soonish, I think, and seeing as though he's the kind of guy to fuck anything that walks, I think it's a safe bet to say he'll bend you over any way you want."

Ilaria grins, her eyes sparkling with excitement. "You really do know the way to a girl's heart, don't you?"

I flip her the bird, and not a moment later, the bell sounds through the school, sending us all back to class and bringing me that much closer to finally getting the answers I need from Tanner.

CHAPTER 13
Brielle

I never realized how much of a needy bitch I was until now. Any normal girl would be using this time to give herself a facial, maybe scroll through socials to add some thirst traps to her spank bank, hell, she might even paint her nails, but not me. I'm standing at my window, staring at Tanner's driveway just waiting for him to get home.

Pathetic, I know. This is what Tanner Morgan has reduced me to.

Does it make me lame that I wouldn't have it any other way?

I hear Mom and Orlando downstairs, arguing about something ridiculous. Well, to be honest, it's more like Orlando arguing and ranting at her while she's probably on her knees, begging him not to leave her. If I hadn't needed this space from Tanner to think, I never would have stepped foot back inside this house. There's just something so humiliating about being here. The way Orlando has been looking at me over the last few days has been … weird. It's a strange sort of smugness mixed with deep irritation and intrigue. I don't like it. I don't like it one fucking bit.

If I didn't have Jensen keeping me company, I would have gone insane. He came and barged his way through my door last night, arms full of candy and popcorn, demanding we Netflix and chill, without the chill. He dragged an oversized bean bag through the door, plonked it at the foot of my bed, and that's exactly where he stayed while I did everything I could to not focus on Tanner's bedroom window.

Like I said, pathetic.

Letting out a heavy sigh, I'm just about to give up when I hear the familiar rumble of Tanner's motorbike coming from down the street. A thrill shoots through me and my back straightens, more than ready to bolt down the stairs and throw myself out the front door.

The bike grows closer and with it comes the intense anticipation I've felt all day, only now it's so much worse. Despite living next door and seeing him in the hallways at school, I've missed him this week. I hate the divide between us. Yes, I was the one who put it there, but now that I've had a moment to understand how he is nothing but a victim in this, I'm ready to move forward. I just hope I haven't hurt him by asking for this space.

The sound of his bike is almost deafening as Tanner flies up the street and pulls to a stop in his driveway.

Then just like my very first day in Bradford, he looks up at my window, that sleek black helmet concealing his eyes beneath but doing nothing to mask the feel of his intense stare locked on mine. Nerves settle deep in my bones, and I curl my fingers into my palms, pressing my nails against my skin to distract me from what I'm about to do. It doesn't make sense to be nervous—it's Tanner—but here I am, feeling as though I'm about to shit myself.

He reaches up and removes his helmet as he relaxes back on his bike, looking like a fucking treat with his black shirt clinging to his skin and stretching around his biceps. He doesn't say a word, just stares up at me, knowing damn well the kind of effect he has on me. It's always been this way, and always will be. I don't think anything will ever change that. Tanner Morgan has got one hell of a hold over me, and I wouldn't have it any other way.

My need for answers pulls me from the window and all the way down the stairs. A million questions filter through my mind, but by the time I hit the front door adrenaline pulses through me, and I can't remember a single one of them.

I'm being ridiculous. Tanner was open with me about what happened that night, and I have no reason to doubt that he won't be open with me now.

Stepping out through the front door, I immediately glance over to Tanner's driveway to find him in the middle of putting his bike in the garage. I walk across, skipping over the small hedge between the two properties before stepping into the opening of the garage. He kicks the stand down and balances the bike before hooking his helmet over the handle.

Tanner glances back at me with a heaviness in his eyes that nearly brings me to my knees. He indicates toward the interior door with a small nod. "Come on," he mutters.

He holds out his hand and I willingly take it, allowing him to lead me inside. He presses a button on the wall to close the garage door as we enter the house, and I let him pull me into the kitchen. "Are you hungry?"

I shake my head, my appetite completely gone, though I'm sure that's not the case for Tanner. He's always starving after training. I take a seat on one of the chairs around the island counter while Tanner dives deeper into the kitchen, becoming one with the refrigerator.

He pulls out a container of leftover takeout and grabs a fork, not even bothering to heat it before digging in like some kind of psychopath. "Where is everybody?" I ask, watching as he lifts the fork full of noodles to his mouth.

Tanner shrugs his shoulders. "Addison said something about going to a friend's house after school, but really, I think she's trying to avoid being here in case Hudson shows up to talk about her little spontaneous make-out session, and Mom has some fundraiser meeting at the country club."

"So, we're alone?"

His brow arches and a cocky grin stretches across his gorgeous face. "All alone," he says, his tone thick and suggestive.

I roll my eyes. "What's with men and their one-track minds? Does everything have to be about sex?"

"No, not always," he says, digging back into the take-out container. "But we try to keep it at a respectful eighty to ninety percent, otherwise we'll get kicked out of the sleazy men's club. When that happens, they take our license to fuck, and no one wants that."

I shake my head. "How do you even say that shit with a straight face?"

Tanner shrugs his shoulders and walks around to my side of the island, sitting down beside me as he continues to annihilate his noodles. "I can't tell you all my secrets now, can I?"

"Maybe not," I mutter, a seriousness coming over me. "But there are some we need to talk about."

Tanner nods and puts the container down on the counter, pushing it away from us before swiveling on his seat. "Are you okay?" he murmurs, grabbing my knees and swinging me toward him to put us face to face. "What I told you the other day, it wasn't my intention to scare you."

I shake my head, reaching up and cupping the side of his face. "I'm not scared of you, Tanner. I was just … I was heartbroken." His brows furrow, not having expected that response. "I've painted this picture of you in my head of this untouchable, incredible guy who could do no wrong, and it's probably one of the reasons why I was so taken aback that night you lost control at the track. You made me realize you had flaws just like the rest of us, and so when you told me what you'd been involved in as a kid and how you never stood up and reported it, I was in shock. It's not something I ever thought you'd be capable of. I was so angry, I couldn't understand how you'd gone so many years without doing something about it, but after you explained why you couldn't, and I had some time to process that information, I started to see the bigger picture. You're just as much of a victim in this as the mother and her child were."

Tanner shakes his head. "No, I wouldn't go as far to say that," he tells me. "I still helped break into that house, and I still looted the place when they told me to. I could have walked away the minute I realized it wasn't a house party."

"That might be true," I tell him. "And I don't want to justify what you did, but you were just a kid getting pressure from the Hardin brothers. They had no business taking you there or even hanging out with you in the first place."

"Either way, I'm no victim, and while what I did can't even compare to the horrors they put that woman through, I still have a lot to make up for."

I nod, agreeing with him wholeheartedly. "I get you're coming from a good place, but I honestly doubt there's anything you can do or offer that could ever make up for what happened that day. She lost her child and was raped beside his dead body. She doesn't need you to try and make up for it. She needs justice and closure, just like Addie does."

Tanner nods, his gaze dropping to where his hands rest on my knees. "You're right," he tells me. "But I don't know how I can give her the justice she deserves without putting you and my family at risk."

"I know you don't want to hear this, but sometimes the risk is worth the reward."

"No, absolutely not," he says. "I told you this. If I go to the police, they will come for my family, come for you, my friends, me. I'm not putting us through that. Fuck, Killer. I nearly just lost you, Addie, and

Jax. I watched you bleed out in my hands. These guys are no joke, Bri. The shit Colby did ... that's nothing compared to them." He shakes his head, panic beginning to plague him. "I only just got Addie back. What do you think it would do to her if they got their hands on her? I just ... I fucking can't, okay?"

"Okay," I say, grabbing his hands and squeezing. "Okay, we'll figure it out, but one way or another, that woman is getting justice. I can't live with myself knowing the truth about this and not doing anything to help her."

Tanner nods, able to agree with that. "We will," he says. "I promise you that. I don't want to be that guy who stands back and allows this shit to go on. After everything Addie went through, it's opened my eyes, and I've realized how fucking wrong I've been to hide from this." He swallows hard, his lips pressing into a firm line as indecision plagues his stare. "There is one thing I've been thinking about, but I don't know how to make it happen or where to even start."

My brows furrow as I trail my thumb over his knuckles. "What is it?"

He brushes his hand back through his hair and lets out a heavy breath. "It's nowhere near enough but I was thinking, with her permission of course, I could open a foundation in her son's name to help prevent crime in less fortunate areas and which also supplies a safe place for victims just like her who have nowhere else to go. Maybe if they just need someone to speak to, there could be counselors on hand, or other survivors to talk to."

Pride swarms through my chest, and I pull him in toward me,

pressing my forehead against him. "I think you're the most incredible man I have ever met," I tell him. "I think it's a great idea, but like you, I have no idea where to even start with a project like that. But you know who would?"

Tanner pulls back, weariness in his eyes. "Who?"

"Your mom."

"Fuck."

"You're going to have to talk to her about this at some point."

"I know, but … fuck. That's not going to go down well."

"I know," I tell him. "But as long as you're still holding on to this, you'll never be able to move past it. Consider it personal growth, or hell, just doing the right freaking thing for a change."

He gives me a pointed stare before finally letting out a breath. "You're right. I'll figure out a way to tell her. But for now, are we cool?"

I nod as my gaze shifts to the counter, my brows furrowing as I consider what I need to say. "There's just a few things I haven't been able to figure out." I pause, waiting for his reaction, and as he watches me with openness, I go on, knowing I'll get the complete truth from him. "How the hell did Orlando come across photographs of that night? And why hasn't he said anything until now?"

Tanner scoffs, irritation burning in his dark eyes, but there's something else too, something I can't quite put my finger on. Whatever it is, I don't like it. "There are so many fucking reasons, Killer. I'm the brother of his client's victim. I almost broke his jaw. I'm dating his new stepdaughter. Take your pick, there's so many reasons he'd benefit from having my obedience," he says, shifting his eyes from mine as though he's trying to hide something, which doesn't make sense as he's being an open freaking book right now. Every question I've asked, he's answered with complete honesty. "As for how he got them though, that's a fucking mystery to me. But down in those cells, he mentioned something about my father. I just can't figure out why."

"Your father?" I cut in, unable to work out how the hell the two things could possibly relate.

"Mmhmm," he murmurs. "My guess is that my father somehow found out what I had been involved in and asked Channing to bury the evidence. After all, that's what he does best, but my father never mentioned any of this to me. Surely if he knew, he would have beat my ass for it."

Pressing my lips into a hard line, I try to wrap my head around it all.

Tanner fucked up, that much is clear, and despite the work he promises to put in to make it right, Orlando still plans to blackmail him. But for what exactly? His silence? His obedience? Or is it something much worse, something neither of us could possibly imagine? All I know is I'm not about to let that shit slide. "So, what do we do?"

"Huh?"

"This isn't just going to go away," I tell him. "Orlando is going to hold this over you until the day he dies, so what do we do? I'm not just going to sit back and let it happen."

Tanner grins, his brow arching high. "Yeah?" he questions, slowly standing and reaching down to my hips. He hauls me up onto the edge of the island counter and pushes between my legs. "You want to get your hands dirty for me?"

He presses right up against me, and the fly of his jeans rubs my clit, sending a shot of electricity pulsing straight to my core and flooding me with need. With a gasp, I sink my teeth into my bottom lip as he grinds against me. "Well, you know how I like to get dirty for you."

Tanner groans and dips his head, his lips pressing to the base of my throat and moving over my skin, sending shivers scattering over my body. "Fuck, Killer," he groans, taking my hips and yanking me impossibly closer. "Tell me we're all good so I can fuck this tight pussy right here in the kitchen."

"We're so fucking good," I pant, already desperate for him.

Before the words even get a chance to linger in the air between us, his lips are on mine. Tanner kisses me deeply, and it's like coming home for the first time all week. I've missed him so fucking much, missed the easy way we get to be together. This week seriously fucked with our vibe, but I feel as though we're coming out the other end stronger, and now the only thing left for us to do is seal the deal with one hell of a thorough fucking.

He reaches between us and I can already feel his cock straining against his fly. Tanner grips the waistband of my pants as his arm curls around my waist, lifting me just enough to tear my pants down my thighs, right along with my black lace thong. I work on kicking them off my feet as I hastily grab the front of his pants, desperate to release the monster I know is waiting to destroy me in all the right ways.

My sweatpants hit the floor, and I push my legs wider just as Tanner's heavy cock springs free against my thigh. Taking hold of it, I curl my fingers around his thick base, the sound of Tanner's low groan doing wicked things to me.

I feel his fingers at my entrance and just like that, he pushes them deep inside me. "Oh, fuck," I breathe, his fingers curling just right, making my eyes roll back. He does it again, before gripping my chin and meeting my stare, holding me captive in every possible way. The hunger burns between us as he refuses to break eye contact, and just as the intensity grows, he moves his fingers just right, massaging my walls until my soul leaves my body.

"Tanner," I pant, unbelievable pleasure rocking through my body, and just when I think it can't get any better, his thumb stretches up and presses against my clit, rubbing small, tight circles. "Oh, God yes. There … right there."

He watches me so closely, reading my body like a fucking book, and when his lips pull into that cocky smirk … holy shit. He's absolutely everything. "You like that, Killer?" he questions in that deep, raspy voice, his confidence making me want to impale myself on him and fuck him until the sun comes up.

My hand works up and down his thick cock, but it's not enough. If he doesn't stop teasing me and working my pussy like this, I'm going to come on his fingers, and as glorious as that would be, that's not what I want. I need him inside me. I need him to fill me, to stretch me, and only after he's thoroughly fucked me can I come.

"Tanner," I warn, tipping my head back as the satisfaction overwhelms me. "I need you inside me."

A low groan rumbles through his chest and his desperation has me dripping wet and ready for more. I mean, fuck. How do you politely say *impale me?*

He pulls his fingers from within me as his other hand takes his cock, stroking it twice and making my mouth water before lining himself up with my entrance. He takes my hip to hold me steady and with a forceful thrust, he slams that thick cock deep inside me.

I cry out in pleasure as my walls stretch around him, only stopping when he physically can't go in any further. He pauses, closing his eyes as the softest curse slips from between his delicious lips.

"Don't stop," I beg him, my hand curling around the back of his neck to hold him close.

Tanner pulls back as his thumb works my clit, and when his eyes open, his desire hits me like flames igniting my skin. I suck in a gasp, everything clenching inside me as my anticipation builds. When he slams into me again, his jaw flexes, and he grips my hip with his other hand. "So fucking tight, Killer."

A thrill shoots through me as he picks up his pace, both of us panting heavily and clinging onto the other as though we'll never get a chance like this again. Tanner fucks me hard, and I tip my head back as my pussy clenches around him, getting close to the fucking edge.

"Oh God, Tanner," I groan. "More. Don't fucking stop."

He gives it to me just how I need it; hard, fast, and raw. It's fucking everything. Every thrust, every touch, feels like ecstasy pulsing through my veins, until finally, I detonate and my world explodes.

My whole body shakes as my orgasm tears through me like a fucking bullet, and I cry out his name, digging my nails into his warm skin. Tanner comes with me, grunting in pleasure as my pussy contracts around him, but he doesn't dare stop. He keeps fucking me, keeps moving and rubbing circles over my clit as my high claims me—body and soul.

Then finally, I crash hard, sagging against Tanner's chest as he holds me tight, keeping me from falling to the ground. I struggle to catch my breath, and just as I go to tell him we'll be doing it all over again, the familiar *BANG* of the door echoes through the house followed by Addison's raging voice. "Oi, Tanner! Where are you?" she calls, quickly walking this way. "You wouldn't fucking believe the shit I've had to put up with this afternoon."

My eyes go wide as I meet Tanner's stare, knowing damn well we won't have time to get dressed. "Well," he says with a heavy sigh, an apology in his eyes. "This is going to be interesting."

And sure enough, the very next thing I hear is Addison's disgusted scream. "OH, FUCK NO! ON MY KITCHEN COUNTER? That's where I cream my bagels."

Tanner laughs, cupping his junk as I do my best to cover up. "After all this time, we finally have something in common," he says, his tone preparing me for the worst. "This is where I like to cream Bri's bagels."

Well … fuck.

CHAPTER 14

TANNER

Who would have known an afternoon full of crazed make-up sex would have Brielle sleeping like the living dead? She didn't even get to eat her dessert before she crashed on the couch. Can't blame her though, I did make sure she was thoroughly fucked. You know, after my sister ran away to gouge her eyes out with a rusty fork.

Hearing Mom in the kitchen, I reach over and grab the bowl of melted ice cream that's been wedged between Brielle's waist and the couch before lifting her legs off my lap. I take the discarded dessert into the kitchen, walking past Mom who's trying to reach the chocolate she hides from us on the top shelf. The problem is, when she chose this hiding spot, she failed to consider the fact that I tower over her, and every time I open the cupboard, I see it staring right back at me.

"You okay, my love?" Mom asks, turning her back and trying to be discreet about her chocolate.

"Yeah, fine," I respond, walking over to the sink and rinsing out the bowl before stacking it in the dishwasher. "Bri crashed on the couch, so I'm going to take her up to bed."

Mom gives me a dopey smile and I roll my eyes, knowing her over-the-top-mom-loving is coming at me full force. "Do you have any idea how happy it makes me to see you falling in love with such a beautiful, kind-hearted young girl?"

I groan and let out a heavy breath. "Yes, Mom," I say as she discards her chocolate and walks over to me, throwing her arms around me and refusing to let me go. "Soon enough, you're going to be moving out of here and going to college. Being the star I know you are, I just hope you don't forget about poor old Mom back at home."

A fond smile pulls at my lips and I hug her back, knowing just how much she needs it. "You're acting as though you won't have Addie here keeping you busy. With all your fundraisers and country club events, you'll be the one who has to remember to check in with me."

"You're right," she says, a soft chuckle in her tone. "I am a busy woman. My social life is much more interesting than yours. You know they're considering me for the event coordinator position at the club? Seems I've got a knack for it."

I nod, feigning surprise but knowing more than I let on. I may have been the one to subtly suggest it to Heather Fox, knowing her father is the president of the country club. "That's amazing, Mom. No one throws a casino party quite like you do."

"Too right," she laughs. "Who would have known at my age, I'd be cooler than my kids?"

I scoff. "Bossing around a bunch of bored, money-hungry moms is hardly the definition of cool."

"Oh, stop," she says, finally releasing me from her crushing embrace. "You wouldn't know cool if it hit you in the face."

I roll my eyes and let out a shaky breath, thinking about everything Bri and I spoke about this afternoon, and knowing she was right. I won't be able to move forward and make amends until I'm honest about everything that went down. I just hate that in the process of moving forward, I'm going to break my mother's heart. She doesn't deserve this, especially with all the stress she's already been facing with Addie and her son possibly being a murderer, but I know at the end of the day, she's still going to love me. And despite probably wanting to beat the crap out of me, she'll figure out how to help me.

Leaning back against the counter, I glance up at Mom, the heaviness of what I have to tell her weighing down on my shoulders. "Mom, do you have—"

A soft knock sounds at the door and her gaze shoots up to mine. It's after 10 p.m. Who the hell would be knocking on the door at this hour? Mom's brows furrow. "Are you expecting someone?"

I shake my head, unease pulsing through me. "It's probably just Hudson," I lie. "He and Addie had a weird moment at school today. I'll check the door. You stay here."

Mom nods as I break away from the kitchen, making my way to

the front door, but the closer I get, the more my hands shake. The only time someone knocks on the door this late at night is when someone is either desperate for help … or it's the cops.

Reaching for the handle, my stomach twists. There would only be one reason the cops would be on my doorstep. Had Colby woken from his coma, I would have received a call to let me know I was off the hook, but if it warrants a visit late at night, that could only mean one thing. He's dead, and that blood is on my hands.

Pulling the door open, I prepare for the inevitable arrest that's about to go down, only to come face to face with something equally as horrifying.

Rachael Jacobs, Colby's older sister.

"The fuck?" I grunt, standing in the open doorway, gaping at the biggest mistake of my life.

"Ummm," she says nervously, glancing anywhere but at me as she unconsciously picks at her fingernails. "Can I come in?"

I narrow my eyes and try to figure out the best way to say fuck no, but Momma raised me right. If she's here to tell me I killed her brother, the right thing to do would be to let her in, rather than having to break news like that on the doorstep. I'm not always a complete asshole.

I cautiously step out of the doorway and wave her into the foyer, but there's no way in hell she'll go any further than that. I don't trust this girl one bit, especially considering she shares DNA with Colby Jacobs.

Rachael walks in, and I make a point to keep a good distance away as she takes in the larger-than-life foyer. I keep a hard stare trained on her, knowing what kind of effect it can have on people. "What are you doing here?" I demand, my tone suggesting I'm not in the mood to be fucked with.

Rachael's stare flicks to mine and her eyes widen just a fraction before taking a hesitant step back. "You put my brother in a coma."

"He raped my sister while she screamed for him to stop."

She presses her lips into a hard line and glances away, not denying it despite the bullshit Channing fed to the judge. "I'm not here to fight with you."

"Then why the fuck are you here?" I demand. "You're not welcome in my home, especially the home where my sister sleeps."

"I really thought we'd be able to talk like adults, but your hostility is making that impossible."

"Do you blame me?" I question.

"I did nothing wrong," she seethes, stepping closer as she narrows her eyes at me. "Stop looking at me like I'm personally to blame for my brother's fucked-up decisions. I'm not him. You don't have the right to treat me like shit. My brother's life is hanging in the balance because of you."

"Because of me?" I scoff, appalled by her audacity. "He came to us. He was the one who had the knife. He was the one who stabbed Addison in the bathroom and tried to rape her, *again*. He was the one who punctured my cousin's liver. And he was the one who made sure the fucking love of my life nearly bled out in the grass. I did what I had to do to protect the people I love," I growl, spitting each word through my teeth. "Tell me he didn't fucking deserve it. Tell me after drugging and raping my sister, wrapping Bri's car around a fucking tree, attacking Addison in the hospital, and everything he did at the fucking track that he didn't deserve it. If that asshole dies, then consider it a favor."

Tears well in her eyes, but she's too angry to let them fall and she desperately tries to blink them back, not wanting to appear weak in front of me. She just doesn't realize I haven't held high opinions of her since the moment I heard about her using me to cheat on her boyfriend when I was sixteen. If she wants respect from me, that ship has sailed.

She doesn't respond and so I step into her, getting a fucked-up thrill out of the way she retreats, not stopping until her back is pressed up against the wall and she's got nowhere to go, trapped like a rabid bunny. "I'm going to ask you one more time. Why the fuck are you here in my house?"

Rachael watches me for a moment, her brows furrowing as she stares back at me. "You really have no idea, do you?"

"The fuck are you talking about?"

Something comes over her, and the fear fades into something sinister and crude. "Our son, Tanner. Congratulations, Daddy. It's a boy."

I shake my head, not believing her one bit. I saw her at the courthouse, saw the way she looked at me. It's as though I could see the pieces of her fucked-up little game falling together. "You're full of shit," I tell her. "That kid ain't mine and you know it."

"Deny it all you want, Tanner Morgan, but I know the truth, and after what you've put my family through, it's time we finally get what we deserve."

I scoff. "Money? Is that what you want? You're going to throw your kid to the wolves for a fucking payday?"

"Don't act like you know me," she seethes. "I'm not asking you to care for him. I'm not asking you to be his father, just pay the child support you owe, and you won't have to hear from me ever again."

I laugh. "You're fucked in the head. No wonder your family sent you away."

This time she steps into me, trying to appear menacing, but she really can't pull it off. "You saw him at the courthouse. Don't be stupid about this, Tanner. I know you saw the resemblance. He looks just like you. He's got your eyes and everything, and what scares you most is that you know I'm right. I saw the way you were looking at him, saw the fear in your eyes. You know it just as well as I do. He's your son, so do the right thing and—"

"Get your little manipulative hoe-bag ass away from my son," Mom seethes, storming into the foyer, clearly having overheard every last word of our conversation. I gape at her, feeling as though some kind of alien life form has taken over my mother. She never speaks like that. Hell, maybe Bri is starting to rub off on her.

Mom barges past me, shoulder charging me on her path to push Rachael away from me. Seeing the anger in Mom's eyes, Rachael hastily backs up, going awfully quiet for someone who had so much to say. "Don't you for one second think you can extort money out of my son. I will bring the law down on your entire family so hard, you won't even see it coming."

"But it's true. Tanner is my son's father."

"Forgive me for not believing a single word that comes out of your mouth," Mom tells her. "We will be doing our own private paternity test through reputable lawyers, not the dirty ones your family uses. If the test comes back as a match, then Tanner will happily pay what he owes in child support, but you better be prepared to give up your son fifty percent of the time. We will be fighting for equal custody."

"Absolutely not," Rachael says as the reality of all of this begins to sink in. Could she be telling the truth? Could her child really be mine? Is my life about to change in the biggest way, and fuck, if it is, have I really missed the first year of my son's life? Fuck. "Tanner is a murderer. He'll never get custody of our child."

"Well, fortunately for us, that decision is not yours to make. It will be decided upon by a judge, and taking into acount your hostile home environment, and the fact that your brother will be charged with three counts of attempted murder, it doesn't look good for you." Mom walks to the door, grabs the handle, and yanks it open, her intentions crystal clear. "Now, you have disturbed my night quite enough. See yourself out of my home and expect to hear from our lawyers."

Rachael fixes me with one last look as my head begins to spin, panic tearing through my chest at the minuscule possibility that she's telling the truth. Looking back at my mother, Rachael strides out of the house, and the second she can, Mom slams the door behind her before turning her ferocious stare on me.

"Wow, Mom. *Manipulative hoe-bag ass.* Who knew you had it in ya?"

She storms toward me, her finger poking hard into my chest. "Is it true?" she demands. "Is there any small possibility that the words from that girl's mouth were truthful? And I swear to God, Tanner Morgan, if you even think about lying to me right now—"

"I don't know," I tell her, cutting her off before whatever ridiculous threat she's cooked up can spew out of her mouth. "I mean, yeah, I slept with her two years ago, but I was safe. I swear, I used a condom."

"Oh, Tanner," she groans, putting her fingers to her temples and rubbing. "When was he born?"

I shake my head and shrug. "I don't know."

"You don't know?" she demands, her face turning red. "You didn't think to ask?"

"Excuse me for being too freaked out to think straight."

Mom lets out a heavy breath, trying to calm herself. "Okay, okay. It's fine," she says, her tone getting higher and becoming desperate. "We can back-date it. It's nothing a little math can't handle. When did you sleep with her? Was it only once?"

"I don't know, Mom. It was two years ago, maybe a little less," I tell her, matching her level of wild panic and desperation. "It was a party and I was drunk. I don't know what to tell you."

"Think Tanner. When was the party? Surely you have to remember something. I can't tell if this is all fabricated until I can confirm the dates don't line up. Do you know anybody who knows her or could tell us when he was born? Brielle is from Hope Falls, maybe she knows someone."

"Mom," I say, stepping into her and taking her shoulders. "I'm not about to go and wake Bri over this. There's nothing we can do about it tonight. We're not going to get any answers unless you'd like to go back out there and interrogate Rachael. I'll hold her down while you beat it out of her."

"Oh, stop," Mom says, shoving me away, trying not to grin. "That's not a very good joke."

"You're right," I say, trying to take my own advice and calm down. "It wasn't, but you needed it."

Mom lets out a heavy breath, trying to find peace. She's usually so good at control. Although, at least I know where I get my ability to fly off the rails from now. "Okay, here's what's going to happen," she finally says. "Sleep on it tonight, and in the morning I'll make an appointment for us to go and speak with our lawyer and find out everything we need to know to get this paternity test done. Until then, keep your mouth shut about it. The last thing we need to deal with are misinformed rumors. Can you imagine what those hoity-toity women at the club would say?"

"Just ten minutes ago you were boasting about how cool you were to have a social life with those same hoity-toity bitches."

Mom rolls her eyes and starts to walk to the stairs before stopping and turning back, fixing me with a hard stare. "I am more than aware of the manwhore you've been over the last few years, which is why I'm so thrilled to see you settling down with Brielle. But I swear to you, that better be the only random woman I find on my front doorstep insisting you're the father of her child."

"Promise," I tell her. "I'll make the others use the back door."

The glare I get from her is like none other I've ever received, and damn, this woman is not happy, but she can't help but love me anyway. She turns without another word, her glare enough to silence my bullshit.

I turn to head back to the living room to get Bri off the couch when I find her standing in the hallway, leaning up against the wall with her arms crossed and a look of death in her eyes. "How much did you hear?" I ask, walking toward her, hoping to God this isn't what breaks us.

"Enough," she tells me, not giving anything away.

"And?"

"And nothing," she says, shrugging her shoulders. "We'll get a paternity test and if the kid is yours, then we'll deal with it."

"You're not freaking out?"

She presses her lips into a tight line and shakes her head. "Nope," she says, lying right through her teeth. She's definitely freaking out.

I step into her, taking her waist and pulling her in close, feeling the way her body vibrates with unease. "And if the kid's not mine?"

She scoffs, her tone expressing exactly how she feels. "Then I'm going back to my Hope Falls roots and jumping her bitch-ass in a back alley."

I laugh and curl my arm over her shoulder, pulling her into me before leading her back to the stairs, more than ready to take her to bed. "There's my girl," I tell her. "But do me a favor and take Addie with you. She could use a scrappy girl fight."

"It'll be my pleasure."

CHAPTER 15
Brielle

Tanner's hand lingers on my thigh as we drive home from the Friday night home game.

It sucked. Like really fucking sucked.

With everything going on, and the bomb Rachael dropped on him last night, Tanner's head really wasn't in the game. Shit, it wasn't even halfway there. He fumbled and fucked around which only served to frustrate him and his teammates, and with Jax already out for the count, it wasn't good.

They still managed to scrape through by the skin of their teeth and hold the lead, keeping them at the top of the leaderboard and ensuring they remain in the prime position for the season, but it wasn't pretty. The way Tanner plays is usually ruthless yet poetic, but today it was scrappy and desperate. I can't blame him. He's had a lot going on and I haven't helped. I'm just glad we've come out the other end and we can work on making things right.

"Are you sure you don't want to go to that party?" I ask, closing my hand over his and giving it a gentle squeeze. "Maybe it'll be good to chill with your friends and get your mind off all the bullshit."

Tanner glances at me as we drive down the street, turning onto our road. "The last time I thought I'd go out for a drink, you, Jax, and Addie nearly died," he says. "Besides, I'm not feeling it tonight. I just wanna chill with you."

"Oh, thank God," I breathe, relief pounding through my veins. "I was hoping you'd say that."

Tanner laughs and glances at me quickly, just long enough to shake his head. "Then why'd you ask if you didn't want to go? If I said yes, you would have felt inclined to go."

I shrug my shoulders and give him a stupid grin. "The things I do for you," I say as we approach his house, only to find Orlando's black Aston Martin parked in the driveway next door with both him and Mom only just getting out of the car, looking as though they've spent the first half of the evening at some fancy, over-privileged event. "Ugggggghhhhh," I groan. "If they're staying home tonight, maybe we should go out."

Tanner scoffs. "What does it matter? We'll chill at my place. You won't even notice them."

"Oh please," I scoff. "You can't tell me that you don't hear them arguing every other day."

Tanner grins as he pulls into his driveway. "I wouldn't call it arguing," he says thoughtfully. "I mean, it takes two to argue, right? It's usually more of a one-way ranting at your mom while she just silently takes it."

"Pathetic, right?" I mutter as I watch Mom struggle to heave herself out of the Aston Martin in her tight gown, Tanner's comments mimicking the same ones that had gone through my head just yesterday.

Tanner glances at my mother, his lips pressing into a hard line. "How are things going with her? You haven't said much about it."

I shrug my shoulders. "Honestly, I don't know. It took her two days to realize I'd been sleeping in their house this week, but apart from that, she hasn't done anything in particular to offend me."

"Oh, so no red marks across your face?" he says with a nasty sneer, taking a stab at her. "That's good."

An unladylike grunt tears from the back of my throat as I turn my attention back to my mother, watching as she finally manages to pull herself out of the car. She quickly glances my way, but the window tint on the Mustang is far too dark. Hell, it's so dark I'm sure it's probably illegal.

If Mom senses me watching, she doesn't let it show, and turns her back to make her way around the Aston Martin. I follow her every step, the resentment eating me alive when I catch sight of her bare arms and back covered in finger-shaped bruises. My eyes widen and anger like I've never felt bursts through my chest. "Seems I'm not the one wearing red marks," I spit, shoving the door open hard and throwing myself out of the Mustang

"Oh, fuck," I hear Tanner grunt, knowing damn well if he doesn't move his ass, he's about to miss the excitement.

I fly over the small hedge between the two properties, and by the time Mom and Orlando notice me coming, I'm already right in front of them, a bull ready to charge. I grip Mom's arm and shove her away, forcing her behind me as I slam my hands against Orlando's chest with such force that he fumbles back, quickly trying to catch himself to avoid falling into the grass. "You absolute piece of shit. How dare you put your hands on my mom!" I roar, not giving a shit if every last bastard on the street can hear.

"BRIELLE!" my mother shrieks.

Orlando comes back at me, anger and humiliation taking over. His hand whips out toward my arm but Tanner is right there, pulling me out of the way. "Put one fucking hand on her and I'll fuck you up so fast not even you could get yourself out of that shit," he says, his tone so calm and controlled, it's eerie and sends a shiver sailing down my spine.

Orlando stops, knowing he's no match for Tanner. Hell, he's already experienced his wrath once before, and that was barely scratching the surface. So instead, he gets right in Tanner's face, his whole body shaking with rage. "You watch yourself, boy," he mutters. "You're in no position to be making demands. It would be a shame if certain photographs found themselves in someone else's hands."

"Fuck off with your bullshit threats," I spit, pushing my way back in front of Tanner, not ready to let him be the star of this particular showdown. "My mother might be a fucking pushover and willing to accept your shit, but I'm not."

"Brielle," my mother warns again, her tone suggesting I should shut the fuck up before I take things too far. "You need to stop."

I scoff, barely glancing over my shoulder at her. "Look at yourself," I seethe. "I'm not fucking blind. I can see the bruises all over your back and arms. Are you so fucking desperate for a social standing that you'll put up with that? Pack your bags and leave. Why do you stay here? He's treated you like shit since the day we moved in." Turning my attention back to Orlando, I step forward, getting stupidly close. "Does it make you feel like a man? Hitting her? Grabbing her arm and knocking her around like a fucking ragdoll? Or do you just get off seeing the marks you leave on her skin?"

Orlando clenches his jaw, barely holding himself back from beating me to a fucking pulp. "You stupid girl," he spits. "You don't know what the fuck you're talking about."

"I know you're a piece of shit who likes to exercise his power over other people, and soon enough, the whole fucking world will know it too. You're a dirty lawyer and an even dirtier husband. You're nothing but a cancer, infecting everyone with your bullshit," I tell him, letting him hear the repulsion and venom in my tone. "You put your hands on her ever again, and Tanner won't be the one you'll need to watch out for. It'll be me."

"Bri," Mom snaps, gripping my arm and spinning me to face her. "That's enough."

"Excuse me?"

"Where do you get off thinking you can speak to my husband

in this way?" she demands, her face turning red. "You don't know anything about the inner workings of our relationship."

"I know you decided to humiliate yourself and push me away to protect this new, fucked-up lifestyle of yours."

"Is that what you truly think of me?" she questions, hurt in her eyes.

I stare at her in horror, unable to understand how she can't see the effect of her own actions. "Are you kidding me?" I question. "Can you honestly not see how far you've pushed me away? How things have changed since you allowed yourself to be manipulated and controlled by this asshole? Come on, Mom. You used to be so strong. Where's the mother I had in Hope Falls? She was incredible and my best friend, but you … You're nothing but a stranger to me now."

Mom gives me a hard stare before stepping toward me, venom in her eyes. "You can't be here. You need to leave," she warns, her words lingering in the air between us. Her voice trembles and before she continues, the venom in her eyes morphs into fear, her hands shaking at her side, and it puts me on edge. There's something more going on here, I just wish I knew what. "Get your things and never come back here."

I'm taken aback, her words slamming right into my chest and spreading the vilest of poison through my heart. Guilt lingers in her eyes and she can barely look at me, and if it weren't for Tanner at my back and his hand on my hip, I'd probably have crumbled into a million pieces by now.

I shake my head, staring back at her in the worst internal agony

I've ever felt. "You don't really mean that."

"Don't I?" she argues before indicating the grand home behind her. "Look at this lifestyle Orlando has so generously offered us. Your schooling, this home, your clothes, the goddamn brand-new Maserati that you've left wasting away in the garage. He has given us the world, and you repay him with these hurtful allegations and nasty behavior. I tried to turn a blind eye, hoping you were just adjusting to the changes, but this has gone on long enough, and now I see that you are simply being ungrateful. Is it really that hard for you to be happy for me?"

I inch forward, trying to get closer. "He hurts you, Mom. What did you expect? I can't sit back and watch as you allow this to happen. Is he … is he holding something over you? Are you too afraid to leave? Too ashamed to admit you made a mistake? Because if that's it, I don't care. Screw your pride, that's what you always told me, right?"

Mom steps closer, and I flinch as she raises her hand to press it against my cheek. Her expression overflows with such love that for a moment, I could have sworn I saw the woman she used to be. "I love you, Brielle. I love you so, so much," she whispers, giving me a sad smile, "but if you don't vacate this property, I will have no choice but to file trespassing charges against both you and your boyfriend."

My brows furrow in confusion as Orlando just stands there and smirks like he just won some prize I didn't know we were competing for. "Mom, no, I—"

"Come on," Tanner says, pulling at my waist. "Whatever you and your mom need to sort out, it isn't going to happen here. Let's go."

"But—"

"No, Killer," he says, a strange understanding in his tone that sends a wave of betrayal slicing right through to my soul. "Your mom *needs us to go.*"

He says the words with such intensity that the fight fades out of me, and despite everything that's been left unsaid, I allow him to pull me away. We cross back over the small hedge toward Tanner's front door, and I can't help but glance back over my shoulder, watching as Mom walks away.

My gaze shifts, finding Orlando standing right where we left him, not moving a single muscle as he stares after us, the poison in his eyes sending shivers down my spine. For the first time, I truly fear for my mother inside that house. Surely nothing will happen while Jensen is there. Orlando couldn't be that stupid … Right?

Orlando catches my eye and his stare is like taking a shot of lava, burning everything in its path. His lips kick up into a wicked grin and rage rocks through me as my nails dig into Tanner's hand. Tanner glances back at me, sees what has my attention, and pushes me past him into the house.

The door slams between us, locking me inside, and as I scramble to open it again, Tanner holds it from the other side. I hear muffled words through the door and the bite in Tanner's tone suggests that whatever he's saying was never intended for my ears.

I bang on the door, demanding Tanner open it, and when he finally does, I prepare to break past him. Only Tanner's reflexes are like lightning, catching me before I even get one foot out the door.

Tanner lifts me off the ground as I try to break free, but his arms are like two steel bars across my chest. He moves into the house, getting far enough inside to slam and lock the door behind him. Before I even know what's going on, Tanner's already halfway up the stairs, carrying me right along with him.

"Put me down," I cry, the desperation in my tone dragging me into a raging, neverending fog of despair.

Tanner doesn't respond, just clenches his jaw and keeps walking. He reaches the top of the stairs, and with each step he takes down the hallway toward his bedroom, I take a breath, my emotions growing wilder by the second.

By the time he's pushing into his bedroom and closing the door behind us, tears are welling in my eyes. The soft thud of the door sounds through the room and Tanner releases me, gently lowering me to my feet and pulling me into his chest. His arms close around me once again, only this time it's a warm embrace, and I fall into him, my tears already soaking through his shirt.

"He's going to keep hurting her," I cry, never having felt this type of intense helplessness before.

"I know," Tanner says, his voice grim and thick with devastation. "That's why she needed you to go."

"What?" I breathe, pulling back and looking up at him. "What the hell are you talking about? She told me to go because she didn't want me accusing her fucktard husband of being an asshole."

Tanner shakes his head. "I don't think so," he says. "It took me a minute to see, but after you asked her if he was holding something over her, it clicked."

"What clicked?" I demand, stepping out of his arms and hastily wiping my face. "I don't understand."

"I … fuck," he says with a heavy breath, moving across his room and running his hand back through his hair. "There's something I need to tell you, and you're not going to like it. Hell, you'll be even more pissed that I haven't said anything about it, but I think once you know, it might help you understand what's going on with your mom. At least, what I *think* is going on. I could be wrong."

I clench my jaw, nerves pulsing through my body. "What do you mean there's something you need to tell me? I thought we got everything out in the open yesterday? There weren't supposed to be any more secrets between us."

"I … it's not exactly a secret. I didn't want to tell you because I know how this will make you feel."

"What the hell are you talking about?"

Tanner sighs and drops onto the edge of his bed. "Come here," he says, patting the space beside him.

I shake my head and make a point of crossing my arms over my chest and remaining exactly where I am. "Spill it, Tanner."

He presses his lips into a hard line and nods before scrunching his face, not wanting to talk about whatever the fuck this is, but he's backed himself into a corner and I won't be taking no for an answer. "You know when I was being held in that cell and Channing came to chat?"

"You mean blackmail you?"

"Yeah, that," he mutters darkly. "Yesterday you asked me what his reasons were for threatening me with exposure—"

"Because you're the brother of his client's victim," I finish. He mentioned a few other reasons, but I know damn well that is the most likely option. "You know as well as I do, this is his way of trying to get payback for the fist-sized bruise you left across his jaw."

"It's more than that."

Unease rocks through me, and I don't like the way his eyes harden. "What do you mean?" I ask shakily, watching him closely for every little change in his expression.

"In the cell, he was saying how I was being so bold for someone whose girlfriend lives under his roof, so when I subtly let him know the things I would do to him if he ever touched you, he implied that he had bigger plans for you."

"Huh?" I grunt, not understanding where the hell this is going.

"He said you're nothing but a careless woman whose sole purpose is to cater to a man, and once he's had his fill of your mom, he'd be taking you too." Bile burns up my esophagus. "He said that my job was to wine and dine you, keep you warm and well-trained until he's ready for you. He said something about teaching you how to become a perfect wife in public and a fucking whore in bed."

Tanner glances down, unable to meet my eye. "And when you told him how that was going to go down?" I question, knowing damn well a suggestion like that would have been met with nothing short of a million fatal threats from Tanner.

"He threatened to release the photographs."

I nod, the very thought of it making me sick, but while I want to throttle him for not telling me, I understand why he didn't … couldn't.

Me knowing doesn't serve any purpose other than to make me want to throw up. It's not something that will ever happen, not even close, but what I don't understand is how he thinks this has anything to do with my mom. "Okay, so Orlando is a dirty pervert who wants to use me as some kind of prize in public and a personal sex slave at home, but how does this have anything to do with Mom kicking me out?"

"Because I think she knows, and I think this is her way of trying to protect you, trying to keep you away from that house."

"No," I say, shaking my head. "No, it's not possible. She'd never let it happen."

"But what if she had no choice?" he says. "What if she was forced into a marriage with him and now she's doing everything in her power to keep you away from the same fate?"

I shake my head again. "I would know. She wouldn't hide that from me."

Tanner shrugs his shoulders before getting off his bed and crossing the room. He wraps his arms around me, pulling me into his chest as I feel my world spiral out of control. "I could be wrong," he tells me. "Your mom could have really been kicking you out because she's fucked in the head, but that doesn't sound like the woman who raised you. And deep down, I think you know that."

Letting out a heavy sigh, I glance out Tanner's bedroom window to the house next door, chills sweeping over my body while hoping to God he's wrong. Because if he's not and my mother has been protecting me this whole time, trapping herself in an abusive marriage solely to keep Orlando away from me, I'll never be able to forgive myself.

CHAPTER 16

TANNER

Most days, Riley is a blessing in disguise. But today, the thought of knocking his teeth in is getting me hard. The fucker won't stop talking, even in the middle of bench pressing. I swear, the asshole just likes the sound of his own voice. If I could walk out and leave him here, I would. The only issue is I stupidly agreed to do this at my home gym and not his.

I've been best friends with the guy for years. I know him better than I know myself, and when he's like this, it usually means he either just had the best fuck of his life or he's met a brand-new woman to torment with his undying messed-up brand of adoration. And seeing as though he's been with me all morning—and I can guarantee I haven't fucked him—it could only be the second option. Though, the fact he's been running his mouth all day and hasn't found a second to mention this mystery woman makes me wonder what it is about her he's hiding. Hell, maybe she has a third tit and he's gatekeeping her, hoping like fuck the boys don't try and take her off his hands.

"—and so, Logan was trying to get one up Chanel in the Jacuzzi," he says, talking shit about last night's party Bri and I skipped out on. "But she was all like 'Nah, babe, everyone can see,' and Logan laughed it off, but you know what Chanel is like. Once the idea was put into her head and she had a minute to think it over, she was so down. I swear, they're denying it, but they were definitely fucking in the Jacuzzi, like right fucking next to me! Can you believe it? I mean, fuck. If you're gonna mess around right next to a guy, the least you can do is extend an invitation."

I scoff, picturing it so perfectly. Chanel sitting on Logan's lap in the Jacuzzi with Riley sitting beside them doing everything he could to make it awkward and uncomfortable while they tried to hold a conversation, pretending Logan's cock wasn't buried deep inside her cunt.

"Right, so while that was going down, Jax was sitting across the party at the bar watching Arizona like a fucking hawk. I was counting on him for a good night, but fuck man, the kid has got it bad. He's seriously fucked up over her. He just sat there all night and moped about the fact she was trying to spread her legs for some other guy."

"Huh?" I cut in, one of the few words Riley has let me get in during our workout. "The fuck you mean she was trying to spread her legs for some other guy? She's been frothing at the mouth over Jax and swears she can't get over him."

"Oh yeah, Arizona ain't stupid. Everyone could see Jax was watching her, so she played him at his own game, let him get a taste of what it's like when she had to watch him fucking around with other chicks. I doubt she let the other dude fuck her, but as far as Jax could tell, she was down for anything and it drove him fucking mad. He was drinking the heavy shit, and you know what he's like when he's drunk and depressed. That shit ain't fun."

"Shit," I mutter, watching as Riley lowers the bar to his chest again, knowing he'll be getting close to his limit. "Wait. Jax is still on medication. He shouldn't have been drinking."

"Try telling him that," he says with a grunt, pushing out another rep, trying to be a hero. "But for the record, that's the last time I count on any of you fuckers for a good night. You bailed, Jax moped, and Logan was too far up his girlfriend to remember to pull out."

I try not to laugh. "Bullshit. Logan's not that fucking stupid."

"You sure about that?" he questions, racking the bar and glancing up at me. "Think about it. Where the fuck would he have stashed a rubber? We were in the fucking Jacuzzi and the swim trunks he was wearing left nothing to the imagination. They were so fucking tight I could see the outline of his balls through the material."

"Fuck bro, I could have done without that image in my head," I mutter, hating how fucking right he is, but Logan knows better. He's asking for trouble. The idiot needs a reality check.

Riley sits up and takes a quick drink of water as I walk around the side of the bench press, adjusting the weights for the next round. We get back into position, and just as Riley's hand curls around the bar, the sound of my phone cuts through the silence. "Hold up," I say, fishing my phone out of my pocket and seeing an incoming call from my father.

"What the fuck?" I murmur, staring at it as it rings, unsure if I can be fucked getting into some bullshit argument with the bastard today, though having said that, I sure as fuck need some answers from him.

"Who is it?" Riley questions, hearing the bite in my tone.

My gaze flashes up to him, letting him see the pure irritation in my stare. "My dad."

"Huh," he grunts, just as confused as I am. "What the fuck does he want?"

"How the hell am I supposed to know?"

Riley gives me a pointed stare. "Here's an idea," he says mockingly. "Maybe answer the fucking thing and find out."

Rolling my eyes, I let out a heavy sigh and hit accept before bringing the phone to my ear. "What did I do to deserve this call?" I say, letting out a heavy sigh.

"Helloooooow," a child booms through the phone, confusing the absolute shit out of me.

My eyes go wide as I pull away from the phone, glancing at the screen and double-checking I haven't taken a few too many hits to the head during football. It definitely says Dad across the screen, and I doubt he got a new number. He has too many business associates to deal with the hassle that comes from changing numbers. "Umm, hi," I say awkwardly, my brows furrowed, putting the phone back to my ear as Riley sits up and watches me, picking up on the hesitation in my tone. "Who is this?"

The little girl laughs and it only confuses me more. "It's me, silly."

The fuck? Who the hell is *me?*

"Okay," I say, trying to figure out why some random kid would have my father's phone, while also trying to figure out if I care enough to try and guide her back to wherever she stole it from. "Where'd you get this phone?"

"Dada's pocket," the little girl says with a cheeky giggle, knowing she's probably done something she wasn't supposed to do, while unintentionally dropping a lead weight right onto my chest. "Wash your name?"

My gaze shifts back to Riley as a daunting feeling begins growing deep in my gut and spreading through my veins, plaguing me with unease. "I'm Tanner," I tell her, swallowing hard, a sharp edge to my tone. "Tanner Morgan."

She laughs again, only this time it's so high-pitched and squeaky I have to pull the phone away from my ear to keep it from bursting my eardrum. "That's wike my name," she says, her excitement knowing no bounds. "We da same."

"Are we?" I question, Riley now watching me back, his eyes narrowed to slits, having no fucking idea what's going on, but that would make two of us. I could have sworn she said this was her dada's phone. "What's your name?"

"Roni," she says so confidently. "Roni Morgan."

Morgan.

Fuck.

My mouth goes dry as my stomach clenches, threatening to throw up the chicken kebab I'm now regretting. "Morgan, huh?" I ask, hoping like fuck this is some twisted coincidence and that my father isn't out there somewhere with another fucking kid. "How old are you, Roni?"

"Ummm," she pauses, really thinking about it. "Umm, fr … free."

"Three?" I question. "You're three?"

"Uh-huh."

Riley stands and steps closer to me, staring at me with the oddest concern, a look I've only seen from him out on the football field after I take a nasty hit. "Who the fuck are you talking to?"

I shake my head, not wanting to miss a damn thing this little girl says, only the sound of a screaming baby in the background has me on edge, my hands fucking shaking, but with what? Rage? Confusion? Betrayal? I don't fucking know. "Who's that baby, Roni?" I ask, putting the phone on speaker, knowing Riley won't stop badgering me until he gets an answer, no matter if I'm in the middle of a conversation or not. "Is that your brother?"

"Uh-huh," she says, sounding almost distracted. "I have two of them. They're twinnies."

Riley's eyes widen, putting the pieces together with the little bits of information he's heard from the one-sided conversation. His gaze snaps back to mine, his jaw hanging open as he slowly shakes his head, the thoughts going through his mind mirroring the ones in mine.

"Twins, huh?" I breathe, my voice breaking.

"Yeah, dey kinda fat."

I scoff, trying not to laugh. "You know, my sister Addie was kinda chunky when she was a baby too, she was like a miniature sumo wrestler."

"What's a sumo wrestler?"

"It's a—" I cut myself off, hearing the baby screaming again, and decide I really don't want to get into that right now. "Where's your mommy at? Is she looking after the babies?"

Roni sighs and despite not being able to see her face, something shifts in the conversation. "She's always looking after the babies," she tells me, her voice sad. "She always plays with dem now. Not me."

I try to say something, but I'm lost for words. I don't do little kids. I wouldn't know where the hell to even start when trying to console one, that's Addie's department. She's always been good at that shit. Me? Not so much. I'm awkward as fuck. "I um, I'm sure your mom loves you very much," I say, scrunching my face and looking at Riley for approval, but he gives me a blank stare and shrugs his shoulders, just as lost as I am. "What about your daddy?" I question, my stomach dropping right out of my fucking ass, the anticipation of her response sending me spiraling into a black abyss. "Does he spend time with you?"

"Dada works lots."

"Yeah, mine too," I tell her, feeling as though my legs are about to give out beneath me. "What's, um … What's your dad's name?"

"Twenton," she says, unknowingly detonating the bomb that's going to destroy my world and shred Mom and Addie's hearts to pieces until they're nothing but dirty scraps on the floor.

Trenton Morgan. My goddamn father.

My knees finally give out and I fall back, catching myself against the wall as the betrayal rocks through me. I've never had a close relationship with my father, not since I hit my teens, but I never imagined he could do this to us. I never thought he'd do this to Mom. He's not just cheating on her, he's got himself a whole new family.

Riley watches me as Roni continues talking, but my head is spinning so erratically that I can't make out her words. The one thing I know for sure is this little girl is my sister, and as for her chunky twin brothers who've stolen her mother's attention, well fuck, they're my brothers too.

Riley gapes at me, having no fucking idea what to say to make any of this okay, and I don't expect him to because fuck, I haven't got a damn clue what to say either. I try to tune into Roni's voice, knowing in the back of my mind this could be my only chance to get information on this family I never knew I had, but a woman's voice cuts through the phone. "Roni, baby, where are you?"

"Uh-oh," she laughs before the phone is plagued by the rustling sounds of Roni bolting through her home.

"Roni," the woman calls. "Where are you—oh no, not again. You know you're not allowed to touch daddy's phone." Roni laughs, all too proud of herself as her mother chants in the background. "Oh, shit, shit, shit, shit, shit."

A baby starts crying again, but the rustling gets louder, drowning the baby out until I hear what must be my father's side piece yanking the phone out of Roni's hand. There's a short silence before a panicked curse. "Oh, crap, Roni. You're calling people again?" she says before her voice is much louder, speaking to me. "Hello? Hi, I'm so sorry, my daughter likes to call people. Who is this?"

I pause, unsure how to handle this. I have no idea what this woman knows of me or if she even knows of me at all. Does she think my father is a knight in shining armor giving her the world, or does she know he's betrayed the family he has back home, a family who very much believed they were his only priority? "I think the more appropriate question is, who are you?"

"Ex ... excuse me?" she questions, taken aback by my question. "Who is this?"

"My name is Tanner Morgan. I'm the son of the man you're currently living a double life with."

There's a pause and I swear, I can almost hear the rapid beat of her heart. "I ... Ummm, what?" she breathes, sounding as though I'm playing some kind of wicked prank on her. "What are you talking about?"

"Your boyfriend—"

"Husband," she cuts in with an accusing tone, as though trying to insert some kind of dominance over this conversation.

I laugh. "Holy shit, he's really got you fooled," I tell her, almost pitying the woman. "I'm sorry to break the news, my father has been married to my mother for twenty-three years, and despite how much I despise the man, they're still very happily married. So, I'll ask you again, who the hell are you?"

"I'm ... I'm his wife. We've been married for five years. I just had his babies."

I cringe. "Well shit, hey! This is awkward," I say. "I suppose you better check the legality of that wedding certificate, but in the meantime, could you let him know he has a wife and daughter back home who've been desperate for his return?"

"Uhhh …"

I close my eyes, the weight of my father's infidelity weighing down on my shoulders. How the fuck am I supposed to tell Mom and Addie about this? I suppose I could simply do it without tact like I just did to this woman. I don't even know her name and I just blew up her world in the space of two seconds, just as her three-year-old daughter did to me. I mean sure, I probably owe her an apology, but she's not going to get it today.

There's nothing but the soft cries of the woman's babies in the background and then just like that, the call goes dead, and I realize there's a good chance I will never get the answers to the millions of questions flashing through my head. Who the hell is she? When did my father's affair start? Will my half-siblings ever be a part of my life? And will that little girl ever truly know who I am to her? Because even though I've never met her, never even laid eyes on her, I feel this strange need to protect her, exactly how I feel about needing to keep Addison safe from the ugliness and horrors of this world.

The phone falls from my fingers, crashing to the ground and cracking the screen as my hands come up and slowly drag down my face. "Fuck, Tanner," Riley says, his voice thick with hesitation, trying to find the right words. "You good?"

I shrug my shoulders, the overwhelming need to have Bri in my arms plaguing me. "I don't know, man," I say. "It's not me who's going to be hurt by this."

"I know," he says, knowing just how much Addison idolizes my father, and how my mom longs for him when he's away on his so-called business trips. "Are you going to tell them?"

"What kind of prick would it make me if I didn't?" I ask him, hating this position I've somehow put myself in. I stand, needing to get this over and done with quickly, starting with Mom. I'll let her decide how she wants to break the news to Addie, but I won't hide this from them. I won't stoop to his level and betray their trust like he does, and I sure as fuck won't protect his secret, no matter if he's been doing the same for me about that night with the Hardin brothers. I don't care what it costs me; I won't hide from this.

Grabbing my water bottle, I'm just about to tell Riley I think it best if he jets out of here when I turn and find Mom sitting just outside our home gym in the adjoining living room, her hand over her mouth as tears stream down her face, doing everything in her power not to fall apart. "Fuck," I whisper, coming to a stop.

Riley glances up and swallows hard, seeing the broken woman before us and sighs, heartbreak flashing in his eyes. "I'll leave you to it, man," he says, grabbing his shit, and without another word, he walks out of the gym and crosses to my mom. He doesn't say anything, just simply leans down and wraps his arms around her, giving a gentle squeeze before pulling away and giving her space.

Riley vanishes out the side door, leaving me with my mom.

I join her on the couch and take her hand, holding it in my lap and trying to figure out how to talk about this, despite it being crystal clear she heard more than enough of my conversation. "I don't know what to tell you," I say, my voice breaking with pain, the lump in my throat making it hard to breathe.

Mom pulls her hand free from mine before hastily wiping her eyes and standing up. She makes a show of straightening her outfit before giving me a fake smile while trying to appear encouraging. "You don't need to tell me anything," she says. "I'm your mom. I should be the one consoling you, but I know how you hate to be coddled."

I stand in front of her and pull her into a tight hug, hating the broken sob that tears from her throat as she curls into me. "It's okay to be sad and hurt," I tell her. "You don't need to be strong for me. I got you."

Mom cries for a moment, her tears staining my shirt and then finally, she pulls herself together and wipes her eyes again. She gives herself a moment to breathe before giving me another smile, though this time, there's a little more warmth to it. "I'll have to break this to your sister," she tells me. "It's going to break her heart."

"It will," I agree.

"I don't know how much more hurt Addison can take," she confides.

"I know, but it'll hurt her more if we keep it from her, and I won't do that."

Mom nods, reaching for my hand and squeezing. "You're right," she says before allowing a quiet moment to pass between us. "I'm sorry you had to find out like that. That's not a conversation anyone ever wants to have, especially someone your age. I think you handled yourself well."

I give her a blank stare. "You're fucking with me, right?" I laugh, a grin pulling at my lips. "I was an ass to that woman."

"Language," she scolds. "But yes, you were a bit of an ... ass. However, you gave her the information she needed to make her own decisions. You didn't need to do that. It wasn't your responsibility to shoulder, but you did, and that shows what a remarkable young man you've become."

I give her another blank stare. "Don't give credit where it's not due," I tell her. "There was nothing remarkable about it. I was hurting and I wanted her to feel it too. She had a smug tone, the way she called him her *husband,* and I wanted her to feel the sting just like you and Addie were going to. I wasn't kind, Mom. I wanted her to know she wasn't the only one in his life, wasn't special enough for him to have ended things here. That doesn't make me a saint, it makes me a bastard."

Mom nods. "Either way, this is only the beginning. Something tells me there's about to be some big changes around here, so buckle up, kid. The three of us need to stick together." And just like that, she gives me one more smile, one that doesn't reach her eyes, and not a moment later she walks away, barely holding herself together.

CHAPTER 17
Brielle

One messed-up drama after the next. When the hell will life go back to normal?

I can't even wrap my head around everything that's been going on. I'm pretty sure there's some kind of rule about not being stressed out while trying to heal from a stab wound. You know, because it's not good for you and all that. But hell, let's go ahead and throw a bigamist asshole with a double life, second wife, and children on top of the ever-growing pile of shit to deal with. Not to mention the even bigger asshole next door who thinks I'm about to become his personal sex slave. Like what the fuck is going on around here?

I knew Tanner's father was an asshole the second I met him. He didn't think I was good enough, but all those bad vibes would never have led me to believe he'd be the type of man to build another life across the other side of the world, while still maintaining a marriage and family here in Bradford. He seemed distant while he was here, not that I saw much of him. But from what I did see, I thought he loved his wife and daughter, the apple of his eye.

I just wish I'd been here for Tanner when he found out. If I'd known, I would have raced right back here, but I was holed up in the library, smashing out another assignment while Tanner was working out with Riley. He's been so busy trying to be the shoulder for his mom to cry on that he disregards his own feelings in his need to be her hero. Sure, a part of me loves that about him, but he won't be able to help anyone if he doesn't process and deal with the hurt himself. I know Tanner likes to be the protector of his family, but sometimes he needs to put himself first.

It's been a strange afternoon in the Morgan household. I've been chilling with Tanner while his mom took Addie down to the big comfy couches and broke the news to her. At first, Addie seemed numb, but then the tears started, and now she's pissed. As for their mom, she's just broken. I don't blame her though. I can't imagine how it would feel learning your husband of twenty-something years created a family across the world with someone else, learning he had three young children with another woman and had supposedly married her. If it were me, I'd be asking how many other women there had been and how long it'd been going on. I'd be re-evaluating my whole life and trying to figure out how the hell to move forward.

It's creeping toward dinner time when I walk up the stairs, looking for Tanner to figure out what our plans are for the night, but I come to a stop, finding him standing in Addison's doorway, murmuring some kind of encouraging words to make her feel better about the bomb she was blindsided with. I don't bother them and instead, detour to Tanner's room. He knows I'm here, despite not making a sound. I don't know how, maybe he can sense me. Hell, I wouldn't be surprised if he had hidden a GPS tracker on me somewhere, and that goes for Addie too.

Tanner is protective, and since Colby decided to surprise us with a little knife play, that protectiveness has only become more intense. I won't lie, most of the time, that protectiveness is hot as fuck, but at other times, it's simply overbearing. I'm sure, given time, he'll be able to relax, but while it's still so fresh and those memories continue to haunt him, he won't be able to find peace.

Pushing through Tanner's bedroom, a figure in the window has me pulling up short. My eyes widen, and my heart kicks into gear, but the second I see my brother's stupid face grinning through the window of the second story bedroom, a cheesy smile rips across my face.

"Holy shit! Damien!" I shout, rushing over to the window to let him in, only the fucker laughs and straightens up before whipping his dick out and slamming it up against the glass, proving once and for all he's spent way too much time living around a bunch of dudes.

I scream and turn away from the window, my eyes burning at seeing all too much of my brother. He squishes his balls up against the glass as he laughs so damn hard the moron almost falls back and tumbles right off the roof.

"BRI?" Tanner roars, storming down the hall at the sound of my scream, only to bust through the door to find my brother's version of a squashed frog up against the glass. Not being able to see his face, Tanner is just about ready to end his life, only Damien pulls back and leans down again, grinning at Tanner like a thirteen-year-old boy who just saw his first set of tits.

Tanner stops, his expression morphing into bewildered glee as he shakes his head. "What the fuck, man?" he says as I step up to the window, flicking the latch and opening it wide for the asshole to climb in.

A laugh comes from the door and I whip around just in time to watch as Addison lowers her phone and starts hashing out a text, clearly having captured one of the worst moments of my life, right below getting stabbed, being in a car wreck, and tearing off my meat curtain with hot wax. "Oooh, Ilaria's night is about to get a whole lot better." And just like that, she hits send on her message and I shake my head, never so mortified in my life.

Damien's feet hit the ground and he smirks at me, so damn proud of himself. "What's up, dork?" he says, crashing into me and pulling me into a tight hug.

I fight against him, desperately trying to shove him off me. "Eewww," I shriek. "Get off me with your dirty dick hands. What the hell is wrong with you?"

Damien laughs and eventually releases me, but not before making a point to rub them all over my face, making me gag. I shake my head, never wanting to pulverize someone so badly in my life. Don't get me wrong, I love my brother, I adore him, but it's times like this that make me wish I were an only child. I mean, who the hell made it a rule that big brothers are supposed to torment their little sisters? Whoever that was deserves a cactus right up the pee hole.

Stepping away from Damien, I walk toward Tanner's private bathroom. "Excuse me while I bleach my face," I mutter. I swear, I have no idea what Ilaria sees in this douche-canoe.

"Sure," Damien says, ignoring my glare as though it simply bounces off him. "When you're done, you can explain why the hell Mom just told me you're living here now, and after that, we're getting fucked up." He turns to Tanner. "Know any parties going on tonight?"

Well, fuck. Looks like my night just got a little more interesting.

Precisely eight minutes later, I'm standing in the cold with my face scrunched in distaste. "Are you sure we really need to bring him?" I ask, hovering in Orlando's backyard and staring up at Jensen's bedroom window. "He's such an ass."

"Why, that's your big brother you're talking about," Damien says in his version of a Southern drawl, only it just makes him sound like a bigger ass than Jensen. "You wouldn't dream about leavin' me behind now, would ya, lil darlin'?"

"First off, he's our *stepbrother*," I remind him, rolling my eyes as Addison scoffs behind me, knowing damn well how I'm about to answer that question because if the tables were turned, she'd answer it the exact same way. "And second, do you really want the answer to that while the memory of your dick hands on my face are still burning their way through my brain?"

"Good point," he murmurs before making a step out of his hands and bending low. "Now, quit fucking around and get your ass up there."

I groan before stepping into him and shoving my hand against his shoulder. My foot drops into his hands and Tanner moves in behind me, more than ready to help hoist me onto the roof. "I swear, If I find that asshole doing anything unholy in his room, you're both paying for my therapy."

Tanner scoffs. "Really? After everything that's been going down, that's what you think will put you into therapy?"

I roll my eyes, but before I can get another word in, Tanner and Damien hoist me up and a piercing squeal tears from deep in my throat. I clutch the edge of the roof as they push me all the way up, and I scramble to get my knees firmly on the roof. "Holy fuck," I mutter, commando crawling across the rough shingles, certain I'm about to fall and drop to my untimely death. I crawl right across to Jensen's window before pulling myself up against the frame and peering in.

My face scrunches, taking a look at the hot mess before me, and while I'm glad not to see him jerking off into an apple pie, there's definitely porn paused on his laptop. I bang my knuckles against the glass. "Oi, fucker," I call through the glass.

Jensen's head pops out of his bathroom, his toothbrush hanging from his mouth. "What the fuck?" he says, catching sight of me at his window. He gapes at me, shaking his head before ducking back into his bathroom and spitting a mouthful of toothpaste into the sink. He ditches the toothbrush and wipes his mouth before striding out again. "What the hell are you doing?"

"Grab your shit," I tell him, not exactly wanting to explain the bullshit that led me right up to this moment of my life. "We're going to a party."

"Fuck off, like I'd wanna spend my night chilling with you."

Fucking liar. "Non-negotiable, asshole. Let's go."

I turn and scramble my way back to the edge of the roof, more than ready to shove my foot up Damien's ass if he even thinks about dropping me. Just as I plonk my ass on the edge and get ready to jump, I hear Jensen's window opening behind me. He peers past me to see the crowd gathered below and his whole demeanor changes, now suddenly more than ready for a night of wild partying. "Aye," he says, cheery fucking McGee. "When the fuck did you get back?"

"Just now," Damien responds. "I was caught by Mom in the driveway long enough to know I didn't want to walk through the front door, so hurry up. We're getting fucked up."

"Yeah, alright," Jensen says, clearly having some kind of man boner for my stupid brother. "I'm down."

"Don't be stingy," Damien tells him. "Bring the good shit."

Jensen chuckles and disappears from view, leaving me to launch myself off the roof and right into Tanner's arms, and thank fuck for that because Damien definitely wasn't paying attention. We walk around the house, meeting Jensen at the front door as he locks up. "You know my dad and your mom took off like ten minutes ago," he tells us. "You could have used the fucking door."

I glare at Damien. I should have trusted my gut when the asshole insisted Mom and Orlando were still home, but he just shrugs.

"Consider it all part of the adventure." I roll my eyes as we cut back across to the Morgan property. Just as Tanner hits the button for the garage door and Damien gets sight of the black Mustang waiting patiently for a little love and affection, he grins wide and holds his hand out for the keys. "I'm driving."

Jensen sits up front so me, Tanner, and Addie squish into the backseat, and dammmmmn, Tanner doesn't seem impressed by this turn of events. He doesn't strike me as a backseat kind of guy, especially in his own car. He likes control, and more than that, he likes to be the big guy on campus, so this really doesn't sit well with him, but it's a little too late for that. What's one ride, though?

"Alright," Damien says, glancing up and meeting my stare through the rearview mirror. "Catch me up. What happened with the Jacobs' kid? Did he get locked up?"

My eyes widen and I cringe, knowing damn well I haven't been giving him updates about Colby, being stabbed, or any of the other bullshit that's been going on around here. "Ummm," I say, awkwardly glancing toward Tanner, not knowing how to answer this. "He's certainly paying for what he did, if that's what you mean."

Sensing the strange tension now filling the car, Damien narrows his eyes. "What the fuck is that supposed to mean?"

He's met with silence from the backseat, but apparently Jensen has no reservations and is more than happy to fill in the details. "Oh, you haven't heard?" Jensen questions. "Man, things have been fucked up since you left. So, you know my dad was representing Jacobs and somehow got him off the rape charges, which by the way, I've been looking into that shit and I've got no fucking idea how he did it. It doesn't make sense to me, but what do I know?"

"Shit, he really got off?" Damien questions, glancing up at me again before trailing his gaze to Addison beside me who studiously stares out the window, pretending she can't hear the conversation around her. I nod and Damien cringes. "Fuck, that sucks."

Jensen continues. "Yeah, there's no fucking question Jacobs did it, so your sister's boyfriend took it into his own hands like the dumbass he is and got himself locked up for a forty-eight-hour hold—"

"Wait, what?" Damien says, now looking at Tanner. "How the fuck did you manage that?"

A sly grin cuts across Tanner's face, his eyes sparkling with the memory of his fist slamming against Orlando's jaw. "Let's just say Channing won't be able to eat without thinking of me ever again."

Jensen chuckles, knowing just how right Tanner is. "You should have seen my old man after he took that hit. I've never seen him so angry. Man, his jaw was messed up, but not as messed up as Jacobs after he stabbed the girls and Jax."

Damien slams on the brake, the car screeching to a halt as traffic weaves around us, laying on their horns and hollering abuse out their windows as they barrel past us, but all I can do is cringe, especially as Damien whips around to gape at me. "What the fuck did he just say? Stabbed, Brielle? You got fucking stabbed by that bastard?"

I cringe some more before adjusting myself in my seat and raising my hips. I pull up the hem of my shirt and push my pants down just enough to show him the angry red scar still causing havoc over my body. Damien's eyes bug out of his head before shifting to Addison who does the same, pulling up her shirt to see the scar high on her ribs.

"Holy fuck," Damien breathes, shaking his head. He whips back around, sitting in silence before the rage takes over and he slams his hand down over the steering wheel. He shoves his door open in the middle of the road and gets out, pacing in front of the Mustang and creating abstract shadows as he cuts through the headlights.

I take a heavy breath and as cars zoom around us, a strange awkward silence fills the car. Jensen reaches across and turns on the hazard lights, the irritating click, click, click of the flashing lights grating on my nerves. I clench my jaw before finally letting him have it. "Really?" I demand. "You had to go and tell him we got stabbed?"

Jensen shrugs unapologetically. "How was I supposed to know you failed to tell your brother you were dying in the hospital from a stab wound? Seems to me like the kind of information people usually share."

Addison nudges me. "He's got a point."

"Damn it."

A moment passes before Damien comes striding back to the car and drops into the driver's seat, putting the Mustang back in gear and turning off the hazard lights. "Okay," he finally says, hitting the gas simply to give himself something to do other than bitch me out. "We'll be at Riley's place in less than three minutes, and you have until then to tell me every fucking thing that's happened here since I've been gone, and after that, I'm getting fucked up."

Sounds like the best fucking plan I've ever heard.

The next three minutes are horrible as we go over everything from the stabbing to Tanner putting Colby in a coma, which I'm not surprised to find that Damien is thrilled about. We explain how the few days after that went down, and how I moved into Tanner's place with Jax to heal. And just to throw salt on the wound, I tell him about Orlando's plans for me and how we believe Mom trapped herself to save me. Hell, Addison also makes a point to tell him about Tanner's baby daddy issues, which naturally, is also news to Jensen. Though surprisingly, Jensen doesn't seemed shocked about his father's desires to fuck me at all.

By the time every last word has been said, all secrets divulged bar one, Damien is pulling up in the center of Riley's extravagant driveway. He cuts the engine and gets out before holding the door open for me and Addie as though he's some kind of perfect gentleman. He fixes me with a scathing glare and it's only then I realize just how much trouble I'm really in.

Thank fuck for alcohol.

CHAPTER 18

TANNER

The second I can, I snatch the keys to my Mustang right out of Damien's hands. Don't get me wrong, I'm more than happy to let the guy drive her. Sure, he likes to fuck around, but when people's lives are in his hands, especially his sister's, he ensures they're safe. Besides, he's not a bad driver, but from the sound of it, he'll be in absolutely no state to drive home tonight.

Music pours from Riley's home, and I have to give the bastard credit. There wasn't going to be a party tonight, or at least, nothing worth our time, and the minute I called and said we were down to party, he pulled this shit together. It's been twenty-five minutes tops since that call and there's already people swarming through his house. Riley is a lot of things, but inadequate is not one of them.

Making our way through the house, we head straight out back to where the boys are bound to be. We pass Chanel and Ari spiking the punch and find Hudson on the way. He pauses for a minute, looking over Addison before shoving his hands deep in his pockets and falling in behind us. The two of them awkwardly pretend everything is cool between them, but we all know things have been awkward since Addison kissed him in the cafeteria.

She's avoided him like the plague, and while he's tried everything he can to get back to where they were, things have shifted between them, and I honestly don't know if it's good or bad. With how stubborn they both are, it could be years before one of them finally gives in and admits defeat.

Bri's hand remains in mine as we find the twins and Riley claiming the area by the pool. Ilaria sits with them, and I notice the exact moment she realizes Damien has tagged along. I scoff, watching as she sits up and fixes her hair and adjusts her tits in her black bikini top, trying to make them appear bigger than they already are.

Seeing us getting closer, Riley meets my stare and holds it, his eyes narrowing in question. The second we reach them, he stands and steps right into me, grabbing me and slapping me on the back, trying to appear as though he's just saying hello, when in fact I know it's much more than that. "You good?" he murmurs, keeping his voice low. After all, the last time I saw him, he was hightailing it out of my place after finding out my father had another whole family across the other side of the globe.

"Yeah, man," I mutter, not really wanting to talk about this now. "I just wanna get fucked up and not think about it."

"Alright," he says, pulling away. "Just say the word and I'll break out the weed."

I shake my head and indicate to Damien and Jensen. "Save your stash," I say, not really into it. "These assholes brought more than enough to go around."

"Fuck yeah," Riley says, moving across to Damien as I take Bri's hand again, leading her over to Jax and Logan to sit down. Riley walks right into Damien, throwing his arms around him and clapping him on the back as though they're best friends who haven't seen each other in years. "What's up, man? When did you get back?"

"'Bout an hour ago," Damien tells him, his gaze already shifting toward Ilaria. "I'm home for a few weeks then jetting off again."

Riley grins and I groan, recognizing the mischief in his eyes. After all, that very look has gotten me into a world of trouble before, the kind of trouble that gets people thrown into the back of cop cars and locked up until they remember their own freaking name. "So, what you're saying is we've got only a few weeks to get a lifetime of fucking around squeezed in?" he questions. "I hope you're ready for this."

Damien smiles, his eyes sparkling and locked on Ilaria's. "I'm ready if she is."

Well fuck, I don't think I've ever seen Ilaria blush like that. Her whole fucking head ducks as her cheeks flame the brightest shade of red. "Fucking hell. Could you lay it on any thicker?" Bri mutters. "Hold up, the dude we used to rent DVDs from at Blockbuster couldn't quite hear your desperation. Try it again, but this time, why don't you just drop your dick into Ilaria's hand?"

Damien grins. "Don't tempt me," he says. "That tight ass and gorgeous face are all I've been able to think about for weeks. You go and put ideas like that in my head, little sister, and I might not be able to resist."

Bri gags and throws herself to her feet. "If I have to put up with this shit all night, I'm going to need a drink." She searches out Addie. "Wanna come?"

Addie spares a glance toward Hudson before flying to her feet and stepping in beside Bri. "Fuck yeah," she says before turning a pointed look on Ilaria. "I assume you're not coming?"

Ilaria shakes her head, her cheeks still flaming bright red. "Nope, I think I'm good right here," she says, unable to stop perving on Brielle's brother.

The girls take off and Jax calls out after them. "Hey, if you see Ari anywhere, tell her to quit avoiding me. I know she's here."

Bri doesn't bother looking back at him but flips him off as she makes her way back inside, most likely to where we saw Ari and Chanel spiking the punch.

It takes less than thirty minutes before everyone starts to chill out and the drinks really start to flow. The girls strip down to their bikinis and take over the Jacuzzi, while Ilaria stays on Damien's lap with his lips permanently attached to her neck. I mean, fuck. I know these military guys wouldn't be getting any pussy at bootcamp, but shit, I wasn't expecting this motherfucker to go this hard so soon. There's no doubt about it, he's got game, and a shit-ton of it. More than I've seen from Riley and Jax combined. Ilaria's in good hands though. If any of us thought he'd screw her over, we would have cock blocked him until he was sent packing again.

The boys pass a joint between themselves, and the more hits Jax takes, the harder he stares at Ari. Fucking pathetic, really. "Dude," I say, kicking back and nodding across to the Jacuzzi. "If you want her, take her. She's right there waiting for you to man up. We all see you're messed up over her."

He shakes his head and glances away. "Don't know what you're talking about," he says. "I don't want her like that."

"Sure," I say, forcing myself not to grin at his misery. "So, which one of these bitches are you fucking then? The red head has been eye-fucking you since I got here. Go tap it."

Jax glances at the girl and his face scrunches up in distaste. "Nah, not feeling it tonight," he says, wanting nothing to do with the girl at all. Hell, if he wasn't so messed up over Ari, he would have fucked the red head right here beside me.

Riley scoffs. "Right, how's your dick lately? Still rocking a semi everywhere you go?"

Logan laughs. "Nah, he's jerking off in the shower every morning. I hear him moaning Ari's name every few hours. I'm surprised his cock hasn't fallen off with how often he's pulling it."

Jax punches his brother hard enough to give him a dead arm. "Fuck off, Logan. You had blue balls over Chanel for ages before you manned up and wifed her," he says before looking at me. "And don't get me started on the bullshit we had to endure before Bri decided yours was the only dick she wanted to jump on."

Logan scoffs while rubbing his arm. "Yeah, but at least I never carved a hole out of the bar of soap in the shower," he mutters before giving him a sarcastic grin. "If I were you, I'd be hitting up the bodywash or conditioner. Less friction, more slide."

The boys laugh and that only rubs Jax the wrong way, but hell, he's gotta get rubbed somehow since it's not gonna be by Ari. Having already punched his brother, he turns his glare on me. "You're one to fucking talk," he says, more than happy to dish out the bullshit, but unable to handle it when it's coming back at him. "Should we call you daddy from now on? How's your kid?"

Okay. Good mood, officially ruined.

"He's not my fucking kid," I say, letting Jax hear the hitch in my voice, a clear warning that he's crossed a line. "Rachael's a liar just like her piece of shit brother. She just wants me to pay for what I did to Colby, but the second that paternity test comes back without a match, she'll be the one to pay."

I down the rest of my beer and get up, needing a hit of fresh air and probably a hit of that joint that's been getting around too. I make my way over to the Jacuzzi and reach down, grabbing Bri under the arms and hauling her ass out. She screeches, not knowing who's got her, but the second she realizes it's me, she scrambles for her drink before it's too late.

I grab a towel and wrap it around her before pulling her into me. "Come and shake your ass for me," I murmur into her ear, my whispered words having her head tilting to the side and leaving me prisoner to her every need. My lips close over her warm skin and she presses back into me, her sweet ass grinding against my cock.

Her body moves as she dances against me, sipping her cocktail and winding her free hand up behind my neck. My fingers graze her thigh and slip up beneath the towel, but that's not good enough for her and she pulls the towel right off.

My arm circles her toned waist as she looks up at me over her shoulder. "Have we shown our faces here long enough?" she questions. "Because I have no issue with slipping away so you can fuck me in some dirty back alley while I scream your name."

My fucking cock springs to life as though it's got a mind of its own and judging by the devilish grin pulling at Bri's lips while she grinds her ass against me, she damn well knows it.

I'm just about to take her up on her offer when a booming voice cuts across the property. "Where the fuck are ya, boy?"

My back stiffens as my head snaps up, searching out Riley across the pool. He looks fucking sick, like his whole world is about to come caving in on him. "Who the hell is that?" Bri questions, watching the asshole push his way through the bodies.

"Fuck, stay here," I say, releasing Bri and stepping around her. "It's Riley's dad."

I start cutting across the yard and I'm not surprised to find Bri walking right behind me, half jogging to keep up with my long strides. "Like fuck you're leaving me behind, assface," she mutters at my back. "*I lean, you lean,* remember? You don't get to preach that and then leave me behind while you handle your shit. We're in this together. Your fight is my fight whether you like it or not. If your knuckles are getting bloody, then so are mine."

I clench my jaw, not having time to deal with this, not if Riley wants to get through this without another broken nose. I've had to cover for Riley far too many times due to the abuse his father puts him through, although not quite so much now that Riley's bigger than the fucker. When he talked back to him, Riley got a black eye, when the team lost a game, Riley got a broken arm, when he accidentally ordered pizzas instead of Chinese, Riley was hospitalized for a week.

And each one of those times, I've taken the blame.

Riley hates his father. He's humiliated by his abuse, and I don't blame him. Telling everyone your father beat your ass so bad you ended up in surgery isn't exactly something Riley wants circulating the school. Besides, I don't want to find out what his father would do if he thought Riley had been telling people. Instead, Riley calls me.

Riley and I beat the shit out of each other all the time. Coming to school with a split lip and stitches across our jaws isn't news to anyone, so Riley knows to call me. He punches me hard enough to draw blood and the next day, we walk into school together, claiming it was nothing but a spat between friends, and no one even bats an eyelid. Although something tells me the gig is about to be up.

I've come face to face with Cory Sullivan plenty of times. He knows exactly what I think of him, and I'm sure he's not so fond of me, especially since I'm the one who first convinced Riley he was big enough to fight back. I'm sure the first time Riley knocked him out cold came as a bit of a surprise, but at least the beatings seemed to ease after that. Now, Cory saves it for special occasions like when he's drunk as fuck. Times like now.

Riley looks out to the crowd, desperation and panic in his eyes as he searches me out. I'm only a few feet away, so it doesn't take him long to find me, and despite knowing he can handle this himself, he still seems relieved to have me ready and waiting at his back.

Cory beats me to Riley, barely able to stand straight on his feet. He's in a business suit, looking disheveled with his tie pulled loose and his shirt spilling out of his pants. He's the CEO of some big company and his favorite hobby is taking his shitty mood out on his son.

"The fuck is this?" Cory demands, haphazardly waving his hand around at all the people crowding his home. "You think you can invite your fucking friends into my house for a rager like you own the damn thing?"

Riley's hands go up, panic in his eyes, trying to defuse the situation before shit gets all too real. "Dad, it's cool. We'll take it somewhere else. Don't make a fucking scene."

"A scene? *Don't make a fucking scene?*" he demands, stepping into Riley and gripping the front of his shirt. "I'll show you a fucking scene, you good for nothing piece of shit."

His fist rears back and I hear the audible gasp coming from innocent bystanders as Riley's eyes widen, more than capable of handling a sloppy punch from his father, but that fact does nothing to take away the years of fear and power this motherfucker held over him.

I go to step in, more than ready to put this asshole in the ground, but a bikini-clad blonde shoots in front of me. "Hey asshole," she calls, loud enough to demand his attention.

Cory pauses, whipping his head to meet her furious stare as his fist hovers in the air. My heart races with fear. I know he won't hesitate to hit his son, but I don't know where he draws the line, and I sure as fuck don't want to use Bri to figure it out.

Before he even gets a word in, Bri storms in front of him, shoving him hard enough to make him wobble back, forcing him to release his hold on Riley. "You fuck with Riley, and you fuck with me too, and trust me, you don't want to do that."

Riley's hand goes to Bri's waist, ready to throw her out of the way, but she stands her ground, not moving a fucking inch, even when Cory comes back at her. "Mind ya business," he spits, getting right in her face, but she doesn't even flinch. Damien, on the other hand, looks like he's about ready to throw down. One hand on our girl and I'll happily spend the rest of my life behind bars, and I don't doubt Damien would be right there beside me. Cory's whole body seems to vibrate with rage. "This is between me and my son."

"Look around you," Bri says, her gaze as cold as ice as she indicates to the hundred or so pairs of eyes locked on us, phones in hands, more than ready to expose this motherfucker for exactly what he is. "Shit's getting cozy. It's between all of us now." Bri smirks, knowing she's got him right where she wants him. "Ball's in your court, so what's it going to be? You want to beat the shit out of your son in front of all these people?"

Cory growls, leaning in toward her, but Bri still holds her ground, her unwavering determination to protect Riley standing strong. "I suggest you get the fuck out of my house before it's you who ends up black and blue."

There's a collective gasp around us and my hands ball into fists, not taking kindly to threats against my girl, but still, she pushes back. "Hmm, I wonder," she says, glancing around us. "Show of hands how many of your parents are colleagues of Mr. Sullivan's?"

To my surprise, at least three hands raise high into the sky and Bri arches a brow at Cory, never looking so damn smug in her life, even more so as she lowers her voice and steps even closer. "I wonder how quickly they'll destroy you."

Fucking hell. I don't know whether to be worried or turned on. All I know is that there's a reason I stopped calling her Killjoy, and this is why. My girl is a killer through and through.

Cory's hand whips out, his fingers snapping around Bri's arm as he yanks her into him, spittle hitting her face. "Listen here, you little slut," he growls just as Damien leaps to his feet with determination to end him. But it's Riley I need to watch out for.

Time slows as my gaze snaps to his, a familiar look burning in his eyes. A look I've seen far too many times. It's one thing to threaten Riley, but fuck with someone he cares about, and it's the end of the fucking road for you.

I don't waste a fucking second.

Lunging forward, I throw my arms out, reaching for Bri and yanking her out of the way just as Riley's closed fist flies through the air with the force of a fucking cargo train. His father doesn't even see it coming, still focused on bitching out Bri.

Riley's fist slams into his face, not a hint of warning. His nose snaps like a twig with the most satisfying crunch I've ever heard and blood gushing out like a waterfall, splattering across the pavement as his head whips around with the force. Cory roars in pain, but the momentum has barely hit him yet. He falls back, and just to add insult to injury, Jax's foot accidentally-on-purpose slips out, tripping the fucker before discreetly pulling it back as though he didn't do a damn thing.

Cory falls into a row of vacated chairs, spilling abandoned drinks and making an even bigger fool of himself, and as the crowd of onlookers laugh at his expense, he tries to scramble to his feet.

Gripping onto his bloody nose, Cory stands and glares at his son. "You'll fucking regret this, boy," he says before spitting a mouthful of blood onto the ground.

Riley steps forward, not a hint of fear in his eyes. "Will I?" he questions. He holds his father's stare, and seeing his son has the upper hand, he turns and storms back into the house to the crowd's delight.

Riley lets out a breath as Bri breaks from my grasp, rushing into him and gripping both of his arms, demanding his attention. She looks up at him with big blue eyes and I can only imagine what he sees in them. "I'm so sorry," she says. "I had no idea. If—"

Riley shrugs her off, his stare hardening as he looks over her head to the DJ. "Turn up the fucking music." The guests all cheer as the music is cranked up, and without another word, Riley steps away from Bri to grab his drink. He lifts the glass to his lips, downs the contents in seconds and throws the glass against the pavement hard enough to shatter it. "Is this a party or what?" Riley calls out to his guests. "Someone get me a fucking drink. I'm getting fucked up tonight."

CHAPTER 19
Brielle

Our night went from amazing to shit in the span of three seconds. The moment Riley's dad accepted defeat and took the high road, our night turned into babysitting Riley and making sure he didn't do anything stupid. Well, anything stupider than normal. Luckily for us, he seemed intent on drinking the hard shit while staring into oblivion until he needed to throw it all up into his father's wood-fired pizza oven.

It's been a long-ass night.

Damien and Jensen got just as fucked up as they hoped to get, while Ari ended up crying in the bathroom because Jax had the audacity to smile at her. I have no idea what went down between Ilaria and my brother, but I know there was a good hour when they both disappeared. When I saw her next, her cheeks were flushed and she looked like she was about ready to float off into the clouds. Though when I asked her about it, she pretended like she had no idea what the hell I was talking about.

Liar. She's just as bad as my brother.

We got home a few minutes ago and Tanner had to help Jensen and Damien out of his Mustang and into Orlando's house. I waited out front, refusing to enter that god-forsaken mansion. Tanner was only gone for a minute, but it felt like the longest sixty seconds of my life.

I hate everything about that house and what it represents. I hate that my mother could be trapped and abused, but what I hate more is how she refuses to talk to me. If Tanner is right and she really is doing all of this just to protect me, then she should have come to me. We could have worked it out together and saved that bond we've always shared, but I don't know if we'll ever get it back now.

Fuck, I hate how much I miss her.

Addison had absolutely no desire to wait out in the cold for Tanner to get Damien and Jensen inside. She took off the second the car door closed behind her, leaving me alone with nothing to do but stare up at the house of horrors.

When Tanner finally stepped out into the night, a wave of relief slammed through my chest and he took me home to put this bullshit day to rest. Only now, walking into his bedroom, I'm not sure I'm ready for any kind of rest.

Tanner drops down on the end of his bed as I walk across his room, making a point of pulling the curtains closed. After all, the last thing I need is to have my brother peer through the window at the wrong moment and be blinded by the filthy things I'm about to do to Tanner.

Turning around, I pull my phone out of my pocket and hit play on my Spotify playlist as Tanner holds out his hand to me, wanting to pull me into his lap like he usually does, but I shake my head, my eyelids becoming hooded as I watch him.

I place my phone down and start swaying my hips to the soft music, loving the way his eyes roam over my subtle curves. "You wanna dance for me, Killer?" he murmurs, his voice so thick and raspy, it's doing wicked things to me.

I don't respond and instead, slowly peel off my tank and drop it to the ground behind me, leaving me in my black bikini top and loving how his greedy gaze eats me up. I'll never get enough of this, enough of him. The way he looks at me, it's intoxicating. It's as though I'm the only girl in the world.

The music is slow, and I move forward, standing between his knees. Tanner reaches up to touch me, but I shake my head. "Patience," I warn, moving a little closer so that my knee gently presses against his hardening cock while I pull the string for my bikini top. "Hands off the merchandise."

A soft groan rumbles through his chest, but he's not one to back down from a game. He makes a point of leaning back against his palms, opening himself up for the best lap dance he's ever received.

The bikini top falls to the ground between us, and his eyes darken with hunger, sending a wave of shivers over my skin. Turning around,

I slip my thumbs into the waistband of my pants and glance over my shoulder, watching him as I slowly push them down over my hips and take my bikini bottoms with them. I bend lower, taking my time, and the further I get, the deeper he groans. It sends a rush through me, and my heart starts to race, the anticipation swelling in my chest the longer I dance for him.

Straightening up, I step out of my pants, completely bare for him, and as I turn around to face him, I really start to dance, rolling my body and pressing into him until I'm dripping wet. I see the long, thick column of his cock through his pants, straining to be freed, and while it freaking kills me not to have his hands on my body, I'm having too much fun.

My fingers trail over his skin, leaving goosebumps in their wake, and while seeing the reaction my touch has on his body is one of the most thrilling things I've experienced, it's nothing compared to the unequivocal desire burning in his eyes. Just seeing how badly this beast of a man wants me does wicked things to me, and I fucking love it.

God, what I would give to be able to keep him forever.

Tanner's groan signals his wavering patience as the need to touch and throw me down becomes more than he can bear. But this is my game, and he'll play by my rules whether he likes it or not. If he can't, I'll be sure to make him suffer the consequences. Though that doesn't mean I can't have fun. This bitch is thirsty.

Dropping to my knees in front of Tanner, I look up at him as I spread my legs wide, sending my desperation soaring. Tanner watches me, his chest rising and falling with quick, sharp breaths, and as I reach for the front of his pants, his eyes flutter with anticipation.

Tanner doesn't look away, watching me from above and from the angle he's at, I don't doubt he can see absolutely everything, right down between my legs to how fucking needy I am.

I slowly drag his fly down, and with every passing second and gasp of breath, the tension in the air intensifies. My heartbeat rages in my ears, drumming erratically, and I reach inside his pants to graze his velvety skin. Tanner's eyes flutter as I curl my fingers around his thick shaft to release him from the confines of his pants, and a low groan rumbles through his chest.

He sucks in a breath, the anticipation putting him right on the edge, but the second my tongue rolls over my lips, he fucking crumbles. "Killer," he rasps, breathing heavily. "You're fucking killing me."

I lean into him and grin, slowly working my hand to the tip of his cock and circling my thumb over his tip. My eyes become hooded as I meet his heated stare. "Is this what you want?" I question before flattening my tongue against the base of his cock and licking all the way to the small bead of moisture at the top, refusing to look anywhere but at his dark, hungry stare.

Tanner groans as a shiver rocks through his body, his hands balling into tight fists, but he's being a good boy and following my 'no touching' clause. Though, something tells me it won't last much longer. Tanner may have a lot of patience, but he lacks self-control, and right now, I'm counting on his inability to keep himself grounded.

My mouth closes over his tip as my hand tightens around his base. I work him with my tongue and try to keep my composure as he adjusts his hips, wanting me to take him deeper, and so I do just that, taking him right in the back of my throat until tears well in my eyes.

My head bops up and down as my tongue works its magic, but my fucking pussy is getting desperate. I need him to touch me, need his fingers inside of me, need his mouth closing over my clit and sucking. Holy fuck, I need it all. Bend me over the fucking desk and slam into me until I feel the walls shaking and taste color.

I work him hard, giving the performance of a lifetime, and when his body tenses, he can't hold out any longer. His hand comes to the back of my head, his fingers weaving into my hair and gripping tight as I continue to fuck him with my mouth. His hips rise higher and in a flash, he stands.

I come up higher on my knees to reach his new height as his other hand snaps out and braces against the wall, keeping him upright. He watches me with fire in his eyes, spurring me on as the hand in the back of my hair tightens. He pushes against the back of my head and I take him deeper, unable to look away.

I pick up my pace as my tongue roams over his thick cock. His responding groan is enough to give me life. "Fuck yeah, Killer. Just like that."

Pride swells in my chest, and I can't help but wonder if this is the start of some kind of praise kink I never knew I had. Either way, I like what his approval is doing to me, but I like it even more that despite being on my knees, I hold all the power.

I pump my hand up and down, while my other locks onto the base of his cock, keeping a firm grip, and as his body tenses, excitement shoots through my veins. His cock hits the back of my throat one more time and as my eyes flash up to meet his, he detonates, spurting hot cum into my mouth.

I swallow him down, not stopping until I'm certain I've claimed every last drop. "Fuck," he grunts, bracing himself against the wall as he tries to find his composure.

Pulling back, I let him fall from my lips as I lower myself back down, my ass hovering just slightly above the soft carpet as I rest against my feet. My pussy clenches, desperate to be fucked as my knees remain spread. I make a show of wiping my lips as I look up at him. "I hope you're not finished because I'm only just getting started."

Tanner takes his cock, gently stroking it as he watches me on my knees, his eyes burning all over again. "Mmm, I like you on your knees like this," he murmurs, his eyes hooded. He steps around me, and I feel his intense gaze roaming over my body.

"Oh yeah?" I question. "A perfect little whore, willing to suck your cock at your say so?"

Tanner laughs as he steps in behind me and in a flash of lightning, he's on his knees, his wide chest pressed up against my back and his rock-hard cock slipping right between my crack, and fuck me, if I push my hips back just as inch, I'll feel him right against my needy cunt. "No," he breathes, his lips right at my ear as his strong arm curls around my body, his fingers diving between my legs. "A greedy little slut who'll bend over and let me fuck her into oblivion."

Oooooooh, fuck. I'm screwed in all the right ways.

Then without even a hint of warning, Tanner's fingers plunge deep into my core, making me cry out in unbelievable pleasure. My hand slams down on his knee beside my thigh, and I dig my nails into his skin, feeling his hand at my ass as he strokes his delicious cock. "You ready for me, Killer?" he questions, curling his fingers inside me and making my whole body jolt as I desperately try to lower myself further onto them.

Looking back over my shoulder, I reach up and curl my hand around the back of his neck, gripping his hair and holding him still. "For you? Always."

Tanner groans and fuses his lips to mine, kissing me deeply as his fingers continue working, sending my body into a complete tailspin. "Tanner," I groan, knowing damn well I won't be able to hold out for long. "Don't make me wait."

He grins against my lips before finally pulling back. He winks and everything inside of me crumbles. "Wouldn't dream of it."

I have no idea what he plans to do, but fuck, I'm ready for it. When I feel his hand pressing against my back, pushing my chest to the carpet, the thrill that shoots through me is enough to see me to my grave. My tits hit the carpet but he keeps pushing me down, not stopping until my ass is perfectly offered to him, my glistening cunt right there for the taking.

Tanner grunts and I look back, watching him as he takes me in, his fiery gaze locked on my pussy. He reaches down, the heel of his palm resting against my ass, and I gasp as I feel his fingers at my entrance. "You want this?" he asks, teasing me.

"Fuck, Tanner," I moan, trying to push back against his hand.

"Please."

His eyes flame and he watches himself slowly pushing his fingers deep inside my cunt, and I suck in a gasp, my walls clenching around them. He slowly pulls out and does it again, and it quickly becomes one of the most erotic experiences of my life.

He goes again. And again, and fuck yes, he doesn't stop, slowly torturing me with the sweetest, yet filthiest torture I've ever had the pleasure of enduring. The heel of his palm presses against my ass and I groan, more than ready for him to claim me there too.

Done playing games, he adjusts himself behind me and the moment his tip hits my entrance, I see my whole fucking life flashing before my eyes, knowing damn well this is as good as it's ever going to get. No moment will ever feel better than this, and then he slowly pushes into me, stretching my walls wide, going deeper and deeper until I think he may physically break me.

I feel his balls press up against my clit and gasp, unable to resist reaching through my spread legs and pressing my fingers against my clit, gently rubbing to relieve the pent-up tension that's desperate to be released.

Tanner pauses, seated impossibly deep within me, giving us both a moment to adjust. "Fuck, Killer. This right here—your fucking sweet cunt, this is my goddamn temple." I groan at his words, and his hand spanks down on my ass without warning. He pulls back before slamming straight back into me.

"YES," I pant, forcing my knees even wider as his fingers dig into my hip. "Oh, God. Please, again."

He thrusts into me again, both of us groaning with the intense pleasure as my pussy jolts and spasms, already losing control. His fingers mix with my wetness, feeling himself as he pulls out of me, and I gasp as he draws that wetness up to my ass.

Tanner's thumb presses against me, gently pushing inside as I rub tight circles over my clit. My whole body relaxes, and fuck, it feels good. I push my ass back, wanting to take more, and he gives me exactly what I crave, stretching me wider.

He continues to fuck me, but now the thought has entered my head, and I can't shake it. I always knew I wanted to try this with him, just didn't know when I'd be ready. But if I don't feel his cock pushing into me soon, I might just go out of my mind.

"Tanner?" I pant, hoping to God he's down for this too.

"Hmmm?" he groans, slamming into me again, making a needy gasp tear from between my lips.

I look back over my shoulder, meeting his hungry stare. "I need you to fuck my ass."

He falters, pausing for only a second and screwing with the perfect rhythm of his cock thrusting into my pussy. His eyes shoot to mine, his brow arching with interest. "You know I'm fucking down to claim every inch of your body, but are you sure?" he questions, diving a little deeper with his thumb, testing me.

I groan and push back harder, my eyes rolling in pleasure. I don't need to give him an answer, he can see it written all over my face.

Tanner grins wider, a newfound excitement brimming in his eyes. He continues fucking me, only now, he works my ass just a little harder, pushing his fingers deep into my cunt, stretching it wider around his cock before dragging that wetness up to my ass and preparing me.

When I'm finally ready for him, he pulls free of my pussy and lines his cock up with my ass. Nervous anticipation pulses through me, and I do what I can to relax. "Keep rubbing that clit, Killer," he mutters, his voice so low it sends vibrations rocking straight through me.

He starts to push against me and my ass begins stretching around him. "You good?" he questions, taking his time. I nod, letting out a breath. It burns, but it's a welcome burn, and the more I relax, the easier it is to take. "Push back against me, babe."

I do as he asks until he's finally seated as deep as he can go. He stops there, giving me a moment to get used to his size, and the more I rub my clit, the quicker the burn begins to fade. "Okay," I tell him. "Just take it slow."

Tanner pulls back just slightly, and I gasp. The feeling is like nothing I've ever experienced before. He continues, slowly moving in and out as my eyes roll and he pushes my body to its limits, and just when I think I couldn't possibly handle anymore, he reaches down between my legs and pushes two thick fingers inside my cunt, gently massaging my walls. "Tanner," I breathe. "I've never … shit. So good … I … oh fuck. I'm gonna come."

"Give it to me, Killer. I want to feel you squeezing me."

Holy hell, his words are my undoing, and I come hard, my whole world exploding with undeniable pleasure. Satisfaction rocks through every inch of my body, my eyes clenching as my toes curl, but it's nothing compared to the way my pussy shatters, convulsing around

Tanner's fingers as my ass clenches around him.

"Oh fuck," Tanner grunts, pulling out of me before spilling hot cum over my back, his tone deep and gravelly. "I hope you liked that because I plan on claiming that ass every fucking night for the rest of our lives."

I grin, my face squished against the carpet. "I'm so down for that," I mutter, feeling his cum sliding down my back and right down the center of my ass. "But if you don't clean your cum off me so I can get up, you'll be fucking nothing but your hand."

That same hand in question comes down against my ass. "Watch your mouth, wench, or I'll be forced to teach you a lesson."

"Oh yeah?" I challenge. "And what lesson would that be?"

Tanner grins and without warning, his arm locks around my waist, flipping me over. I squeal in shock, knowing damn well we're going to need a carpet cleaner in here after this, but the thought is gone from my mind the moment that dirty mouth of his closes down over my clit.

CHAPTER 20

TANNER

The sun has barely risen when my bedroom door slams against the drywall with a loud *BANG!* My eyes barely get a chance to spring open before my father storms into my room, his face red in uncontrollable rage. "What the fuck did you say to her?" he booms, spittle flying across the room as he grips my arm and yanks me toward him.

Bri flies up out of bed with a squeal, scrambling for the blanket to cover herself as my fight or flight instincts kick into gear. This asshole must have gotten on a plane the second his new wife ended the call to me.

I throw myself to my feet, towering over my father before slamming my elbow down over his arm, breaking his hold. Anger drums through my chest, knowing he's only here to try and save whatever shred of dignity he has left after his very own daughter outed him as a fucking low-life piece of shit.

I don't allow him one more fucking word before I shove into him, pushing him back against my bedroom wall as Bri hovers in the corner. Her whole body shakes as the trauma of everything she's been through comes roaring back to the front of her mind. "Who the fuck do you think you are coming in here and making demands?" I spit, never having hated this motherfucker more than I do right now.

Dad pushes back, trying to pull his usual intimidation tactics, but that bullshit hasn't worked on me in years. "Answer my fucking question before I make you."

I scoff and shove him back into the wall. "Or what?" I question. "You'll go running back to your new family like the spineless piece of shit you are? Look around ya, old man. We haven't needed you here in years."

His fist comes out of nowhere, smacking into my jaw and rocking my head to the side as Bri lets out a rage-filled gasp, her fear only pushing me closer to the edge. How fucking dare he act like this in front of her. "What the fuck did you say to your mother? What does she know?"

My hand drags down over my face as a wicked grin pulls at my lips. I was more than prepared to keep him in the dark just as he's done to us over the past few years. Keep him wondering and fearing for what we know, terrified that at any moment Mom will see she's better off without him. But fuck it, there's no time like the present.

I lean into him, letting him see the absolute delight in my eyes, knowing just how much joy his misery brings me. "I didn't tell her a damn thing," I say, pausing and allowing a moment for relief to pound through his body before dropping a fucking bomb on his ass. "I didn't need to. She overheard the whole fucking conversation. Congratulations, asshole. You did this to yourself."

His face drops, and I can practically see the panic claiming him. There's a lot of shit my mother was willing to put up with over the years, but this? He's fucked. My father has always clung to Mom. She was his first love and the person who's always kept him grounded, but not anymore. There's no way Mom will look the other way, not when he's married another woman and started a family with her. She'll never forgive him, and call me a fucking psychopath, but I can't wait to sit back and watch him burn.

"You're lying," my father rumbles, poking me hard in the chest. "I don't know how you did it, but this is on you. You told her. You're responsible for breaking her heart. She was fine with me being away, she was coping, but this is going to destroy her."

"This is on me?" I scoff, laughing at his bullshit attempt to put his affair on me while grabbing a pair of boxers and stepping into them. "Oh yeah, my bad. I forgot. *I* was the one who flew to Australia, and *I* was the one who fucked a random whore and knocked her up. Tell me again, how the hell did I manage to marry her while still married to someone else?"

His fist comes at me again, but I won't be his fucking punching bag. My hand comes up, catching his fist and twisting it away. "Here's what's going to happen," I spit, getting right in his face and letting him see the real me, the monster who lives inside. "You're going to divorce Mom. You're going to give her everything she wants, and you'll never step foot in Bradford again. You'll tell Addison how much you love her and admit you're a terrible father, and then you'll fuck off. We don't need you, and after the bullshit hurt you've caused them, we sure as fuck don't want you. Understand me, Trenton, if you even try to screw them over again, I will hunt you down."

"You've got a lot of nerve trying to threaten me, boy," he growls, pushing off the wall and forcing space between us. "If you knew the things I've had to do to keep your nose clean, you'd be keeping your ungrateful mouth shut."

Understanding hits me like a fucking wrecking ball. I've gotten into plenty of trouble, but only once have I ever been involved in something so horrendous it made me sick. Channing mentioned my father's name, but I didn't believe it, not until right this minute. My gaze narrows and my father shrinks back, finally understanding just how far I'll go to protect this secret. "You knew," I accuse. "All this fucking time, you knew what went down that night and you didn't say a fucking thing."

My father nervously glances toward Bri in the corner before fixing himself with the kind of untouchable confidence that is no doubt how he got into this mess in the first place. "Of course I fucking knew. Orlando Channing came to me the second this shit was about to go public. Who do you think paid off the authorities to lose that evidence?"

I shake my head, unable to believe what I'm hearing. "I was a fucking kid. I should have been charged for my involvement in that, but you … fuck, Dad. Paying off the authorities meant the Hardin brothers got away with what they did in that fucking house, and that's on you. You're just as fucking guilty as I am."

"Don't you put me on the same fucking level as you, Tanner. You're a fuck up. Always have been."

I scoff, more than ready to take him out when Addison barges through my door. "What the hell is going on—" she stops abruptly when she finds Dad in my room, and her demeanor shifts. She glares at him, the hurt from his betrayal on full display. "You shouldn't be here."

"Addie," Dad says, taking a hesitant step toward her, his hand raised as if to express some moronic show of innocence. "It's not what you think. I swear to you, my sweet girl, just give me a chance to explain everything."

"Are you or are you not having an affair?" Addison demands, tears welling in her eyes, but there's no way in hell she's about to let them fall for him.

"That's not fair, sweetheart," he says, a strange tone in his voice as he tries to tiptoe around the question. "It's a little more complicated than that."

"Yes or no, Dad," she shouts, her jaw clenching. "It's not a hard question. Did you or did you not screw around on Mom while she was waiting here for you every fucking day, praying for you to be here with her, *with us.*"

"Honey—" he says, not denying it one fucking bit.

The tears finally fall and it breaks my heart. "I hate you," she says, swallowing hard as her voice breaks. "I never want to see you again."

Addie goes to bolt from my room but my father's booming tone keeps her locked in her place. "Don't you walk away from me."

She wipes her eyes on the back of her sleeves. "Why not?" she throws back at him. "You walked away from us first. You replaced Mom with some Australian bitch and got yourself a whole fucking tribe of kids to replace the two fuck ups you already have. Are we not enough for you? Are we damaged goods, not worth your time? Not obedient enough? What, Dad? What is it about us that you couldn't stand to be around?"

Dad just stares at her, not having a fucking clue what to say, but why would he? He's never here. He doesn't know how to console her, especially now after everything she's been through. He's no father to her. "I … I don't want you talking like that, Addison. I love you all, you know that."

"THEN WHY DID YOU REPLACE US?" she cries, her hands trembling as the pain makes her voice shake. She doesn't hang around for a response, turning on her heels and taking off like a bat out of hell.

"Fuck," I mutter under my breath, turning to Bri, but she's already grabbing her phone off my nightstand and racing for the door.

She holds her phone up, not bothering to even look back at me. "Already calling him," she says, reading my mind and knowing a situation like this calls for none other than Hudson Bellamy. Relief pounds through my chest, but I catch my breath as Bri comes to a stop and glances back at my father with a condescending smile.

Oh fuck, this isn't going to go down well.

"Killer," I warn, but she's not having a bit of it.

Despite her smile, she manages to look at my father with such hatred it almost knocks me clean off my feet. "Respectfully," she starts in a sugary sweet tone just as the loud BANG of Addison's door slams down the hallway, "you're a piece of shit who never deserved this family, and I hope to God you spend every day of the rest of your life despising yourself for hurting them like this." Her smile widens and she's right back to looking like the sweetest angel. "As always, it was such a pleasure seeing you again."

Ahhh, fuck. And now I'm hard.

Bri doesn't spare me a single glance before taking off after Addison, and I don't make a move until I hear the door opening down the hall and softly closing behind her again. Finally, I ball my hands into fists and take a calming breath, not prepared to lose myself again.

I take a step toward my father just as he spins around to face me, rage burning in his eyes. "What did I tell you about screwing that gold-digging whore?"

My fist rears back and I—

"TANNER!" my mother snaps from my open door, still tying her silk robe at her waist, looking disheveled with puffy eyes from a night of drinking and crying. "You dare raise a fist in my house, and I will show you the door."

Shit.

I reluctantly lower my fist, but before I get a chance to defend myself, my mother's stare turns to stone as she faces my father. "You have a lot of nerve showing up here, Trenton," she says. "I want you out of my house."

"Sara, no," he says, shaking his head and stepping toward Mom. "We can talk about this. Don't just throw away twenty years of marriage."

"Marriage?" she laughs. "What marriage? You're living it up with some other woman in Australia, giving her your time, patience, and love. Hell, you gave her three children as well. We have no marriage. What we have is a lie, a sham. You've made me the laughingstock of Bradford. You've humiliated me."

"Please, Sara. You're the love of my life," he says. "I never meant to hurt you. It just happened. I didn't mean to fall in love with her."

"I want you out of my house," she says, crossing her arms over her chest and fixing him with a venomous stare. "Pack up your shit and never come back here. I don't ever want to see you again, and in case you haven't caught on, I'll be filing for divorce the moment my lawyer's office opens."

Mom turns on her heel and stalks away, but Dad isn't finished with her yet, determined not to allow it to end just like that. "Sara?" he shouts, storming out of my room after her.

I step out in the hallway just as Mom walks back to her room, closing the door behind her and flicking the lock. Dad hurries after her, his fist slamming against the hardwood. "Sara," he booms. "Open the door. I'm not through with you." He bangs again, getting more aggressive by the second. "I'm not walking away, Sara. Open the fucking door."

"You're being childish, Trenton," Mom calls from within just moments before the door springs open and Mom shoves a pre-packed duffle bag into Dad's arms, clearly having already thought this through. "I've wasted years waiting on you. I've allowed you to walk all over me, but I'm through. There is no coming back from this. Now go! Leave your key on the way out."

Mom slams the door in his face and he's left standing in the hallway, banging on the door once again. "Open the fucking door. You don't get to decide when you're through with me. You're my wife. You obey me."

Oh, hell no.

I storm down the hallway, determined to put this fucker in his place. No one speaks to my mother like that and gets away with it. "The fuck did you just—"

The door tears open and my mother comes storming out, shoving my father in the chest. "Excuse you?" she spits, stepping into him and forcing him back as his eyes widen, realizing way too late what just came out of his mouth. "Where the hell do you get off speaking to me like that?"

"Sara, I—"

"OUT. NOW," she roars, her whole body shaking with rage. "If you step foot in this house again, I will call the authorities to have you removed. Do not make me ask again."

"You won't even hear me out?" he questions.

"There is not a single word that could come from your mouth

that I wish to hear," she tells him, not wavering for even a second. "You destroyed our marriage. You lied to me. You bedded another woman and betrayed my trust. You took our vows and regarded them as nothing more than trash. Get out of here, Trenton. Go back to your little whore across the globe. Go and enjoy your new children and leave mine the hell alone. I just hope you don't screw them over like you did us."

With that, Mom storms past him, shoulder charging him as she goes. She makes her way downstairs, refusing to look back and give him the satisfaction. As of this very second, Trenton Morgan is dead to my mother. Hell, he's dead to me too.

My father turns, desperation in his eyes as he glances toward Addison's closed door, but I take a step to my right, blocking his way. "Addison made it clear she doesn't want a damn thing to do with you," I remind him before indicating the duffle bag in his arms. "Looks like you've got everything you need. For what it's worth, I hope your new wife is smart enough to take her kids and run. They deserve a shitload better than a fuck up like you."

I watch as my father swallows, his Adam's apple bobbing up and down as I do everything in my power to ignore the heavy sobs and murmured whispers coming from the other side of Addison's door. I don't doubt Hudson will be breaking down the front door any minute now, determined to be the shoulder Addie cries on.

Without a single card to play, my father finally realizes he just lost the best thing to ever happen to him. No matter how many wives or children he has, he'll never be able to replace what he had here with

Mom and Addie. He shoots me one last stare and there's still a fight in his eyes, but he knows damn well I will put him in the ground.

He hangs his head, his shoulders falling in defeat before silently walking back down the long hallway, clutching the duffle bag in his hand. He passes in front of me, and I watch him go, an odd hollowness in my chest. He gets halfway down the stairs when I move closer to the railing, watching him closely. "Dad?" I call after him. He pauses to glance back up at me. "Don't let the door hit you on your way out."

And with that, I turn around, hoping like fuck I never have to see him again.

CHAPTER 21
Brielle

"You know what?" Sara says as we sit around the dining table, Tanner on my left and Hudson on the right while a puffy-eyed Addison sits directly opposite me. "I've always wanted to open a bakery, but I've never had the guts to do it. I've always waited around for Trenton, waiting on him to tell me what our next steps will be, but why should I hold back? There's nothing stopping me from going after that dream now."

"I say go for it," Tanner says while scooping a bite of risotto into his mouth. "There's no denying you're the best baker in Bradford. The things you make are sophisticated and elegant, much better than the shitty bakery down by the school. Their chocolate eclairs look like someone took a shit on the baking tray."

"Tanner!" Sara scolds. "Watch your mouth. I'm not doing this to be some kind of competition to every bakery in town, or because I think I can do a better job. I just want to wake up every day and enjoy what I'm doing. I want to have purpose."

"And what about those country club bitches?" Addison asks, propping her elbow on the table and resting her chin in her hand. "I doubt they'll be accepting of you when you walk in wearing a dirty apron with flour in your hair."

"Fuck them," Sara says, her lips pulling into a smirk as her children gape at her casual use of the word fuck. "They can go to their hoity-toity events and live their lavish lifestyles, but every night, they'll go home to husbands who won't ask about their day. They will never know what it feels like to live a rewarding life, but I will."

"Damn straight you will," Tanner says. "And if they have a problem with it, you could always shit in their eclairs."

Sara blanches, gaping at Tanner in horror. "I'm going to pretend I didn't just hear that," she gasps as Tanner and Hudson giggle like misbehaving children.

"Come on, Mom," Addison says. "We all know those country club women would take one taste of your pastries and hire you for every event until their dying days. You're just that good."

Sara gives her daughter a fond smile, pride shining through her eyes. "Thank you, my love," she says just as a knock sounds on the door.

Sara goes to stand, but Tanner waves her off. "Finish your dinner," he says, getting up from the table. "I'll get it." Tanner doesn't wait for a response before striding out of the dining room and through the kitchen.

Sara continues talking about her bakery as I listen for Tanner, hearing the soft click of the lock and the front door creaking open. I hear a man's voice, too soft to make out the words from this far away, but curiosity claims every inch of my soul. I lean back in my chair, peering up through the long hallway and into the foyer to see two men standing just inside the door.

I gasp, recognizing them immediately. "It's the cops from the hospital," I say, my eyes wide, cutting off whatever Sara was saying as panic tears at my chest. "The ones taking Colby's case."

Addison straightens in her seat, her eyes widening as Sara flies to her feet, gaping at me. "Are you sure?"

I nod, pushing out from the table and getting to my feet. "Certain," I tell her, walking around the big table, determined to hear what's going on. "Their faces are ingrained in my mind."

Sara follows me with Hudson and Addie trailing behind. Addison looks like she's about to pass out, her nervousness making her brave enough to clutch Hudson's hand, refusing to let go. We make our way into the foyer and the detective's voice trails off when he sees Sara approaching. "Mrs. Morgan," he says, tipping his head like a gentleman. "We apologize for barging in on your evening like this. I'm sure you were all sitting down for a meal, so we'll keep this short."

"What's this about?" she questions as I move in beside Tanner, almost cowering behind his big shoulder, too scared to hear what they have to say. After all, good news doesn't prompt an in-person meeting like this. Whatever this is, it's not something we're going to easily shake off. I grip Tanner's hand and he squeezes mine in return, holding it tight.

The detective gives Sara an encouraging smile, but it doesn't reach his eyes. "We've regrettably come to provide your son with an update on Colby Jacobs' state."

Sara's back stiffens as I grip Tanner tighter, feeling him starting to sway on his feet, the color already draining from his face. "Just give it to us straight," I tell them, needing them to rip it off like a Band-Aid.

The detective meets my stare and gives me a quick nod before lifting his haunted gaze to Tanner's. "Would you prefer to talk in private, son?"

Tanner glances toward Addison, fear in his eyes while Addie just looks ... broken. Tanner shakes his head. "No, it's fine. Whatever you have to say to me you can say in front of my family," he tells them, his voice thick with sorrow. "What's the verdict?"

The two cops share a glance before the officer takes a step back, allowing the detective to take point on this. "I'm sorry, Tanner. Colby was pronounced brain dead in the early hours of this morning and his family made the decision to turn off his life support. As of a few hours ago, Colby Jacobs was confirmed dead."

Addison gasps, dropping to her knees as Hudson hovers around her, dropping his hand to her back and doing everything he can to comfort her as the wild emotions rock through her. Tanner falls back against me, stumbling before quickly catching himself. "I killed him," he mutters, barely able to meet the detective's eye, disbelief thick in his tone.

"Yes," he confirms.

A tear falls from Sara's eye, and she hastily wipes it away before meeting the detective's stare. "So what now? Will Tanner be charged for his involvement?"

The detective shakes his head. "No, ma'am, I do not believe so. Tanner was clearly acting in self-defense. However, it is up to the discretion of Colby's family if they wish to push this further, but given the evidence, I do not think any judge in his or her right mind would convict your son of any wrongdoing."

"So it's over?" Sara questions. "All the hell Colby Jacobs has brought down over our family is finally over?"

"I understand this isn't the type of justice you were searching for, but yes, Colby Jacobs cannot hurt your family ever again. However, it would be foolish to assume the scars of his brutal attack won't live on." The detective turns back to Tanner. "If you feel you would like to speak with a professional, I can offer you the names of a few local therapists who would be willing to sit down with you and talk through it all. Taking a life … whether innocent or guilty, it's not something you can simply shrug off. It will haunt you and it will take a toll on your mind. It's best to be prepared for that. It will hit you when you least expect it."

Tanner nods and my hand slips up the back of his shirt, pressing against his warm skin as a reminder that I'm here for anything he needs. The cop slips his hand into his pocket and pulls out a business card. He hands it to Tanner with a tight smile. "If you have any questions, just let us know."

Tanner nods. "Thank you," he murmurs, the words sounding as though they cause him physical pain.

The detective spares a forced smile for Sara before the cops turn and make their way back out the door when Addison gasps and flies up off the ground, her eyes wide. "Wait," she rushes out, lunging forward to catch them. The cops turn and look back at her with furrowed brows, waiting patiently as Addison tries to find the strength to go on. "What about Erica?" she asks. "This isn't over until she's been punished for what she did."

"Erica?" the detective questions, glancing at the other cop for a quick second.

"Erica Sawyer," I confirm, clinging to Tanner's side. "She acted with Colby, helping to drug Addison the night she was raped, and then fabricated evidence to pin it on me."

"Ahh, yes," the detective says. "Unfortunately, there simply wasn't enough evidence to continue pursuing a case. It's been dropped, unless you have something substantial to add. Something that could hold up in court?"

Addison shakes her head. "What … What are you saying? She just walks away from this with nothing more than a slap on the wrist? She drugged me, right along with Colby. She egged him on, laughed when I could barely stand up. And you just … you let her go?"

Tears spring from her eyes as Hudson steps into her side, pulling her into his side and holding her close. The detective gives her a forced smile, trying to figure out what the hell to say in this situation, but not having a damn helpful thing to say, he simply bows his head. "I'm sorry, Miss Morgan. Our hands are tied. I wish there were something more we could do to offer you justice."

Addison shakes her head as my chest truly starts to ache. The bombs this man has dropped on Tanner's family tonight will never be forgotten. I mean, fuck. How much more can these people take? Rape. Coma. Arrest charges. Bigamy. And now this.

The cops leave, closing the door behind them and not a moment later, Addison falls into Hudson's arms, crying into his chest as he holds her tight. "It's not fair," she sobs as Tanner falls back a few steps and crumbles onto the second bottom step, dropping his face into his hands.

I sit down beside him as Sara desperately tries to console both her children, not a single one of us capable of easing the pain in the room. Taking his hand, I curl into Tanner's side and am relieved when he welcomes me in, putting an arm around me and pulling me in closer. "I killed him," he murmurs so softly I have to strain to hear him.

Reaching up, I take his chin and force his broken stare to mine. "It was self-defense, Tanner. You did what you had to do to protect the people you love. If anybody else was in your position, they would have done exactly the same thing. It could have easily been Riley or Logan. You're not a monster, Tanner. You're the love of my life and the reason I get to wake up each day. If it weren't for you, I'd be dead right along with him."

Tanner knocks my grasp off his chin and looks at me with such pain in his eyes it nearly kills me. His fingers trail down the side of my face, pushing a stray lock of golden hair behind my ear. "You look at me like your hero, like I'm deserving of your love, but the truth of the matter is I lost control. I couldn't stop. I beat him until he stopped breathing, all while you and Riley screamed for me to stop. But I couldn't stop, Bri, and more than that, I didn't want to. I wanted him to die. I wanted him to feel the consequences of what he did. I wanted him to hurt and know that I was the one who did it. I killed him, Bri. There was nothing heroic about it. I'm a killer, just like the fucking Hardin brothers."

He pauses, shaking his head as he comes to terms with the words falling from his lips. "I promised you that you'd never have to see me lose control like that again. You deserve so much better than this, you deserve—"

"Don't tell me what I deserve," I snap, pulling away from his touch and getting to my feet, standing on the bottom step to look him in the eye. "I know what I want, so don't get all high and mighty on me now, Tanner Morgan. Pulling away from me is doing nothing but punishing us both, and that right there is exactly what I don't deserve. I'm not letting you go, Tanner. We're going to face this together." I drop down in front of him, resting my hands against his knees. "I know you lost control out there. I saw you, Tanner. I saw the look in your eye. You wanted him dead, but after what he did … it's justified. The way he hurt the people you love, the way he hurt your sister. You'd just watched him stab Jax and boast about hurting Addison again. I will never hold that against you. Yes, you lost control, and that's something we'll work on. Hell, we have been. The other day at school, you held yourself back from that asshole in the hall instead of beating him black and blue. You're not the monster you think you are, Tanner. You're the best man I've ever known."

Tanner reaches forward, gripping my arms and yanking me hard into his chest, wrapping his arms around me as though he'll never let go. "You're my whole fucking world, Killer. I can't do this without you."

Lifting my head from his chest, I press my lips to his. "You'll never have to."

Tanner presses his forehead against mine and pulls me into his lap before dropping his head to my shoulder and holding me there, neither of us willing to move an inch. My arms wrap around him, hating the heaviness resting on his soul. I don't know how to help him, how to ease the pain of realizing he's killed a man, but I have to hope that this is enough, that *I'm enough*.

I'm just about to ask if he wants to go upstairs when Addison pushes back from Hudson behind me. "No, this isn't right," she seethes. "I can't ... I can't just sit back and let Erica walk away from this. She might not have physically touched me, but she holds some responsibility for what happened to me that night. If she hadn't been there, if she hadn't encouraged Colby to fuck with me, I would have walked out of that party fairly unscathed."

"I know," he tells her. "But what can we do? We don't have the evidence to support it. It's our word against hers, and it's not like we can trust the courts anyway. They let Colby walk free despite all the evidence."

Addison shakes her head, fresh tears appearing on her cheeks. "But it's not fair," she cries. "It's not fair."

Her chest heaves with fast gasps and within the space of a few seconds, she starts hyperventilating, having some sort of panic attack. Her hand goes to her chest as everyone's eyes begin to widen. "Fuck," Tanner rushes out, more than ready to throw me off him in order to get to his sister, but Hudson is right there, his hands gripping her arms and pulling her in close.

"Look at me," he tells her, keeping calm and focusing his whole attention only on her. "Focus on me, babe."

Addison looks up at him, her panicked stare locked on his. Her brows furrow and I hate the fear I see deep in her eyes. She watches him as though he's her whole world, relying on him to make everything okay, and I don't doubt he's the only person on the planet who has the power to do so.

When the panic doesn't subside, he steps in closer, weaving his hand up around the back of her neck. "I got you," he tells her, his voice velvety smooth as it sails through the foyer. "You're safe here."

She nods, her eyes locked on him as though they're the only two people in the world, and just like that, she inhales deeply and finds peace, somehow managing to pull herself out of the storm. She doesn't look away, watching him as though he's her knight in shining armor, but the look in her eyes—she's still scared. Terrified, in fact. She wants him so bad. She wants to be his world, but she's not able to make the move herself. She needs him to take the reins and give her the push she so desperately craves.

As if reading her, Hudson inches in the final step, refusing to look away as her body finally begins to relax and just when I think he's about to give her whispered words of wisdom, he closes the gap, bringing his lips down on hers in the softest kiss.

Addison's whole body melts into his and his arm closes around her waist, holding her to him. He takes his time, not wanting to push her farther than she's willing to go, but his intention is crystal clear. If she couldn't see what she meant to him before, she sure as hell can now. She might not understand just how deeply it runs, but these two are end goals.

Wanting to give them some privacy to figure out this new, crazy status of their relationship, I crawl off Tanner's lap and take his hand. "Come on," I tell him, noticing the way Sara ducks away, slipping back toward the dining room. "Let's give them some space."

Tanner stands and loops our joined hands over my shoulder, pulling me into his side. "Yeah," he mutters, clearly not in the mood for his usual smartass quips and remarks. We start walking up the stairs to his bedroom, and with each step we take, the heaviness weighs down further on my shoulders, knowing damn well this is going to be a long road through hell and back.

CHAPTER 22

TANNER

The ball flies from my hands, sailing through the air like a knife through butter. At least, it looked that way until it started to fall flat. The ball doesn't even make it into Logan's waiting hands, only serving to frustrate the shit out of me.

Jax stands at the sidelines beside Coach Wyld, his arms outstretched and disgust etched across his face. "The fuck was that?" he spits as Coach scoffs an agreeable grunt. I know I deserve it, but fuck, Jax's attitude makes me want to wring his neck.

He's been just as frustrated as I've been, having to sit out every day, watching his teammates get to take advantage of the field while he's forced to sit on the sidelines, but healing from a stab wound isn't supposed to be easy. Hell, Addie hasn't been cleared to dance yet, and

I'm sure if Bri had been involved in sports, she'd still be waiting for the stamp of approval too. The three of them are lucky to be allowed out of the house to attend school every day. I'm sure if their doctors knew they were going out partying and fucking around, they'd have something to say about it. So for now, I bite my tongue while trying to put myself in his shoes, but every day it gets harder to have sympathy for the fucker.

I tear my helmet off and drop it to the grass before dragging my hands down my face. My game has been off all fucking week, ever since the cops showed up at my place to let me know I'd murdered a man. Despite how the fucker deserved it, the knowledge that I've taken a life has darkened something inside me, taken away the light from within and left me haunted.

I killed him with my bare fucking hands and they haven't stopped shaking in three fucking days.

Logan stands downfield, staring back at me with the same disgusted stare as his brother, and if Jax hadn't already said something, Logan would be spouting the same shit. He starts jogging back, knowing damn well Coach Wyld is about to ask us to do it again.

Riley strides past, scooping my helmet off the ground and shoving it into my chest. "Head in the fucking game, bro," he says, meeting my eyes with a pointed stare before glancing toward Coach who's shaking his head, looking stressed. "Just pull it together for ten more minutes so we can get out of here before the sun goes down."

My cheeks blow out as I exhale loudly, but I nod, pulling my helmet back over my head and watching as Logan scoops the ball up off the ground. He launches it to me and I catch it with ease. "Run it again," I tell him before Coach has a brain aneurysm from having to scream at me again.

"Yeah," Riley cheers, clapping and trying to pump me up while darting out of the way, giving me the space I need to hopefully not fuck this up again.

Logan nods, and I jog back a few steps, giving myself a slight run up, and I can't help but glance toward Coach, seeking out his approval despite knowing I don't need it. I don't need anyone's approval, but for some reason, what Coach Wyld thinks of me matters.

He doesn't look happy, and after talking to him earlier in the week and explaining what happened with the cops over the weekend, he's been taking it easy on me, but that's not what I need. I don't want his pity. I want him to push me, to treat me just like he usually does, to give me some kind of normalcy when out on the field. Fuck knows everything else has been a mess lately.

Rearing back, I give it my all, and as the ball flies down the field, Logan takes off at a sprint. He keeps his eye on the ball, pushing himself harder as Riley goes in for the tackle, doing his best to push Logan harder.

Logan evades him with ease before effortlessly catching the ball and making a point of laughing at Riley as he crash-tackles right into the ground, leaving grass stains up his arms and legs. Hell, I can hear his muttered swearing all the way down the opposite end of the field. Riley should have known better. Logan is a fucking rocket on the field. Once he gets into a sprint, no one can catch him.

It wasn't a great throw, but just as I'd hoped, Logan has a way of making me look good, at least good enough that Coach Wyld lets us off the hook. Though I don't doubt he'll ask to speak with me at some point between now and the end of the week, making sure my head is screwed on right so I don't nearly cost us another game.

"Alright, wrap it up, boys," Coach says, indicating the field full of training equipment before fixing a pointed stare on me, the weight of his concern and pity slamming into me like a fucking freight train. "Morgan. I want to see you in my office first thing in the morning."

Shit.

I nod, knowing damn well there's no way out of this one. If I don't attend his bullshit checkup, I won't play, and I simply can't get down with that.

Jax jogs out onto the field, going for the training equipment, sliding through on a technicality as packing up the field isn't technically a part of our training. He passes by me, making sure to whack me right in the guts. "Poor form, man."

"Fuck off," I mutter, ripping my helmet off again. "At least I'll be playing on Friday. What'll you be doing?"

Jax runs past me, whipping around to jog backward as he flips me the bird. "Your fucking mom if you're not careful."

I groan, shaking my head and trying to remember that somewhere deep down, I really love the bastard. "What in the Alabama? She's your aunt. That's messed up."

Jax laughs, his gaze filling with the worst kind of enjoyment that I prepare myself for the bullshit about to come falling from his mouth.

"YOLO!" he calls before flipping around and jogging across the field, the worst rendition of *Sweet Home Alabama* pouring out of him while going as far as to mimic the guitar riff in the song.

I don't know how he does it. One minute I want to smack him, and the next, he's the most endearing, entertaining motherfucker I've ever met. He has a certain charm, there's no doubt about it. If only he didn't have to go and put that mental image of him and my mom in my head. That one is going to need a stiff drink to process.

Knowing I'll get my ass kicked if I don't start helping pack up, I get to it, trying not to rip Daniel Carter's face clean off his body. I know I got a good punch in after he called Addison a whore in the hallway, but that wasn't nearly enough damage to ease the rage burning inside me. Every time I see him out on the field, claiming to be some kind of team player, I want to destroy him. It's assholes like that with egos and God complexes who make life hard for girls like Addison. Clearly, he doesn't have a sister. If he did, there's no way he would have made those comments in the hall.

After twenty minutes of slave labor, I stand in the locker room shower, attempting to hide out in my cubicle as Jax walks up and down the narrow corridor, trying to justify why he shouldn't be asking Arizona out.

I don't know how the fuck I got dumped with him. He started with Hudson, but that bastard is so fucking loved up with my sister after finally finding the balls to really kiss her that the only response he could give Jax was to follow his heart. And let's be honest, that's not the kind of answer the moron was looking for. He knows better than to try this shit on Logan, so Riley was his next culprit, and I'm not surprised that didn't go well either. From what I could tell, Riley just wanted to talk about their threesome out by the lake, which clearly wasn't the conversation Jax was aiming for. Apparently the fucker is feeling a little sour after sharing his toys. Sounds to me like someone is getting a little more attached than he's letting on.

Logan stands in his cubicle, staring hard at the wall and ignoring his brother as he continues marching up and down the corridor behind us. "Do you ever fucking shut up?" Logan groans, probably having heard this shit all night. After all, most of the time, it's just the two of them at home in that huge house, except for when Chanel comes over, and when that happens, I doubt they're chilling together. Logan would have his girl up in his room spread out on his bed like a buffet, leaving Jax all alone. I suppose before everything went down, he'd have Ari to chill with, but … I suppose life would be pretty lonely right about now.

Jax glances at his brother, giving him a nasty glare. "I'll make a deal with you," he says, stepping into the empty cubicle between mine and Logan's. "I'll shut up when you stop acting like a pussy-whipped little bitch."

Logan rolls his eyes, having had enough of Jax's bullshit for today. "I'm the little bitch?" he questions. "Remind me what you were doing while we were out on the field? Putting in your application for official benchwarmer? Or would you prefer something with a little more excitement? Waterboy, perhaps?"

In the blink of an eye, Jax reaches over the shared wall between their cubicles and grabs a firm grip of his brother's junk, and judging by Logan's grunt of pain, I can only assume Jax is giving it a good, thorough squeeze. "How's that for a fucking waterboy," Jax spits, venom bursting in his tone.

"Alright, fuck," Logan says, glaring at his brother, not needing to say anything further. Jax knows he's won this round fair and square.

He releases his brother's dick and makes a point of holding his hand under the water of Logan's shower. "Gross," he mutters. "Who knows what diseases you've got festering down there."

"Then don't fucking touch it," Logan spits.

"Fucking hell," I mutter, dropping my head forward into the spray of hot water. "Do you two ever stop arguing? You're like a broken record."

Jax lets out a heavy sigh and turns toward me, resting his arms over the wall between us, and if I weren't so confident in his sexuality, I'd be nervous about the way Jax's gaze drops, checking out the merchandise. "The fuck do you want?" I question, reaching for the tap and turning it off.

"I just—" He lets out a heavy sigh and stares off at the wall behind me. "Do you think Ari's been fucking around with other guys?"

Grabbing my towel, I quickly dry off and wrap it around my hips. "I think the second you told her it was never going to happen between you two, you lost all right to know."

"Yeah but … fuck. Come on, man," he whines, following me out of the showers as Riley passes on his way in, his phone in one hand and a suspicious bottle of cream in the other. "Surely Bri has said something to you, right? She'd know if Ari's fucking someone."

I stop at my locker and look back at Jax, giving him a hard stare. "If it bothers you so fucking much, go and ask her yourself," I tell him. "Bri hasn't told me shit."

He looks at me as though he knows I'm lying, and he'd be right. I am, but I'm not about to tell him that Ari is still messed up, still living in a world of hurt over his rejection. Hell, I don't think I've ever seen a girl longing over someone the way Ari longs for Jax, but I have to give it to her, she does a good job hiding it.

Letting out a sigh, Jax sits back on the bench, sulking as I quickly get dressed, determined to get out of here and spend the rest of my afternoon buried deep inside my girl. After stuffing my training bag with all my shit, I grab my phone and keys out of my locker and turn back toward Jax, hating that he's so down about all of this. "Have you considered that maybe there is something there with Ari? Something real? You're too messed up over her for this to be nothing."

"The fuck are you talking about?" Jax says. "I've told you, I don't think about her that way."

"Right," I mutter. "You've been obsessing over whether she's been fucking someone else for the past twenty minutes, and yesterday, you were wondering what she was doing while you were busy keeping the bench warm. And the day before that—"

"Alright," Jax rushes out. "I get your fucking point."

I arch a brow as I reach for the strap of my bag. "Do you, though?"

Jax rolls his eyes as though I'm the one being unreasonable, and just as I go to lift my bag onto my shoulder, Riley comes striding out of the showers rocking a semi with his phone still in his hand and a satisfied grin across his face. Hell, the asshole didn't even bother to cover up with a towel.

"Awwwww, fuck no," Hudson says, noticing Riley at the same time I do.

Riley gives him a dopey grin and holds up his phone, flashing us the screen to see some random Instagram model. "I'm in love," he says with a sigh, stopping by Jax and dropping down on the bench beside him, stretching out so that his dick flops down between his legs, just dangling there for everyone to see.

Here we go again. This wouldn't be the first Instagram model Riley's fallen in love with, and it won't be the last, but hell, anything is better than him frothing at the mouth over Brielle. I'll take it any day.

Logan tries to avert his eyes as Jax reaches over and snatches Riley's phone out of his hand. He glances over the screen, checking out this girl's page. "Fuck, man. This chick is hot," he says, finding a bikini pic and stopping his scrolling as he checks out the way her tits practically spill out of her top. "Where'd you find this one?"

Riley shrugs as Logan tosses a towel at him, covering his dick. "Don't know, man. She liked a few of my pics and that was all it took."

"When are you meeting her?" Jax questions as he holds the phone out for me to glance over.

"I, ummm …. I don't know," Riley says with a strange hesitation in his tone as I take the phone and scan over the girl's name, @Bad_GirlZoe18, and immediately shake my head. Trust Riley to fall madly in love with a woman who calls herself a bad girl. I haven't even scrolled further and I already know they're practically soul mates.

Out of habit, my thumb reaches to the top right of the phone, clicking on their private messages and my brows furrow seeing it completely blank. "Wait," I say, my gaze shooting up to Riley's. "You haven't messaged this chick yet?"

He glances away so fucking fast I have to laugh. "Holy fuck, man. What's wrong with you? Sliding into a chick's DM's is your signature move. You haven't even sent her a picture of your cock."

His cheeks flush—*fucking flush*—like a teenage girl as he reaches up to yank the phone out of my hands. He looks away, unable to meet my eyes. "I just umm ... I ... I just didn't want to, alright? I'm taking my time with this one. Waiting until the moment is right and then I'll shoot my shot."

Logan booms a belly laugh. "Dude, she has to know you fucking exist to be able to wait for the moment to be right."

"Like you'd fucking know," Riley shoots back at him. "It took you a fucking year to even find the balls to look Chanel in the eye. So what if I want to take my time with this one. Look at her, she's fucking gorgeous. She must have assholes like me in her DMs every fucking day. I need to do something to stand out, something that'll get her attention, and the standard thirst trap ain't gonna make the cut."

I gape at him, feeling as though I'm looking at a complete stranger. The guy sitting before me looks nervous, but the Riley Sullivan I know has never been nervous a day in his life. Hell, he even looks like the thought of reaching out to this girl is going to make him throw up.

What the fuck is going on here?

Hudson laughs, snatching Riley's phone off him to check out the girl. "Awww, Riley doesn't know how to talk to the pretty girl," he teases, barely sparing her a glance before handing the phone back, not interested in some other chick's bikini pics. "But don't worry," he says with a wink, a mischievous grin pulling at his lips. "Leave it to us. We've got your back."

Real fear shines through Riley's eyes as he throws himself to his feet, his dick jumping right along with him. "If you fuck this up for me, I swear to God, I'll make sure you never use your fucking dick again," he says. "You'll be pissing into a plastic bag for the rest of your life."

Jax laughs as he stands up, hooking his arm over Riley's shoulder, a wicked sparkle hitting his eyes. "Don't you worry 'bout a damn thing," he says, his mischievous tone confirming my exact thoughts. "We've got it covered, and besides, a little fun never hurt anybody."

I laugh as the endless options start working their way through my mind. This really is going to be fun. Jax is right, a little fun never hurt anybody, except maybe Hudson who'll end up pissing into a plastic bag, but considering everything, is that really such a terrible thing? After all, one day he'll be wanting to take that thing near my sister, and I can't have that happening now, can I?

CHAPTER 23
Brielle

Jensen leans up against the doorframe of his bedroom, his foot crossed over the other as he watches me with a stupid grin across his face. "What the fuck are you doing?" he questions as I slink down the hallway, trying to be as sneaky as possible.

"Getting the drop on Damien," I tell him. "What else would I be doing?"

Jensen's grin widens and I don't like it one fucking bit, but he's not my problem. It's the asshole who's been messaging my friend all day, making her all kinds of hot and bothered during school. He needs his head kicked in and naturally, I'm the perfect person to do it. The fact I'll really enjoy beating his stupid ass has nothing to do with it. It's simply an added bonus.

I creep like some kind of stalker, trying to ignore the way Jensen shakes his head at my performance, though he simply doesn't understand. Jensen doesn't have siblings, so he'll never get the extraordinary lengths a younger sister will go to ensure her brother's untimely demise, and he'll never understand just how much joy it brings her.

Today's plan—ultimate wedgie. If I don't at least tear the fabric, it'll be considered a fail, and those who know me understand failure is simply not an option.

I make my way down the hall, passing the shared bathroom which none of us actually use and past the linen cupboard Tanner used to use to make my life a living hell. I mean, who the hell builds a crawl space into a bedroom like that? Is that not a million kinds of messed up? But hell, when in Rome, right? After all, this is Orlando's home, and I don't doubt there are even more fucked-up horrors still to undercover in this place.

A shiver sails down my spine, remembering the conversation I had with Tanner only a few nights ago, confessing one of Orlando's more sinister plans. It's gross, there's no other way to put it. If the asshole thinks there's any chance in hell I would willingly marry him and become his perfect little wife or sex slave, he's got another thing coming. There's no way I'd ever submit to him like that. I mean, first up, he's like a million years old and probably has a wrinkly ball sack. He's also married to my mom and technically my stepfather. Does that count as incest? Not to mention, he's fucking weird and creepy. The word pedophile is flashing in big red lights in my head. Sure, I might be eighteen already, but barely just legal. I wouldn't put it past the asshole to be interested in younger girls.

Another shiver sails down my spine, and I try to put it aside. There's nothing I can do about the Orlando situation right now, but there is something I can do about Damien, and I won't be leaving until I know for a fact his asshole is burning.

Turning the corner, I spy his door at the end of the hallway and glance back, finding Jensen behind me, still able to see me from his door. He looks far too happy, and it puts me on edge, but I won't allow him to ruin this for me. I've been planning it all afternoon.

Reaching Damien's door, I curl my fingers around the handle and take a breath, determined to open this door faster than it's ever been opened in its life. This is going to be a mission. Damien has fast reflexes and can be ready to whoop my ass at a moment's notice. I need to make this fast. Get in, get out, and run like fucking hell.

After mentally pumping myself up, I prepare myself for a world of domination.

In three, two, one.

I twist the handle and shove the door open, slamming my hip into it to give it the extra oomph it needs. The door crashes against the drywall with a loud bang as I fly into the room, my eyes wide and frantic as I look for Damien.

My heart pounds, deep in enemy territory. Barely a second has passed, not even time to blink and I'm already in the center of his room. His desk and couch are empty, so I whip my head toward his bed and come to a screeching halt. A horrified scream tears from deep in my chest. "AHHHHHHHHHHHH," I bellow, my eyes turning to lava inside my head, completely scarred as I find my brother mounted on top of Ilaria and drilling into her.

Damien whips around, his eyes wide as he finds me gaping at the horrific sight.

"MY EYES!" I cry, bile rising in my throat as Jensen's loud, booming laugh practically shakes the foundation of the house. "Holy fuck, what are you doing to my friend?"

Ilaria laughs before slapping a hand over her mouth. "He was rocking my world if you really must know."

"Oh God," I groan, holding a hand over my eyes, able to smell their sex in the air which makes me want to throw up all over the expensive carpet. "Please don't talk to me while my brother's dick is still buried inside your skanky vag."

Damien laughs, so not understanding the horror of this moment, or if he does, he certainly finds my pain amusing. "What would you prefer I do? Pull it out?"

Yep, I'm definitely going to be sick. I have never regretted anything more in my life. I cry out, my feet slamming against the floor as I bolt back down the hallway, my hand cupped over my mouth.

Oh no. I'm not going to make it.

I barge through the bathroom door just as vomit erupts from my throat like a goddamn fountain, and though I try to block it with my hands, the force is just too great. Vomit spurts through my fingers, spraying the bathroom like some kind of bloody murder scene. And the smell. Fuck!

Finally making it to the toilet, I hang my head into it and violently redecorate the bathroom as Ilaria appears in the doorway with a blanket wrapped around her. "Oh no," she says with a soft chuckle in her tone, holding a hand over her mouth as she looks at the mess.

I raise my head long enough to give her a nasty glare. "I hope you know what this means for you."

Ilaria presses her lips into a hard line, her eyes sparkling with laughter. "Bring it on, baby."

Damien and Jensen show up at the same time, both with stupid grins on their stupid boy faces. Jensen has the decency to at least pretend to feel for my current predicament. My brother, on the other hand, has no such reservations. A bellowing laugh tears from him as he loops his arm over Ilaria's shoulder, his other hand trying to cover his junk, but considering he's still hard, he's not doing a very good job. And hell, just seeing it has me dry retching again.

"Holy fuck," I mutter, breaking into a sweat. "For the record, I hate you all."

Damien laughs and grabs Ilaria, throwing her over his shoulder. "I'm cool with that," he says before spanking her ass and bolting back to his room, Ilaria's giggles echoing down the long hallway.

I shakily get to my feet, glaring at Jensen who remains at the bathroom door. "Don't even think about fucking off without cleaning this shit up," he says, scanning the room. His expression becomes more and more horrified the longer he looks, even glancing up toward the ceiling, unsure whether to be mortified or impressed.

I roll my eyes and start cleaning up after myself. "The least you could do is grab me the mop," I grumble. "This is basically all your fault.

Don't pretend like you didn't know I was about to walk in and see that."

Jensen shrugs his shoulders. "Sorry, but after hanging out with your brother, I've decided he's a shitload cooler than you. We're bros now."

"Ahh, fuck," I mutter.. "And what exactly does it mean to be bros?"

Jensen shakes his head, giving me a tight smile. "Don't ask questions you simply can't understand. It's a deep, deep kind of friendship. It's like our spirits are living on the same fucked-up level that you just can't complete with. Accept it now. It'll be easier in the long run."

I groan and give him a blank stare. "Just give me a warning if I'm about to walk into a room and see you and Damien creating a human centipede. I can handle seeing him fuck one of my friends, but I don't think I'd ever recover from that," I tell him. "That's just taking the whole stepbrother thing a little too far."

Jensen laughs and slips his hands into his pockets. "Ahhhh, jealousy doesn't look good on you, little sister."

"Jealousy?" I laugh. "Jealous of what? Your desire to fuck my brother? No thanks, you can have him all to yourself."

"I ... no, that's not what I meant."

"You said so yourself," I tease. "You're experiencing a deep, deep friendship, and honestly, I didn't know you could get that deep inside my brother. But it's cool, whatever floats your boat."

"Fucking hell," Jensen mutters. "He warned me you were tricky, but I underestimated you."

I give him a wide grin. "Most people do," I tell him before arching a brow. "Now, how about that mop?"

CHAPTER 24
Brielle

Okay, so hear me out. I kinda left while Jensen was getting the mop, but who can blame me? At least I did a half-assed cleaning job, but the moans, groans, and giggles coming from Damien's room made me need to shower in bleach. Though I don't know what that's going to do for the memories etched into my brain.

I skip over the small hedge between the houses and break into Tanner's place. "Addie?" I call from the bottom of the stairs, having learned my lesson about barging into people's rooms uninvited, especially now that she's getting handsy with Hudson. "Are you here?"

Addison's head pops over the banister, looking down at me. "What's up?" she questions, her hair falling around her face.

A wide grin stretches across my face as I feel a war brewing in my veins. Hell, walking in on my brother and Ilaria must have messed with me a little more than I thought because before that, I was determined to let this one go, but the more I think about it, the more I can't sit back and do nothing. "You wanna go fuck someone up?"

Her eyes sparkle with excitement, knowing exactly what I'm thinking. "The boys aren't going to like this."

"The boys can kiss my ass," I tell her, knowing damn well what the boys think about this. We've spent the last few days listening to all their reasons as to why we shouldn't. But fuck them. If Addison isn't going to get justice, then we'll take it for ourselves.

We sit in Tanner's stolen Mustang, knowing damn well he'd have something to say about this, but he'd have to find us first. We cross over the border into Hope Falls, the windows down and the wind blowing in our hair.

Hey Violet blasts through the speakers, preaching about *Fuqboi's*, and we scream the lyrics at the top of our lungs, feeling free for the first time in weeks. "Is this seriously where you used to live?" she questions, her face scrunching as she looks at all the litter scattered across the road, the chains and boards around peoples' homes, not to mention the graffiti on every available surface.

"Yeah, it's just peachy, right?" I laugh, hating the thoughts that are probably rummaging through her mind, judging the lifestyle I once lived.

I see the familiar yellow beetle up ahead and nerves filter through me, making my hands shake. "She's home," I tell her, nodding up ahead to Erica's house, relieved that neither of her parents' cars are there.

I bring the Mustang to a stop a few houses down and glance toward Addison, who seems to have gone very quiet. Turning down the music, I give her a hard stare. "Whatever you want," I tell her. "I've got your back."

She nods, letting out a heavy breath, and I can't help but wonder if she's nervous. This isn't exactly something Addison has done before, and I suppose neither have I. Well, kind of. Growing up around here, I've been forced to do things I never wanted to do. Mostly, I've been lucky. I haven't been jumped or fucked with, but I've certainly witnessed it.

"I, umm…" she says, her words falling short. "I don't think I want to hurt her."

"Okay," I say slowly, wondering where this is going.

"I want to expose her though. Maybe humiliate her a bit too. Make her feel just a fraction of the humiliation I've endured."

I nod, a grin pulling at my lips as her eyes start to light up with a plan. She quickly tells me all the ins and outs, and by the time we're falling out of the Mustang, my stomach is hurting from laughing.

We cut across the lawn, and if we were anywhere else, we would have garnered the attention of the neighbors, but not in Hope Falls. Here, people have learned to mind their own business because the consequences are generally a lot worse.

"Back here," I tell Addison, leading the way through the backyard of Erica's home, knowing damn well the kitchen door is unlocked and the only one in the house that doesn't creak. After all, I've snuck through it a million times before.

Loud music blasts from inside, and I grin knowing just how easily we'll be able to get the drop on her. We duck past the back windows and slip inside. Addison hovers behind me, not as confident with the layout. We peek around the corner of the kitchen, double-checking the bitch isn't stuffing her face, and just as we do, we hear Erica's off-key singing coming from her room.

I relax a bit and grab one of the dining chairs, placing it right in the center of the living room before rummaging through the junk drawer. Finding masking tape, I silently hold it up with a grin, each piece of our plan quickly falling into place.

"You ready?" I mouth, indicating down the hall.

Addison lets out a shaky breath before nodding. "Let's do it."

And just like that, we barrel down the short hallway and barge into Erica's bedroom. She stands by her closet, picking out an outfit for who the fuck knows what and sees us through the mirror. Her eyes widen in shock, but before she can even get a scream out, we're on her.

She whips around and smacks me in the face, but I catch her arm as it flails about. Addison is the brains of this operation, and she goes for the legs, kicking the bitch's knees out and watching her crumble to the ground with a loud oomph.

We each grab an arm and drag her out to the living room as she screams, the music easily drowning her out. "Let go. Let me go, you dumb bitches," she wails, kicking her legs out, but it's no use. We're up near her head and she's definitely not flexible enough to leave any damage.

We tackle Erica into the dining chair, and Addison quickly gets to work strapping her down, breaking the masking tape with her teeth and wrapping it around enough to ensure she'll never be able to break through it. "Holy fuck, this is such a rush," Addie says, enjoying this far too much.

After Erica's ankles and wrists are bound to the wooden chair, I stand back, surveying our handiwork, pretty impressed with our efforts. "Well, hey there, bestie," I chime with a wide smile. "Long time no see."

"What the fuck do you want?" Erica spits. "You're nothing but a backstabbing little slut."

I laugh, almost snorting. "Oh, I'm the backstabbing slut?" I scoff. "Might I remind you that you're the one who fucked my boyfriend behind my back, but good riddance. I'm sure you heard the fucker is dead."

Erica clenches her jaw, but I continue. "I'm sure you remember my friend Addison?" I question, glancing at the girl beside me who watches Erica with venom in her eyes. "Remind me, have you been officially introduced? I know the last time you saw her, you were hopped up on drugs and pumping her full of them. Wait … was that before or after you suggested Colby should fuck with her?"

"Hmm," Addison says. "Pretty sure it was before because after she pumped me full of drugs, she was busy watching me scream for help as Colby dragged me away."

"Ahhh," I say, nodding as Erica's face turns white, recognizing just how much trouble she's in here.

"What do you want with me?" she spits, focusing on me because she can barely look at Addison. "The cops dropped the charges against me. It's my word against yours, and like you said, you were pumped full of drugs. Who'd believe you?"

I laugh and glance at Addison, pointing to my lips while nodding toward Erica. "Would you mind?"

"Oh," Addison says with a cheerful glee. "Of course. What was I thinking?" Addison steps up to Erica, stretching out a piece of tape and slamming it down over her face, then she adds a few more pieces just for good luck.

Erica tries to argue through the tape, but all that comes out is a muffled grumble. Knowing her parents are bound to come back at some point, we get to work. I rush down to Erica's room, finding a bunch of markers and her phone.

I hand a marker to Addison and together, we scribble words across her skin, covering her clothes and every available bit of flesh. We tell the story on her skin, writing down her shame for everyone to see.

Betrayal.
Backstabber.
Cheater.
Liar.
Fraud.

GUILTY.

The list goes on and on and by the time we're done, tears are welling in Erica's eyes. It's almost hard to look at as the years of friendship claw at something inside of me, but she doesn't deserve my pity. She doesn't deserve to be let off the hook. Addison needs justice to be able to move on in this world, and I won't stop until she gets it.

Addison and I look over her before glancing at one another. "Umm," I say, my gaze narrowing. "What are we supposed to do with her now?"

Addison shrugs, neither of us really thinking this part through. "I mean, we could lock her up in the school for everyone to find in the morning."

I shrug my shoulders. "I don't know," I tell her. "Security got pretty tight there after someone brought a knife to school a few years ago. There are too many cameras. Oh—" I say, grabbing her phone and entering the passcode that still hasn't changed. I scroll through her recent texts before a wide grin stretches across my face. I turn the screen to show Addison. "She was getting ready to go out before we got here," I remind her. "Fancy a visit to Hope Falls' local hangout?"

A wicked grin pulls at Addie's lips. "Today just keeps getting better."

Scanning over her texts, it looks like all the Hope Falls rejects are partying at the basketball courts tonight. The text says to show up just after eight, and seeing as though it's already after five, we start getting a move on. After all, we don't want anyone to spot us and the longer Erica has to sit there alone and vulnerable, the better.

Fuck, that makes me sound like a bitch, but I can't find it in me to feel bad about it.

"Ummmm, question," Addison says, scanning her sharp gaze over Erica. "How are we supposed to get her in the car?"

"Hmm," I mutter, clearly not having thought this part through either. I walk around the back of her and yank the chair toward me, tipping it back. "You think we could carry her?"

Addison shrugs and moves into position, her hands curling around the legs of the chair. "Remember," she smirks. "Lift with your knees."

I bark out a laugh and just as we're about to lift, the sound of a roaring motorbike cuts through the house, loud enough to hear over Erica's ridiculous music. My back stiffens and I meet Addison's stare. "Oh shit."

"WHAT THE FUCK ARE YOU DOING?" Tanner's booming tone rattles my fucking eardrums, and I glance over my shoulder to where he hovers in the doorway, his hands balled into fists, freshly showered after football training.

Busted.

Addison releases the chair and straightens up, crossing her arms over her chest and fixing Tanner with a nasty stare. "I think the better question is what the fuck are you doing? And how the hell did you know where to find us?"

"Yeah," I agree, pushing the chair back up and fixing him with a stare. "We didn't breathe a word to anyone about where we were going. How did you—OH HELL NO," I blurt. "You put a tracker on our phones."

A guilty expression crosses his stupid, lovable face, and I want to strangle him. "Can you blame me? Every time I turn my back, one of you ends up in the hospital."

My mouth drops, gaping at him in horror. "So you put a fucking tracker on us? Not cool, Tanner. That's such an asshole move."

He shrugs, the guilt quickly slipping away and morphing into indifference. "Yeah, well, considering you're halfway through kidnapping that bitch, I'd say it was time well spent. Now, back to my original question. What the fuck are you two doing? Do you have any idea how messed up this looks?"

"It's not how it looks," Addison says, shrugging it off.

"Oh really? You didn't break in, then bind and gag the bitch who had a part in your attack?"

Addison grins. "Okay, well maybe it is how it looks, but for the record, we didn't gag her, just taped her mouth shut. But in our defense, she's a mouthy bitch and had a little too much to say. We were just problem solving."

"Look," I say. "We can stand here and argue about this, or you can shut the fuck up and help us carry this bitch out of here. We need to move on to stage two of this plan, and if you're going to stand around looking pretty, you might as well be helpful."

Tanner groans before letting out a heavy sigh. "Fine," he finally says. "But don't think you're off the hook just yet. You stole my Mustang, and I can guarantee you listened to your bullshit chick songs in it. She's a beast. She only plays my shit."

I roll my eyes and fix him with a hard stare. "You can take it out on me tonight with a thorough fucking," I tell him. "As for now, be a good little criminal and grab the hostage."

Ten minutes later, Erica is laid across the backseat of the Mustang, chair and all, her face only a few inches from the ceiling. "Yeah, we really didn't think this through," I laugh as Addison climbs in the passenger seat.

Tanner walks around the front of the Mustang, straddling his bike and pulling his helmet over his head, though he makes sure to give me a pointed stare, narrowing his gaze on me. He starts the bike and takes off down the streets of Hope Falls. I follow after him, the momentum making Erica's chair rock back. I try to overcompensate by hitting the brakes, but instead of straightening her out, she rocks forward, her face slamming into the back of my chair and getting stuck dangling over the leg space of the back seat.

"Whoops," I say with a cringe as Addison slaps a hand over her mouth, muffling a booming laugh.

We drive like that, letting her dangle for the next few minutes and before I know it, we're pulling up at the deserted basketball courts. I cut the engine beside Tanner's bike. He climbs off and walks to the back door, pulling it open and pausing as he catches sight of Erica.

"The fuck?" he mutters to himself as Erica tries to scream through the tape.

Reaching in, he grabs her and drags her out of the car before adjusting the chair in his arms. Still shaking his head, he walks across the courts and sits her down right below the spotlight, knowing that the moment the sun goes down and the automatic lights turn on, she'll be the center of attention for everyone to see … and read.

We follow Tanner onto the court while Addison flips Erica's phone between her fingers. "Now what?" Tanner questions, glancing back at his sister, wanting her to get the justice she deems acceptable despite not agreeing with our tactics.

"Ummmm … just one more thing," she says before unlocking the phone and bringing up the camera. She stands in front of Erica before turning the camera on herself. "Hi," she says to the screen. "My name is Addison Morgan, and over the summer, I was drugged and raped by Colby Jacobs. My body went into shock and for six long weeks, I lay comatose in Bradford Private hospital. Upon waking from my coma, the flashbacks destroyed me, and I remembered how this bitch behind me had a hand in my attack. She encouraged Colby to fuck with me, laughed as they both pumped me full of drugs, and when I was dragged away to be raped, she stood back and didn't do a damn thing about it." Addison pauses, trying to regain control of her voice as it starts to break. "A few weeks ago, Colby was cleared of rape in front of a judge due to a dirty lawyer tampering with evidence, and barely a week later," she says, pulling the neckline of her shirt down enough to show her scar, "he attempted to rape me again, only this time instead of mental scars, I escaped with a physical one. He stabbed me, punctured my lung, and put me in hospital for the second time. That night, Colby also stabbed two of my closest friends and they nearly lost their lives. If it weren't for my brother … I wouldn't be here. Colby is gone now, and while that wasn't the justice I deserved, at least I know he can never hurt anyone again."

Addison takes a breath, adjusting the camera to see Erica more clearly in the background, the words written on her skin clear as day. "A few days ago, I was informed the police had also dropped the charges against Erica Sawyer, and again, I lost my chance for justice. So I say fuck it. I'm taking justice into my own hands, and I am well aware the police will be knocking on my door for this, but I don't care. I'll accept it because I know Erica will finally be exposed for the monster she is. The world will know what she did that night. So this here is a call out to the authorities to do better. To the judicial system—do better. The police, lawyers, the principals in our schools—do better. Because girls like me are suffering. We're terrified and carrying scars you couldn't even dream of while monsters like Colby and Erica are freely walking the streets, looking for their next victim. And that is on you."

With that, she wraps up the video and sends it to herself and then everyone else in her fucking address book. Both mine and Tanner's phones beep with incoming texts, and as we pull them out, Addison instructs us to send it to everyone we know.

Once the video posts to all of Addison's socials, we get back into the Mustang, leaving Erica alone on the court. The video is already spreading around the globe, her call for justice trending worldwide.

CHAPTER 25
TANNER

"Hope you're ready for me, @Bad_GirlZoe18," Jax says, slipping his hand into Riley's bag and scooping out his phone as Riley speaks with Coach Wyld about his college options for next year. "Hope you're ready for me because I'm about to fuck your fucking world."

I shake my head, but I can't lie, the idea of messaging this chick for Riley has been playing in the back of my mind since the moment we learned about her. I don't know what it is about her, but she's already got my best friend by the balls, despite the fact he's too chicken-shit to even talk to her.

It's cute really … nah, fuck that. It's lame as shit. The dickhead needs to grow a pair of balls, but if he won't do it, then we'll happily step in for him. The only issue we've had is that since finding out we were planning to make this happen, Riley has been gatekeeping his phone like it was his only lifeline. But honestly, the fucker should have a little more faith in us. Well, me at least. Hudson, Logan, and Jax have had their own girl issues. Not me though. I know exactly how to satisfy my woman and keep her coming back for more.

Logan comes barreling through the locker room. "If we're doing this, it's gotta be now," he tells us. "Wyld had him close the door and sit down."

I cringe. When Coach asks you to close the door behind you, that means you're in for the long run. Though it's game night, so it can't be any longer than twenty minutes. After that, we need to get ready and get our heads in the game, no ifs or buts about it. That stands for Coach too.

Jax sits on the bench as Hudson hovers over his shoulder, watching with a close eye. After all, if anyone is going to fuck this up for Riley, it'd be Jax. That idiot couldn't even shave his balls without busting a nut.

"Umm, okay," Jax says with the kind of confidence that has me groaning. He holds the phone up, reading it out as he types. "Hey little Baddie, you caught my eye. But just between you and me, the only reason I'd kick you out of bed is to fuck you on the floor."

"Aww, fuck no," I say, snatching the phone out of his hands before he can hit send. "The hell is wrong with you? You send her that shit and you'll get blocked in seconds."

"What the fuck would you know?" Jax questions. "You have no

fucking game. I'm the one reeling in all the bitches. How many chicks have you fucked in the past few weeks? Oh what's that? Fucking crickets. You have one. Me? I could score with every chick in town. Hell, I already have."

Logan smacks his brother up the back of his head. "Bullshit. All you've fucked is your hand since the lake. Besides, I don't think Riley just wants to fuck her. He wants to date her and then fuck her."

"Bullshit," Jax says. "Riley doesn't date. He fucks and then bails. Trust me, let me work my magic and I'll have Riley slipping one in by the end of the night."

Hudson holds his hand out for the phone. "Sorry, man, you would have struck out with that shit," he says. "Give it to me."

I shake my head as I hand it over, knowing damn well Hudson won't be able to pull anything worthwhile out of his ass. He hits the backspace, holding it down until the screen is clear. "Alright," he says with a moronic grin. "You guys ready to see the master at work?"

Jax scoffs, getting salty that his efforts were disregarded faster than the chicks he usually fucks. Hudson gets on with it, reading out his message and typing just like Jax had. "Hey girl, I couldn't help but notice your ass in that red bikini. I'm not gonna lie, you've had me rocking a semi for days," he says, making me gag. "What do you say we do something about it? Your place or mine?"

Pride settles across Hudson's face as he turns the phone around for us to read over the screen and I can't help but notice the multiple spelling errors. "You're fucking kidding, right?" I question, letting out a heavy sigh before taking the phone back. I glance toward Logan.

"Do you want a chance to embarrass yourself, or should I just take it from here?"

"What?" Hudson grunts, so sure he'd gotten it right. "What was wrong with that? It was forward, let her know he's down to fuck, and asked to meet up."

"Your game is just as pathetic as Jax's."

Hudson's eyes widen with hurt. "What? What do you mean? My game is spot on. It got your sister, didn't it?"

"My sister clearly doesn't know what's good for her," I mutter. "But you didn't pick up Addie by hitting on her with bullshit lines and suggesting you'd whip your dick out for anything. You treated her like a fucking human, just like this chick wants to be treated. Do we even know if she's available? She might have a boyfriend, and if she does, she'll fuck Riley off so fast, he won't even get a chance to say hello."

"Okay, genius," Jax mutters as I delete Hudson's bullshit lines. "If you think you're the fucking pussy whisperer, let's see what you've got."

I give Jax a blank stare before writing out the message, not bothering to read it out loud like the boys had done. "Hey, what's up?" I flip the phone around and show them the simple message. "That's how it's done," I tell them. "It's simple, she's not being treated like a fucking pussy factory, and she's not going to block him for being a fucking creep. She'll be able to figure it out all on her own."

Jax scoffs and rolls his eyes. "BOOOOORING!"

I shrug and hit send before any of them get the chance to fuck this up then toss the phone into Logan's hands, assuming he's the only responsible one right now. "Just wait and see. She'll hit him back the second she gets online."

Logan shakes his head, certain that I've fucked it up. "Bullshit," he mutters to himself, before turning around and slipping Riley's phone onto the top shelf of his open locker, but I've never been so confident. Had I been messaging some random chick for myself, I probably would have ended up sending some bullshit pick-up line thinking I was all that, but since being with Bri, there's a lot of shit I've had to learn. I mean, sure, there would be a handful of chicks who are down for the dirty pick-up lines, and some might even find it endearing or adorable, but majority of women just want to be treated like a fucking human.

Standing in front of my open locker, I peel off my shirt and get ready for tonight's game. I shove my phone, wallet, and keys on the top shelf before rifling through my bag for all my safety gear. I'm just about ready when my phone buzzes on the shelf. The vibration against the metal locker draws my attention immediately.

We're only ten minutes out from our pre-game rituals, and though I consider ignoring it, I know it's probably a text from Mom or Bri wishing me luck for the game. Usually, if it's Bri, it'll come with a dirty picture attached, and I simply can't resist.

Scooping my phone off the shelf, I unlock the screen and pause, seeing a new email from my lawyer. "Ahhhh, fuck," I mutter to myself, my stomach dropping right out my fucking ass. There's only one reason he'd be e-mailing me on a Friday night, and I don't fucking like it.

I've been actively doing everything I can to avoid this. I haven't chased him down to get results quicker, and I sure as fuck haven't been waiting on the edge of my seat. I already know the test was a waste of time, but I can't avoid it any longer. Besides, it's in the best interest of the team to get this out of the way. I've played like shit since the second Rachael showed up on my doorstep claiming her son was mine, and now I can finally put this shit to rest, and the second the game is over, I'd be more than happy to rub it in her face. Besides, it's nothing but a ploy to extort money out of me and my family. Though one thing is for sure. Despite how supportive Bri has been, I know it's been on her mind, and the quicker we can get back to normal, the better.

Knowing damn well what I'll find inside this email, I quickly open it and scroll past my lawyer's message to go straight for the attached results, certain I'd be able to understand the technical terminology. I can respond to it properly after the game, but for now, there's only one thing I'm interested in.

My cell service is shit in the locker room and it takes a moment for the multipage document to load, but when it finally does, I don't hesitate to scroll through the many pages of information explaining what I'm about to see.

I get to the third page titled "DNA Test Report" and there's a table filled with numbers I can't even begin to understand, but I keep scrolling to the bottom until I find the words *Probability of Paternity: 99.98%*

My whole fucking world stops, everyone fading out of reality around me as I become locked in the moment, staring at the too bright screen.

99.98%

Fuck.

I shake my head, barely breathing.

How could I be the father? I used a condom, and fuck, I don't even remember finishing. She was a dud lay, and I was bored after three minutes. This can't be right. I can't be her child's father, but this test is saying I am, and who the fuck am I to question it?

I'm eighteen, not even having finished high school, and I've got a one-year-old son. A son whose first year I've been absent for.

FUCK. Fuck, fuck, fuck.

Colby was my child's uncle, his flesh and blood, and I'm the man responsible for murdering him. I killed my own son's uncle, my child's family. What kind of monster am I?

My stomach twists and I heave, needing to throw up, but I hold it down and grip my phone tighter before racing out of the locker room. "Yo, Tanner. Where the hell are you going?" I hear Hudson calling after me. "We've got a fucking game."

Running through the school, I race toward the field, my gaze snapping from side to side, trying to find that one person through the thick crowd climbing the grandstand. I search desperately, my heart racing faster than ever before as panic takes over. My knees fall to the grass, and I barely catch myself, the screen of my phone still staring up at me with the haunting DNA results.

"Tanner?" I hear in the distance. "TANNER!"

A set of soft hands grip my arms, pulling me to my feet. I can't find the words, but her hands move to my face, forcing my stare away from the phone, her bright blue eyes filled with concern. "What's wrong?" Bri rushes out, swaying as people shoulder past us to fill the grandstands, desperate to find seats before one of the biggest games of the season.

I take her waist, pulling her in closer, unable to look away from her frightened eyes. "I'm sorry," I whisper, hating the thought of breaking her heart, but I can't keep this from her. I have to tell her. It's me and Brielle against the fucking world. Who am I if I don't have her in my corner? "I never thought … I didn't—"

"Tanner, breathe," she says calmly, her hand sliding down my arm and gripping my hand. "What's going on?"

"The paternity test," I tell her, my voice shaky, knowing damn well she has every right to walk away from this. I hand her my phone, watching as her brows furrow and she turns it around to look at the screen. "I'm sorry. I … I'm his father."

Bri sucks in a silent gasp, and I see the hurt in her eyes. She keeps her stare locked on the screen, reading over the words a million times just as I had, and a part of me wonders if it's because it's too hard for her to look me in the eyes. "It's okay," she finally says, glancing up, trying to hold herself together. "The second Rachael came to the door, we knew this could be a possibility. You'll be okay. *We'll be okay.* We just need to figure ourselves out."

"How the hell am I supposed to do that?" I question, keeping my voice low as to not break the news to the whole fucking school.

Bri shakes her head, her grip tightening on my hand. "I don't know," she confesses, her voice breaking. "But what choice do we have? I know you, Tanner. You can't mess this up. It's not possible. You're this kid's father and you're going to be his whole world, but right now, you have a game to get through. Focus on that and being the best fucking quarterback this town has ever seen, then when we get home, we can start working on this. Until then, just know that I love you."

I shake my head, my heart breaking as I confess what's buried deep inside. "I missed the first year of my kid's life. Fuck, I don't even know his name."

She pushes up onto her tippy toes and presses a kiss to my lips. "And you'll make up for it," she tells me. "You don't need to be afraid of this. You're the most incredible, amazing person I know, and this little boy is going to be lucky to have you in his life."

"You sure?" I question, absolutely terrified.

Bri nods. "I've never been so sure. It's not being a father you need to fear, it's getting home and having to tell your mom."

Bri's words are like a bucket of ice water coming down over my head. "Oh fuck," I breathe, terror like I've never known rocking through my chest. "She's going to kill me."

"Better her than me," Bri mutters.

My brows furrow and I grip her chin, tilting it up until she meets my eye. "Are you okay with this?"

She shrugs her shoulders, uncertainty in her beautiful eyes. "I just need a minute to adjust," she admits, being honest. "But don't worry about me. We'll work it out together. Just go back to the locker room, kick ass in your game, and tonight, we can figure out how we're going to make this work."

"You're sure?"

"I'm sure," she tells me. "The good, bad, and the ugly, Tanner. I'm not going anywhere."

"Okay," I tell her, finally able to take a deep, calming breath.

Bri smiles up at me before squeezing my hand again. "Go," she says before indicating to the girls crowded behind her, each of them watching with concern. "We need to find our seats, but if you don't kick ass on that field and make me proud, then we'll really have issues."

A smirk kicks up the corner of my mouth, and I drop a kiss to her lips before turning and sprinting back to the locker room, more than ready to make her proud.

CHAPTER 26

TANNER

Sweat drips from my brow as we face the team from Haven Falls. We have eight minutes left on the clock, and that time is quickly slipping away. The first half was neck and neck, but moving into the second, my boys pulled us through, and we've been holding on to the lead ever since. But one minor fuck up and we could lose it all.

We jog across the field, quickly making our way back to Coach Wyld after the Haven Falls coach called a timeout. I don't blame them though. They need every advantage they can get right now. This game is too close not to utilize every card you've got up your sleeve.

My guys look rough. They're exhausted, but looking around, I know they still have enough gas in the tank to get us through to the end. It's been a fast game, but we're not done yet.

Coach Wyld is red in the face, but it's nothing new. I'm surprised he hasn't lost his voice after all the yelling he's been doing, but this is standard practice for a game night. He gives it his all, and it's part of the reason I respect him so much.

"Logan," he says as we quickly huddle around, Jax jumping up from the bench to give his two cents wherever he can. "Keep doing what you're doing. They're fast, but they won't be able to catch you. Work those reflexes, be ahead of the game."

Logan nods and Coach quickly moves on, working his way around the circle. "Bellamy, watch that footwork. Number 19's been coming for you all night. Don't let him take the advantage."

Hudson nods. "Yes, Coach," he says, barely getting the words out before Wyld starts in on someone else. One by one, he quickly spits out his orders and I find myself lifting my gaze to the grandstand. Bri's eyes are already on mine, and the moment her lips split into a wide, dazzling smile, I feel like I've been injected with the most potent drug.

"Tanner," Coach snaps. "Where's your fucking head?"

"In the game, Coach."

"Really?"

Fuck. "Yes, Coach."

"Because it looks like it's up in the stands with your girlfriend."

"No, Coach. It's in the game."

His gaze narrows on me, and I know I'm going to pay for this come Monday during the afternoon training session. "That's what I thought," he finally says in a low tone filled with the kind of authority that has me bending to his every will.

Knowing what's good for me, I keep my fucking mouth shut and pay attention as he continues his way around the circle. Jax bounces at his side, desperate for a little action, though we all know he has no chance in hell.

A bottle of water sails across our huddle, and I quickly catch it and take a sip, splashing some onto my face. As the whistle blows, Coach gives one final nod, ready to send us back onto the field, but as I turn to run back into position, one of my linebackers goes down like a sack of shit.

"Oh fuck," I mutter, my eyes going wide as I race toward him. "We need a medic!"

People swarm from everywhere—our coach and the assistant coach, the first aid team, the fucking water boy, even a few people from the stands. "What the fuck happened?" Coach Wyld calls out, shoving some nosy asshole out of the way to get to his player.

"Don't know," I say from my knees beside his head, jamming my fingers against his throat to check for a pulse. "He just collapsed. He's got a pulse but it's weak."

"Thank fuck," Coach says, getting down on his other side before quickly checking him over for himself. "WHERE'S THAT MEDIC?"

Within seconds, there's a whole team of medics getting on their knees beside us, and I hastily move out of their way, letting them do their thing. One of them attaches a pulse ox to the linebacker's finger while another straps a blood pressure cuff around his arm. They talk among themselves while our assistant coach does everything in his power to try and shoo the crowds away, giving my linebacker the space and privacy he deserves.

"What's the diagnosis?" Coach asks the senior medic as the two others heave our player onto a gurney.

"Looks like heat exhaustion, maybe dehydration," the medic says. "You need to put a new player in."

"Fuck," Coach says, running his hand through his thinning hair as he presses his lips into a tight line. He glances over the line of reserves, knowing not a damn one of them has the skill level needed to help win this game.

Jax is straight on his feet.

"Hell no," Coach grunts, shaking his head before Jax even gets a chance to plead his case.

Jax races toward him, his eyes wide and desperate. "Come on, Coach. Put me in. You know I've got this," he pleads. "You have no other option, not if you want to win this."

Wyld scrunches his face as if he's actually considering this before finally realizing how fucking stupid it is. "Sorry, kid. We spoke about this."

"Oh, sure," Jax grumbles. "Just hand them the win then."

Coach clenches his jaw, glancing back at the field. He's running out of time. If he's going to make a decision, it needs to be done now. "FUCK! Jax, you're in."

"YES!" Jax cheers, fist pumping the air before bolting toward the field. He stops in front of me, grabs my helmet and smashes his against it as I just gape, horrified by Wyld's decision to play him. "FUCK YEAH! Let's do this."

Jax takes off at a sprint, the whole crowd roaring for him as he makes a fucking spectacle of himself, and within seconds, they're chanting his name. "The fuck?" I hear Logan calling from across the field as I step toward Coach.

"Are you sure about this?" I question. "One hit and he'll be fucked."

Coach shakes his head. "Sorry, kid," he says, dropping his clipboard to the bench to focus on the game. "My hands are tied. He gave me his medical clearance first thing this morning. His doctor signed off and Jax assured me he's good to go."

"Medical clearance?" I question. "What fucking clearance?"

"Not the time or place, Tanner," he says, staring past me and to his players on the field. "Get your ass out there. If you want to undermine my authority and question my decisions as the coach of this team, you can do that after we win this fucking game. Understood?"

Fuck.

Anger bursts through my chest, and I reluctantly jog back into position, barely getting there with only a few seconds to spare. There's no way Jax got clearance. He walked out of his check up a few days ago just about ready to take his doctor out. If he was cleared, he would have screamed it from the rooftops.

Despite the chanting and cheers coming from the grandstand, one cry of outrage sounds over everything else, and I glance up to the girls, finding all of them up on their feet. Addison and Bri look like they're about to be sick with Coach's decision to play Jax, while Arizona looks as though she's about to wring Wyld's throat. Ilaria, on the other hand, has her nose buried in her phone, probably without a clue of what's going on down here.

Bri meets my eye, and without a word spoken between us, I know she's begging me to watch out for Jax, and I will do my best, but trouble can happen in a split second. I can't always be exactly where he needs me, not in such a fast-paced game.

"What the fuck are you doing?" I hear Logan cursing out his brother. "You're going to get hurt."

"Lay off," Jax says, getting into position. "I'll be fine."

Logan goes to respond, but the whistle signals that the ball is back in play, shutting us all up. The ball moves from player to player, and Haven Falls quickly makes their way down field, getting a little too cocky for my liking.

The ball is swiftly delivered into my hands and I rear back, letting the bastard fly, knowing Logan will be exactly where he needs to be. But just as he jumps to catch the ball, he's brought back to the ground with a devastating blow, leaving the ball wide open to sail straight into the arms of Haven Falls.

"Fuck," I mutter, clenching my jaw and taking off again, my boys pushing themselves even harder.

Haven Falls tries to make a run for it, but my guys are too fast, coming in hot. He dodges and weaves as the crowd roars, but his footwork is lacking and in the most humiliating moment of the whole season, he fumbles, dropping the ball.

Jax is on it like hot cakes, catching it before it even hits the ground and taking off like a fucking rocket. He tucks the ball securely in his arms, and we all take off with him, adrenaline coursing through our veins. This is it. This is our game-winning play, and it's about to be the biggest showstopper of the season.

His feet slam against the grass, propelling himself further up the field, dodging and weaving like the fucking pro he is. I move into position, ready to have his back wherever he needs it, just as Riley and Hudson do the same. But there's too many of them.

Riley slams into one as number 19 sidesteps Hudson, getting on his nerves for the last fucking time.

"Go, go, go," I chant, my sharp gaze whipping side to side as he creeps closer to the end zone. He pushes himself faster and just as he goes to adjust his hold on the ball, preparing for the best touchdown of the season, three Haven Falls players come out of nowhere.

Logan goes for one as I slam into another, but the third makes it through, crashing into Jax like a fucking freight train, his big-ass shoulder making fucking mincemeat of his stomach. The momentum of the hit has Jax flying off the ground and his agonized cry has me pulling up short, the game the furthest thing from my mind.

I double back, my eyes widening as I watch Jax go down hard, his back slamming into the ground as the fucker comes down on top of him. "FUCK," Jax cries as Logan and Riley start bolting toward him. I reach them first and I grip the Haven Falls guy by the back of his shirt, ripping him off Jax and throwing him aside like a fucking ragdoll as Jax lets out a pained groan, curling into a fucking ball.

"JAX," I shout, dropping down beside him, looking over him as the whistle signals another timeout. Jax scrambles, reaching for me and clutching onto my arm with everything he's got, barely able to fucking breathe.

"FUCK," he grunts, sucking in quick, sharp pants through his teeth, agony tearing across his face. "Something's wrong. I can't … I … fuck."

He clutches his stomach as Logan's knees slam down into the grass at his head. Logan screams for the medics, and I've barely had a chance to check over him before Logan's hands are at Jax's waist, tearing his shirt up and getting a look at the damage.

There's deep bruising and it's quickly spreading across his abdomen, a clear sign of deep internal bleeding. "FUCK," Logan grunts, panic in his eyes as he glances up at me, almost begging me to tell him this is all some kind of fucking nightmare.

"You fucking idiot," I berate, reliving that night all over again as I grip onto Jax's hand. "What the hell were you thinking?"

Tears well in his eyes from the pain. "I had to play," he chokes out.

"And now look at you," Logan says. "I can't fucking go through this again. I can't fucking lose you."

"It's … it's just a hiccup."

"JAX," Arizona screams from the sidelines, the assistant coach struggling to hold her back. Tears stream down her face, and there's only ever been one other time I've seen her look so terrified. "Jax, you big fucking idiot."

"Shit," Jax grunts. "She's gonna have my balls for this."

"Out of the way," the medics order, Coach Wyld racing in beside them. We all scramble back and it happens so fast. One second, he's in agony on the grass and the next he's being loaded into the back of an ambulance with Ari somehow at his side.

I stand with Logan, Riley, and Hudson, watching as the ambulance pulls away, the sirens blaring through the night as the girls come crashing into us. Chanel throws her arms around Logan. "He's going to be okay," she promises him, but we all know that's not a promise she can make.

Logan shakes his head, a million different emotions swarming in his eyes. Anger. Frustration. Terror. "That should be me in there," he spits, pulling out of Chanel's arms. "Arizona has done nothing but fuck with his head for weeks, and now when it counts she wants to be the one by his fucking side? He's my goddamn brother. My twin. I'm his family, not her."

"Logan," Coach Wyld says, jogging to catch up to us. "I've spoken to your father. He'll be on the first flight home. As for the rest of—"

"The fuck were you thinking playing him?" Logan demands, getting in Wyld's face. "He wasn't cleared. Wasn't even fucking close."

Coach shakes his head. "I'm sorry, Logan, but Jax gave me his clearance this morning. Said his doctor signed off on it."

"Bullshit," Logan spits. "Did you call his doctor or just take Jax's word for it? He's dying in the back of that fucking ambulance because you played him."

"Logan," I warn. "Don't."

"Don't what?" he roars. "Don't call people out on their bullshit when I see it? My brother is fucking dying, Tanner. Dying. He's not taking a fucking vacation. He'll be back in surgery, with another six months of recovery. What about college, huh? He'll get dropped so fucking fast."

"Stop," Chanel says, forcing his stare back to her. "We don't need to be thinking about that now. All that matters is making sure Jax gets through his surgery unscathed. After that, you can point your finger all you like. For now, can we just get out of here? They're going to need you down at the hospital. You're his closest family."

Logan looks back at Coach Wyld. "You better hope he's alright," Logan spits before gripping Chanel's hand and taking off toward the student parking lot.

Coach clenches his jaw, shaking his head in disbelief, no doubt struggling with the guilt of playing Jax when he knows damn well he shouldn't have. Hell, I even tried to warn him, but once his mind was made up, there was no going back. But I'm not fooled. Jax would have done anything to be able to play tonight. They're both to blame, but at least Coach didn't do it consciously. Jax knew damn well he hadn't been cleared and went to great lengths to submit a forged clearance.

"He just needs some time to cool off," I tell Coach.

"Yeah, I know," he says before nodding toward the field. "Right, get back in there. We have four minutes left in this game and you know damn well those reserves can't pull off this win. There's nothing you can do for Jax right now."

I gape at Coach Wyld. Is he fucking kidding himself? He wants us to play right now?

"Yes, Coach," Hudson says before making a start for the field.

"The fuck?" I grunt, catching his elbow and pulling him back.

"We're not fucking playing. We're going to the hospital."

"It's four fucking minutes," Hudson argues. "Coach is right. There's nothing we can do for Jax right now, and besides, if Jax is going down for this game, the least we can do is fucking win it for him."

Shit. I hate it when he's right.

Mom's heels click against the cheap linoleum as she races toward us in the waiting room. "Oh, Logan," she cries, rushing into him and throwing her arms around him, forcing him to stop pacing for just a moment. "I came as soon as I heard. Have there been any updates?"

Logan shakes his head. "Nothing yet. Just that there's a lot of internal bleeding. They'll need to locate the source and then try to get it under control, but apart from that, we know nothing. I've tried getting an update, but they won't tell me shit."

"It's okay, my sweet boy," she says. "I'll deal with them and work out the paperwork. You just focus on keeping calm. You're not helping anybody by getting all worked up, okay?"

Logan mutters a barely audible "Mmkay," before dropping down between Chanel and Hudson, and true to her word, Mom takes control of the situation. "Have your parents been called?" she asks Logan before quickly glancing at me.

I nod. "Coach Wyld called Uncle Linc straight after, but I don't know if he's had any further updates. Not sure about their mom."

"Okay," she says, stepping into me. She pulls me into a quick hug, rubbing her hand in a circle on my back. "How are you holding up? Are you okay?"

"Yeah, I'm fine. I'm just—" I cut myself off, shaking my head. "This shouldn't have happened."

"I know," she tells me, pulling away and giving my hand a firm squeeze. "But the why doesn't matter right now. We'll worry about that once Jaxon is out of surgery. I'm sure there will be some kind of internal investigation at school. But if Jax really did forge a doctor's clearance, he could be looking at some real trouble, and not just the kicked off the team kind of trouble."

Mom gives me a tight smile before dropping her hand. "I'm going to check in with the nurses and see if I can get us an update."

She takes off as I drop down beside Bri, taking her hand and pulling it into my lap. "You okay?" I murmur, glancing across the room to where Ari sits alone with tears on her face after Logan decided to take his frustrations out on her.

"Yeah, I'm just worried about him," she tells me. "We should have seen this coming. He's been too upset about having to sit out, and plus all the mind-fuck stuff with Ari. He's been silently spiraling. I should have known he'd pull a stunt like this."

"There was no way you could have known. None of us did," I tell her. "Jax is always so happy and shrugs off anything that comes his way. He never lets on if he's hurting or struggling, just goes about his day as if it were like any other. But don't worry, I don't think this was a cry for help. I think Jax was just being a careless idiot, thinking he's invincible like he always does. Only this time, he realized he's only human, just like the rest of us."

Bri lets out a heavy breath and scoots back in her seat before curling into my side and resting her head against my shoulder, watching as Ilaria gets up to try and chat with Arizona for the tenth time, only for Arizona to tell Ilaria to leave her alone again.

Riley and Hudson quietly talk between themselves, trying to include me in their conversation, but my gaze is locked on Mom, watching as she speaks to the nurses and tries to get some kind of answers out of them.

They talk for about ten minutes before Mom comes back, and the second she does, we are all on our feet. "It's touch and go," she tells us, not sugar coating anything. "Jax has lost a lot of blood, but they're confident he will be alright with enough blood transfusions. He should still be in surgery another few hours, and then Logan will be able to go and sit with him as he wakes."

A weight drops from my shoulders, and for the first time all night, I feel as though I can finally breathe.

"Oh, thank fuck," Logan says, dropping back onto his seat and pulling out his phone. "I should give Mom a call and let her know."

"Good idea," Mom says, reaching over to him and giving his shoulder a gentle squeeze. "Let her know I'll be staying here if she needs anything."

Logan nods and gets busy with his call as Mom settles into a chair directly opposite me. "How was the game before Jax got hurt? Were you doing well?"

"Yeah, it was fine," I tell her, giving her a tight smile and knowing it's now or never. I have to come clean about the paternity test because waiting is only going to hurt her, but is now really the best time? I don't want to drop another bomb on her while she's already stressed and worried about Jax, but I need to get this out. I need her to tell me what the fuck I'm supposed to do. "I, umm … I got the paternity test results."

Her back stiffens and she becomes impossibly still, her hands pausing midair as she gapes at me. "And?" she questions, a slight panic in her eyes.

I swallow over the lump in my throat. Why is it suddenly so hard to breathe again? Is the air getting thinner in here? "And, Rachael was right," I tell her, feeling as though I'm stabbing her right in the back and twisting the knife. "I'm his father."

I prepare for my mother to rain down hell over me, to tell me how stupid and careless I was to get some random girl pregnant, but instead, she just gives me a sad smile. "Oh, Tanner," she coos, leaning forward in her seat and squeezing my knee. "It's going to be okay."

I shake my head. "How can you say that?" I ask her. "I missed the first year of my kid's life."

"Because I know you," she insists. "And I know you will do everything in your power to make up for it and be the best father that baby could ever ask for."

"I don't know the first thing about being a father."

Mom laughs. "Do you think I knew the first thing about being a mother when I had you?" she challenges. "I'd never felt so lost in my life, but when you hold your baby in your arms, something just clicks and you work it out. You're going to be just fine, and if you need help or you're struggling, you know I am always there to help. Though, I'm not going to lie, I'm far too young to be a grandmother. You know I'm only twenty-three!"

I laugh and roll my eyes. "Yeah, sorry about that."

She smirks, always proud of herself whenever she gets away with shit like that. "So, I think first thing in the morning, after we know Jax is okay, we'll contact our lawyer and see about getting a custody arrangement put in place, and I'm sure there will probably be some child support payments which will need to be sorted out," she tells me. "Now, I haven't had any experience with this myself, but I would expect this type of thing can take a little while to hammer out those finer details, so until then, we can work on putting together a nursery for him in the spare room."

A weight slams down over my shoulders, crippling me. A nursery. Spare room. Custody arrangements. Holy fuck. This shit is getting real. Not only am I this child's father, but I'm going to have to care for him, be responsible for his health and wellbeing, and make sure he grows into a respectable, strong young man.

Fear pounds through my chest, but the moment Bri reaches across and takes my hand, it seems to settle. "You've got this, Tanner," she tells me. "I'll be right there the whole time. *I lean, you lean.*"

They're the magic fucking words, and just like that, I feel as though

I could face down the whole damn world. "Okay," I tell them both. "First thing in the morning, we make this happen."

CHAPTER 27

Brielle

Sitting in the waiting room and waiting for Jax to wake from his surgery is going to be what kills me. We've been here for five hours already, and I've never been so hungry. The only issue is the thought of actually eating right now makes me want to throw up.

Jax came out of surgery an hour ago, and it was a major success. The second he could, Logan took off to go and sit by his side. But since the moment the doctor came out and told us he was in recovery, it's been crickets. Logan's phone died hours ago, so we haven't even been able to get a text from him, just letting us know the idiot is still breathing.

The waiting room has transformed into our living room. Hudson sits across the room with Addison laying across three chairs, her head on Hudson's lap and her body curled into a ball, trying to fit. I've never seen anybody look so uncomfortable in my life, yet somehow she's fast asleep. I could never. If there's no bed beneath me, there's no chance in hell I'll be able to sleep. Well, I suppose that's not entirely true because I have no issue sleeping with Tanner beneath me.

Riley and Arizona sit on the floor, slumped against the wall, and it's moments like this I'm really proud of the giant asshole. Arizona hasn't spoken a word all night apart from telling us to leave her alone, but Riley wouldn't take no for an answer. He just sat down beside her and played a movie on his phone, holding it at an angle she could watch without having to admit defeat. That movie ended hours ago and now they're just sitting there in silence, but at least she has company.

That just leaves Ilaria and Chanel who've all but emptied out the vending machine. They sit opposite Hudson and Addie, both looking sick from how much junk food they've consumed, but I can't blame them. We all handle stress in different ways, and for those two, the deliciousness of a chocolate bar and soda is what does the trick. I just wish I could do the same. I've sat in the same seat for so long my ass hurts.

I'm just about to get up and go interrogate the nurses for information when Arizona hastily gets to her feet, gaping at her phone. "Shit, I have to go," she mutters to no one in particular.

Tanner straightens beside me. "Everything alright?"

She shrugs her shoulders, her attention focused on her phone. "Yeah," she finally says with a breath of relief. "My dog just set off the security alarm at home, but Mom and Dad are out of town for some big work event, so I have to disable it before the neighbors assume there's an escaped prisoner making his way through our street."

Tanner laughs and stands. "Do you want me to give you a ride?" he questions, always the gentleman of the group, concerned about her being out in the middle of the night alone.

"Is that okay?" she questions. "I don't want to keep you from being with Jax."

"It's fine," Tanner says standing before glancing back at me. "I'll be back in ten." And not a moment later, they're out the door.

Without Tanner right beside me acting as a distraction, my numb ass becomes too much to bear. As I get up to stretch, Riley's phone chimes with an incoming message. His brows furrow as he checks it out, but when the words, "Aww, fuck no," fly from his lips, he has my full attention.

Hudson chokes back a laugh before Riley can even get his next words out. "Who the fuck messaged Zoe?" he demands, glaring daggers at Hudson.

His hands fly up in a show of innocence. "Don't look at me, bro. I had nothing to do with it," he says, though the grin on his face would suggest otherwise. "It was Jax's idea. Just be happy Tanner stole your phone before he could send some bullshit line about wanting to fuck her on the floor."

"What the fuck are you guys talking about? And who the hell is Zoe?"

"Oh, haven't you heard?" Addison asks from Hudson's lap, peeking through one eye, clearly not awake enough. "Riley's in love with an Insta model, but he's too much of a pussy to actually talk to her, so he just jerks off to her pics all day."

My brows arch as I turn my stare back to Riley, finding a guilty smirk across his face and—what the fuck? Is he blushing? "Oh, hell no," I say, marching across the waiting room and plonking myself right in front of Riley. "You've gotta show me this chick like right fucking now."

A wide grin stretches across his face as his eyes light up with excitement. "Yeah?" he questions, almost coming across nervous about it.

"Ummm, duh," I say.

He's on his feet in two seconds flat, Zoe's profile already up on the screen.

Riley sidles up next to me, my shoulder practically squished into his chest as he holds the phone out. "This is her," he says, clicking on her picture and showing off this girl who he's apparently falling in love with despite never having a single conversation with her. "Isn't she hot?"

I take the phone from him to get a closer look, and holy fuck, this chick is stunning. She's the perfect match for Riley, beach blonde bombshell with gorgeous green eyes and a few stray freckles across her nose. Though, in the world of social media and filters, who knows if they're actually real.

"Holy shit, Riley, she's freaking hot," I say as Ilaria pushes into my other side and glances at the screen. "Fuck, I follow her," she says. "She has this awesome nighttime skin routine I follow religiously."

"Oh yeah?" Riley asks, probably the first time he's ever been enthusiastic about skin care.

"Yeah," Ilaria says with a wide smile. "Have you seen her TikTok? She's super cute and goes live all the time."

Riley's whole face drops, his eyes widening as though someone just handed him the keys to the universe. "She goes live?" He gapes. "How the fuck did I not know this?"

Ilaria scoffs. "Because you decided to tell your asshole boys about her instead of us," she quips. "Like come on, that's the biggest rookie error I've ever heard of."

I scoff, scrolling to her next picture. "I think there's bigger things to deal with right now," I say. "Like why the fuck haven't you closed the deal on this one yet?"

Riley hesitates, looking as though he's about to shit himself. "Because she's like … way out of my league. Fucking look at her. She'd have pricks in her DMs all the time. Besides, there's nothing special about me. I couldn't hold her attention no matter how hard I tried."

I gape at him. "You've got to be kidding, right?" I question. "You know if Tanner hadn't swooped in with the whole *I'm going to watch you through your bedroom window and jerk off* and put on a show-stopping performance, I would have totally fallen in love with you."

Riley scoffs. "Liar. You were practically drooling for his dick the second you ran into him at my end of summer party."

I laugh. "Ahhhh, good times," I say before giving him a real smile. "But it's true. Any woman could so easily fall for your charm. You're hot as hell and you have this ridiculously sexy smirk that—oooft." Just to prove my point, I make a show of fanning my face, unable to avoid laughing as I do it.

"Oh yeah, I know the one," Ilaria says. "You know I was totally crushing on you junior year, until I figured out just how much of a slut you were. If it weren't for that, I would have totally followed you anywhere. But luckily for you, she hasn't got a clue you're a walking STD, so shoot your shot. You've literally got nothing to lose."

"You really—"

"HE'S AWAKE!" Logan's booming voice fills the waiting room, and we all whip around to face him.

"Oh, thank fuck," Addison breathes, pushing up from Hudson's lap.

"I know." Logan sighs a breath of relief before a seriousness comes over him. "Now I can fucking kill him." And with that, he turns on his heel and bolts back toward Jax's room.

A smile pulls at my lips as I hand Riley his phone before dashing back to my seat to grab mine. I quickly bring up Arizona's number and hit call before pressing the phone to my ear. It rings twice before she answers and before she can even get a word out, the wailing of her home alarm deafens me.

"Holy fuck," I curse, pulling the phone away from my ear.

"Hold on, hold on, hold on, hold on," she chants before I hear four little beeps. The alarm cuts off and relief fills my eardrums. "Shit, sorry," she pants.

"It's fine, but is Tanner still with you? He hasn't come back yet."

"No, he left straight away," she says "He should be there by now."

"Oh, really?"

"Yeah, don't stress. He's probably just getting some fresh air or calling Coach Wyld. He said something about needing to give him some updates."

"Yeah, probably," I say, shrugging it off. "Listen, I'm calling because Jax just woke up."

"No way," she breathes as I hear her dog barking in the background. "How is he? Was he alright? Is he in pain?"

"I don't know," I tell her, feeling like an idiot for not getting those answers before rushing to call her. "Logan just came out here screaming about him being awake and then threatened to kill him and ran back. Didn't actually tell us anything about how he was, but I'm assuming he's okay, otherwise Logan wouldn't have come out."

"Good point," she says before the barking gets louder. "No, Daisy. No, get down—ahhhh, fuck, ya big bastard." The alarm blares to life, wailing through the phone as I hear Arizona calling after the dog again. "Shit, DAISY, COME BACK!"

There's loud rustling through the phone before I hear Arizona panting down the line. "I have to go," she calls over the noise of the alarm. "If you speak to Jax, let him know I'm going to kick him in the balls when I see him next, and don't, under any circumstances, let him know I was a wreck during his surgery. Let him think I went home and slept like a baby."

I roll my eyes, but she's gone before I can get a response out, and as I slip my phone back into my pocket and glance up at my friends, I find them all getting to their feet, packing up their shit. "What's going on?" I question. "Are we going somewhere?"

Addison rubs her eyes. "Yeah, the nurses caved and said we could go see Jax, but I think they just wanted us out of their waiting room."

Excitement drums through my veins and I glance back at the door, certain Tanner should have come through it by now. "Okay, I'll just go find Tanner and meet you there."

She nods and as one, they all take off down the hall. Knowing we probably won't come back here, I scoop up Tanner's things he left on the seat and stride to the exit, wondering where the fuck he could have gotten too.

I walk out through the automatic doors and out to the hospital parking lot before stopping and quickly scanning, trying to remember where the hell we parked. We were in such a rush that the finer details of our night quickly escaped my mind. Luckily, there aren't too many cars here tonight, and it doesn't take long to find the tail end of Tanner's Mustang.

As I make my way toward it, slipping through the other parked cars, I hear Tanner's muffled voice from the other side of the Mustang. I pause, not liking the sound of it. "Come on, man. Don't be fucking stupid," Tanner says, a strange hesitation in his tone. "It's not worth it."

"Oh, I think it is," a voice says, pulling at something inside me. There's a strange familiarity with the voice, though I can't figure out where the hell I've heard it before. "You see, maybe you could have persuaded me, but then you went and fucked up my boy, and now you leave me no fucking choice. An eye for a fucking eye."

A chill sails down my spine as goosebumps spread across my skin.

Something warns me to keep quiet, that whatever is going on isn't something I should be involved in. I should tuck and run, but not when Tanner is involved.

I hold my breath, my heart racing erratically in my chest as I slip through the parked cars, walking on my toes to keep as quiet as possible.

The closer I get, the clearer their voices become. "An eye for an eye?" Tanner scoffs. "Man, it's too fucking late for that. He raped my sister, attacked her in hospital, then tried it all over again at the track. Should I go on?" he demands. "Because there's a whole fucking list of people he's hurt."

"You don't know what the fuck you're talking about," the voice says. "From what I heard, your sister is a fucking whore. She wanted it. He was doing her a favor."

My blood runs cold, and I cut through the cars a little faster, not knowing what kind of position Tanner is in, but the fact I haven't heard this guy getting the shit beat out of him yet is challenging everything I know about Tanner.

I reach the back of the Mustang and creep up beside it before having to slam my hand over my mouth to keep me from making a damn sound, seeing my whole world about to crumble. Tanner stands in the vacant parking space in front of the Mustang, his eyes locked on Roxten Hargrove, Colby's best friend.

They stand facing one another, with Roxten's back mostly to me, but there's no mistaking the gun held firmly in his hand.

Fear rocks through me as my hands shake, desperate to do

something … anything that will get that gun away from Tanner's chest. Tears well in my eyes, quickly falling down my cheeks as I keep hidden, having no idea what the hell to do.

"Would you be saying that if it was your little sister who'd been raped? What about your mom or your girlfriend? Would you have their backs or would you call them whores and tell them they asked for it because of the clothes they were wearing or the way they smiled at him? Or would you go to the ends of the fucking earth to destroy the bastard who violated them? Because I know I sure as fuck would."

"It's too late to plead your fucking case, Morgan, so save me the bullshit. I'm not interested."

Oh fuck.

Oh, fuck, fuck, fuck. He's going to shoot him.

Tanner shakes his head. "Walk away, man," he says, his tone dropping dangerously low. "Otherwise you better shoot to kill because I will come for you, and when I do, I will slaughter you like a fucking animal."

Ahh, fuck. FUCK. Why does he have to go and provoke the bastard?

Desperation courses through my veins, and without thinking, I slip into the open driver's seat of Tanner's Mustang, the adrenaline gripping me by the balls and convincing me I'm braver than I really am. Finding his keys and phone still in the center console, I grab the key and shove it into the ignition. The engine roars to life and regret pours over me, knowing my cover is well and truly blown.

Roxten whips around and I blind him with the beaming headlights, the gun now trained on me as Tanner stares with wide eyes, shaking his head. I rev the engine, giving the bastard one hell of a warning as Tanner takes a hesitant step back, putting distance between him and Roxten.

"Don't be fucking stupid, bitch," Roxten roars over the sound of the engine. "I'll fucking shoot you both."

I rev the engine again, daring him to fucking come for me, and I see the very second he goes for it. I duck down just as the bastard pulls the trigger, the loud bang echoing through the parking structure. Rage burns through me, and the second my head comes flying back up over the dash, my foot slams down on the gas.

The tires screech and the car lunges forward as Roxten's eyes widen with fear. He lets off two more shots and as Tanner dives for cover, the car takes off like a fucking bat out of hell, flying across the short space and slamming directly into Roxten.

The momentum lifts him off the fucking ground and he slams against the windshield, cracking the glass, but I hit the brakes, throwing him off. He's launched into the air before violently smashing against the side panel of Logan's RAM, caving in the back door.

Roxten drops lifelessly to the ground, the gun clattering against the pavement as I sit wide eyed, my heart pounding in my chest. "BRI?" Tanner roars, racing toward Roxten and grabbing the gun, his eyes coming right back to mine. "Killer, baby, tell me you're okay."

I swallow hard, nodding. "I, umm … yeah, I think so," I say, my hands shaking on the steering wheel. "Is he dead? Please tell me I didn't kill him."

Tanner bends down, checking Roxten for a pulse and relief shines through his eyes. He blows his cheeks out wide before walking around to the driver's door and opening it. He crouches down and takes my hand in his. "He'll be okay," he says, forcing me to meet his eyes. "He's just knocked out cold. Maybe a few broken bones, but nothing permanent."

I let out a heavy breath, unable to believe that shit just happened. "I ran someone over," I mutter, trying to come to terms with what I've done.

"And you saved my fucking life," Tanner says, squeezing my hands and silently willing me to come back to him. "I saw it in his eyes, babe. He was going to pull that fucking trigger. If you didn't show up when you did …"

Tanner trails off, the same thoughts reflected in my own head. "He shot at me."

"Trust me," he grunts, a strange tone in his voice. "I fucking know."

A small smile pulls at the corner of my lips as people start to come running out of the hospital, Riley and Hudson right in the front. "You're mad at me, aren't you?"

Tanner smirks and rolls his eyes before reaching into the car and pulling me into his arms. "So fucking mad," he tells me.

"Just to clarify," I tease, already knowing the answer as Tanner reaches into the car and cuts the engine. "It's because I put myself in a dangerous situation, not because I just messed up your car."

Tanner shakes his head and stands up before pulling me out of the car. "We better find a doctor for this asshole," he tells me, glancing over my head at the people coming to see what the fuck is going on out here. "I'd suggest we run, but I think we've already had enough trouble with the cops lately."

"Shit," I gasp, my gaze snapping up to his. "What if they think I did it on purpose?"

Tanner shakes his head, tucking me back into his chest. "They won't," he tells me. "The fucker chose the worst possible place to do this. I can count at least ten cameras, and that's only in this section of the parking structure. You're good."

Relief blasts through my chest as I crumble against him. "Thank fuck," I say before remembering the reason I was out here in the first place. "Oh, umm, by the way, Jax woke up, and if and when it comes up later with your mom, I only now just realized I told Riley about your little exhibition kink of watching me through your window while jerking off, and she definitely wasn't asleep."

Tanner gives me a tight smile, "Well, shit," he breathes. "Thanks for that."

I beam up at him as the crowd finally reaches us. "Anything for you, Tanner Morgan."

CHAPTER 28

TANNER

Jax is a fucking idiot. There's no other way to put it.

He was released from the hospital less than an hour ago and instead of lying in bed, recovering from surgery, he's hosting a fucking party, and judging by the scowl on Logan's face, this party definitely didn't get cleared with him first. Though, we shouldn't be surprised. This is nothing but typical Jax behavior.

I sit with the boys around the fire pit, watching as more and more guests arrive, each of them beelining straight for Jax to check he's still alive. After all, when Bradford's poster boy for a good time goes down in front of the whole school, his recovery is guaranteed to generate a bit of interest.

"JAXON MORGAN," I hear Brielle from across the party as she

storms toward us, her glare locked on Jax and unintentionally sending a wave of relief pounding through my veins. She's been with the cops all afternoon, discussing her little accident in the hospital parking lot with Roxten. If it didn't go well, I'd be able to see it all over her face, but she looks fine. In fact, she looks fucking perfect. "What the hell is this? You're supposed to be in recovery, locked in your room watching porn for the next few weeks."

Jax groans, glancing over all the girls as they trail in behind Bri. "Shit, you really are a killjoy, aren't you?" he says, a cocky smirk pulling at his lips, one I have no doubt Bri could knock right off his face in two seconds flat. "If I wanted to chill with the fun police, I would have asked my parents to stick around."

"Ha-ha," Bri says, stepping between my knees and dropping down on my lap as the rest of them make themselves comfortable around the fire pit. "I'm just looking out for you. It wasn't that long ago Addie and I were going through the same thing with you. I remember the pain as though it happened yesterday, so quit trying to fool everybody. I know you're hurting, and if it weren't for the painkillers you're strung out on, you'd be in a ball, crying on the ground."

Jax rolls his eyes before staring across the fire pit at Arizona. "Yeah, well I'd rather be messed up over this, than anything else."

His words are loaded with accusation, and Arizona couldn't miss it even if she tried. Her head snaps up, and she shoots a venomous glare at Jax. "What the hell is that supposed to mean?" she demands, her hands balling into fists as she flies back to her feet. "You're not the one who's been messed up, you're not the one who's not enough, and you're not the one who's had to watch the person you're crazy about fuck around with every bitch with a pulse. So sure, go ahead and boast about how you'd rather get stabbed than have to deal with me and my bullshit feelings."

Ari goes to storm away when Jax clenches his jaw, knowing damn well he said the wrong thing. "Fuck, Ari." He pulls himself up and everyone's eyes widen with fear.

"Holy fuck, Jax, don't," Ilaria rushes out, but Jax isn't having any of it. He's too determined to say what he needs to say.

He curses with the pain but doesn't stop going after her. "Ari, stop," he says, each step taken with an agonizing cringe, but his pleas fall on deaf ears. "For fuck's sake, you stubborn bitch. That's not what I meant and you know it. Now, turn the fuck around so we can talk this shit through."

Ari stops, more than ready to beat his ass to a pulp, but as she glances back over her shoulder, tears already staining her cheeks, she sees Jax on his feet. Her eyes bulge out of her head. "What the fuck are you doing?" she spits, racing back to him and grabbing his waist, certain he's about to fall flat on his face and tear his brand-new stitches. "Go and sit your stupid ass back down."

"Fine," he mutters. "But only if you come and sit with me and talk. I'm done with this bullshit between us."

Ari clenches her jaw as everyone seems to watch with bated breath, more than ready for them to just kiss and make up, but it's really not that simple. There's hesitation in her eyes and I see the exact moment she's about to cut and run when Jax grunts, exaggerating his pain and making a show of needing her help, not only pulling at her heart strings, but successfully pulling off the best guilt trip known to man.

She lets out a huff before rolling her eyes and giving in. "Fine," she mutters, tightening her grip on Jax and helping him back to the fire pit. She holds onto him so he can sit slowly, but the second his ass is in the chair, he locks his arms around her waist and pulls her down onto his lap.

Ari squeals and tries to scramble off him, but he holds on to her legs, keeping them hooked over his knee so she can't get too far. "Are you a fucking idiot?" she demands as he rests his hands on her thigh. "Are you trying to break your stitches?"

"Maybe I am an idiot, or maybe I just miss having you close."

Ari shakes her head as Logan rolls his eyes. "Don't," she warns him. "I'm happy to talk, but don't lead me on and make me think there's a chance when we both know there's not."

"I'm not trying to lead you on, Ari. I'm trying to be honest," he says. "You've been one of my best friends for the past ... I don't even know how fucking long, but I miss you. I hate not having you around, and I hate seeing you at school every day and not being able to drag you into the stairwell. Not to mention, watching you try to chat up random fucking losers at parties is driving me insane. It's a fucking miserable life without you in it, Ari. I want you back."

"You can't have something you never had, Jax," she says. "You want the easy fuck, someone to drop to her knees every time you glance her way without the worry of a stage ten clinger, but you don't want *me*. You're too fucking scared of your own heart to want anything that could potentially be real."

He shakes his head. "But maybe I do want something real."

Ari narrows her eyes on him, anger burning within them. "Really?" she challenges. "I. Am. In. Love. With. You. Do you understand that, Jax? I'm in love with you. You have my whole fucking heart, every last piece of it. Are you ready for that? Because that's what it means to have something real."

Jax clenches his jaw and reaches across to her, gripping her waist and hoisting her toward him until she's straddled on his lap, the two of them facing off in the greatest war this town will ever see. "I. Want. You," he says, articulating every damn word so she understands him clearly. "I don't want some other bitch on her knees for me. I want you, and only you. Am I in love with you? I don't know," he says honestly. "Maybe I am, but I'm fucking willing to find out. The question is, are you?"

Arizona hesitates, everything she wants sitting on a silver platter, just waiting for her to grab it with both hands. "You're going to hurt me, Jax," she says, her voice soft and filled with pain. "You've already destroyed me so much. How can I just willingly offer myself up to you like that again?"

"Because I was a fucking idiot then," he insists. "I didn't know how much you meant to me until I didn't have you there, and I don't ever want to feel that way again. But you're right, I am fucking scared. I'm terrified. The thought of hurting you kills me, which is what I meant before. I'd rather deal with this fucking stab wound than deal with the fact I've been hurting you."

Ari cries as she takes Jax's face and leans forward. She kisses him, and watching it almost kills me. This isn't the *holy shit, we're about to be the happiest couple in the world* kind of kiss. This is something else.

Bri grips my hand, glancing at me for a moment, the look in her eyes telling me she's seeing what I'm seeing, and as I look around at our group, I see nothing but sadness for our two friends. "I'm sorry, Jax," Ari whispers, gently pulling back from him as he grips her waist tighter, silently begging her not to say what she's about to say. "I have to think about this. You might be scared to let yourself feel something real, but I'm terrified of handing myself over for you to break me. I wouldn't survive it, Jax. These past few weeks have taught me that much."

She pushes off him and goes to walk away but Jax catches her hand. "Ari," he whispers, the silent plea for her to stay shining through his tone.

"I'm sorry, Jax," she whispers, letting her hand fall away. "I just … I need to think about this."

He nods and lets her walk away, the girls all getting up to follow her, probably to get blind drunk.

Logan nudges his brother's foot and lifts his chin, demanding Jax's attention. "You good, bro?" he questions, knowing from experience just how much that kind of rejection hurts. Though luckily for Jax, it wasn't a flat-out no. "That was rough."

Jax shrugs his shoulders. "It is what it is," he mutters, switching out his bottle of water for something a little stronger, despite the painkillers he's on. He doesn't expand on that, but I don't expect him to. Though the pressure dissipates when Riley throws himself to his feet, gaping at his phone.

He jumps right up onto the edge of the fire pit, holding his phone and flipping it around so we see the screen. "HOLY FUCK," he blanches, panic in his eyes. "She responded. Zoe fucking responded. What do I do? What do I do?"

Jax grunts, not able to be happy for Riley right now. "Fucking message her back, dickwad."

A smirk pulls at my lips as I try to get a closer look at the screen. "What'd she say?"

Riley grins. *"Not much."*

My brows furrow. "Huh?"

"To the message you sent," he tells me, shoving his phone closer to my face so I can scan over it properly.

Riley - Hey, what's up?
Zoe - Not much.

"Huh," I breathe, glancing up at Riley and trying to push his phone out of my face. "Yeah, umm … I don't know what to do with that."

"The fuck, man?" he panics, trying to push his phone into my hands. "You started this. You need to finish it. I don't know what the fuck to say to this girl."

"Well, figure it out, and do it now before she puts her phone back down and loses interest."

His eyes widen, realizing I'm right. "Fuck," he says, jumping down from the edge of the fire pit and backing up to his seat, not bothering to even look before he sits in it. His fingers hover over the screen, moving closer before hesitating and pulling back again. He goes on like this for at least five minutes before frustration gets the best of him. "FUCK! This shouldn't be so hard."

"What the hell is wrong with you, man?" Logan questions. "You never strike out. Just have a normal fucking conversation with her and seal the deal already. Just leave the bullshit pick-up lines out of it and act like a normal fucking human being."

Riley groans, bunching his hands into fists before taking a breath and trying to relax. "Fine, okay," he says, letting his fingers move across the screen. He hits send before his gaze snaps up to mine. "Holy shit, I did it," he says, his face white as a fucking ghost.

I laugh. "What'd you say?"

"Asked her what she's doing," he says before blanching again. "Oh, fuck. She's seen it," he says before his eyes widen further. "OH FUCK. SHE'S TYPING!"

I shake my head, not prepared to watch Riley freak out over his phone for the next hour, but I'm saved when Damien and Jensen come striding through the party, wide grins on both their faces, already drunk as fucking skunks. "Yo, what's crackin' bitches?" Jensen says, raising a beer he swiped from the kitchen. He doesn't wait for a response before turning to Jax. "Nice to see you still breathing, asshole."

Jax rolls his eyes, clearly not in the mood after Arizona's dismissal. "What's going on?" I ask as the moron just grins back at me.

Damien takes pity and finally clues us in, throwing his arm over his new stepbrother's shoulder, both of them grinning ear to ear. "This fucker just got accepted into Brown, that's what," he says just like a proud big brother would.

"Fuck yeah, man," I say, getting up. I go to congratulate him, pulling him in and clapping him on his back. "That's fucking awesome. Have you told Bri yet? I'm sure she'll be thrilled to get you out of town."

Jensen scoffs a laugh. "I bet she would," he says. "But nah, only just found out on the ride over."

"Congrats, man," I say, really fucking proud of the bastard despite kinda hating him. I suppose Bri has unintentionally brought us back together like when we were kids. I know last year was hard for him, finishing his senior year, only to have some girl falsely cry rape to avoid her parents' wrath. He was dropped from all his college options and left with nothing despite clearing his name. At least now he's finally getting back on track.

"Yeah, yeah," Damien says, cutting off our conversation. "Where's Ilaria?"

I roll my eyes and point across the party to where the girls are already shit-faced—all the girls except for Bri.

I start searching for her, scanning through all the bodies when a text comes through on my phone. I pull it out and glance down at the screen.

Killer - Hey

Suspicion rears its ugly head as I respond.

Tanner - Hey to you too.
Killer - I've got a surprise for you.
Tanner - Oh yeah?

A photo comes through a moment later and I groan, taking in the fishnet stockings pulled up her gorgeous thigh, leading up to a black lace thong with a black garter belt connecting the two. My dick fucking jolts to life like someone hit it with defibrillator paddles.

Another text comes through.

Killer - It's all yours … if you can find me.

Not even a cheetah could catch me now.

I run inside, trying to look closer at the background of the photo to figure out where the fuck my dessert lies. This house is fucking huge. The twins' parents didn't spare a single expense when building this mansion and it shows. I've always loved it, except for right fucking now. They have thirteen spare bedrooms! This isn't going to be easy, but that's assuming she's actually in a bedroom and not one of the private offices, living spaces, or theater rooms.

Screw my uncle and his fucking money. I need to taste that fucking pussy right now.

Skipping up the stairs two at a time, I can't help but wonder what I look like to the people down below, barging through the crowd, desperate to get upstairs. Hell, it's probably nothing good. I'm sure they think I'm about to shit myself and need to get to a private bathroom before I redecorate the Italian marble tiles.

Getting up to the second floor, I start throwing doors open, not bothering with an apology as I disturb not one, but three different couples fucking in the twins' parents room. Hell, I don't even wait a moment to try and figure out if this was some twisted version of an orgy and they don't quite understand the whole togetherness part of it.

Continuing on, I burst through three more doors before coming to the furthest spare bedroom on the second floor. I twist the handle and swing it wide to find Bri standing in the darkened room, just enough light spilling in from the hallway to see the perfect silhouette of her body in her lingerie.

I groan low, never having seen these before, but with the fishnet stockings and garter belt, I almost fall to my fucking knees in the doorway.

Bri stands by the window, looking out at the party below, her back to me and showing off that delectable ass in her thong. My mouth goes dry. "Killer," I groan, stepping through the door, not wanting to close it behind me in fear of blocking out the light and not being able to see her.

Bri glances over her shoulder, her eyes locking onto mine, and for only a moment, I think this is going to be one of the best nights of my life. But those delicious pouty lips quickly pull into a wicked smirk, and before she's even made a sound, I realize this isn't anything at all like what I thought it was going to be.

"What the he—"

"SURPRISE, FUCKER!" she calls, whipping around so fast, I nearly miss the gigantic strap-on dildo protruding from her hips. She braces her hands against her waist, posing like fucking Superman, her cock so fucking big, I almost feel like less of a man … *almost*.

I gape at her, having no fucking idea what to say.

"I've been thinking," she says, her eyes sparkling with mischief. "It's not fair for me to have all the fun, right? You got to claim my ass, so I think it's only right I get to claim yours."

My heart races, not wanting to ever break her heart or tell her no, but fuck, there's always a first for everything. "Ummmm," I say, the real words I need to say getting caught in my throat when I see a sparkle at the tip of the dildo. "Is that thing pierced?"

"Yep," she says proudly. "You like it? I thought it added a little something special. After all, it's a party. Everyone and *everything* should look their best for a night out. Addie helped me with it."

"She what?" I demand, my eyes bugging out of my head. "Holy shit, you've corrupted my sister."

"Oh, please," Bri laughs, wiggling her hips just to see the strap on dance. "Actually, speaking of piercings, where do you draw the line for that? Because dammmmmn. I played with this thing this afternoon and I'm not above sneaking into your room in the middle of the night to pierce yours. Though I'm kinda hoping you'll get it done by a professional, cause like, I wouldn't trust my ability to get it straight."

"I ummm … holy fuck, Killer," I mutter, closing the door behind me and flipping on the lights. "I swear, I fucking love you, but if you don't take that thing off, you're gonna see a grown man cry and I really don't want that to happen. This visual is already scarred in my mind."

Bri laughs as she loosens the buckle for the harness, letting the whole contraption slip down her thighs, the dildo hitting the ground with a heavy *thump*. "Relax," she tells me, stepping out of the harness, her heels gently clicking against the tiles as she makes her way over to me. Her hand presses against my chest as she reaches up to brush a kiss over my lips. "I'm just fucking with you."

I let out a heavy breath and take her waist, pulling her in hard against me. "I hope that doesn't mean you're not down to fuck because you look like a goddamn meal in this," I say, my hands roaming over her body and grabbing a perfect handful of ass.

"You're damn right, I am," she says just as a message pops up on my phone.

I ignore it, determined to get my fill of Bri, but a second message comes in followed by a third. "Fuck, sorry, babe," I say, slipping my hand into my pocket and pulling out my phone once again. I find three texts from Mom and my brows furrow before a slight panic sears through my chest.

I spoke to her just before Jax demanded to throw a party tonight, and when I did, she mentioned something about wanting to chat with our lawyer about pushing through the custody arrangement. She feels we've already missed enough time with our newest addition.

Quickly checking her messages, I open them up only to be blindsided by the photographs of me inside that Hope Falls house, staring at a boy's lifeless body as one of the Hardin brothers lays on top of the little boy's mother, forcing her legs apart.

Bile rises in my throat but I force myself to read the accompanying messages.

Mom - Get your ass home.
Mom - NOW.

CHAPTER 29

TANNER

My palms sweat as I pull my bike into the driveway with Bri plastered against my back. My head hasn't stopped spinning since the second Mom's texts came through, and I'm not so proud to admit I was forced to run to the bathroom and throw up everything in my stomach.

I've been dreading this moment since I was fourteen, and I've avoided it like the fucking plague. But here it is, right on my fucking doorstep, staring me in the face. There's no going back now. I promised Bri I would come clean, that I'd finally talk to Mom about this and learn how to move past it, but the very thought of it has crippled me to the point of physical pain.

It killed me letting her know I was the father of Rachael's child.

I've never wanted to disappoint her, and while she took it in stride and held her head high, I knew a part of her was breaking. She's always feared I would fuck up and lose myself in the process, but now that she's seen how bad my mistakes are, nothing will ever be the same between us.

Knowing I can't sit out here all night, I take a shaky breath and cut the engine. Bri releases her hold around my waist and climbs off my bike, hovering close as I do the same. "You're going to be okay," she murmurs, taking her helmet off and hanging it over the handlebar with mine. "She's going to be broken, but just know that it can't get worse than this. Once the words come out and she has time to process, it will get easier."

I look up, meeting her stare. "You sure about that?"

Bri presses her lips into a tight line. "No," she admits. "But I wasn't about to tell you that you're about to break your mother's heart and that she'll never forgive you. Positive thinking, Tanner."

"Right," I mutter, hitting the remote for the automatic garage door. It slowly begins to roll up and I start pushing my bike inside. Half of me wants to get this over and done with while the other part of me desperately wishes to get back on this bike and never come back. Though, I'd have to take Bri with me because there's no way in hell I'd leave her behind. Hell, I might even send Addie the occasional postcard. Maybe a text if I'm feeling generous.

"Come on," Bri says, seeing the hesitation in my eyes. "Like a Band-Aid."

I nod. "I've always hated that metaphor."

"Well, tough shit," she says. "Get a move on. Your Mom probably heard your bike from a mile away, and now she's sitting in there wondering why you're being such a bitch and not walking through her door."

"Shit," I sigh, hating how right she is.

I go to reach for Bri's hand but she pulls back with a cringe. "I umm … I think I should give you and your mom space to talk this through. I don't want her to feel as though she has to play the part of perfect doting Mom because I'm there when all she probably wants to do is rip you a new asshole."

My brows furrow and I step around my bike, pulling her into me. "You sure?"

"Yeah," she says, nodding toward Channing's place. "I'll sneak back into my room and sleep there tonight. They won't even know I'm there."

A chill sails down my spine. "You know how I feel about you staying there."

"I know," she whispers, pushing up on her tippy toes and brushing a kiss over my lips. "But I'll be okay for one night. I'll lock my door and you could always come and join me when you're done talking to your mom. You know, if you're still alive."

Fuck.

"Yeah, okay," I say, blowing my cheeks out with a heavy breath. "Do you want me to walk you over there?"

"It's two steps away," she says, giving me a blank stare. "Stop avoiding your mom and go give her the answers she needs." With that, she steps back, pulling her hands free of mine and letting them fall away. She gets to the opening of the garage before pausing and glancing back at me. "Just remember I love you and you're an amazing man. No matter what happens in there, I've always got your back. Nothing that happened that night could ever change the way I feel about you."

Warmth spreads through my chest, and before I can tell her how much she means to me, she's gone, slipping into the darkness and crossing to Channing's property. Needing to get this over and done with, I close the garage door and make my way through the internal door.

All the lights are off, but I see a soft glow coming from the formal dining room right down the hall. I swallow hard. We don't use that room, not even for formal dinner parties, so the fact she's decided that will be our interrogation room already has me wanting to run.

An eeriness comes over me as I stride down the hall, trying to make a little noise so she can prepare herself. Only as I turn into the dining room, I realize that she's not only prepared, but she's ready to fucking go.

A bottle of wine rests on the table, nearly empty, and her lipstick stains the rim of her glass. She's been going hard on the bottle, so hard there's a condensation circle around the bottom, directly against the table, which is unheard of from my mother.

"Sit down," she says, not even looking up at me.

I nod and walk past her, quickly scanning the photographs on the table and the other paperwork I didn't even know existed, but from here there seems to be some kind of statement, and my guess would be it's from the mother or a neighbor who witnessed the break in. All I know is that for it to be on this very table, it must have my name written all over it.

Taking a seat just down from her, I prepare myself to face the firing squad, and as I glance up, I see the almost empty bottle of white rum sitting beside a tall shot glass.

Fuck.

Mom lifts her glass of wine to her lips and takes a sip, still not able to look at me before putting it down a little too hard. "Talk," she spits.

"Mom," I say, something breaking inside of me as I brush my fingers over the photographs. "This isn't who I am. I never wanted to be a part of any of that, and had I known … fuck, Mom. I screwed up. I was young and stupid with a chip on my shoulder, and I … I swear to you, I've felt sick about this since the day it happened."

Mom's head snaps up, her sharp glare locking directly onto mine. "I don't want your excuses or to hear your groveling. You've had four years to come to me with this. I want to know what the fuck happened and why the hell you were in that house. I want every last detail, right down to your specific involvement, and why the hell these documents anonymously showed up on my doorstep. You're not to stop speaking until I physically ask you to. Is that clear?"

"Yes, Mom," I say, never having felt this low in my life. But just as she asked, I give it to her straight, not skipping out on a single detail, just as I'd done with Bri. I give her the ins and outs, the very thoughts that were going through my head at the time, and the way I almost pissed my pants when that gun was pointed at that little boy and rang loudly through the house.

Mom sips her wine with bloodshot eyes, refilling it at least three times, her lashes wet from the stream of tears spilling down her face.

I tell her every last detail of that night, right up to the Hardin brothers cornering me on the way home, threatening my family and beating the shit out of me. I tell her how Riley all but saved me that night and how up until a week ago, I was unaware my father knew all about it.

Every now and then, she pipes up with a question which I answer quickly and factually before continuing with my story. Only those questions become more frequent when I tell her about my visit from Channing in the precinct cells.

"You think these papers came from him?" Mom demands.

I shake my head. "Dad and Channing are the only ones who know about this, and I doubt the Hardin brothers are stupid enough to keep this kind of evidence on hand," I tell her. "Honestly, it could have come from either of them. Channing is determined to fuck with me because of Bri, and Dad … well, I wouldn't put it past him to try and punish me after his little performance last week."

"Bri?" she questions, her gaze snapping back to mine. "What does she have to do with this?"

I quickly explain everything Channing said to me about Bri, word for fucking word and by the time I'm done, Mom looks as though she could tear him limb from limb, but we're not nearly done yet.

Getting back on track, I explain my reasons for why I haven't told her, my true and very real fears about the retaliation from the Hardin brothers and for the first time all night, I see just a hint of understanding in her eyes. "I swear, Mom," I tell her, letting her see just how broken up I am about everything that's happened, letting her see how I shoulder the guilt despite having been a misguided child myself. "I'm doing everything in my power to make sure she's taken care of, even though I know it'll never be enough. I paid for a proper burial from my trust for the little boy, and I've made sure his grave stays clean. I pay her rent, and make sure she has everything she needs, but I just—"

"That's not nearly enough," Mom tells me, her broken heart resting in pieces before me. "She lost everything that night, and you think you can make up for it by throwing a bit of money at the problem? That is such a childish view of the world. You're a father now, Tanner. How would you feel if that had been Bri, and your child ran in to save her? Would you accept anything less than justice?"

I shake my head, knowing damn well she's right.

"While I'm sure she is appreciative of the help you have given her, it is also an insult to rub your money in her face. Every time the cash shows up, I wonder what goes through her head? That some rich kid is paying for his guilt? Giving her hush money to keep quiet? None of that is ever going to erase the memories of that monster forcing himself inside her, and it sure as hell will never bring her son back to her."

I hang my head, the weight of everything I've done paralyzing me.

"That woman needs justice, and you need to start making amends for what you've done," Mom tells me. "I don't know how, but I know that you're better than this. You're not that scared little boy anymore, Tanner, and I refuse to let you be anything like your father. You will acknowledge your mistakes and then you'll learn from them. Is that clear? Even if it means putting yourself in a less than respectable position. Nothing is more important than giving that woman the closure and justice she deserves; no football career, no college, nothing. She is your first priority. Do you hear me, Tanner Morgan? Standing back and doing the bare minimum is unacceptable."

I nod. "I hear you, Mom," I tell her. "I want to do better, I just don't know how. What am I supposed to do? How can I start to make this right without putting you, Addie, and Bri at risk?"

Mom shakes her head. "I'm sorry, love, but that's not for me to decipher. I don't know how to fix this, and I can't give you the answers, but just know that I have faith in you to do the right thing."

With that, Mom stands and glances down at the papers spread across the table. "Clean this up, please," she says. "I don't want Addison stumbling across these photographs. She adores you, and the last thing she needs is to learn her big brother had a hand in seeing an innocent woman being raped."

I couldn't agree more.

Reaching across the table, I start gathering the papers as Mom turns and starts walking out of the dining room with her glass in hand. I find myself calling to her, every last piece of me torn to shreds, though if this is how I'm feeling, I can't even imagine what it's like for her. "Mom," I murmur, hoping to God she still loves me. She turns back and meets my eyes, the usual spark absent from her gaze. "Are we okay?"

She presses her lips into a hard line and truly considers her response. "I'm hurt, Tanner. Every step I take, my world crumbles just that little bit more. First your father, and now this. It's a lot to process, but just know that I love you. You are my son, and I am so proud of the man you've grown into, but your actions and deceit have hurt my heart." She pauses for just a moment, gathering herself. "I just need time to process, Tanner. I'm sure you can understand that."

I nod and let her go, desperately wishing things could be different.

CHAPTER 30
Brielle

The thought of leaving Tanner to deal with his mother's wrath kills me, but this is something he needed to face alone. They needed a private, deep, and personal conversation. I just hate how I left him there in the garage. I felt like I was betraying him in some way, like I was leaving him to face down the flames of hell by himself. I just hope to God he doesn't get burned.

I skip over the small hedge between our properties and stare up at Orlando's house. The last thing I want to do is stay the night here, but what choice do I have? I'm sure climbing the tree and scaling Tanner's roof isn't in my best interest tonight, not when his mom has so much going on that needs to be worked through.

Walking up to the door, I let out a heavy breath before reaching up and feeling the top of the doorframe for the spare key. It looks like all the lights are out inside, so maybe I'll be lucky enough to get through the night undetected.

Turning the key, I unlock the door and slip inside, trying to be as quiet as humanly possible. It's pitch-black inside, and I grope along the wall, searching for the railing for the stairs.

My foot hits the bottom step and just as I go to make my way upstairs, a voice cuts through the silence. "What do you think you're doing sneaking in here in the middle of the night?" my mother questions.

I pause, whipping around and searching the darkness, and if I squint just enough, I can make out her silhouette in the living room, sitting in the dark with nothing but the glow of the streetlight through the window.

I cut across the foyer to the entrance of the sitting area, my brows furrowing as I take her in. "Why are you sitting here in the dark?" I question, hesitation thick in my tone. I creep a little closer, my gaze sweeping the rest of the room, making sure we're alone.

Mom turns to face me and I gasp, falling back against the wall as I see the dark bruises and swelling around her eyes. "Oh, Brielle," she cries. "My sweet, sweet angel. I am so sorry I got us involved in all of this, but you shouldn't be here. *You can't be here,* do you understand me? I can't have you here."

"I know," I say, my heart breaking as I rush deeper into the sitting room, dropping to my knees before her. I take her hands and look up at her, my heart breaking seeing the state that asshole has left her in. Despite the bullshit that's lingered between us over the past few months, I still love my mom, and I can't bear to see her like this, nor will I sit back and do nothing about it. "You need to get out of here. You can't stay. I won't let you, not when he's hurting you like this."

She rests her hand against my face and gives me a tight smile, her eyes expressing every emotion passing through her. "It's not that easy," she tells me. "If there was a way, I would have packed us both up and taken you away a long time ago, but there's no where I can go where he won't find us."

"Mom," I say, using a firmer tone. "I don't care what he wants or thinks, you are not staying here."

"I'm sorry, my sweet girl, I know you don't like seeing me like this. I know our relationship has been strained over the past few months, but just know there has been a reason for everything I have done. All I want is to protect you, even if it means hurting you. Just trust me when I tell you that you need to get out of this house. You need to get as far away from this place as you can. Go and be free, enjoy your life with Tanner and be happy."

I shake my head and stand up, pulling at her hands. "Come on," I insist. "I'll help you pack. We'll find a cheap motel and pay cash. We'll go somewhere he can't track us."

"Believe me," she says, pulling back on her hand, refusing to budge. "If I could, I would, but there's so much more going on that you simply don't understand, and I don't want you here to find out the hard way. Just please, Brielle. Please just go."

I scoff, anger starting to burst through my chest, hating how hard she's making this. I can't save her if she doesn't want to be saved. "You mean his sick fascination with me?" I spit, watching as her face drops, realization in her eyes. "You mean how you've married him simply to keep him from doing the same to me? I know it all, Mom. I know what you're doing, and I don't want you putting yourself in this position to save me. You can't live like this. It's getting worse. The bruises are getting harder to hide, and soon enough, he won't be able to stop himself. How much of this can you take before he kills you? I just … I don't understand why you'd put yourself through all of this. Does he have something on you? Is he threatening you?

Mom sobs and I rush in, throwing my arms around her, knowing I'm right, and whatever it is, it's enough to push mom to strength lengths. "How long have you known about all of this?" she questions.

"A few weeks," I admit. "Orlando made some comments to Tanner, threatening him and boasting about his plans for me, and we've been putting together all the little pieces. I get it, Mom. You've been hurting me to force me away, pushing me out the door and making me not want to come back, but you're my mom. I love you, and no matter how much you push me away, I'm going to keep coming back. I just wish I knew how we got here."

She shakes her head, pulling back enough to wipe her eyes, only to cringe when she touches the swelling. "Honestly, honey," she says, completely defeated. "I don't even know myself. The first few dates seemed authentic and I truly believed we were starting something real. He was charming and the perfect gentleman, promising to save us from Hope Falls and give us this luxurious new life, but then I started to see through the cracks and he became controlling and dangerous. One second, I was falling for him, the next he was threatening to expose some ugly truths about the woman I was before I had you and your brother, and I just … please trust me when I tell you those things cannot see the light of day."

"Mom," I whisper, searching her eyes.

She shakes her head, refusing to get into details with me. "I saw him looking up your socials, zooming in on your images, and when I confronted him about it, he just … snapped. It's why I took off to Paris without you and married the bastard. I wanted to put distance there and tie him up in legal documents, yet the more I keep you away, the more he becomes obsessed with this idea of having you close. You should see him, honey," she says, devastation in her tone. "When you'd come home and hang out by the pool with your friends, he'd stand at the window watching you, and I'd have to come up with an excuse to pull him away. It's sickening. He thinks I'm jealous of his little obsession, and for the most part, I just let him believe that because it's better than him finding out how I've been purposefully pushing you away. I just … I'm terrified I'm not enough to hold his attention and sooner or later, he's going to get bored and go searching for something only you will satisfy for him."

My mind reels with all this information, but one thing rests against my soul, darkening it with its ugliness. "But last week when you kicked me out, you did that in front of him."

Mom presses her lips into a hard line and glances away. "Yes, I did," she says. "And I paid greatly for it, but I don't regret it because it meant you were no longer expected to come home and live under his roof every night," she sobs, wiping her eyes again. "Do you have any idea how many nights I've laid awake, terrified of him slipping out of bed and forcing himself into your room? I would check your door every night, making sure it was locked."

My heart shatters for everything she's had to endure in order to protect me. "What do we do?" I question, gripping her hands.

She gives me a sad smile. "If I knew the answer to that, I'd already be doing it," she promises. "I just hope you can forgive me for allowing this monster into our lives."

Mom pulls me into a tight hug, holding onto me with everything she's got, and I hold her right back, every last piece of me completely broken. I can't stand by and allow this to continue. I have to put an end to it, even if it's the last thing I do.

Guilt soars through my chest. For months I've hated on my mother, not knowing the horrendous abuse she was going through just to keep me safe. She sacrificed her own safety, her happiness, and her relationship with me to make sure I was protected from this monster. And in return, I hated her. I treated her like shit and spat hurtful words while wishing things could be different. She took the fall for me, throwing herself under the bus to save me from suffering this fate.

I should have trusted her, should have known my mother would never turn her back on me for a lifestyle with a man who was less than perfect. "I'm so sorry," I whisper through the dark room. "I've treated you so badly and you didn't deserve it."

"You didn't know," she argues. "If anything, your anger and

frustration only helped make my dismissal seem all that more authentic."

"I—" I stop abruptly as a plan begins to form in my mind. I might not be able to get Mom away from Orlando, but maybe I can get Orlando away from the world. "Do you think you could get him out of town tomorrow?" I question. "I think I have an idea."

Mom pulls back, her eyes wide as she looks at me. "Oh, honey. No," she breathes, the fear in her eyes all too real. "Whatever you're thinking, no. It's too dangerous. I don't want you to have anything to do with this. I can handle it myself. I'll … I'll come up with something."

"Mom, please," I insist, desperately wishing I knew what he was holding over her. "You need to let me try. If I can just find what I'm looking for, we'll be okay. I swear, all I need is him out of town for the day to give me freedom to look. I won't disrupt anything. He'll have no idea I was looking, but please, Mom. This could be our only chance to save ourselves. You have to let me take it."

She presses her lips into a hard line, resignation in her eyes. "I don't like this."

"I know you don't," I tell her. "But we've always been a team, and I'm not about to let you shoulder this burden on your own. Let me help you."

She watches me a moment longer before letting out a sigh. "Okay," she finally says. "The Country Club has been advertising an art exhibition in Broken Hill. I can suggest a day trip out for that and perhaps dinner afterward. He likes to show off his money and always boasts about how many clients with deep pockets he can screw over in Broken Hill."

"Perfect."

"I can't guarantee that he'll go for it, but I will try."

I squeeze her hand. "Thank you, Mom."

She nods and just keeps staring at me, her eyes filling with tears all over again. "It's killed me not to be your support system over the past few months. With everything that's been happening with Colby and getting stabbed. You'll never know just how much it broke me not to hold you in that hospital and be there for you. It killed me to see my little girl hurting like that."

"It's okay, Mom," I whisper. "I understand now, but it's over. Colby is dead. He can't hurt me or anyone else ever again."

Mom gives me a fond smile before standing, pulling me up with her. "As much as it pains me to send you away, I truly think it'd be best for you to sleep at Tanner's place tonight. I wouldn't forgive myself if something happened to you here. Not to mention what your brother would do."

I gape at her in horror. "Why hasn't Damien done anything about this already?"

"Oh honey, I can't let him see me like this. He's got such a promising future ahead of him, and I worry—"

"That he'll kill Orlando."

Mom presses her lips into a hard line, the truth right there in her eyes. "He's been having a good time here with Jensen. They're out partying all the time and enjoying life, and in a few weeks, everything is about to become very serious for the both of them out in the real world. I want to give him this time to be young."

I nod, not wanting to tell her just how messed up I think that is, and after giving me one more firm hug, she sends me on my way. I slip out the front door, being careful not to make a sound before cutting back across the lawn and over the hedge.

Addison and Hudson pull up at the same time, and as Addie bails out of his car, I hear her laughing about Riley's conversation with Zoe. Apparently he managed not to screw it up and has been talking to her all night.

"What are you doing out here?" Addison asks, walking up to the front door with me. "I thought you guys left ages ago."

"Oh yeah," I smile. "I umm, I just wanted to check in on my mom."

"Really?" she questions, pushing the door open. "I thought you kinda hated your mom."

Not knowing how to respond, I just give her a tight smile before walking in behind them and bailing straight up the stairs, hoping to God Tanner has wrapped things up with his mom. I make my way down the hall and gently knock on his door before pushing it open.

Tanner sits on the edge of his bed, his elbows braced against his knees as he hangs his head. He glances up and his brows furrow. "What are you doing here?" he questions. "I thought you were sleeping in the devil's lair."

"Yeah, I was," I murmur, stepping into him as he takes my waist, "but I ran into Mom and we talked. She thinks it's best I sleep here. You know, in case Orlando decides to take a stroll into my room in the middle of the night."

His brow arches as he looks up at me. "I'd kill him."

"I don't doubt that," I tell him.

"You spoke to your mom?"

"Mmhmm," I mumble.

"You wanna talk about it?"

I shake my head. "You wanna talk about the discussion with your mom?"

"Fuck no," he says. "I'd rather gouge my eyes out with a rusty fork."

I give him a beaming smile. "Good," I say, kicking my shoes off and climbing into his bed. "Then we agree." And with that, he scoots in beside me, pulls me into his warm arms, and holds me tight, both of us ready to put tonight behind us.

CHAPTER 31
Brielle

Okay, so maybe the black hoodie and tights were overkill, but what else was I supposed to wear to break into Orlando's office? If I'm going to live the criminal lifestyle, I might as well dress the part, right? Though I have to admit, I kind of hoped that getting through the door and past security would be a little more challenging. I mean, damn, I didn't even get an adrenaline rush. The code to disable the security system is exactly the same code that he uses at home. Where's the fun in that?

My gaze wanders around his ridiculously big office space as I walk deeper through the foyer. This place is definitely way more than what he needs, but men like Orlando are all about comparing the size of their dicks. They have to have the biggest and the best to compensate for the fact that he ain't shit.

There's an extravagant reception area with a few chairs set out for clients to wait, and as I walk past the foyer and into the main part of the office, I find ten separate offices, all separated by glass panels with their own little secretary desk right outside the door. It looks like a scene out of *Suits,* though Orlando can only dream about being that successful.

There's one massive office at the end, and I press my lips into a tight line.

Bingo.

I make my way into his office and shake my head as I take it all in. Extravagant doesn't even begin to cover it. There are two separate lounge suites, an attached conference room, a bar, and of course his desk is surrounded by floor-to-ceiling windows overlooking the city. I suppose this is what you get for being one of the top lawyers in the country.

It's a shame I'm about to fuck that up for him.

Not wanting to be here any longer than necessary, I start hunting, his office becoming my playground. I go straight for his desk and power on his computer, and as it does its thing, I start digging through the drawers, yanking them open and quickly rifling through them. Only there's nothing out of the ordinary, nothing that's going to give me what I'm looking for. But why would it? Orlando wouldn't be so stupid as to leave shit like that laying around for anyone to find. Especially with the kind of people he's been dealing with.

I search the desk from top to bottom, even going as far as to make sure there are no hidden compartments. When I find absolutely nothing, I move onto the computer, only to be hit with a six-digit passcode. "Well fuck," I mutter, staring at the blank screen.

What the hell could it be?

I start to type in Mom and Orlando's wedding date and get halfway before I hit delete. It's definitely not that. He doesn't care for Mom enough to have it as a passcode. Hell, I bet he doesn't even remember what the date was. But what else could it be? Jensen's birthday? The number of cases where he's narrowly escaped the law? Fuck, who knows?

"Think, think, think, think," I murmur, glancing around his office for some kind of clue when I see a framed photograph of his first wedding to Jensen's mom, the one that actually mattered. A grin stretches across my face. "Gotcha, motherfucker."

Now, the only issue is figuring out when the hell they got married. Though, I'm sure it's nothing Google can't handle.

Three minutes later, I'm in.

I start digging through files and programs, not having a damn clue what I'm actually looking for, but there's bound to be something. The only issue is, this is a go-hard-or-go-home situation. If I find only one document proving he's a dirty lawyer, he'll find a way to get out of it. What I need is substantial evidence, something the police cannot ignore, even the dirty ones who've been paid off. I need an open and shut case.

Fifteen minutes quickly turns into two hours when I finally come across a locked folder titled *Vacation*. Call me crazy, but the only people who need to lock their vacation pics are the ones who are going on those vacations with someone other than their wives.

When I click on the folder, another password pops up, and I let out a heavy sigh as my fingers dance carefully across the keys. Access Denied. Of course, it wouldn't be his wedding date again; that would be too easy. It tells me I've only got two more tries before permanently locking me out.

"Fuck," I mutter, before pulling out my phone. I scroll down my contacts until I find Logan's name and hit call.

It rings three times before he answers. "Bri?" he questions, a strange tone in his voice. "You good? You never call me."

"Yeah," I say, hearing Jax in the background with a bell. I mean, damn. Who the hell gave that idiot a bell? "I, um … shit. This is going to sound bad, but you're good with computers right?"

"Yeahhhhh," he says slowly.

"Say I found a locked folder and didn't know the password. How would I break into that?"

There's a pause as he considers his response. "You're not fucking around on Tanner's computer are you? Because you're cool and all, but I'm not about to help you go searching for dirt on my cousin."

"Why? What's on Tanner's computer that I need to know about?"

I can picture the look on his face as he stumbles to find the right words. "Oh, um, nothing. I just … you know, in case you might have been snooping around and found something you shouldn't."

I scoff. "As if I'd do that to him," I tell him. "Besides, I'm not interested in seeing the dick pics you've sent him over the years. This is something else, but I swear, I wouldn't ask you if it wasn't important."

"Shit, okay," he finally says. "What kind of computer is it?"

Logan rattles off instructions and it takes me far too long to understand what the hell he's trying to say, but the minute I'm in, my heart starts to race. "Hooooooly shit," I breathe, hitting the jackpot. "I'm in," I tell Logan. "I'll talk to you later. Thanks for your help."

"Yeah, yeah," he mutters, ending the call and leaving me to my pot of gold. I search through the files, each one more horrendous than the last, but as I come across a sub folder labeled MORGAN, my stomach begins to cramp. Images upon images of that night fill the screen, and my heart shatters. I came here hoping to find this, but I didn't consider how it would feel to actually see the horror of what happened inside that house.

Not wanting to see anything more, I select all of them and hit delete before moving across to the trash can and permanently deleting them all from the system, making it impossible for Orlando to recover the files. I remove the sub folder as though it was never there and just as I wipe the tears off my face, another sub folder catches my attention.

ASHFORD

Sucking in a gasp, my brows furrow and I open the folder. My hand covers my mouth and my chest starts to ache, finding the screen filled with videos and still photos of my mother working as a prostitute. I flick through the pictures, the tears streaming down my face. She would have only been fifteen or sixteen in these images, much younger than I am now. Her skin is pale and her cheeks hollow. She has dark bags under her eyes and her hair looks as though it hadn't been washed in weeks. Not to mention the bruising and needle marks inside her elbow.

I can't bear to look at it another second and drop the whole folder into the trash can, permanently deleting the files just as I'd done with the evidence against Tanner. I make a vow to myself never to bring this up, never to burden my mother by letting her know what I saw here. I don't want to destroy her.

This right here will go to the grave with me.

Letting each of the images fall from my memory, I insert my flash drive and copy every last remaining file from the locked folder.

After getting everything I need, I slip the flash drive into my pocket and turn off the computer before standing up and checking over his desk, making sure every last thing is exactly how I left it. I can't risk Orlando finding out I was here.

Confident that everything is just right, I stride toward the office exit, pausing when a canvas on the wall catches my eye. It's a picture of a big vase filled with tulips, and while it's a gorgeous print, there's something off-putting about it the longer I stare.

It hits me a moment later. Orlando's whole house doesn't have one cheap art print, and certainly no cheap frames. I mean, sure, the whole place is decked out with extravagant artwork by famous artists, but he'd never hang a vase of flowers on the wall. It's not his style. This print seems like some kind of quick fix, as though he's hiding something.

The second the thought makes its way through my head, I step up to the wall and grip the sides of it. The fucker is heavy but nothing I can't handle.

Setting it down on the ground, I stare up at the wall, a grin plastered across my face. Today really is my lucky day. What are the chances of hitting a jackpot twice?

Orlando's safe stares back at me, and I crack my knuckles, more than ready to get to work.

My fingers shake over the keypad as I inhale slowly. One mistake and it could be all over. I hold my breath, cautiously punching in each number of the anniversary date. There's no way to know what he keeps in here, but I assume there are hard copies of the evidence against Tanner, and I'm not about to let those fall into the wrong hands.

Entering the last two digits is like stepping out of a plane, not knowing if your parachute is going to open, but when the safe makes a beeping sound and the light flashes green, I almost piss my pants out of pure relief.

Grabbing the handle, I quickly turn it and pull it open, only to have to catch the files as they begin to spill out. "Holy shit," I breathe, quickly arranging them to be able to hold them better and seeing the names of old cases scrawled across the front of the manila folders.

It's everything I just saw in the locked folder on his computer and knowing just what these papers could do for Tanner and my mom, I take every last one of them, clearing out the safe before closing the door and rehanging the cheap flowers.

My heart races as I double back to the door, pausing to look over the office. Everything is right where it should be. I just have to hope Orlando doesn't decide to go searching through his safe before I have a chance to do something with these.

After double-checking the flash drive is securely in my pocket, I lock up the office as though I was never here and hurry out to the parking lot. I unlock the stupid Maserati Orlando gifted me, feeling sick for having to use it, but what other choice did I have? Tanner doesn't exactly know what I'm up to right now, and after running his Mustang into Roxten's bitch ass, it'll be out of order until the body shop is able to complete the repairs, though it's really only the windshield that took most of the damage. Besides, there's something sweet about using the Maserati to get revenge.

Without a moment to waste, I dump the files on the passenger seat and get my ass moving. On the way back to Tanner's place, I haphazardly make a last-minute right turn instead of a left, driving back toward downtown. I'm almost on autopilot when I pull up outside the precinct, not sure if I can stomach what I'm about to do, but when it comes to Tanner and my mom, there's nothing I wouldn't do to protect them.

A thick silence settles over me when I cut the ignition. So much could go wrong here. The file folders I have pulled into my lap are heavy, and I imagine walking in there and putting this all into the hands of a dirty cop, but I have to take my chances. I have to try, even if it means slamming these papers down and making a scene so that every last cop in the building knows what's happening. They can't all be in Orlando's pocket, can they?

Thumbing through the files, I take out the ones that incriminate Tanner, but as I scan through them, I find a folder labeled JACOBS, and my curiosity shoots right through the roof. I can't wait and pull the file out of the big pile, setting it on my lap and quickly thumbing through it. There's a shitload of paperwork and evidence from the night Addison was raped. Evidence that never saw the light of day, but the one piece of paper that has my attention is the report from the rape kit confirming a perfect DNA match for Colby Jacobs.

Gotcha, motherfucker.

Not wanting to risk this document falling into the wrong hands and disappearing again, I pull out my phone and take photos of every last page before closing the folder and resting it right on top of the pile. Having everything in order with the people I love protected, I let out a shaky breath, grab the pile of manila folders, and make my way into the precinct.

The Maserati drives like a wet dream on a late summer's night, and it's a shame it'll get locked back in the garage, never to be touched again. A smile rests across my face, and with every new street I turn down, I crank the music up, never feeling so elated in my life.

Orlando Channing is going down, and everyone I love will receive the justice they deserve.

I fly down the street—past the tree that still holds the scars of my Honda slamming into it—and turn onto my road. As I pass Tanner's house and pull into Orlando's driveway, my very pissed-off boyfriend pushes off the edge of his mother's car. He's staring at me with crossed arms and a dark expression—as if he knows exactly what I've been doing.

I swallow hard and consider hitting the gas and taking off again, but Mom and Orlando will be back soon enough, and the last thing I want is to get caught in the act.

Pulling into Orlando's driveway, I sit patiently, waiting for the garage door to open all the way before slowly creeping in, and by the time I cut the engine and get out of the car, Tanner is right there, his calculating stare locked on mine. "What the fuck are you doing?" he questions.

I give him a wide smile. "Oh hey," I beam, guilty as shit. "I thought you were working out with the guys?"

"That was hours ago," he states, fixing me with a hard stare. "What are you doing?"

I try to smother a smirk as I narrow my eyes at him. "Why?" I question, more than prepared to be a shady bitch. "What do you think I'm doing?"

Tanner rolls his eyes and drops his arms. "Babe," he says with a pointed stare. "Why were you calling Logan and asking how to break into locked files?"

My mouth drops and I gape at him. "That little snitch."

"Bri," he warns, trying to get me back on track.

I shake my head and let my smile fly free before nodding toward Orlando's front door. "Come on," I tell him. "There's something we need to do."

His brows furrow, but I take off before he gets a chance to stop me. With no one home, Tanner races after me as I hurry through the house, beelining for the one room I've never been in—Orlando's home office. "Killer," Tanner says, following me into the obnoxiously big office. "What the fuck is going on? We shouldn't be here. It's only going to backfire on us."

I whip around, fixing him with a wide smile as I tear my phone out of my back pocket and bring up the images of the rape kit report. "Look what I found today," I tell him, handing it over before digging out every last incriminating photograph of him in Hope Falls and dropping it onto Orlando's desk.

Tanner's brows furrow as he reaches over to take my phone, flicking through the pictures, and the more he sees, the quicker his lips pull into a victorious smile. "Where the fuck did you get this?" he questions, before skimming over the photographs on the desk. "Are these—"

"Every last hard copy I could find," I tell him.

"What?" he questions. "How?"

I glance away, knowing he won't like what's about to come out of my mouth. "I, uhhh, may have broken into Orlando's office and wiped his computer clean of everything to do with you while also maybe copying every incriminating document onto a flash drive and handing it over to Detective Daniels."

His eyes bug out of his head. "What?"

"Yeah, good times," I grin, all too proud of myself. "Raiding his safe was the cherry on top though."

Tanner presses his fingers to his temples, pacing the office. "Holy fuck," he breathes before snapping his head back to me. "You showed them these pictures?" he questions, waving my phone around.

"No," I tell him. "They're our personal copies, but I made sure to give them the original report, signed and dated by whoever the dude was that tested the rape kit."

Tanner storms into me, grabbing me around the waist and yanking me into his strong chest, the happiness in his eyes warming everything inside me. "She's going to get her justice."

I nod, looking up at my whole damn world.

His lips crash against mine, but before we get carried away, I push against his chest, pulling back from his kiss. He looks down at me, his brows furrowed in concern, but I quickly clear things up. "Umm, so, now that the cops have everything they need, I can almost guarantee they'll be getting a warrant to raid this place, and I kinda figured we should double-check it first and make sure there are no more photos of you at … you know."

His eyes widen, realization dawning. "Oh fuck," he says, his arms falling from around my waist as his gaze starts shifting around the office. "Where?"

I shrug my shoulders. "Look for a safe," I tell him as I dart around the back of his desk. "I'll check the computer."

Twenty minutes later, Tanner swipes his arm across Orlando's desk, watching as everything goes flying across the room, computer and all, and not a moment later, he slams my chest down against the mahogany table, naked as the day I was born.

Smoke fills the room as every last piece of evidence against Tanner burns to ashes on the carpet, but all that matters is the way he kicks my legs wide.

"Oh God," I groan, his hand coming down against my bare ass with a hard spank as the other curls around my hair, pulling my head right back. Then before I can even tell him how I want it, he lines his thick cock up with my dripping entrance and slams it deep inside me.

"Fuuuuck, Killer," he groans, that deep rumble doing unspeakable things to me.

He fucks me hard and fast, knowing at some point we need to get out of here before the smoke kills us, but he's determined to make me come first.

Tanner slams inside of me, stretching me wide and pushing me to my limits as my body crumbles to his every will. My hand grips the edge of the desk, holding on for dear life as my eyes roll in the back of my head. "Yes, Tanner. YES! More."

He rises to the challenge, thrusting balls deep, and I swear, just one more inch and I'd feel him in my fucking throat. He spanks me again and I groan, pushing back against him and taking everything he's got like the perfect greedy whore.

I take all of him, and just as I feel that familiar tightening deep in my core, warning me what's to come, the fire alarm blasts through the mansion and water rains down over me. "Oh shit," I gasp, realizing it's the fire sprinklers.

I go to push up from the desk but Tanner holds me down. "Oh, no you don't," he mutters, a deep growl in his tone, only fucking me harder.

My face drops back against the desk, and I look back over my shoulder, watching him as he fucks me, dripping wet from the sprinklers, and good God, it's the most erotic thing I've ever seen. The alarm continues to wail, and I don't doubt this place will be crawling with firemen in less than two minutes, but we won't even need one.

It builds and builds, becoming more intense by the second, and every thrust of his thick cock deep inside me only makes me want to scream. He doesn't relent, giving it to me just right, and as my walls clench around him, he pushes me right over the edge. "Oh, fuck," I cry, my pussy shattering into a million pieces.

My eyes clench and my knees go weak, feeling my orgasm tearing through my body. "So. Fucking. Tight," Tanner grunts each word as my pussy convulses around him.

He thrusts into me one more time, coming hard and shooting his hot cum deep inside me, making me feel like the most desired woman on the planet.

My orgasm still wreaks the sweetest havoc over my body just as the office door whips open and I find both Jensen and Damien staring at us. My eyes widen but I can't fucking move, not unless I want Tanner's cum dripping out of me in front of my brother.

"Oh hey there," I say awkwardly, watching as they take in the scene before them—the fire, the smoke, the sprinklers, and us.

Damien looks as though he's about to tear Tanner in half, but Jensen just shakes his head and presses his lips into a hard line. "Why am I not surprised?" he questions before turning his gaze on Tanner. "Once you've blown your load, you should probably think about getting out of here. You know, smoke inhalation and all that."

Tanner nods and just like that, Jensen reaches back in, grips the door handle, and pulls it closed like the perfect gentleman, leaving his new stepsister to continue getting railed.

CHAPTER 32

Sara

A lifetime of memorabilia spills from overturned boxes across the bedroom floor—the bedroom I used to share with the love of my life. A photo of us when we were young and inseparable catches my eye, and I take another swig of wine to wash away the taste of his deceit.

I've been searching for hours through every family photo, every souvenir keychain, and every letter Trenton lovingly wrote in our first few years of marriage. I need to find the moment everything went wrong, the moment he stopped looking at me like I hung the moon. The moment the lies began.

It feels like my entire world is on fire.

Trenton wasn't just having an affair; he had a whole family. A wife, children—everything sacred between us, he had with another woman.

A tiny pair of white baby booties stare up at me from the bottom of an empty box, and my heart falls to the floor. Our babies. Even if he didn't love me anymore, how could he do this to them?

Tanner and Addie have gone without, their father absent while he doted on his new wife and children, leaving them to fend for themselves through the hardest year imaginable. While Addison lay comatose in the hospital, recovering from a violent rape, Trenton was taking his daughter to play dates, and while Addison was coming to terms with her rapist walking free, Trenton was hiring a babysitter so he could wine and dine his new wife.

I've never felt so foolish. Twenty-three years of marriage just washed away. How am I ever supposed to trust again?

Letting out a sigh, I try to focus on sorting Trent's shit into three piles: claim as my own, mail to the sorry bastard, and burn in a fiery pit of hell. So far, the fiery pit of hell pile is looking pretty full.

When the well of tears inside me has finally run dry, I push the empty box aside and grab another, tipping it upside down unceremoniously. An old phone falls out, and the screen cracks as it tumbles over twenty-three years of junk. There are things in these boxes I haven't seen or thought about in years, and while some come with fond memories, the rest just leaves me aching.

The longer I stare at the old iPhone, the more foreign it looks. Trenton has always been a Samsung user, and the phone definitely never belonged to me. I scoop it up and turn it over in my hand, pressing the power button and holding it down for a moment. The

Apple logo appears on the screen, sending a rush of relief coursing through my veins, but not even a second later, the screen goes black again.

Letting out a heavy sigh, I toss the phone to the side. That'll have to be a job for another day. It needs one of the old Apple chargers, and I can guarantee I don't have one of those hanging out in a drawer anymore.

A soft knock sounds at my bedroom door as I'm shoving yet another armful of crap into the burn pile, not even bothering to look over the contents. My brows furrow as I glance up. "Come in," I say slowly, wondering who the hell that could be. After all, neither of my children have ever knocked on my door in their life. They prefer the more subtle approach of just barging right in.

The door opens and Brielle's face appears in my room. "Hey, sorry. I was just wondering if you had a second?" she questions hesitantly before scanning over the array of crap before me. "I can come back if now isn't a good time."

"Oh no, sweetheart," I say, trying to force a welcoming smile across my face but it feels so fake. "Come in."

She presses her lips into a tight line, and as she steps into my room and closes the door behind her, I see something in her eyes. Whatever this is, it's hard for her.

Brielle walks across my room as I get to my feet and step out of the pile of crap. I can't help but notice papers in her hand, and for some reason, it puts me on edge. "How can I help you, darling?" I ask, offering her a seat at the end of my bed.

She cringes as she sits down, looking up at me sadly. "I think it's more about how I can help you." I arch a brow, but the reluctance in her tone suggests this isn't anything I actually want help with. "Umm, yesterday," she says, visibly swallowing. "I kinda broke into Orlando's office and found some things I thought you should have."

I pull back in surprise. "Me?" I question. "Are you sure? I've had nothing to do with Orlando, only my children."

"I know," she murmurs. "Which is why I found this so … strange."

Brielle hands me the papers, and as I skim over them, my brows furrow. "What is this?" I question, never having seen these papers in my life.

"They're your divorce papers," she tells me at the same moment I see both my name and Trenton's printed across the paper. "They were signed and dated seven years ago."

My gaze snaps up in horror. "What?" I breathe, flipping through the pages. "That's impossible. We're still married." Brielle gives me a tight smile as I reach the final page, finding my signature along with Trenton's. Only it's not my signature at all; it's been forged.

I gasp, pain slicing through my chest as though someone is physically shoving their hand through my body and squeezing my heart with a death grip. "How … how is this possible?" I whisper as tears begin to well in my eyes.

Brielle reaches across and takes my hand, giving it a gentle squeeze. "Judging by everything else I found in his office, it's clear Orlando is a very dirty lawyer. I can only assume Trenton hired him to make this happen without your consent. I found a ledger mixed in with all the papers I stole from his safe, and there was a big payment from your husband around the same time those papers were signed. I can't pretend I know what it costs to file divorce papers, but lawyer fees for something like that definitely shouldn't be that high."

I drop the papers into my lap and place my hand over my mouth to keep from sobbing in front of this sweet girl. "Thank you for bringing this to me, Brielle," I whisper, realizing this was how he was able to get away with marrying this other woman in Australia.

She awkwardly stands and gives me a tight smile, though the heartbreak in her eyes only makes it harder to meet her gaze. "For what it's worth," she says, "I handed everything I found over to the police yesterday, including proof that Orlando messed with the results from Addie's rape kit, so he'll be going away for a very long time."

My eyes widen just a fraction in disbelief. "What about Tanner?" I question, my heart still so broken after discovering what he'd been involved with as a fourteen-year-old boy. "Were you able to find the hard copies of those ... photographs?"

Brielle nods. "Yeah, I found them and Tanner destroyed them, but I still think he needs to come clean about what happened that day."

"As do I," I tell her. "But it's in his hands now, and I need to trust that he'll do the right thing."

Brielle smiles. "I'm sure he will."

With that, she starts to walk back to the door, but a thought occurs to me. I reach down and scoop up the old iPhone off the carpet. "Brielle, sweetheart," I say, glancing up as she stops and looks back at me. "Would you do me a favor and ask Tanner if he has one of the old iPhone chargers for this? I found it in a box of Trenton's things, and considering everything else I've discovered about the man, I feel it's in my best interest to see what else he has kept from me."

"Oh, sure," she says, walking back and taking the phone from me before quickly flipping it over to check what the charging port in the bottom looks like. "I, uhh … I think I might actually have one of these. I'll have to double-check, but for some reason, Mom used to keep a box of old chargers and cords that never actually fit any of our devices. I'll sneak back in and see what I can find."

I give her a fond smile. "How are things with your mom?"

Brielle shrugs her shoulders. "Who knows?" she mutters, a real sadness in her eyes. "The things she's had to put herself through over the past few months to protect me from him … I can't even tell you how much that kills me, but despite all of that, I still feel so angry with her."

"Oh, honey," I say, pulling her into a quick hug. "Everything is going to work out for the best. It's completely normal to feel angry. She pushed you away, and even if her intentions were good, it still hurts. It's perfectly fine for you to take your time healing."

Bri hastily wipes at her eyes before pulling back and giving me another tight smile. "Thanks," she murmurs, before holding up the phone. "I'll see if I can get this working for you."

And with that, she's gone.

An hour later, I make my way downstairs with an empty bottle of wine, knowing all too well that if I'm going to make it through the next ten years of memorabilia, I'm going to need to start fresh on a new bottle.

Making my way to the kitchen, I stop to find Tanner and Brielle slaving over the hot stove, and my gaze snaps to the clock. I suck in a horrified breath. "Oh my goodness, dinner!" I rush out. "I completely lost track of time. I'm so sorry. Go sit down, I'll finish up."

Tanner shakes his head. "It's fine, Mom. We've got it under control. Sit down and relax."

I gape at my son. Who the hell is this stranger standing in my kitchen? Though, I suppose that's a bit of an unfair comment. Ever since Addie was hurt, Tanner has really stepped up to become the man of this house. He was there in my darkest times and kept my chin up when I thought about giving up. He's really been my rock over the past few months.

"I—"

"Don't even think about arguing," Tanner mutters just as he takes the vegetables off the steamer and nearly drops them, pulling a face before pretending everything is cool.

I roll my eyes and reluctantly take a seat at the island counter. While they may have it under control, a little supervision wouldn't go astray. I'm not familiar with Brielle's abilities in the kitchen, however I'm more than familiar with my son's, and it's not a good mix.

"Oh, hey," Brielle says, putting down the spatula and crossing the kitchen. She unplugs the phone laying on the counter and hands it to me. "I managed to find a charger. It's old and slow, but it's doing the trick."

"Ahhh, thank you, sweetheart," I say, dropping my attention to the phone as I hold down the power button. Just like before, it takes a few seconds before the Apple logo appears on the screen, but this time, the ancient device does what it's supposed to do. It clearly hasn't been used in a while and takes a little longer than my patience can handle, but the moment the home screen finally loads, I'm ready to dive in.

My stomach twists with unease, but it's now or never. If I truly want to learn my husband's secrets, then this is how it's going to happen. Though, I can't see how it could possibly get any worse than secretly divorcing me and starting a new family across the planet.

Letting out a shaky breath, my finger hovers over the photo gallery before finally mustering up the courage to press down. It opens to an array of images, each one more horrifying than the next. My husband with strippers, licking their bodies and snorting cocaine off their breasts. My husband at parties, hooking up with random women, drugs spread out on tables. There are dick pics and photos of other women in compromising positions, clearly images sent on request.

Bile rises in my throat, but I keep looking, unable to stop until I come to a video of Trenton, holding the camera up as he screws some woman on a table. I exit out of it, the noises coming from the video making me want to die.

Tanner meets my gaze over the top of the phone, and I simply shake my head, not wanting to hear whatever it is he has to say about this, though also not wanting to submit Brielle and Tanner to this filth. I exit out of the photo gallery, determined to revisit this when I'm alone.

Instead, I move onto the text messages.

My hands shake, but determination has a death grip on me, and I open it up to a slew of text messages from random women with names like Candy, Stacey, Tiffany, and Starlight. I'm trying not to gag when a name in the inbox draws my attention like a black hole in the sky.

Rachael.

"What in the ever-loving hell is this?" I mutter under my breath. The comment has Tanner whipping around from the stove to watch me with curiosity, but I pay him no attention, needing to see what the hell this is about.

My stomach twists and clenches. The messages are dated from two years ago, and I pray this isn't the same Rachael who's the mother of Tanner's child.

I scroll up to the beginning of the conversation and start reading, each word like another knife right through my chest.

Rachael - What am I going to do? Please, Trenton, you have to help me.

Rachael - Answer me. This is just as much your problem as it is mine.

Rachael - I didn't get pregnant by myself you know. If you don't do something about this, I'm telling everyone what you did.

Trenton - Okay, alright. Settle down. Don't go and make any rash decisions. We can figure this out. You're only seventeen. No one can know about this. I'll make an appointment and handle it.

Rachael - Appointment? What for?

Trenton - An abortion. You can't have that baby.

Rachael - Missed call.

Rachael - Missed call.

Rachael - Missed call.

Rachael - WHAT DO YOU MEAN ABORTION? I'M NOT HAVING AN ABORTION! ANSWER ME!!! Sooner or later, people are going to realize I'm pregnant, and they'll ask questions. What the hell am I supposed to say?

Trenton - Stop calling me. You have to have an abortion. I'm not having this kid with you. You're on your own, but if anyone finds out about this, you'll regret it.

Rachael - You're not exactly in a position to threaten me, Trenton. I'm seventeen, remember. Underage. Pretty sure that's considered rape in a court of law. And for the record, me and my boyfriend broke up, so you can't use him as your scapegoat.

Trenton - Fuck.

Rachael - Missed call.

There's a few more missed calls and a slew of raging texts from Rachael, and then finally a response from Trenton almost a week later.

Trenton - Calm down. Here's what you're going to do. My son is going to a party tonight. His name is Tanner. Seduce him. Do whatever you have to do to fuck him. I don't care how it happens, just do it.

Rachael - That's insane. I know of him. He's barely sixteen. Are you really trying to pin this on your son? Besides, do you even know your son? He's the most popular guy at Bradford. I'm some poor bitch in Hope Falls. He's not going to fuck me. Not to mention, the dates won't line up. I'm already eight weeks.

Trenton - I'm not going down for this, Rachael. Just do it and don't tell him you're pregnant. I'll give you some money to disappear for a while, long enough for the dates to be foggy in his mind, then hit him with it. Say it was born premature. Get him drunk enough he doesn't remember what happened that night. There'll be a paternity test, and as long as no one knows to look any deeper, the paternity test will confirm Tanner is the father.

Rachael - What? That doesn't make any sense. How will the test confirm Tanner is the father?

Trenton - Because Tanner shares my DNA. A common paternity test will show mutual characteristics between the DNA and confirm Tanner's DNA matches your child's. They'll only seek further testing if they know there's a chance I could be the father. You can't let that happen, Rachael. Tanner's DNA is enough to bring a positive paternity result and put enough doubt in their minds to be believable. Do you understand me? Just stick to the plan and it'll be fine.

Rachael - This is ridiculous.

Trenton - Your other option is an abortion, otherwise you're on your own.

Rachael - Okay, fine. I'll do it.

Trenton - Good. Now don't message me again. No one can know about this.

Horror settles into my chest, and as I lift my gaze from the phone, I meet Tanner's concerned stare. "Mom?" he questions. "You don't look so good."

"Here," I say, passing him the phone, a strange hollowness inside my heart. "You need to read this."

CHAPTER 33
Brielle

"OH FUCK. GO, GO, GO," Addison yells as she races down the hill of Bradford Private toward the student parking lot, school security hot on her tail.

"Oh, shit," Tanner laughs, shoving the key into the ignition and starting the engine as I dive into the backseat of the Mustang, making space for a quicker getaway.

Tanner throws the car in reverse and hits the gas, flying out of his spot before reaching over and opening the passenger door just in time for Addison to fly through it. The door slams behind her, and Tanner puts his foot to the ground, skidding out of here like a bat out of hell, only narrowly escaping school security.

"What the fuck was that?" Addison demands, whipping around

to fix me with a hard stare after receiving a very shady text from me to meet us in the school parking lot and make it quick. But hell, once I received the heads up, I wasn't about to waste a perfectly good opportunity.

"You'll have to wait and see," I tell her as Tanner grins, knowing damn well what's coming her way. "But I promise, it's worth the after-school detention we're all about to get."

Addison groans, trying to get comfortable in her seat. "I didn't even think about that."

A smirk stretches across my face as I rest back in my seat, and it doesn't move the whole ride into the city, despite Addison's endless demands to be told what the hell is going on.

We pull up across the road of the office I was only just rummaging through a few days ago, and I grab a bag of popcorn, shoving it into the front seat. "Here," I say, dropping it into her lap.

Addison's whole demeanor shifts, unease and nervousness flashing in her eyes. "What the hell are we doing here?" she demands, recognizing Orlando's office. "I wanna go home. I don't like this."

Tanner rests his hand over his sister's. "Just sit back and watch the show," he tells her. "I promise, it'll all be worth it."

Addison groans and sits back in her chair as my knees bounce, the anticipation of what's about to happen almost killing me. My phone buzzes and I stop breathing, terrified I'm about to be told this isn't going ahead, but when I pull my phone out, I find a new text from Miranda, a girl I used to go to school with.

I open it to find a video, and I quickly read the text before pressing play.

Miranda - Dude, you should see this shit. That video your friend posted last week made the rounds big time and now Erica is getting her ass handed to her. She just got booed out of the cafeteria and then escorted off school grounds. She won't be showing her face here again.

What the hell?

I hit play on the video and the sound of the entire student body of Hope Falls fills the Mustang, and I watch as Erica is escorted out of the cafeteria by the assistant principal, dragging her by the arm as the students boo and throw food at her back.

"Holy shit," I breathe, my gaze glued to the phone.

"What's that?" Tanner questions, glancing at me in the backseat.

I scoot forward in my seat and hold my phone out. "Here, check this out," I tell them, starting the video from scratch as Addison and Tanner lean over to get a better view. A few seconds play before they understand what's going on, and I watch as Addison's brows arch. "I know it's not exactly the justice you were hoping to get with her, but at least she's being held accountable now."

"Yeah, I guess, I just—" Addison freezes, her gaze drawn out the window as no less than twenty police cars come screeching down the road, every single one of them coming to a stop around the building. Some stop out front while others go around back, making sure no one from inside can make a break for it. "What's going on?" Addison rushes out, sitting up straighter with her eyes glued out the window.

Excitement drums through my veins as I tear open my bag of popcorn. Show time.

I shove a handful of yummy goodness into my mouth like some kind of rabid animal. "I might have found a little dirt on one particular dirty lawyer that may or may not put him away for the rest of his life while also convicting Colby of exactly what he did."

"What?" she breathes, her eyes wide, watching as the cops bail out of their cars and race through the door, kicking it down, and raiding the place as though they're in some kind of movie. "Holy shit. You found the real rape kit report?"

"She sure did," Tanner says with a proud, boastful grin. "Along with every other fucked-up thing he's ever done. Orlando Channing is done for."

Addison laughs and rests back into her seat, watching the show like it's prime time television. She scoops a massive handful of popcorn into her mouth. "Oh my God," she cackles, just as more cops show up and start taping off the area to all the press who have come crawling from every direction. Big camera crews and reporters are all rushing around to get the money shot. "This is amazing."

Tanner glances back at me, his eyes so bright and happy it makes me want to kick Addison out and screw him right here and now. Fuck getting written up for indecent exposure. It'll all be worth it.

Barely a few minutes have passed before two cops come striding out of the office with Orlando in handcuffs. They shove him hard, pushing him toward a police cruiser, and before I even know what's happening, Addison's window is down and she's calling out to him.

"HEY, ORLANDO," she hollers, making sure he hears her loud and clear. Her hand flies out the window just as Orlando's head snaps up, and she flips him the bird, grinning wide so he knows exactly who's responsible for his downfall. "FUCK YOU, ASSHOLE. ENJOY PRISON."

Just as Addison sits back in her seat, Orlando's head disappears into the back of the cruiser. "You're right," she says with a satisfied grin. "That was totally worth the after-school detention."

We sit and watch the show, and as the minutes pass, Addison's phone starts blowing up. She opens her texts, and I watch her brows furrow. She quickly searches for something on her phone and sure enough, her face is plastered all over the internet for the second time in as many weeks. Only this time, instead of demanding the justice system to do better, she's half hanging out the door of Tanner's Mustang waving her middle finger around for the world to see.

Tanner laughs. "Nice."

"Ahh shit," Addison groans. "After-school detention and a rant from Mom. Just perfect."

"I don't know," I muse. "After Orlando helped your dad secretly divorce her, your mom might be cool about this one."

Tanner glances at Addison. "She's right. Hell, Mom might even be proud."

We watch the show for the next twenty minutes, watching as box after box of files are taken from Orlando's office, each one hopefully holding all the evidence the cops need to give justice to all the people Orlando has screwed over during his long career.

We're just about to go when a text comes through on Tanner's phone. He pulls it out, checks it and laughs before holding it up for me and Addie to see.

Mom - Get your asses back to school, NOW!!

Addison scoffs as Tanner starts the engine. "Right, Mom's really going to be proud," she mutters to herself, rolling her eyes.

Tanner smirks and hits the gas, pulling the Mustang around in a wide U-turn and heading back toward school so we can all face the firing squad and be handed our detention. Though hopefully that's all we get.

Addison cranks up the music, trying to make the most of the ride just as Tanner slams the brakes and pulls off to the side of the road, nearly sending me right through the fucking windshield. Though at least this time a broken windshield wouldn't be my fault. Tanner only just got the Mustang back from the shop yesterday.

"What's wrong?" I rush out, leaning forward in my seat, getting closer to Tanner as he stares out the window, his hands tightening on the steering wheel.

He nods out the window, and I follow his gaze to find Rachael and her mom stepping out of a designer store, probably spending the money Tanner was forced to pay for a child that isn't even his. Rachael pushes a stroller as her child sleeps, her shopping bags dumped on top of him.

Anger drums through my veins. There's so much wrong with this picture, I can't even focus. That baby might not be Tanner's child, but he's still his half-brother, still shares his DNA, just like the three babies living in Australia. And despite how they all came to be, I don't doubt there's nothing Tanner wouldn't do to protect them. Family means everything to him, and it's not their fault their father is a lying, adulterating piece of shit.

Tanner is out of the car in no time, but I'm right there with him.

"Oh shit," I hear Addison behind us, scrambling out of the Mustang and racing to catch up with us as we cross the road, looking like a pack of fucking wolves going in for the kill.

Colby's mom spots us first, and before Rachael even has a chance to look up, her mom is rushing across the street, her hand whipping out and smacking hard across Tanner's face. "You … you murderer," she spits at him. "You killed my baby boy."

I'm more than ready to tell her what I think of that, but Addison is on fire and comes racing in like a knight in shining armor, shoving her hands hard into the woman's chest and sending her flying away from Tanner. Addison keeps on her, forging ahead and getting in her face. "Your piece of shit son deserved to die for what he did to me," she spits, rage like I've never seen flying from her mouth. "He drugged me and threw me down. Pulled my fucking pants off while I screamed for somebody—anybody—to fucking help me. I begged him to stop, begged him not to touch me, and you know what that bastard did? You wanna know? HE FUCKING LAUGHED IN MY FACE and then got away with it. He walked free because of that dirty fucking lawyer, but he couldn't handle the shame of what he'd done. Couldn't handle the fucking world knowing what a piece of shit he was, so he tore the fucking breathing tube right out of my throat as I laid in a fucking coma. Is that the little boy you were trying to protect?" she spits, tears springing to her eyes.

Addison steps even closer, her voice lowering with the deepest, raging anger. "The night Colby came to the track and held a knife up against my throat, he was ready to fucking touch me again. Oh, he fucking wanted it. He wanted to throw me down and force himself inside me all over again. I should have killed him myself. Fuck, I wish I had killed him myself because maybe then it wouldn't be so fucking hard to close my eyes at night. He deserved it for what he did. He stabbed me that night right through my chest, and when he didn't get what he wanted, he stabbed Brielle and Jax too. So tell me, please for the love of God, tell me why the fuck my brother should feel bad about what he had to do to protect us. He saved our fucking lives because of the decisions your son made, and he'll have to live with the weight of that for the rest of his life."

The woman weeps as Tanner steps in, placing his hand on Addison's shoulder. "Stop," he murmurs, gently pushing her back toward me. "She's in denial. Yelling at her isn't going to do you any good. It just brings up things you don't need to be thinking about," he says before fixing his stare on Rachael. "But right now, we've got bigger issues to deal with."

Rachael stares at Tanner, visibly shaking, and with every step he takes toward her, her eyes widen further. "What … what do you want?" she questions, her gaze snapping nervously toward her son.

Tanner stares at her and the look in his eyes terrifies me. "It seems your mom breeds them all the same."

"What's that supposed to mean?" Rachael spits, discreetly stepping in front of her child.

Her mom recovers, and as if finding her back bone, she scrambles toward her daughter. "Don't you dare touch her, you … you animal," she seethes.

Tanner scoffs. "Been there, done that, and trust me, it's no good. Just ask my father."

Rachael's face turns a sickening shade of white as her mother sputters. "What the hell is that supposed to mean?" she demands.

Tanner laughs. "It seems your daughter has a few secrets of her own," he says, stepping around them and moving toward the child in the stroller. He grabs the handful of shopping bags and dumps them on the ground before crouching down to get a good look at the little boy. "Good looks really do run in my family," he says. "But it's a shame he's not mine."

"Where do you get off claiming that child is not yours?" the mother spits. "How dare you. Haven't you messed with my family enough? You take my son from me and now you want to screw over my daughter as well? Not on my watch, asshole. We have the paternity test to prove it."

Tanner straightens up and turns to Rachael. "Do you want to tell her, or should I?"

Rachael clenches her jaw, her gaze flicking between her mother and Tanner, looking as though she's about to be sick. "I … I don't know what you're talking about," she says. "He's your son and the sooner you accept it, the better for everyone involved."

"Oh, there's no doubt we share the same DNA. Isn't that right, Rachael? It's how you knew the paternity test would confirm me as the father. All you had to do was make sure you fucked me. To be honest, it's almost ironic. Colby attacked my sister as some fucked-up revenge plot for me screwing you, but really, you were the one who violated me that night."

"I … I," she panics, but Tanner just laughs, cutting her off and giving a manic smile to her mom.

"Here, let me clue you in because you're clearly not keeping up," Tanner says. "Your daughter, the little whore that she is, wasn't knocked up by me. She was fucking my father, a married man, and when she discovered she was pregnant, they devised a sick little plan for her to fuck me and claim the baby was mine, knowing a paternity test would still confirm our DNA was a match. After all, they couldn't let anyone know she was fucking him because she was underage, and my father really didn't feel like going down for statutory rape, a problem your son clearly didn't have. Though I'm not gonna lie, it was clever, and she almost pulled it off. The only problem is, my father dearest forgot to delete his messages. Pretty stupid for a man facing jail time."

Rachael crumbles, weeping in silence as her mother gapes at her. "Is that true?" she gasps with disgust. "You were having an affair with a married man and set up his son to take the fall?"

"I … I … I had no choice," she says. "He made me do it. He was going to force me to have an abortion."

They start to get into it, but Tanner decides he's had enough and spares one more glance toward his half-brother. "Well, it was lovely catching up," he says before kicking the shopping bags with his foot and cringing. "I hope this shit is refundable, because in case you haven't figured it out, you'll be paying back every fucking cent of child support."

And with that, Tanner steps between the two of them and starts making his way back toward us, ready to leave, but I haven't quite finished here. "Hey," I say, stepping closer to Rachael, and without warning, I rear back and sock her right in the face. She screams as her mother gasps in horror, blood pouring from her broken nose. "Only I get to fuck with Tanner."

And with that, I turn back toward him, give him a beaming smile, and slip my hand into his. With a huge weight off all of our shoulders, the three of us make our way back to the Mustang, ready to face the firing squad at school.

CHAPTER 34
Brielle

"HOOOOOOOLY FUCK," Riley says, eyes wide as he watches the parking lot of Bradford Private, staring at the white BMW that just pulled in. "It's her. She's here. She actually came. I thought she was just fucking with me, but she actually came."

Jax scoffs, embarrassed to be around him. "Dude, chill. You're never going to get your dick wet like that."

"Uggggghhh," I groan, shoving Jax in the arm. "Why do you have to make everything disgusting?"

"Can't help it," he says as Tanner's arms circle my waist, his lips dropping to my neck. "It comes naturally. Call it a gift."

Arizona lets out a barking laugh. "If that's your idea of a gift, what the hell do you call your ability to fuck?" she says before her eyes widen, realizing exactly what she said out loud.

Her head whips toward Jax who just smirks, pride shining in his eyes as he looks back at her. "It's nothing but a God-given natural talent," he tells her, his arms opening wide as if inviting her in. "And it's all yours, baby. All you gotta do is come and get it."

Arizona just stares at him, more than practiced at dealing with his charm, but when he winks, she freaking melts. "God, Jax. You're such an idiot," she tells him, stepping into his arms and pushing up onto her tippy toes. She brushes a kiss over his lips and pulls back to beam up at him. "Good luck warming the bench tonight," she says, her smile quickly morphing into a wicked grin as she steps out of his arms.

Jax presses a hand to his chest and falls to his knees. "Fuck, that hurt."

She rolls her eyes and glances toward us girls. "Come on, we better find seats before all the good ones disappear."

"Good point," I say, turning in Tanner's arms and looking up at him as people from all over town pour into the school parking lot for tonight's championship game. "You're going to be amazing," I tell him, knowing it right down in my chest. "And listen, if you bring me a trophy at the end of the night, I might even do that thing you like."

His brow arches with interest. "Really?" he questions. "That thing?"

"Uh-huh."

"And if we don't win?"

"Then it'll just be you and your hand tonight."

Tanner looks pained with the thought, but before he can get a word out, Ilaria glances at me. "Isn't that a *Pink* song?"

I smirk. "Damn right it is."

Tanner rolls his eyes and drops his arms, pressing one more kiss to my lips before he pulls away and strips off his letterman jacket. "Fucking perfect," he tells me as he drapes it around me. I glance over my shoulder and nearly come in my pants at the sight of his name and number on my back. "You know what?" he murmurs, adjusting his cock in his pants. "When I fuck you tonight, *and I will be,* I want you in this, and only this."

Holy shit, there really is a God.

Tanner winks before turning and walking away with the guys, only Riley hangs back. He glances at us before flicking his gaze back toward the blonde bombshell stepping out of the white BMW. "Will you guys sit with her? I don't want her to be alone and bored."

"Of course we will," Addison tells him. "Who else is going to tell her about the time you accidentally shit your pants on the train and had to ditch them and run?"

His eyes widen in horror. "No, you can't. I swear, Addie, if you—"

"Chill," she laughs. "As if I'd scare her off with that. Obviously I'll wait until she's crazy in love with you and trapped before telling her. That way it's harder for her to run away. I mean, you should see the list of shit I've got on Tanner that I'm just waiting to spill to Bri."

Riley presses his lips into a hard line and shakes his head, unimpressed with Addie's wicked ways, only he considers her a moment. "Is the nudie run story on that list?"

"You know it," she laughs.

Riley chuckles before looking back at Zoe, and when she glances up at us, the widest, beaming smile splits across his face. He takes off at a jog toward her, and the most wonderful feeling fills my chest. I really hope this girl is everything he wants her to be. I've never seen him so happy.

He speaks with her for a minute before pointing up toward us. She glances our way and gives us a nervous smile, allowing Riley to take her hand and lead her back toward us. As he does, the goofiest, most excited grin stretches across his face.

I can't help but laugh. He's such a dork—but a lovable one.

"Guys, this is Zoe," he says as they approach, stealing another glance her way. "And these are all the girls. Ilaria, Chanel, Addison, Arizona, and Brielle. You're welcome to sit with them if you don't want to sit alone."

Her eyes light up with relief. "Oh really?" she questions, glancing at us. "Would that be okay? I don't want to intrude on your night."

"It is more than okay," Ilaria says, slipping her arm through Zoe's and leading her toward the ginormous grandstand behind us. She glances back at Riley, giving him a pointed stare. "Don't you have somewhere to be?"

He rolls his eyes as the girls laugh, and we all fall in line to find our seats except Chanel, who excuses herself to meet with the other cheerleaders. "Hey," Riley says, reaching out and grabbing my arms, gently pulling me back.

"What's up?" I question.

He presses his lips into a tight line as if reconsidering saying whatever is on his mind. "Would you like … not make me sound like a fucking loser? You know, talk me up as a really cool guy, and make sure she doesn't accidentally fall in love with some other asshole? Because that would really fucking suck."

I laugh and push up on my toes, pressing a kiss to his cheek. "Relax and go enjoy the last game of the season. I've got this," I tell him. "Though, it would really help your case if you killed it out on the field tonight."

Riley winks. "You fucking know it." And with that, he takes off, running toward the locker rooms before Coach Wyld can turn this night into a scene right out of hell.

I catch up with the girls, and as we find the best seats in the grandstand, we chat with Zoe. It only takes three minutes for me to decide that she's absolutely perfect for Riley. Funny, witty, gorgeous, and has a fire in her that shines bright enough to keep up with him. You know, when he finally decides to stop acting like a Muppet and be his true, outgoing, and wonderfully moronic self in front of her.

Zoe sits between me and Ilaria while Arizona and Addison huddle together on my left. We've barely sat our asses down when Ilaria leans over to fidget with her bag. She pulls out a whole bottle of peach schnapps before grinning up at us with a wicked sparkle in her eye. "Anyone down to make this game interesting?"

I grin back at her. Tonight just got that much better.

Nearly an hour later, we're finally down to the final quarter, and watching Tanner dominate the field has been one of the best experiences of my life. We all cheer and scream right along with the rest of the crowd, and my voice cracks and breaks the louder I get, but I can't seem to care. Nothing will stop me from cheering for my man.

It's a tight game. Hillcrest scored the last touchdown, putting them up by two points to take the lead, but it's nothing my boys can't handle. I know they're going to kill it, simply because they're all stubborn bastards who won't accept no for an answer.

Riley intercepts the ball, and suddenly all of Bradford gets to their feet. The atmosphere is insane. The love and support of this team is incredible, and as they really start taking off, the crowd only gets more enthusiastic.

Riley tucks the ball under his arm, holding it as though his whole life depends on it, and just as he's done all night, he puts on a fucking show. He dodges and weaves, and as he takes off at a sprint, Zoe flies up on her seat, screaming his name, and I swear, somehow the fucker must hear her as he pushes himself faster, slipping straight past two linebackers and through to the end zone.

Logan runs with him, having his back at all times, and taking out anyone who stands in his way. Then, in an incredible show of glory, he slams the ball down in the end zone, the whole fucking crowd roaring for their team.

"Holy shit," Zoe squeals, jumping down from the seat while staring out at the field, unable to take her gaze off Riley. "Did you see that? He was incredible."

My heart simply melts.

She goes on, shaking her head in disbelief. "This is honestly the best game I've ever sat through," she tells us. "At first, I was hesitant to come because like, who goes and meets some random stranger they met on the gram, but shit, he's really convincing, you know?"

Arizona laughs from beside her. "Yeah, we know," she says in a teasing tone, sipping on the bottle of peach schnapps. "That guy could convince just about anyone to do anything."

I smother a laugh, knowing damn well she's talking about all the times Riley has convinced Jax to make an Ari sandwich … or is tripod a more appropriate definition?

Zoe glances back at the field, already in love with the guy. "I know you all are super close with him, but I don't know. Have you seen his Instagram? It's full of thirst traps and it gives me a bit of a fuckboy vibe."

"What? Nah, he just likes looking good and wants to show it off," I lie, knowing damn well he's a fuckboy through and through. Though I have hope that Zoe might just be the right woman to put all those games to rest. After all, the way he looks at her is real, and assuming she's able to feel the same way, it could be the love story of the century. "To be really honest with you, you couldn't find a better guy. Riley is the whole package. I mean, just look at him," I say, both of us glancing out to the field and swooning over the smile that lights up his whole face. "He's hot as hell and will make you feel like the only girl in the world. He's funny, cheeky, sarcastic, and has no issue throwing you over his shoulder and spanking your ass if he has to. The woman who ends up with him will honestly be the luckiest girl in the world, and the fact that you have all of his attention … shit, go for it. Whether it's a quick fling or you fall madly in love with each other, it'll be the best thing you ever do."

A smile pulls at her lips just as Riley glances up here, making her cheeks flush the brightest shade of pink. "You really think so?" she questions.

"Hell yeah," Arizona says, leaning around me again. "I don't want to make things awkward, and I'm only telling you this because it's necessary for the decision-making process." Ari pauses just a moment as Zoe's brows furrow, certain she's about to drop some kind of bomb on her little love bubble with Riley. "The guy can fuck, like really fucking fuck. Like blow your fucking mind kind of fuck. Plus, his dick … Goddamn, it's huge and pierced. So whether you want to be with him or not, do yourself a favor and take a ride on that thing because Riley knows exactly what he's doing."

Her jaw drops and her lips slowly pull into an excited grin, her eyes telling me exactly what we need to know. Riley is a done deal. If my string of compliments didn't seal the deal, then Ari sure as hell just did.

The game is ticking close to full-time, and as the crowd settles down, watching the two teams get back into formation, Arizona shoots to her feet, her voice ringing out loud and proud. "YOU'RE DOING GREAT, JAX. KEEP UP THE GOOD WORK."

The crowd roars with laughter as Jax's head snaps up. He flies to his feet, whipping around to stare up at Ari in the stands, his eyes expressing exactly how he feels. She's in trouble, but knowing Ari, it's the kind of trouble that'll get her panties wet. "COME AND SAY THAT SHIT TO MY FACE, BITCH."

She laughs and shakes her head, but Jax isn't having it and starts storming toward the stands, bypassing the stairs to climb right up and over the railing.

"Oh, fuck." Ari squeals, knowing he's about to let her have it right here in front of the whole of Bradford, and she takes off like a lightning bolt through the stands, darting to the stairs and flying down them.

Jax follows her movements, watching every step like a tiger ready to pounce, and the moment her feet hit the ground running, he drops from the stands, landing in a low crouch before taking off after her.

Her squeal echoes through the field, but her short little legs have nothing on Jax's size and speed. He catches her in no time, launching at her as his arms close around her waist. They both go flying, but Jax breaks their fall with his arms, always keeping her safe.

He says something only she can hear and there's an intense moment between them before she finally reaches up and grabs his face. She plasters her lips to his, kissing him deeply as he holds her. The whole crowd cheers for them, everyone but Coach Wyld, who's bitching at Jax to get his shit together.

"ABOUT FUCKING TIME," Logan hollers from the field, making Coach Wyld whip around and bitch him out too.

The boys get back into position, focusing on the game just as the whistle blows. We're up by four, but it's anyone's game, and with only a few minutes left on the clock, it's intense. So fucking intense Jax and Ari stop making out on the ground to watch with wide eyes.

Chanel stands with her squad, their pom-poms not even moving as they remain glued to the game, while the girls and I get on our feet, gripping the railing with bated breath. The crowd cheers and roars with every step as the ball shifts up and down the field.

The clock reaches sixty seconds and the countdown is on, the teams battling it out as though their whole lives depend on it. Though I suppose for some of these guys, this game might be one of the biggest achievements in their lives.

The boys run, their eyes sharp as they look from left to right, aware of every last player on the field. Coach Wyld's face is beet red, yelling orders from the sidelines as Jax quickly joins in, demanding they run harder, play faster, and be the fucking best.

Hillcrest gets the ball and takes off at a sprint, half of the grandstand losing their minds while my heart races faster than it's ever raced before. They pass the ball from player to player with amazing footwork, evading our defense, but they're not better than my guys. A moment later, the Hillcrest linebacker narrowly evades a tackle and passes the ball, not clocking Riley until it's too fucking late. He shoots through the center, leisurely collecting the ball in his arms as though picking a daisy on a Sunday stroll.

Riley doesn't hesitate, whipping around and storming back up the field. He's too far away to risk making a break for it, but his teammates are right there, ready and waiting to have his back. He passes the ball down the line, handing it off to Hudson with a perfect pass, effortlessly dodging a tackle. Hudson storms ahead, gaining another ten yards before passing it along just as a Hillcrest player slams him into the ground, making the whole crowd cringe.

Bradford keeps going, keeps passing, and with every foot they gain, another twenty spectators get on their feet. Finally, the ball lands right in Tanner's waiting hands, and like the best quarterback known to man, he does his thing, rearing back and launching it through the air with everything he's got. The ball flies like a fucking rocket, and Logan takes off, keeping his eye locked and loaded on the ball.

Every player races after it as every spectator holds their breath, the anticipation bursting at the seams. Hillcrest does everything they can to save their game, but it's no use. There's less than fifteen seconds on the clock.

Logan is out there on his own with Hillcrest. No one else is fast enough to get there in time, but Logan's got this in the bag. He launches himself into the sky just as the opposition jumps, both of them reaching for the ball, but Logan takes it, tucking it into his arm and breaking into a hard sprint. Hillcrest desperately dives after him.

Logan escapes and runs ahead, the whole crowd screaming their support, but one last Hillcrest player comes at him right in the end zone.

The clock ticks. Five seconds left.

Logan sidesteps, the opponent coming right for him with the kind of determination that puts people in wheelchairs. He pushes to the left, trying to dodge but the other guy is too quick, following his every move. This is going to be close—too fucking close for my liking.

Three seconds.

Two.

Logan dives, his arm outstretched and just as the opponent slams into his side, Logan's hand comes down in the end zone. The ball slams into the grass just as the buzzer sounds across the field, declaring Bradford the reigning champions.

The whole fucking stands are on their feet chanting as I watch the boys. Tanner and Riley take off at a sprint toward each other, launching into the air and crashing together. They crumble to the ground in laughter, and it's all I can bear before I race out of the stands and down onto the field.

I run as fast as my feet can take me, overtaking Chanel as she barrels toward Logan. Tanner turns, reaching up to pull his helmet off, and the moment he sees me coming across the field, a wide smile tears across his face. He jogs toward me, and as I crash into him, he grips my ass with one hand, hoisting me up into his arms.

My lips crush to his as my arms fly around his neck, holding on with everything I've got. "I'm so fucking turned on right now."

"You're telling me," he mutters. "Try playing a championship game with a hard-on the whole time because your girl looks fucking amazing in your jacket."

I laugh, but before I get a word out, his lips are back on mine.

"Get a fucking room," someone roars from across the field, but there's no way in hell I'm pulling away to figure out which asshole dares to disrupt this moment with my man.

Within the space of two seconds, it seems all of Bradford is on the field, going around and giving their congratulations, and I reluctantly pull away from Tanner, knowing his job isn't quite done yet.

I stand with the girls after somehow managing to pull Zoe away from Riley. Who would have known the girl was just as horny as he is! We stand as close to the field as possible, watching as the boys accept their championship trophy, and the pride that swells through my chest feels amazing.

It's been a hard season for Tanner, and despite already having his college plans sorted out, there was still a lot riding on his shoulders. Yet despite everything, he still pulled through and carried his team right to the end, just as he promised he would.

Once the main part of the award ceremony is done, the team stands for a photo, and as we wait, a text comes through on my phone. I pull it out and quickly glance over it.

Mom - Do you have plans for tonight? Do you mind popping by for a minute before you go out?

Double checking the time, I quickly hash out a reply.

Brielle - Yeah, sure. Is now good?
Mom - Perfect.

The second the boys are excused to enjoy their night, they all race over and Tanner grabs me, spinning me around before putting me back on my feet. "Jax and Logan are having a party at their place. You in?"

"Couldn't think of anything better," I tell him. "But Mom just needs me for a minute first. Is it cool if I meet you there?"

His brows furrow. "Is everything good?"

I shrug my shoulders. "Wouldn't have a clue," I tell him. "I just got a message asking me to pop by before I go out for the night."

"Oh, okay," he says. "If you wanna wait a minute, I'll grab my shit and drive you. I can shower at home while you talk to your mom."

"Sounds good," I tell him, beaming up at my whole freaking world.

Barely even thirty seconds later, I sit beside him in the Mustang as he flies down the road, the windows down and music up. He's got one hand on the wheel and the other resting on my thigh. It simply doesn't get better than this.

We pull up at home, and just as promised, he rushes inside to have a shower and get ready for the night while I skip over the hedge and push through the door of Orlando's place. "Mom?" I question, peeking inside to find the foyer filled with boxes and suitcases. "Mom? Where are you?"

I walk deeper into the foyer, glancing over the array of boxes as Mom comes down the stairs looking as though she's been in the gym all day. Her hair is a mess and she hasn't bothered with makeup. Hell, she looks like the mom I had before Orlando Channing decided to fuck with our lives.

"Oh, hey honey," she says. "How was the game?"

"We won," I tell her, pointing out the boxes. "Are we moving out?"

Mom cringes. "Not exactly," she says, motioning for me to follow her. She walks into the living room and drops on the couch, and I do the same, my curiosity driving me insane. Mom takes my hands and gives me a hesitant smile. "I don't know how much you've been told, but from the sound of it, Orlando will be going away for quite some time, and despite how much I love this house, I simply can't stay here."

"Oh," I say, panic starting to claim me. "Where are we going?"

"Not we," she clarifies. "Me. Unless you want to come with me."

My face scrunches with confusion. "Huh?"

Mom laughs and her smile widens. "I've bought a small apartment with the money I had left from selling our Hope Falls home. However, as long as Orlando and I remain married, this house will remain ours … well, ours and Jensen's of course."

"What's … what are you getting at?"

"I thought you might like to stay here," she tells me. "I know our relationship has been quite strained over the past few months, and that's entirely on me. I want you to thrive, Brielle, and I know taking you away from the place that makes you so happy isn't going to do me any favors. So you can stay, unless you'd prefer to come with me, which is more than okay."

"I, ummm …"

"You don't need to make any decisions right now," she tells me. "Jensen will be attending Brown in the fall, so the place will be all yours. You can move all your things into the master room and keep all those fancy clothes in my closet. I don't want any of it. I just want you to be happy. And this school, this town, and being so close to Tanner and his sister, this place is your home."

I nod. "It is."

She pulls me into a tight hug and I hold her like a little girl, terrified to let go. "I'm so proud of you, Bri. Look at this incredible young woman you've become. I'm going to hate being away from you, but it'll only be a fifteen-minute drive at most. I'll come visit you all the time, and you're always welcome to come and stay with me. I've got two spare bedrooms, one for you and your brother."

Tears well in my eyes, and as I pull back, I hastily wipe them. "What are you going to do?"

She shrugs her shoulders. "Who knows?" she says with a fond smile. "I guess that's all part of the adventure. Something for me to figure out along the way."

A strange mix of emotions rest in my chest. Sadness, joy, pride, and nervousness, but most of all, I just feel love. "I'm going to miss you," I tell her. "I hate that things have been weird, but I'm excited to work on it and get back that old friendship we had."

"You and me both, kid," she says, letting out a heavy sigh before standing and dragging me up with her. "I've got movers coming in the morning to take all of my stuff to the new apartment, and if I don't keep going, I'll never have it all ready."

"Okay," I tell her, reading the signs she wants me to get out of here so she can get herself sorted out. "I need to get going anyway, but I'll text you in the morning and you can show me your new place. Tanner and I can come and help you unpack."

"That would be lovely, sweetheart," she says before pulling me into another tight hug. "Now, if you could convince a few of those other strong boys to come along as well, I've got some furniture that needs to be put together."

I laugh and roll my eyes. "Ahhh, that's what Jensen and Damien are for," I remind her. "But sure, I'll see what I can do." And with that, she gets right back to work, and I glance around this massive house that somehow just became mine.

A knock sounds on the door and as I peer through the foyer, Tanner opens the door and shoves his head through the gap. "You ready?" he questions with a grin, only for it to fall away as he sees all the boxes. "If you're about to tell me you're moving away, heads are gonna roll."

I laugh and shake my head, striding up to him and throwing my arms around his neck, letting him pull me into his warm body. "As if you could get away from me that easily."

He smiles back at me, his lips dropping to mine. "As if I would ever want to."

CHAPTER 35

TANNER

It's the biggest and wildest party of the year. Everybody who's anybody is here and feeling good. I've got my girl in my arms, her body moving against mine as she dances for me, while Riley's had Zoe in the spa for the past hour, their faces now permanently attached to one another's. Hell, I wouldn't be surprised if he's already fucked her in there.

The music is pumping and there are more people crammed into the twins' mansion than I've ever seen in one place before, every single one of them chanting for the reigning champions.

Tonight has been fucking epic. Right from kick off, I knew we were going to kill it. The atmosphere in the air and the fact we were battling it out on our own turf just made it that much better. Not to mention Brielle up in the stands wearing my name and number.

We've all been through hell, but tonight we say goodbye to it all and finally get to take that step to put it all behind us. Orlando is locked up, my father is across the globe—hopefully where he'll stay, Colby is dead, and Rachael … well, Rachael can go fuck herself.

I'm not going to lie, I have four half-siblings I never knew about—three in Australia and one living under the roof of my sister's dead rapist—and maybe one day I'll be able to lose the chip on my shoulder and get to know them. It's still too fresh. My father's betrayal is something we'll all have to deal with for years to come, especially my mom. The fact he divorced her without her knowledge … that's just messed up. But apparently messed up is his new motto, like screwing underage girls, getting them pregnant, and pinning it on his son. All I know is that motherfucker better not show up at my mother's doorstep ever again because I'll have a few things to say, and I have it on good authority that I like to speak with my fists.

The song changes and Bri turns in my arms, smiling up at me and making my chest ache. She's so fucking gorgeous it's hard to look at her sometimes. She pushes up onto her tippy toes, brushing her lips over mine, and I feel a smile spread across her lips. "I think Jax and Ari worked through their issues."

"Huh?" I mutter, my brows furrowed as I pull back to meet her gaze.

She nods toward the house where Jax has Ari pressed up against the wall, the two of them locked in a deep conversation. Judging by the look of pure bliss on Arizona's face, I'd say things are going well.

Though no one could ever be too sure with those two. But one thing is for sure, he paid hell after the game for the performance he put on during the final quarter. Coach Wyld had some things to say about it too, but seeing as though the football season is over and Jax is about to graduate, there's not a lot he can do about it now.

I laugh, shaking my head. "Those two give me whiplash."

"At least they're not as bad as Chanel and Logan," she tells me, sending a pointed stare across the party to where Chanel and Logan are arguing by the bar. It's been going on all night. They fight and then ten minutes later, they're sneaking away to fuck in the pool house. They return with Chanel's hair all ruffled and sure enough, they end up arguing again. At least when Jax and Ari fight, Ari storms off and gives him the silent treatment for a few days, giving the rest of us just a little bit of peace.

"Good point," I tell her as she takes my hand and drags me away from the dance floor. "Where are we going?"

Bri glances back over her shoulder and without murmuring a single word, I know exactly where she's taking me. After all, she's still wearing my letterman jacket, and I have a promise I plan to fulfill ten times over.

We reach the house and just as we go to walk inside, something catches my eye, sending a wave of anger rushing through my body. "Hey," I call out, sending a venomous glare to Hudson as he mauls my sister on the kitchen counter. "Watch your fucking hands, man."

Addison's head snaps up, grinning at me, and I shake my head before the words have even come out of her mouth. "If you think this is bad, you should have seen what I did to him on the hood of your Mustang last night."

Hoooooly fuck. I don't know whether to strangle him, lock her in an ivory tower, or throw up all over the house.

I give it a second, trying to figure out how to handle this as the spark in Addie's eyes only shines brighter, challenging me to come at her, but as Bri tugs on my hand, I get shoved from behind. "Out of the fucking way, bro," Riley says, dripping water from the spa all through the house, his hand shoved down the front of his pants, gripping his cock.

"What the fuck, man?" I grunt as Bri's eyes bug out of her head, horrified by the sight in front of her.

"Sorry, dude. It's an emergency. This chick is freakier than I anticipated. The things she's saying she's gonna do to me. Holy fuck, she's my dream girl. I've never been one to let a chick eat my ass before, but for her, I'd do it. I'd fucking bend over and let her get her tongue all up in there. But listen, I'd love to stay and tell you all about it, but she's been grinding up on my dick for the last hour, and I have every intention of dropping my balls into her mouth, but if I don't go and have a tactical jerk now, I'm gonna blow my load before I even get in there."

I laugh as Bri groans. "Shit, Riley. I didn't want to hear that."

He grins at her, turning around to face us while still jogging away. "It's gonna be great, like two heavenly love nuggets swishing around in her mouth." He stops walking, a seriousness coming over his face as his body starts to jolt. "Oh, no," he panics, clutching his dick harder. A second passes before he lets out a heavy sigh. "Ahhh, shit. I'm good. Almost fucking came just thinking about it."

He gives a beaming smile before spinning around and rushing away.

Brielle looks up at me, her eyes dancing with laughter. "He definitely just came in his pants, didn't he?"

"Oh yeah," I laugh, hooking my arm over her shoulder and leading her toward the stairs.

"Wanna make it a two for one deal?" she questions. "We'll see how fast I can make you come."

Without even a hint of warning, I grab her by the waist and press her up against the wall, my knee slipping between her legs and grinding against her clit. "Fuck no, Killer," I growl in her ear, lowering my lips to the base of her throat. "I plan on taking my sweet fucking time, even if it takes all night."

A soft moan slips from between her lips and her body relaxes into mine, but that doesn't stop her smart mouth. "Oh really?" she whispers, her hand slipping in the front of my jeans and curling around my hardening cock, her thumb brushing over the tip and making me groan. "Because I'd bet everything I have I could get you on your knees before we've even made it to the top of the stairs."

Fucking hell. She could do that and more, but I'm not about to let that happen. Not when I want to taste that sweet cunt first.

I pull back and meet her stare as her grip tightens on my cock. "Unless you want me to fuck you right here in front of everybody, I suggest you unhand me, woman."

She grins wider, rising to the challenge as her fist pumps up and down my cock while making a show of licking her lips. "Unless you want to come right here in front of everybody, I suggest you hurry up and take me upstairs so you can spread my thighs and really fuck me."

I've said it before and I'll say it again. Brielle Ashford was made for me.

Before she can get another word out, my hands are at her waist, hauling that fine body over my shoulder. She squeals, gripping my shoulders as I bolt up the stairs, taking them two at a time. I kick in the first door, and glare at the two freshmen making out on the bed. "OUT."

Their eyes bug out of their heads before scrambling off the bed and racing out of the room, slamming the door behind them. Within the same second, I have Brielle's back pressed up against it with my lips crushed against hers.

She fumbles for my shirt, tugging and pulling, but our bodies are glued together, making it impossible to pull it off. Instead, she reaches around my neck, grips the fabric between her hands, and tears until the fabric falls away.

Her hands roam over my body and it's fucking everything. I'll never tire of her touch. It's like a drug to me, potent and raw, feeding into this wicked addiction I have for her.

My thumbs hook into the waistband of her pants and I push them down her thighs, taking her panties with it as she pulls at her shirt, trying to rid herself of my jacket and tank at the same time. I pull back just a little, shaking my head. "The tank can go, but the jacket stays."

Her grin widens, her gaze darkening with hunger as she adjusts herself, dropping her tank to the ground before fixing my jacket back over her shoulders. "This better?"

My gaze trails down her body, her perfect tits just visible past the open jacket and I slip my hand inside, brushing my thumb over her nipple and watching as it pebbles under my touch. My fingers trail right down her body, past her toned waist and in between her legs and I don't hesitate, pushing them deep inside her. She's fucking wet and ready, her warm cunt squeezing my fingers and making my cock jolt in my jeans. "Fucking perfect," I growl, the words rumbling through my chest.

Brielle lets out a breathy gasp, and I pull my fingers free before lifting them to her mouth. She opens wide, curling her hand around mine and guiding my fingers inside. She closes her mouth and rolls her tongue over them, tasting just how fucking sweet she is.

I pull them from between her lips before leaning in and kissing her deeply, tasting what's left on her tongue as my fingers trail back down her body and slip right back into her sweet pussy. They curl around, massaging her walls until her knees go weak. I smile against her lips. "You ready for me, Killer?"

Her hands fall to my pants, hastily unbuckling my belt before freeing my cock and letting it drop heavily into her hand. She grins against my lips, her tight fist pumping up and down. "Depends," she tells me. "Are you ready to get on your knees and worship me?"

Taking her waist, I pull her body hard against mine. "You fucking bet I am." And with that, I lift her into my arms, her legs locking around my waist. I step away from the door, crossing the luxurious bedroom until my shins brush against the bed.

I throw her on the bed, staring down at her as I grip my cock, gently stroking. Her eyes darken, hunger in her hooded stare. She goes to scramble up the bed, but I grip her ankle and pull her to the very edge, her ass barely hanging off the end, and just as she wanted, I drop to my fucking knees.

"Tanner," she gasps, bracing up on her elbows as I take her thighs and push them wide, putting her on display just the way I like her. "Oh, God," Brielle groans, knowing damn well what's coming.

My tongue rolls over my lips, my hunger for her only getting worse the longer I wait. Putting us both out of our misery, I hook her legs over my shoulders and close my mouth over her clit before flicking my tongue over that tight bud of nerves. She gasps and I slide my hand up her body, cupping her tit and circling my finger around her nipple.

Taking my other hand, I slip it under my chin and push two thick flingers deep in her cunt as I continue working her clit. Her head falls back with a breathy groan. "Oh God, Tanner," she moans, reaching down and knotting her fingers into my hair, gripping on with everything she's got.

I don't stop, working her just the way she likes it, her body jolting beneath me. I grin against her, knowing the adrenaline rush of seeing her come undone is something I have never experienced with another woman.

Her grip tightens in my hair, and I feel her body being pushed to the edge. She's almost there, ready to fucking detonate. I suck her clit, my tongue rolling over it as my fingers dive deeper, curling inside her and making her scream.

She pants, barely holding on but I don't dare stop, pushing her to her limit until she finally explodes, her orgasm tearing through her body. "OH FUCK, TANNER," she cries, tipping her head back as her eyes clench, looking like a fucking goddess.

She's everything, the whole goddamn package, and I'll never let her go.

I keep going, keep sucking, flicking, rolling, and massaging until she finally comes down from her high, her tense body relaxing. "Holy shit," she moans, flopping back against the bed, absolutely spent, but I'm not even close to being through with her.

I get back to my feet, gripping my cock as she watches me, her hooded eyes locked on my body. "I think my soul just left my body," she murmurs, her gaze drifting back up to mine.

I grin, stepping in closer, and as my fist slowly pumps up and down my cock, the movement gains her attention. She stares at it with hunger, and her tongue rolls over her bottom lip. "You got plans to use that thing?" she questions, her voice filled with desire and lust.

"You fucking bet I do," I say, dropping my gaze to her pussy, unable to resist the pure need pulsing through my veins. Leaning down, I curl my arm around her toned waist and pull her up off the bed, whipping her around to slam her back up against the wall, knocking a canvas print off in the process.

She squeals, her legs locking around my hip and as my body presses against hers. I line myself up with her warm cunt and thrust inside her, burying my cock as deep as her body will allow. "Oh fuck," she groans, her arms twisting around my neck and holding on for dear life.

I thrust again, clenching my jaw as pure satisfaction rocks through my body, leaving me wanting so much more. I fuck her hard and fast as her pussy clenches around me, squeezing tight, and making me feel like the luckiest fucking bastard in the world. I've been with other girls and it's never, fucking never, felt as good as it does with Brielle. She's my goddamn Killer, a fucking atomic bomb with the potential to take out every fucking man in sight.

"Tanner?" she breathes. "I need more."

Fuck, yes.

Pulling her off the wall, I take her back to the bed. "Get on your knees."

Her eyes flutter and she does it quickly, spreading her thighs wide before plastering her chest to the mattress, that gorgeous ass up in the air and her glistening cunt just waiting for me. My hand comes down on that perfect cheek and she groans loud. "Now, Tanner."

I'm not one to disappoint.

I slam back inside her, this angle taking me so much deeper. My balls tighten as I pull back, grabbing her hips and holding her still. I thrust hard again, and as her walls clench around me, my fucking knees go weak. She's got a chokehold on my cock and I'd never give it up for anything.

My thumb presses down over her ass, and with each thrust, I apply a little more pressure until she's pushing back against me, silently begging for more. I give her everything she wants as her hand slips down between her legs, rubbing tight circles over her clit.

She's so fucking stunning like this. Absolutely breathtaking.

Everything clenches inside of me. I'm close to the edge, her low groans and desperate panting only pushing me further. I slide inside of her as she tightens around me, and I'm just about to lose my fucking mind when she cries out. "Oh, God, I'm gonna come."

"Give it to me, Killer," I demand, applying more pressure to her ass. "Let me see that pretty cunt come apart."

"Oh fuck," she grumbles, her face squished into my mattress, and as I thrust one more time, she's pushed over the edge, coming hard as her whole body spasms. "Tanner, yes!"

Her pussy convulses around me, squeezing like never before, and it's all I need to fall off the cliff. My whole world detonates and I come hard, shooting hot spurts of cum deep into her sweet cunt, her panting groans only making it better.

I don't stop moving until she comes down from her high, her body relaxing against the bed as she works on catching her breath. Gently pulling out of her, I reach down and take her by the waist, lifting her off the bed before walking around to the top of it.

I sit up in the bed, resting back against the headboard as Bri straddles my lap, both of us utterly spent. Her head rests against my shoulder as my fingers trail up and down her back. "Next time you plan to fuck me that good, you need to warn me first," she mumbles, her lips moving against my neck.

I grin, pride swirling in my chest.

"And why's that?"

"So I can pray first," she tells me. "Because when I came just then, I swear I saw Jesus, and if he's going to be a regular sighting from here on out, I better make sure I'm in good with the big guy. Otherwise, I'm definitely going to hell. Fucking that good has got to be a sin."

"Damn fucking right," I tell her, calling it like I see it.

Bri laughs and she sits up, pressing her lips to mine. "Have I told you how much I love you today?"

I pretend to think about it. "Twice this morning, three times before the game, and including just now," I grin, "five times since the game."

"You're an idiot."

"An idiot who fucks you so good you see Jesus, right?"

"You're not going to let me forget I said that, are you?"

I laugh, pushing her hair back off her face. "Now why would I go and do something stupid like that?"

"Well," she murmurs, reaching down between us and taking hold of my cock, slowly pumping her hand up and down my length before raising up on her knees and lowering herself back down on me, taking me whole. "I guess I have no other choice but to give you something even better and make you forget."

And not a second later, she rocks her hips, and my whole fucking world is blown.

EPILOGUE

TANNER

ONE YEAR LATER

Standing with a heavy heart, I watch as the Hardin brothers are dragged out of the courtroom in handcuffs, where they'll each be spending the next thirty or forty years of their lives behind bars. I should be happy. Justice has finally been served, but there's been so much pain and loss there's simply no room to celebrate. All that matters is they'll be right where they belong, rotting in a cell beside Orlando where they can talk shit about me day in and day out.

The day I knocked on Gina's door, I didn't need to tell her who I was. She recognized me, despite being five years older. I expected her to hit me, yell at me, even be fearful, but what I didn't expect was for her to step into me and wrap me in her warm embrace. She cried on my shoulder before welcoming me into her home. We talked and she cried before sharing with me everything she's been through, confessing she had prayed that one day I would find the courage to come forward and help her put the Hardin brothers away. And that's exactly what I set out to do.

It's been a hard year, and at first, I was terrified. I thought the brothers would come for me and they sure as fuck tried, multiple times, but it wasn't anything I wasn't prepared for. I had so much to lose, but if Gina could face them after everything she'd lost, then so could I.

The doors close behind the brothers, and after standing for the judge to leave, I take Bri's hand and lead her out of the courtroom. "You okay?" she murmurs, looking up into my eyes.

I give her a tight smile, the weight of this still resting on my shoulders. Hell, I don't think it'll ever go away, but I'll spend the rest of my life trying.

Gina walks out with her lawyer and she comes straight to me, giving me a warm smile before pulling me into her arms. "I couldn't have done this without you, Tanner," she tells me. "You really are a wonderful man. Thank you. I'm so glad you managed to put yourself on the right path."

"I'm just sorry you had to go through any of this," I tell her. "Nothing can change what you lost that night."

"No, nothing ever will, nor will it take the memories away, but now I will be able to find peace knowing they won't be able to hurt anyone else ever again. The streets of Hope Falls will be safe, and whether you believe it or not, there are countless families who can all rest easy now that they've been put away."

I nod, giving her a tight smile, wishing I could feel it the same way she does. "Listen, I wanted to talk to you about something," I start, watching as her brows furrow with concern. "I've been thinking about doing this for quite a while but wanted to wait until the trial was over." I pause awkwardly, unsure what she will think of this. "How would you feel if I were to start a foundation in your son's name for the underprivileged families in lower class areas who are dealing with situations like your own? It could be a safe place for them to go after crime or devastation has torn their lives apart, somewhere to heal, or just somewhere they can go to talk, shower, or eat."

"A safe haven for survivors," she finishes for me.

"Exactly," I tell her. "Like I said, I'd like to open the foundation in your son's name, if you're okay with that obviously, and if you were wanting to be a part of it, I'd like to take you on board as one of the directors. I want this to be yours."

She gapes at me as though I've just lost my mind. "Are you sure?" she breathes. "I think this is a wonderful idea and really, Jonah would have gotten a kick out of having his name attached to something so special, but I … I couldn't. It's a very lovely offer, but I wouldn't know the first thing about being a director of something so important."

"Then we'll teach you," I insist. "My mom has been getting her business degree and has just started her own bakery. I'm sure she'd be happy to sit down with you and teach you everything you need to know, and whatever we don't understand, we'll figure out along the way."

"You're really sure about this?"

"Positive," I tell her. "I want you on board with this. It wouldn't feel right without you."

Tears gather in her eyes, and she squeezes my hand. "Then yes," she says as Brielle loops her arm around mine, a beaming smile on her face. "I'd love to."

Brielle

FOUR YEARS LATER

The buzzer sounds throughout the stadium, signaling half time of the best football game I've ever seen.

Tanner has been killing it. It's his second year leading his team as captain and there's a damn good reason why. He's the best. There's no question about it. He's done four years of college football and every game, he just gets better. Hell, the whole world knows it, which is why he's had every professional team in the country treating him like a king, wining and dining him and showering him with lavish gifts, desperate to get him to sign on the dotted line.

Tonight is their championship game, and there's no doubt in my mind he'll be coming home with that trophy, and a shitload more where those scouts are concerned.

Ilaria nudges me before nodding toward the cheerleaders as they race out onto the field, preparing for their halftime routine. "Do you think those uniforms get caught up their asses?"

"Don't ask me," I scoff. "Ask Chanel. She was a cheerleader for four years."

Ilaria rolls her eyes as she cradles her pregnant belly. "I tried to ask her, but she's too busy jerking off Logan beneath his jacket and acting as though it isn't the most obvious thing in the world."

"What?" I laugh, having to lean right around her big belly to see, certain if I accidentally touch it she might pop and make Damien a daddy a few weeks too early. "Really, Chanel?" I say with a gag, getting an eyeful of her hand bobbing up and down beneath Logan's jacket. "If you're going to do it, at least get on your knees for him."

"Who's getting on their knees?" Zoe asks from down the other end of our row, having to lean past the newlyweds, Jax and Ari, and announcing it to the whole freaking stadium.

I can all but see the ridiculous comment forming in Riley's head when booming music cuts across the field. My gaze shifts down to the field to see the cheerleaders shaking their asses, but as I look a little closer, I realize they're not alone.

"Oh no," I laugh, watching Tanner twerking on the field. "What the hell is he doing?"

Cameras zoom in on him and within seconds, Tanner's ass is plastered over the jumbotron. The boys howl with laughter as the rest of the stadium cheers on their favorite player. I have no doubt this is going to make national headlines, just like everything else he does.

He gets halfway through the routine, hitting every single step perfectly, and just when I start getting suspicious of how well he knows the dance, the jumbotron goes to a split screen, showing my face plastered right next to Tanner's.

My eyes bug out of my head as the crowd roars, clearly figuring out the same thing I've just worked out. "Oh, shit," I gasp, flying to my feet and making a break for it, cutting in front of all our friends while Hudson and Addison smirk as though they knew this shit was about to go down. "No, no, no, no, no, no, no, no."

What the hell is he thinking? I'm going to kill him.

"Uh-oh," a voice says over the speakers as I hit the stairs, racing up toward the exit. "We've got ourselves a runner."

Oh, God. How embarrassing.

I glance over my shoulder at the screen to find Tanner staring up at me, a wicked smirk across his stupid face. The idiot is really enjoying this.

My head whips back, and just as I lift my gaze to make sure I don't trip and fall, I come to a startling halt, finding Riley blocking my way with his hands braced on his hips and a stupid smirk on his face. "How the fuck did you—"

"Sorry, shortstack," he says, cutting me off, his arms snapping out and grabbing me around the waist. He throws me over his shoulder before strutting down the stairs, the whole stadium applauding his efforts as humiliation claims me.

"Put me down right now, you big bastard," I say, drumming my fists against his back, even considering going as far as shoving my hands down his pants and giving him an ultimate wedgie.

He gets right to the edge of the grandstand and without an exit right here, he has no choice but to toss me over the edge, right into the arms of one of Tanner's teammates. I'm shuffled around and shoved over someone else's shoulder and marched right out into the middle of the field before being deposited right in front of Tanner.

The asshole just grins as I shake my head. "I hate you."

"I know," he says, taking my hands.

"You said you'd wait until after I finish law school," I tell him.

He shakes his head, his eyes sparkling with joy. "No, you said I should wait until you finished law school, and I specifically remember telling you to get fucked."

"But—"

"Don't even try it," he says, cutting me off. "I've waited four years to be able to call you my wife. I'm not waiting any longer, Bri." Tears well in my eyes as I watch him get down on one knee in front of the whole world. "The second I met you, you intrigued me. You came at me with that fiery attitude, and despite how badly I wanted to despise you, you just kept reeling me in. I fell hard for you, Brielle Ashford. You've been my whole fucking world since senior year, but it's not enough. No amount of time with you will ever be enough. I want to build a life with you, build a home and a family. I want babies with your gorgeous bright blue eyes running around our home, jumping in our bed, and filling it with laughter and happiness, but I don't want any of it if I can't have you." He pauses, pulling out a ring and holding it out to me. "Put me out of my misery, Killer. Let me make you my wife."

My tears spill down my cheeks as a wide smile stretches across my face. "Would it be a dick move to say no in front of all these people?"

"You wouldn't dream of it," he tells me.

"You're right," I laugh, throwing myself at him, crashing into his arms with everything I've got, my momentum sending us tumbling to the ground. He holds me tight, his arms wrapped around me as I meet his stare. I brush my lips to his, kissing him deeply as the crowd cheers for us.

I pull back, elation pumping through my veins. "Becoming your wife would make me the happiest girl in the world."

TANNER

EIGHT YEARS LATER

"Holy shit," my six-year-old son says from his bedroom down the hall, making Bri's eyes widen in horror, her gaze flicking to mine as she cradles our newborn daughter, Eleanor, in her arms. "The tooth fairy gave me three hundred bucks."

Nah, that couldn't be right. I know I was hitting the beers pretty hard with the boys last night, but there's no way I would have fucked it up that bad. "Are you sure, buddy?" I call, quickly grabbing my wallet off my bedside table and peeking inside as I hear him barreling down the hall, sounding like a herd of fucking elephants.

"What did you do?" Brielle laughs, shaking her head just as I realize there's a big wad of cash missing from my wallet.

"Ooooh, shit. The tooth fairy had a little too much to drink," I tell her just as Asher bursts through the door, the cash held tightly between his fingers.

He flies across our room before launching himself into the air and crashing down on the end of our bed, prompting Bri to grip Ellie just a little tighter. After all, Asher is about as wild as they come, and it wouldn't be the first time he came bolting into our room, only to end up in the hospital ten minutes later getting stitches. "I'M RICH!" he booms, filled with laughter. "I'M THE RICHEST KID IN THE WORLD."

His noise has Ellie detaching from Bri's nipple, letting a stream of breastmilk shoot across the bed. "Oh shit," she gasps, nearly squirting the baby in the eye, her casual use of the word shit making Asher burst into another round of uncontrollable laughter.

I take Ellie, curling her into my arms as Bri gets herself cleaned up and not a moment later, Asher slides in between us. "Hey," Bri says, a wide smile across her face as she tickles Ash. "That's my spot."

"You snooze, you lose," he tells her, trying to keep a straight face but laughing as Bri's tickles get too hard to avoid.

I can't help but hold my hand out for a high five. "My man," I tell him as his little hand whips across at lightning speed to connect with mine.

What can I say? I've never been so proud. He's the perfect little clone, right down to the smartass attitude. I don't doubt in another six years, he'll be giving us both hell.

Bri rolls her eyes while shaking her head. "Did you really have to teach him that?"

"Don't look at me," I argue, watching the way her arm slips around Asher's back and he absent-mindedly snuggles into her side. "You've got no one to blame but yourself for that shit." I see the argument in her eyes and shake my head. "Don't even think about it, Killer. You know I'm right."

She rolls her eyes as Ash holds up his cash. "What can I buy with all of this?" he asks, no doubt the wheels in his little head spinning.

"With all of that?" Bri questions, making a show of double-checking how much cash he's got. "Wow. With all of that, you could buy the whole world."

Ash laughs and rolls his eyes. "Don't be silly, Mommy," he says, beaming up at her. "I've already got the whole world right here."

Bri's bottom lip pouts out as she looks at me over the top of his head. "Did you hear that?" she asks, just seconds from breaking down into big heaving sobs, but I shouldn't be surprised. The pregnancy hormones have turned my fiery ball buster into an emotional wreck. Hell, she wept over dinner two nights ago because the carrots were next to the corn and she thought that was just so sweet because they might have grown beside each other in the crop field and it was like some kind of reunion for them.

But even I have to admit, Asher knows how to pull on his mother's heart strings. He learned that shit from me.

Ellie stretches in my arms, and just as I go to wrap her back into her blankets, those little blue eyes close and she falls into a deep sleep on my chest, right where she belongs. "Here," Bri says, a soft smile on her lips as she takes us in together. "I'll put her in her bassinet."

I shake my head and scoot down beside Ash, leaving Ellie right where she is. "No chance in hell," I tell Bri, the thought of giving her up to sleep in her bassinet breaking my heart right down the center. "She's happy right here."

Bri goes all gooey again, her heart hanging out on her sleeve. "Is it bad I'm a little jealous?" she questions.

I shake my head, a wide grin stretching across my lips before indicating for her to scooch closer. "Come on," I tell her as Asher rolls over, curling into my side. "There's plenty of me to go around."

And with that, Bri scooches over, lifting her head over Asher's and giving me the sweetest kiss. "I love you," she whispers before dropping her hand to my chest, her fingers brushing over the words tattooed on my skin, forever claiming prime residence above my heart.

I lean, you lean.

Forever and fucking always.

Bradford Butcher

THANKS FOR READING

If you enjoyed reading this book as much as I enjoyed writing it, please consider leaving an Amazon review to let me know.
https://geni.us/Bradfordbastard3

STALK ME

Facebook Page
www.facebook.com/SheridanAnneAuthor
Facebook Reader Group
www.facebook.com/SheridansBookishBabes
Instagram
www.instagram.com/Sheridan.Anne.Author

OTHER SERIES

www.amazon.com/Sheridan-Anne/e/B079TLXN6K

YOUNG ADULT / NEW ADULT DARK ROMANCE

The Broken Hill High Series | Haven Falls | Broken Hill Boys | Aston Creek High | Rejects Paradise | Boys of Winter | Depraved Sinners | Bradford Bastard | Empire

NEW ADULT SPORTS ROMANCE

Kings of Denver | Denver Royalty | Rebels Advocate

CONTEMPORARY ROMANCE (standalones)

Play With Fire | Until Autumn (Happily Eva Alpha World)

URBAN FANTASY - PEN NAME: CASSIDY SUMMERS

Slayer Academy

Printed in Great Britain
by Amazon